Fig
to
the
Top

By

S.L. Gape

2017

Fight to the Top © 2017 S.L. Gape
Triplicity Publishing, LLC

ISBN-13: 978-0997740578
ISBN-10: 0997740574

This is a work of fiction. Names, characters, places, and incidents are the product of the author's imagination and are used fictitiously. Any resemblance to actual persons, living or dead, business establishments, events of any kind, or locales is entirely coincidental.
Printed in the United States of America

First Edition – 2017
Cover Design: Triplicity Publishing, LLC
Interior Design: Triplicity Publishing, LLC
Editor: Lauren Brady - Triplicity Publishing, LLC

Acknowledgement

I'd like to thank Lisa and Sarah for their help, support and proofreading with this book. As like the others, if it wasn't for you pair, I'm not sure I'd be on the right track for my constant quizzing to make sure there's a few twists in there.

To Jen, who of course everyone thought this was about, thanks for your support.

And of course the editing and management team at Triplicity Publishing, for all their hard work and support in getting my book from my head to the shelves.

Manchester, UK

Chapter One

Georgia walked through the front door of her penthouse apartment, immediately struck by the lights of the city beaming through the floor to ceiling windows. Locking the door, Georgia rested the back of her head against it and sighed loudly. She looked down at her Cartier watch, a little gift from herself with last year's bonus. It was after midnight, "Seriously, this better be worth it" she sighed, dropping her bag to the floor and running her hands through her blonde, cropped, brushed back cut, trying to loosen the hair-sprayed style. The hair regularly likened to Pink and Miley Cyrus, still barely moved from the hold, forcing her to shake her head loosely. *Ouch*. Her head and back were sore. She would have Paul arrange a massage when she saw him tomorrow, as her body was in desperate need for some TLC.

Georgia opened her fridge looking for something to eat. Paul had gotten her a hearty soup for lunch when he went out, but she hadn't had a chance to eat it. "Hmm, you need to start shopping, girl," she said into the fridge looking at a bottle of water, a banana and a half bottle of pinot. Great, no lunch or dinner. She couldn't order take away again, plus it was far too late to do that. She ignored the stomach grumblings and took the bottle of water. *When was the last time I switched on a light, other than my bedroom in my apartment?* she thought as she switched it on.

1

Looking into the mirror, she noticed the crow's feet starting to appear. She always had been incredibly lucky with the delayed aging process, a gift from her mother. But as of late, she was noticing more and more lines appearing. She supposed she shouldn't be surprised, she was 40 years old after all, and working 17 hour days would *not* be helping. Shaking the depressing thoughts from her head, she gently lifted the silver dress jewellery she was wearing. It was one of her favourites; a set consisting of a long necklace, bracelet and matching earrings. Next, she stepped out of her favourite pointed shoe-boots. *I could use a foot massage, too*, she thought as she massaged the balls of her feet. *Note to self, have Paul actually book a full spa day.* Her body was screaming like a bitch, and she needed her bed more than anything. She unzipped the long sleeve, light pink, sheath dress she was wearing, one of her favourite outfits because it complimented her 5'9, lean frame. Paired with the 6 inch shoes, it accentuated her long legs. Georgia was exhausted, but her nightly ritual of cleansing and toning had never been missed. People had regularly commented over the years at what an incredible complexion she had, and in her mind, that was a significant reason why. She cleansed and toned quickly before slipping into bed in the underwear set she was wearing. "Hmm," she groaned heavily, happy it was Thursday, which meant the cleaners had been in. Fresh sheets had been put on, and there was nothing better in the world she could think of right now. She breathed in the scent, appreciating the comfort as she quickly drifted off to probably only a few short hours of content dreaming.

Houston, USA

Chapter Two

Erika zipped up her navy pencil skirt from behind, and smoothed down her ivory chiffon blouse. Slipping on her navy pumps, she fastened her long black hair in a clip and left the room, clasping her watch as she was walking down the stairs. "Darn," she grumbled to herself, noticing the time as she quickened her pace, and tripped on the stairs. "Damn it! Dulcie, what have I told you about leaving things on the stairs?" she shouted.

"Sorry, Mommy." Her daughter looked up wide-eyed from her bowl of Captain Crunch.

"Baby, is it a school day today?"

"Uh huh." She nodded enthusiastically, taking another giant spoonful.

"So, what's going on here then?" She held up the box of cereal, watching her 5-year-old daughter's face turn into a smile. Dulcie had inherited Erika's Italian features: tanned skin, long dark curls, big brown eyes, and the longest eye lashes. She was the double of Erika, even down to the long lean frame. Dulcie was the tallest in her kindergarten class, even taller than some of the first graders. "Sweetie, you know the rules. No Captain Crunch through the week, remember?" She smiled, wiping the milk from her daughter's chin.

"But, I was told I could," she said seriously.

Of course, you were, she thought. "Come on, pumpkin. Go get your backpack. We need to leave," she said, clearing away Dulcie's bowl and sliding it into the dishwasher.

Erika grabbed her handbag before grabbing her daughter's hand and locking up her 4-bedroom colonial. She fastened Dulcie into the car seat of her Mercedes SUV, kissing her cheek quickly and winking at the girl, swinging her feet and smiling widely. Dulcie was so much like Erika in every way; already incredibly academic, loving going to kindergarten as much as Erika loved going to work. She was happy that Dulcie wasn't like some of her friends' kids where school *'sucked'* already. *The prospect of another 5, 10, 15 years in school when you don't like it*, she thought, shaking her head.

Erika pulled up at her daughter's kindergarten. *Shoot*. She was going to be late for this morning's meeting. "Come on, baby. Mommy's gonna be late." Erika unfastened the car seat and grabbed Dulcie's backpack. She ran up the stairs, kissing and hugging her daughter tightly, before handing her over to Miss Addison. Erika rushed down the stairs, waving away the car beeping behind her that she had blocked in. She grabbed her cell and speed dialled 1, "Hey, it's me. Are they there yet?" She swerved out of the parking lot and pulled onto the street. "Darn! Okay, stall them. No, Dan had to leave early, I needed to drop Dulcie off. No. No, its fine; just stall and get everything ready for me. I'll be there in 10," she said, hanging up on Tim, pulling in and out wherever possible to get into work quicker.

Manchester, UK

Chapter Three

Georgia walked through the door at 5:40am. It was ridiculously early, but she had no alternative, so she needed to throw herself into this. She had spent the last five years working towards this, after all.

She felt confident, the marketing was set up, and they really had done an amazing job. She would need to remember to thank Julia and her team when this was done. Equally the same went for the ops team, and the design team. Hell, every team for that matter. But first she needed to make sure everything was ready for the launch.

Georgia had been an Area Director for just short of five years and was now in line as the next Managing Director. God, was she ready for it. At forty years old she had nothing but her work. The company she was incontestably enslaved to; the company that didn't allow for a social life, a love life, friendship… *Jesus, even friendship.* Georgia had nothing but Paul, who technically was her assistant, so she couldn't really class him as anything. Especially as his girlfriend hated her, she smiled to herself as that realisation hit. Granted his girlfriend *was* a bitch! *Georgia realised she was a sad, lonely, awful, boring, sad, did she say sad? Assistant girlfriend hating bitch. Yep, that pretty much summed it up,* she thought.

"Worrying again, boss?" Paul walked in, pulling her out of the daze.

"Of course, not. What could I possibly have to worry about?" she turned to him. "That it all falls apart? That the office doesn't make any money? That the new business that I brought in pulls out as we cut the ribbon? That I don't make the cut? That I don't get the promotion everybody has refused to bet on, simply because it's such a dead cert? That it all goes Pete tong and they sack me? I'll be unemployed, sad, lonely, depressed, won't be able to afford my apartment, Ohhh my beautiful apartment. My beautiful apartment that I never use because I'm too busy working. Working and dedicating my life to a company that will sack me," she said distantly.

"Fuck, Georgia, you're a little ray of sunshine, today. Where the hell has all of that come from? Come on, for God's sake. You are not going to screw it up, it's done. Nothing can go wrong at this point. You always get this way when we do something big. Always! We aren't actually having a whole cutting the ribbon ceremony, are we?" he said aghast.

"*Really*?" she looked at him stupendously. "Come on. We have ridiculous amounts to do, before 10am, and I have got the headache from hell already starting," she sighed. "This better be worth it," she said stomping off.

***

Georgia sat back in her high-backed chair, feet resting on the corner of her desk. She rubbed her temples and looked out to the city around her, carefully resting the tumbler of grey goose in her lap.

"Wow, now there's a Kodak moment if ever I saw one. You know looking like that really does make us lads realise what a waste it is you being gay. Never getting a piece of this, horrifying it is," Glen grinned. "Just wanted to come in and say a huge congrats, boss. You did… well, you did fucking fantastic." He held out his hand. "Unless a good old hug would be more befitting," he smirked.

"Completely! Would be a wonderful way to screw with HR, that a randy old director was getting frisky with his boss." She smiled holding out her hand professionally.

"Congratulations, sexy. I'll call you that before you become my MD, then you'll really be able to fire my arse. And less of the old," he admonished, before sauntering out of her office.

Chapter Four

Georgia missed being with people on nights like this. Work had been a bitch today, but it was Friday night. She lived in, well in her opinion the *best*, but to most the second-best city in England. It was early and she had nowhere to go and nobody to go with. Paul had left early, and she had no option but to allow him. It *was* his anniversary with the 'psycho bitch' after all.

The team had all gone out for drinks. She wasn't really one for socialising with people from work. The only option, after one of the most rewarding days in history was to go home with a takeaway and a bottle of plonk to celebrate. Problem was, that was her *normal* night, not even a Friday night; not even a celebratory Friday night. She sighed as she picked up her tote bag and left the office. "Home with a bottle it is then," she said sadly.

"Good night, Ms. Carson. You have yourself a wonderful weekend."

Georgia looked up and smiled sadly. "Good night, Joe. You too, don't work too hard," she said to the building concierge

"Fine one to talk, miss," he responded, returning to his newspaper.

At what point is it odd and wrong that the building concierge to your office knows your first name she thought walking out the door?

***

Georgia walked down the street from her office, heading in the direction of Sainsbury's. She would order in, since she didn't really fancy waiting in a restaurant on a Friday night at this time. A bottle or two of pink Moet and then order an Indian and celebrate, the day being an incredible success. Why shouldn't she push the boat out?

As Georgia was heading to Sainsbury's, she was pulled from her thoughts quite literally.

"Oh, my god, you made it? That's fantastic," Julia said, pulling Georgia in for a hug. "I don't think I've ever seen you out of that office, certainly not boozing with us reprobates. But, I guess after today it's the best way to celebrate. With your future lackeys." She smiled. "Ohhh, this is great," she said, grabbing her hand and running off with Georgia in tow.

"Erm, Ju… Jul…," Georgia tried, but it was too late, she had been dragged inside and the music and noise was far too loud for her to be able to get her attention. Plus, Julia was on a mission, weaving her in and out of the crowds. *Wow, town is busy on a Friday night* she thought. They stopped short of an area by the bar with a number of her very intoxicated staff. There were cheers and screams noticing Georgia, seemingly everyone was quite… was *quite happy* she was there. And all wanted a piece of her. Georgia didn't get too caught up by it, she was well aware it was the level of intoxication. But as people were hugging her and offering her drinks, it felt quite nice, and she opted to stay for one drink after all. This was a celebration, and realistically she could leave and spend the rest of the weekend at home. Alone.

***

A few hours later, and a couple hundred quid lighter, Georgia was well on the way to an incredible hangover tomorrow. She hated to admit it, but she was having a good night. Many people had left, whether it was the younger staff going to meet their own friends or some off home to their husbands, wives and kids. Left were a few of the directors and amusingly, a few of the younger women trying to get 'into' said directors. Georgia was unaware that this was a regular occurrence, as well as being condemned over the fact that she didn't regularly participate. Highlighting that she was also a 'city worker'.

"I'm telling you, come out with us all and you will meet the woman of your dreams," a colleague was saying to her.

"Especially as we always end up at the village at the end of the night," Julia joked.

"I was just gonna say that Jules. Are we off yet? Or we doing food tonight?" Glen the ops Director asked. He put an arm each around Julia and Georgia, leaning in to talk to them. "Although, I'm not going to lie, I am more favourable of the village this evening. I think I could enjoy watching this beauty at work," he raised his eyebrows to Georgia.

"I am not even slightly surprised that that sentence has left your mouth." Georgia shook her head. "I can assure you. You will, *never* see me 'at work', certainly not in the context you are referring to. But, I er… probably should go," Georgia said checking the time on her iPhone.

"Ohhh no, don't. Just ignore him. He is a pervy, old pest but we love him anyway," Julia pleaded.

Glen held his hands up in defence. "Listen, darling, I was ruffling your feathers, but I genuinely didn't intend to offend, I can assure you," he offered, looking offended.

"Come on, what else you going to do? Sit at home alone? It's late so I can't imagine many of us will last much longer. Come on, we'll walk to the gay village, sober up a little and have a few more there. We will all be ready for our beds in an hour," Julia said.

"Come on," a few others were chiming in for good measure.

"Ohhh, come on then. I need a bank though. You lot have put me out of business with all these shots." She smiled, walking ahead with a few staff.

"So, what changed your mind about coming out tonight then, George?" Glen asked.

"Celebratory, I bet," Julia smiled widely, clearly very proud of how today went.

"Erm, actually not. I wasn't coming at all, I was walking up to Sainsbury's to grab a couple of bottles of champagne to celebrate and saw Julia, having a cigarette and…"

"*Wait*? What? Jules, since when did you smoke?"

"I don't, I was putting another of my pissed lot in a cab when I saw her," she said. "So, you weren't actually coming in? I… just railroaded you? Oh look, I'm really sorry about that," she said soberly.

"Oh, gosh don't be. I, as it turns out, have had a wonderful evening. I did wonder regarding the smoking, I wasn't aware you did. I thought it must have been a 'social' thing. But please, it's seriously okay. I did try to shout to say *no* when you dragged me in the pub but it was far too loud. So, I just left it and thought it wouldn't hurt to have one, especially given the outcome of today," she said modestly. "But honestly, I have had the most fun I've had in a long time," she said, looking down at Julia.

Julia quickly turned away. "Well, can't change it now," she said, and rushed off into the first pub they came to on Canal Street. Georgia couldn't work out what had just happened. They had always had a good working relationship and she always held her own. She didn't know why she seemed to be embarrassed of making her come for a drink. Georgia followed the rest into the bar, as she pondered over whether Julia thought Georgia may fancy her. And that was why she got awkward.

Georgia wasn't unattractive by any means, and she had been blessed with great skin that aged tremendously well. Well, maybe until this last year. Add an air of elegance and style with a spunky hair style to suit. That, coupled with the confidence she had gained through her years climbing the ladder, she knew she wasn't a bad catch, if she had *wanted* to get involved with anyone. But, equally, it frustrated the hell out of her when women assumed that just because she was a lesbian and they were female that she was automatically going to jump on them.

"What's up gorgeous?" Glen asked, looking concerned and handing her a shot.

"Err…," she held out her hand to say no, then stopped herself. *No sod it, I will stay and continue to have fun,* she thought. "Nothing, my darling, cheers," she clinked his glass and downed the shot. *Bleurgh, that was bloody disgusting, what the hell had she just drank?*

"What do you want to drink?" Julia asked squeezing into the bar, even in her 6 inch heels. Her very slight height didn't give her much in the way of tallness. Albeit, unfair of her to say given the equally high shoes, that Georgia was wearing.

"Erm, it's okay, I just had one," she said.

"No that was the shot, I'm getting the drinks. I'm a bit wined out, I think I'm going to have a gin and tonic," she said, passing over the drinks she had already got and ordering more.

"Gin and tonic? How old are you?" Georgia said smirking.

"Thirty-six, you signed my thirty sixth birthday card. And I happen to like it," she said seriously.

"Georgia?"

She heard the voice and immediately turned around, fearful at the recognition swimming through her bones. "Hi! What are you doing here?" Georgia said, looking at her ex in front of her, standing next to what she assumed was her new girlfriend given the way she was 'attached' to her. *Oh seriously. get a grip, you silly bloody dyke, you don't have to be all possessive. I'm well aware she's yours now*, she thought.

"We're out with our friends," she pointed. "How about you? I didn't think you *liked* the village? *Or* socialising? *Or* leaving the office?" she said pointedly.

Jesus it's been three years and you're still pissed? Georgia thought. "Well, you know. I guess things change," she sighed.

"Actually, we're out celebrating. This fine specimen," Julia said, grabbing Georgia's arm, "Just got a promotion today. And so, we've brought her out to have some…well…," Julia looked the women up and down. "Have some *real* fun, with some cute as fuck women. If you wouldn't mind, this is a private party. Shoo shoo," she said, shooing them with her hand, and turning Georgia back around, handing her a drink.

Georgia couldn't believe how abrupt and harsh Julia had been, equally she couldn't stop herself from inwardly laughing.

***

They were all laughing, completely stunned at the direct approach of Julia. "She's actually fearless. If you blew on her, she'd fall over, yet she is doing stuff like that," one of her marketing team said.

"I still can't believe she shooed her. That's the funniest thing I've ever seen. Ohhh, I love this song, come on let's go dance," Glen said, grabbing two of the staff, who Georgia couldn't quite place. Glen equally questioned whether they were actually staff, given they looked barely old enough to be employed. He didn't care though; he was off to the area where the residents had decided to transform in to a dance floor.

Georgia leaned back against the bar, observing everyone as they sang like their lives depended on it. 'Nothing's gonna stop us now,' was the song keeping them all adjoined and loving life. "Not joining them?" Julia said to her.

"Erm, no, not really my thing." She smiled, sipping her drink, clearly not enjoying it any longer.

"Really? You don't like this song? Oh, I love it… 'and we can build this dream together, standing strong forever' I love it. It's the best song for pulling funny faces and singing your heart out, see?" Julia said, pointing to their colleagues laughing.

Georgia leant down closer. "So, why aren't you there with em?" she smirked, realising she'd startled Julia, who now looked embarrassed and stepped farther away from Georgia.

"You know, just because I'm gay doesn't mean I fancy every woman within my vicinity," she said seriously.

"What?"

"Well, you were weird outside. Then I was leaning closer so you could hear me, given how loud you were singing and you flinched like I was going to do something to you."

"Georgia, I'm well aware you weren't about to touch me. Nor, did I think you were outside. You startled me is all. I'm going to dance," she said, leaving her empty glass on the bar and joining the rest of the crew.

Chapter Five

Georgia couldn't remember a time she was up so late. She was going to pay for it the next day, she could already tell. However, she was not drunk enough to let her directors and senior members of staff, who were attempting to discreetly leave with the young women, go unnoticed. They had been hanging off their every word all night. She looked on, bewilderedly knowing that most of them had wives and girlfriends.

"Right, you bailing too?" Glen asked, barely able to stand any longer.

"I think, you should be bailing. But yes. I haven't eaten, and I'm suddenly faced with some very angry tummy rumblings. I think I'm going to go and hunt down a late-night takeaway and go home," Georgia said.

"Ohhh, let's go to curry mile. There's taxis there, and it's open all night. I could murder some Indian. Come on, the last three standing," Glen held up his arms as if championing himself.

Julia looked at Glen, concerned. "Hmm, sure you can manage that, buddy? I'm game, I'm bloody starving, too. I literally had a cocktail sausage and a satay stick from the buffet, but I'm unsure you can do it," she said seriously.

Glen was laughing to himself. "Didn't think sausages were your thing?" he chuckled. "Anyways, yes, it's fine. Come on, Georgia. You can come and have a final supper with us low levellers. I only live close by. I will drink water and eat, and then I hopefully won't get too much of a bashing when I get home." He smiled, falling backwards, causing the two women to grab each arm of his.

"Well, I guess I have no choice, given the state you're in. I am putting my foot down, we are drinking soft drinks," Georgia said seriously, walking him over to the taxi.

"Most of them you can only drink soft drinks, or bring your own booze in now anyhow," Julia said, holding him up the other side.

They got in the taxi and told the driver to go straight to curry mile, both women praying Glen would make it there without being sick.

***

"Glen, you're going to get us thrown out, and we're starving. Come on, wake up," Georgia scolded him. "Is he always like this?" she turned looking to Julia.

"He's always shitfaced, yes. To be honest, he doesn't normally come with us to the final bar. Glen, your wife just called," she said, smirking to Georgia.

"What? Shit," he said, opening one eye, rolling his head around like Churchill the nodding dog. "Stop moving you pair, it isn't funny. Come on, stop playing silly buggers. Stop it! Ohhh, I can't, I must leave. Ladies, it's been a pleasure. I'm deeply troubled that I'm leaving you two alone, and I want stories," he smirked, and pointed to them. "Lots of stories Monday," he said, still smirking and pointing his finger, to what they could only assume was supposed to be them. "But my manhood is far too important to me. She will chop it off if I don't get home immediately," he said, falling backwards. "Ooops. Sorry there, mate," he said, shaking the young man's hand that he had virtually fell on, before he bounced like a pinball out of the restaurant.

"Amazing! What the hell do we do with that food?" Georgia said seriously.

"Well, you may as well take it, if you like it. You can have it over the weekend.

"Why would I need it and you wouldn't?" Georgia asked accusingly.

"Erm, well, you don't have to. I just thought that you…well you work a lot so it means you don't have to worry about food," Julia said shyly. "I'm sorry I didn't mean to offend you," she added quietly, scorning herself for pissing off her boss.

Their starters arrived and the women sat in uncomfortable silence, enjoying the food. "Look, I'm sorry, I was out of line before. It was a nice offer, I just hate people thinking that I'm this sad, lonely spinster because I have chosen to work my arse off and make something of myself. I'm not saying I'm the only one. I know others are making things of themselves, but just because I choose this option and not the whole marriage, two-point-four kids, and white picket fence thing, equally doesn't mean that I can't look after myself." Then she remembered the recollection of her regular empty fridge and polo's diet.

"On the contrary, Georgia, nobody thinks you're a sad spinster. Everyone loves you, we all love working for you. I think people are only concerned and want you to let up, just a little, you know? Do this. Come out with us, just once a month? Get pissed and end up in an Indian at…" She looked at her watch. "Sodding hell, it's quarter to three in the morning! Where did the night go? They…no, we all know and love you, and just want you to have a happy, *healthy* work life balance."

"Yeah, well I guess some of us aren't built that way. Is it really quarter to three? Shit, I don't think I've been awake this late since my twenties, unless it was work related," she said distantly.

"And that's exactly my point. Foods good, isn't it?" Julia said changing the subject.

"Yes very, we may not have anything to wrap up of his," Georgia said pinching more of Glen's starter.

"Good, I was starting to worry you had some eating disorder. You never seem to bloody eat," she said half serious and half joking.

"Yes, I know. I never appear to have time. It's not healthy I know, but when I do eat, I really do as you can see." She smiled, taking more food.

"Well you could do with a bit of feeding up. So, are you up to much this weekend?" Julia asked.

"Oh, you know, I need to do a few bits of work, and then, I will probably just relax. How about you?"

"Do you not even have a break at the weekend?" Julia said sadly.

Georgia had never felt bad about all the work she had put it, since she never really did anything outside of work. Tonight, she'd had a lot of fun, and strangely it was with people who were also highly driven. Hitting home, that maybe she could have a night out once a month and do something other than work, *especially* on a weekend. "Yeah ummm, not really, I guess I lost a lot of my friends and that when I started working so hard. I don't want you to feel sorry for me. Weirdly I have kind of gotten used to it, and like it that way."

"I didn't feel sorry for you, Georgia. I just think it's unhealthy. Well, if you fancy something different, my friends are dragging me to a speed dating night tomorrow.

You are more than welcome to come. The more the merrier," she said, smiling.

"Thanks for the offer. But, I don't think too many men would be impressed that I wasted their two minutes, five minutes or whatever when I end it on, and oh, I'm gay," she laughed.

Julia went to say something when their main courses came up, so she didn't continue.

***

"Sorry, you were going to say?" Georgia said spooning the food on her plate. "As the food arrived?"

"Ohhh, it doesn't matter, it's fine," she said quietly.

"What? No, say it. Please? I suddenly feel that I have done something to offend you. I can be very…blind, so I don't want to worry I have offended you somehow. If I have done or said something, I need to apologise," Georgia said, looking at her Marketing Director seriously.

Julia sighed heavily. Putting her fork down. "There wouldn't be any boys there," she said.

"Excuse me?" Georgia was confused.

"You said you didn't want to come to speed dating because the guys wouldn't be happy. There won't be lads there," she said, tearing off a piece of naan bread and concentrating on her food again.

Oh, you mean…?" she said, turning to look at Julia. "You're gay?"

Julia laughed sarcastically, shaking her head. "Yes, I'm gay," she said.

"Oh bollox, did I know you were gay?" she asked, more a question to herself than Julia. She was racking her brain. They had worked together a number of years, had she told her? Georgia would have remembered. Had Georgia just really offended her?

"No, don't worry, you didn't know, you were completely unaware of my attempts to get you to notice me for my first couple of years here," she said quietly.

"Shit, *what*? You were flirting with me? *Really*? And I missed that. Did you make it clear? I'm so sor...," Georgia said, putting her arm on Julia's and feeling completely awful. She was a very attractive woman, well aside from the fact they would look horrific with the 2ft height difference. But she would never intentionally hurt anyone, and now she felt that she might have been a complete arsehole to this woman.

"George, seriously relax. It was a *long* time ago. I'm over it now. I guess the more you ignored me, the more I wanted you. And you have nothing to apologise for. You are career minded, and you don't let anything get in your way. For the record, I made it very, *very* clear," she said, returning back to her food.

"Career minded. Wow, that didn't hurt one bit," she sighed. "What do you mean, you *made* it very clear?"

"I wasn't looking to offend, this isn't a 'tit for tat'. I genuinely like you as a person. I'm not attracted to you, and it's been great to have you be a part of tonight. But, I'm not after you any longer, so you can relax," she said plainly. "Have you ever seen the movie love actually?" She looked at Georgia.

"The interlinking one? Lots of stories? Christmas?" she responded confused.

"Yes," Julia laughed, surprised that she had time for movies. "Well, in the beginning the American woman, she's into a guy in the office and everyone knows, including him. Well, it was kinda the same. Only, you were

21

the only one whom didn't know," she said, raising her eyebrows as she returned to her food.

"Wow," Georgia said, putting her fork down and pushing her plate back.

"Please don't, I didn't mean to upset you," Julia said, concerned.

"You didn't. I don't know what I'm more bothered about. The fact that I have not noticed a beautiful woman flirting with me, or the fact that I'm seemingly a self-obsessed arsehole, that clearly everyone is aware of," she said sadly.

Julia felt awful. "Listen, you really aren't self-obsessed. I can assure you, *none* of us think that. And… thanks for the kind words," she said, embarrassed. "Come on, let's not waste a good night. It's been a ball. Who knew you could be so much fun?" she smirked, banging her shoulder.

***

After a few minutes arguing over who was going to pay, they eventually left, with Georgia winning the battle on the basis that she was clueless to years of wasted flirting.

"So, which direction do you need to go in? You back in town?" Georgia asked Julia, unsure of where she lived.

"No, I don't live in Manchester, I need to grab a cab as I missed my last train. We can get a couple of taxis down here.

"Why have you missed your train? It's ridiculously late, where do you live?"

"Oldham, and before you start, don't flatter yourself?" she winked. "I do this every month remember, all the *'sociable'* guys, we go out once a month. Each month, I miss my train and pay for a taxi," Julia laughed.

"Oh, Erm. I wasn't thinking that, I wasn't flattering myself. I... I certainly wasn't assuming that you had stayed out just...to try...well, to try and get...well you know what I mean," Georgia said.

Julia stopped, turning to face Georgia. "No, I don't actually," she smirked. "Please enlighten me?"

"Oh, piss off. Come on, you can crash at mine. I know you aren't after me anymore, and I have a room. Tomorrow you can do the 'walk of shame' in the light, and get on the tram for a few quid, rather than forty quid for a taxi," Georgia said, linking her arm through Julia's, enjoying the time she'd spent with the woman tonight.

Julia was ready to object, prior to Georgia linking their arms, but she just went with it. Granted, she no longer had any romantic feelings for the beautiful woman. But they were still two single women, and she *was* incredibly hot, so if an opportunity arose, she certainly wouldn't bat her away, Julia decided drunkenly.

Chapter Six

"Here you go. I've got some PJ's for you, and I was going to ask if you wanted a drink, but it's after three so I don't think that's probably the best idea I ever had," Georgia said. "If you need anything else, help yourself. I have waters in the fridge. You're lucky, I have been shopping. Normally, it's empty. And there are spare, unopened tooth brushes in the main bathroom, just by the front door."

"Blimey, even organised at home. Must have a fair few unexpected guests to have a selection of spare toothbrushes," Julia smirked.

"Piss off. Right, I'll let you crack on, I need to brush my teeth badly. There was far too much garlic in that food," Georgia said, walking past Julia as they both stepped in front of the other at the same time.

"Sorry," they said in unison. Julia sidestepped the opposite way this time, just as Georgia did the same. They smiled at each other.

"This isn't awkward at all," Julia said. "Apologies, I will stand still. You go where you need to."

Georgia shook her head, smirking down at the woman. "My room's this way, therefore, I shall walk to my left," she grinned.

"Wow, was that an offer?" Julia walked backwards, raising an eyebrow to Georgia, who was looking back at her over her shoulder.

She continued looking forward, shaking her head. "You're ever so naughty."

"Ohhh, you don't have a clue, boss."

***

One word, one bloody word was causing this much of a stir inside of her. She knew it was only the drink causing the reaction. This was all very new to her; drinking sociably, flirting, having a single, good-looking lesbian in her home at three-thirty a.m. *You can't do this*, Georgia kept telling herself. Hearing the way she said *boss* in that alluring manner though. It wasn't even the fact she called her 'boss,' many of her staff did. It was definitely how she said it. The way it rolled off her tongue, that naughtiness, the provocativeness to it. It wasn't fair on her. She needed to stop reliving the words she was *'over her now'*. She couldn't dare go near her, it wouldn't be fair. But, God she was horny, she'd not been with anyone for ages. And the stress of the last couple of months...sex would have been the best blow out. *No, behave.* She turned over and covered her head with the pillow, before hearing the knock at the door.

"George, you awake?" Julia opened the door.

Ohhh fuck. She was in the doorway with the light shining through the partially opened door. Wearing only the T-shirt of the PJ set Georgia had given her, resting at her thighs. Georgia coughed, trying to ignore the outfit, or lack thereof. "Yes, are you okay?"

"Yeah, your room is bloody boiling, and I can't reach the window. Seriously, why the hell do architects these days make these funky city centre buildings so weird?" She

25

laughed. "I was going to sleep in the lounge but I couldn't find a cover, sorry to wake you."

Georgia laughed getting up. "I have another spare room," she said, walking out of the room.

"Well, I didn't want to go into your rooms. You may have some kind of S&M room in there for all I know. Although, I wish I had of now, had I known you were going to come out half naked. I definitely would have opted for the former," she said looking Georgia up and down.

Georgia looked at her solicitously before responding. "Yes, of course. I don't have time to eat *or* have a social life. However, I have regular 'live in's' whom are holed up in my very own Christian Grey, red room." She shook her head. "There you are. Is that wide enough for you? The suns on it all day, and because it is predominantly windows, this room particularly gets like a greenhouse." She turned around looking at Julia.

"Well, whatever floats your boat, I don't know what you're in to. You aren't much different to Christian Grey, high earning super exec that works too much. What's it they say? 'All work and no play, makes 'you a very dull person'? Plus, I don't know that isn't your release?" she said engagingly.

"You need to stop misbehaving. My release…for the record, is exercise," Georgia said, walking past Julia.

"Misbehaving? *Me?* Best behave, or you may just have to discipline me," she said alluringly. "And exercise is a good release. You know what the best form of exercise is don't you?" Julia said walking back over to the bed.

Georgia sighed, feeling the pull and knowing it was wrong of her to even consider what she was considering. She was the boss. She was the senior person and she was condemning the guys earlier for fucking about with the young women from the office. Equally, they were all married and in relationships. These two…well, they were both single adults. She turned to Julia, raising her eyebrow as she saw her sitting on the bed with her knees slightly raised, giving off the very slightest view of her right buttock and thigh. She looked straight back up to Julia's eyes, who was smirking, having caught her looking. *Fuck*, Julia was up for this just as much as Georgia was. They were both adults. And she wasn't hurting her if she didn't actually have feelings for her anymore, right? Georgia walked quickly over to the bed, pushing her down against the mattress, with her hands on either side of her head.

"You are so bad. You know this can't happen. I'm your boss. You liked me, I don't want to hurt you," Georgia said more of a question.

"You're the one half naked, holding me down, with your knee between my thighs. Rendering me powerless to you, no less," she raised an eyebrow. "FYI, 'Liked' are the key words here, George. I don't care that you're my boss. I have no interest in sharing this information in the next board meeting. Simply put, I am drunk and horny, and Erm, not blind," she said, looking down at Georgia's body. "You are hot, especially right now. Being all sexy, toned, and dominant. Plus, I'm pretty sure," she paused confidently. "Frustrated as…"

Georgia kissed her hard. *Sod it; like she said were both adults.*

Houston, USA

Chapter Seven

"Are you sure you don't want to come out to celebrate? It's been a hard-going couple months," Tim said to his boss

"Don't I know it? No, I'm good. You go. I am just as good going and celebrating with my favourite girl. And at the moment, sweats, a jersey, Frozen, and a Luigi's Mexicana." She smiled.

***

Erika got in her car and punched in Taylor's number. "Hey, I'm gonna stop by Luigi's. You wanna stay and have dinner with us, or do you have big plans tonight?" she laughed into the phone to her nanny.

"Seriously! You don't even wanna joke about that. I'm pretty sure my future is dark and gloomy, and this dating game is just plain mean," she sighed. "Is Dan not home?" Taylor asked.

"No. Working late. So, game? How's Dulcie?"

"She's great, we have only watched F...R...O...Z...E... N once today, and I even promised a trip to the mall to treat her to any movie she wants to pick out. Yeah sure, I'll stay over for pizza, and I'll give you the update on the public humiliation from last night's date. Are we celebrating? Should I open a bottle? Ohhh, we can watch a grown-up movie," Taylor said excitably.

Erika started laughing "Oh, I can't wait for this. We can celebrate, yes," she said shyly. Erika was sad that it was only her nanny that had remembered and bothered to comment. "Cool, I'll be home soon." She hung up, and punched in another number.

"Hey, it's me; is Dan there please?"

"Hey you," Dan responded, distracted.

"Hi, how's work been? So, how late you working? I was gonna swing by Luigi's on the way home and grab takeout."

"Ohhh, I'm sorry sweetie; I just have so much going on at the office. You guys do it without me, I will order something here. I'll be late, baby, don't wait up. Look I need to go, or I won't be home at all; have a good night, give Dulcie a kiss from me."

"I lo…," yeah, *I love you too*, she said sarcastically into the dead phone line. She rested her head in her spare hand against the car window as she continued her drive to Luigi's.

***

Erika parked her car in the garage and carried the pizza boxes into the house. "I'm home," she shouted to the house.

"Mommy, Mommy," Dulcie said, running into her.

"Ohhh, easy kiddo. Mommy's got dinner," she said, handing the boxes over to Taylor, who had come to her rescue.

Erika picked up her daughter, in her frozen pajamas. *This kid is obsessed*, she thought. "Hey baby, good day at school?" She kissed her, before putting her own down.

"Nooooo, not really," she said sadly, concerning Erika. "It was really kinda tough," she sighed, with her hands on

29

her hips. "They gave us a test," her little feet trying to keep up with them into the kitchen.

Erika spun around looking confused at Dulcie's serious face.

Taylor was behind Dulcie smirking and shaking her index finger to Erika, whispering that it was her who'd got the unexpected test. "Wow, for real?" Taylor picked up Dulcie and put her on the countertop. "That's so weird, Dulcie, me too. I went to school and they gave me a surprise test," she shook her head, pouring two glasses of wine and one glass of grape juice.

"You did? Wow, I mean isn't that odd. Do you got Miss Addison to?" Dulcie asked.

"Maybe I got Miss Addison's mommy. I guess you need a glass of wine like mommy and I too huh?" Taylor asked, giving the grape juice to Dulcie.

"Yeah, I do. It's been a long, hard day," she sighed sipping her juice. "Hmm, fruity."

Taylor and Erika turned their backs from Dulcie, smiling at the little girl's words. "So, little lady. You have been bathed, ate dinner, and this is your last drink before bed. Now go, you have 15 minutes only, okay?" Taylor said, lifting her down. "Go watch the last of your TV show, then you can have a bedtime story from mommy."

"Ohhh, but I wanna stay up with you guys," she whined.

Erika looked at her daughter. The '*behave*' stare, always worked a treat; whether that would remain when she became a teenager, who knew?

"Mommy, can you come watch TV with me for a short while before I go to bed?"

"Of course, baby. Go get our seats warm and I'll be right in," she said, gently kicking her daughter's butt;

evoking a small scream and giggle from her, as she ran off to the second living room.

"How about you go relax and have some time with Dulcie? I'll keep this warm for us, plus I gotta make a few calls. Then we can sit down for dinner, movie, drinks and gossip." Taylor said.

"You are a godsend. Thanks, Tay. Listen, don't feel the need to babysit a lonely old woman on a Friday night. If you have better options, go. Go, have fun," Erika said seriously.

"Well, at this moment in time. Unless George Clooney was to come whisk me off on a private jet to Italy, for a real Italian pizza, I'm pretty confident this is the best offer I have had for a long time." She smiled to her boss and friend.

Erika gasped. "Wash your mouth out," she said, covering the sides of the pizza boxes. "Luigi will be most offended," she smirked.

"Mommy, where are you?" Dulcie called, poking her head around the door.

Taylor held her hands up in surrender. "I apologise to the great Luigi and anyone else I have offended," she smirked. "Go, her ladyship has summoned you," she said in her best British accent, taking a bow, cleaning the kitchen up from the cake they had been baking earlier.

***

Taylor could hear Dulcie's sniffles. Walking into the room she watched the girl crying in her mom's arms, sniffing heavily that she didn't want to go to bed yet. Erika was a wonderful mom, and she worked her ass off. Taylor knew how hard it was for her to leave her daughter every day and not spend every waking moment with her. But as she frequently said, she wanted to make sure that Dulcie knew it was important to dream big, have a solid experience of strong independent women, and provide her with a stable upbringing. Equally, she could feel her pain every time she said goodbye to her baby girl. "Hey, Dulcie; come here a moment, I have secret."

Dulcie looked up at her nanny, still sniffling. "No, I don't wanna," she cried a little more.

"Oh, that's a shame. I have a surprise, and I thought you might like to help me with it?" she said, slowly walking out of the room.

Dulcie looked up at Erika, who shrugged to her daughter. "I don't know, baby. Maybe you gotta go see?" she said.

Taylor stopped and held out her hand for Dulcie to go with her. They walked into the kitchen and Taylor put her on the countertop. "Did you forget the celebration cake we baked today for mommy? I think we should do it now, then you gotta go to bed like a good girl, ok? Mommy needs to have some dinner and then when you wake you guys have the whole weekend together. No work." She smiled.

"For real? No work?" Dulcie said, slowly coming around.

"No work, baby." They both looked around to see Erika standing at the doorway in her pant suit, resting her head against the doorframe. Dulcie had the biggest smile on her face, and Taylor's chest tightened.

"So, tell mommy to go sit back down so we can surprise her," Taylor said with her hands on her hips.

Dulcie's sad face suddenly burst into the biggest of grins. She giggled and kicked her feet excitably. "Go away,

Mommy. We got a surprise for you," she said, wiping her eyes.

"You do? Okay, I'll leave. But Dulcie, seriously, it's getting late, you have to go bed then, okay?"

"Okay," she said quietly, turning back around to Taylor.

Taylor smiled to Erika as they watched her leave. They opened the fridge and grabbed the chocolate cake they had made earlier. The plan was to write 'Congratulations Mommy' on it, however, Dulcie was adamant that she should write the words, and as such they had 'congratulati'. She guessed she could say it was Italian. They have a lot of words that end in 'I', and as Erika was Italian, that could maybe work, she thought. "Okay, you wanna go switch the lights out? I'll light the candles and bring it in," she said, lifting Dulcie down.

"Tay Tay? What do we sing?"

"What do you mean?"

"Well, we can't sing happy birthday. Because it's not her birthday," she said seriously.

"Erm, how about we don't sing. We just go in and shout congratulations, or congratulati." She smiled.

Dulcie ran into the second living room. She pulled her children's seat over to the light switch, standing on it, and switched it off.

"What are you doing, baby?"

"It's a surprise," she said, running out of the room again.

They walked into the room with the chocolate cake and both shouted congratulations. "Wow, what's this?" Erika said, taking the cake so that Taylor could switch the light back on.

"It's your celebration cake. We made it all by ourselves today," she gleamed.

"You did? For me?" Erika said, confused by the word 'congratulati' written across the middle of the chocolate cake.

"Don't ask." Taylor smiled, shaking her head.

Chapter Eight

Erika came back downstairs after showering and putting her daughter to bed. She was feeling relaxed with the comfort of her hair tied back in a high ponytail, and her Brown University vest top and sweatpants. It was a warm spring night, and the seasons were about to change, which was noticeable now. She walked into the lounge and could see the movies laid out on the floor alongside the wine and pizza boxes on the coffee table.

"I feel much better now; my feet have officially fallen out with me. And possibly my stomach. I'm starved," Erika said, sitting on the couch on one of her feet, reaching for her wine and a slice of pizza. Taking a big bite of the pizza she leaned her head back on the couch. "Ohhh, yes, yes, yes. Everything is right with the world. Thank you, Luigi," she mumbled through the mouthfuls.

"You are seriously having some kinda love affair with a pizza, you know, that, right?"

"Heeeey, I'm Italian," Erika smirked. "How rude. Salut? Apologies, I needed food," holding her glass up.

"Cheers," she clinked her glass. "I guess you didn't eat again then, no?"

"I know, I know. Please no more lectures. I can't take it today," she said, rubbing her temples.

"You need a spa day, and no lectures. Two full time stressful jobs. The stress of the job you do, combined with not eating, isn't good for anybody. I'm just saying," she said, holding up her hand to stop Erika from speaking.

"And now; I'm not saying. So… today? Hit me," Taylor said, leaning in for a slice of pizza.

***

Taylor and Erika discussed all the details of the day's events. "You want to open another bottle?" Taylor asked. "Celebrations and all that? Alternatively, I can call a cab."

"Hell no, I am yet to hear the latest dating escapades. You fill a sad old woman's life with so much comedy. I'll grab another bottle," she said as she picked up another slice of pizza and walked to the kitchen, putting the bottle in the ice bucket. "Fancy champers. Celebrations and all that?" she smirked.

"For sure. But, you really do need to stop with the whole *old* woman BS. Seriously, you are only a few years older than me. Also, you're a total MILF, so you can't pull the 'old' card out. Deal?"

"MILF?" she laughed. "Yeah right, in my sweats and hair pulled up? Real sexy." She shook her head and popped the lid of the bottle, pouring them each a glass.

"Lots of people like the relaxed look. And you pull off a very good *work* look. Today's was a particularly good one," Taylor laughed. "Here's to… sexy, over 30, who still got it," she said, clinking Erika's glass.

"You have turned out to be one of the best friends I have ever had you know that?" Erika clinked back. "And here's to over thirty." She smiled.

"Well, I'm guessing the fact you put me through school and have never tried to hit on me, made me a little more than just the babysitter," she smirked.

"I cannot believe you have just said that to your boss," she smirked. "FYI, I didn't put you through school, I invested in my best friend." She smiled. "Anyways, this is all becoming very deep, after, too little alcohol. Tell me about last night's prince charming." She grinned.

"Prince charming? Seriously? Ohhh, you will love this. So, he showed up, looked me up and down, turned to the restaurant, and walked through the door. He didn't even hold it open for me."

"Creep," they both said in unison, laughing.

"So, we sit down, he looks me up and down again, and tells me the 'profile picture looks like you're blonde.' I mean, I know people are specifically attracted to certain types, but to be so rude about it? I have never thought I was too bad on the eye, but really?" She took a sip of the champagne. "Long, story short. He was a jerk. I decided I would be equally as rude, so I responded with 'maybe it's your sight that's going as opposed to my profile pic. I'm light brown and always have been, and had you asked anything about me, then maybe we would have established this fact and not wasted either of our times.'" She paused to take some more wine. "I basically said, 'I'm suddenly not very hungry, so I'll let you get the drinks after wasting my time and being so utterly arrogant,'" she said, looking to Erika.

"You didn't?" she laughed.

"Hell, I did. I mean seriously, who treats people that way? What a jerk. Oh, and then the gas station guy from last week? Yeah, so we went out. He was cute, complimentary, a good sense of humour, had all the same interests I did. I'm like right on, this is awesome, he's checking all the boxes; he says you wanna come back to my place? I was like, ummm, I'm gonna respectfully decline, but would you like to arrange another date? He was like, really? I have pulled out all the stops, tonight's the only night my wife's away. He called me a frigid bitch, threw 30 bucks on the table and said, 'looks like I'm not paying, after all we can go Dutch,' and left. Just like that, he threw the money on the table and left."

"Oh, my God, you're kidding? Oooh, honey. I'm so sorry. What a jerk. Listen, ignore the idiot that wants a blonde and ignore the idiot that wants to get laid. You are stunning, you know that? You are incredibly stunning, come on. You're fresh off a Calvin Klein infomercial. Listen, mister right is close by, who will love you for your beauty and your brains, and all the wonderful things about you. I'm sorry it's been tough. The alternative is you turn into a lesbian," Erika said to her laughing.

"This is a real possibility," she laughed. "But don't sweat it. It's fine, I'm fine." She shrugged. "I'm not looking for love. I am so close to finishing school, so I really should be concentrating on that. I just wouldn't mind a little fun once in a while, you know? Someone to kiss occasionally. And hell, some action," she laughed, topping them both up with more champagne.

"It's not all it's cracked up to be you know? Don't rush it, promise me that?"

"I know, I know. You okay? You and Dan having problems? You know I'm here if you wanna talk, right? Just lemme know?"

"I know," Erika said, resting her hand on Taylor's. "I'm fine, I'm always fine, right?" she said sadly.

"Just because you say that regularly, it doesn't mean I buy it. You work so hard, and you keep everything boxed up. Maybe you should make Dan stay home one night and you and I go out. We can have a girl's night out, or go away for the weekend. You are always stressed, so we could go to a hotel for a couple nights and have a spa day and a drunken night," Taylor said.

"Hmm, that sounds awesome. I could do with some relaxation," she said distantly. Daydreaming about hour long massages, spas, saunas, facials, putting on her little black dress, and nice jewellery, drinking expensive champagne in a spectacular atrium with stunning chandeliers. "I like this idea a lot."

"Well you were either daydreaming about the relaxation or about checking some hot piece of ass out. Knowing you as I do, I'm guessing the former."

"You are so wrong. And, so sex obsessed," Erika said, shaking her head vigorously.

"Hey, nothing wrong with window shopping," she smirked.

Chapter Nine

Erika got up the following morning, her head a little sore from the alcohol and the long ass week she had been subjected to. God, she hoped it would all be worth it. She looked across the bed, and surprise-surprise, Dan wasn't there. Sighing heavily, she looked to the clock. *Damn*, it was after 9, and she never slept later than 6, not even on a weekend. She tried to remember what time Taylor had left, after they stayed up late chatting. She needed to get up and find Dulcie. She'd promised her little girl a work free day, and that she would most definitely get. They could make plans, as presumably, Dan was working again.

Erika quickly freshened up before leaving her room and going downstairs to find Dulcie. She could hear the TV going, *Dan must have left her sleeping and got up with Dulcie*, she thought. *Please lord, not Frozen again*. She walked into the lounge, and found Taylor asleep with Dulcie snuggled into her, watching a movie, interestingly not Frozen.

"Hey, mommy," she said lazily.

"Sssshhhh, baby. You'll wake Taylor," she said.

"It's okay, Taylor's awake. We finished the movie yet, buddy?" Taylor said, sitting up and pulling Dulcie up onto her lap.

"Not just yet," she said, not looking away from the TV.

"Okay, you finish here. I'm going to have some coffee with mommy until it finishes okay?" she said, lifting her up and putting her back on the couch.

"Hey, what are you doing here?" Erika looked over to a tired Taylor, crossing her arms as they walked side by side to the kitchen. "I thought you left last night?"

"I did," she sighed. "I got a call this morning from Dan to look after Dulcie, as you needed to sleep."

"Oh, as opposed to you!" Erika said pointedly. "Thanks, Tay. I wish you had called me. Dan was out of line doing that. But, yet again why use your common sense! I'll pay you extra. I can only apologise. I know you need to study," she said, turning her back to Taylor, and breathing heavily. She was so mad, but it wasn't appropriate to do this now with Taylor or in front of Dulcie, since she had been kind enough to come over.

Taylor walked over to Erika and turned her around. "It's the weekend, and it's *your* time with Dulcie. This? *This* right here," she said, pointing to them both. "This is no big deal. Only if you make it one. Now, go sit down. I'll make us coffee and some pancakes. Dulcie wanted to wait before eating breakfast so that you could eat together, so we can all eat together. Luigi's made me super hungry this morning," she said, switching on the coffee maker. "Oh, and Erika, you will not pay me more money. And I'm okay with my studies, I am keeping on top of it, okay? Look, unless you have anything else planned for today, why don't the three of us go to Katy Mills? I promised her I would take her to the mall to buy a new movie, we *need* a new movie," she rolled her eyes. "And do a girl's lunch? Maybe rainforest café?" Taylor said making the coffee.

"That's very kind, but I can't ask you to do that. It's your weekend, too. *You* need some free time, too," she said, thanking Taylor for the drink.

"Cut it out already. You didn't ask me Erika. If you want time alone with your daughter, say that and I'll happily leave it. However, if you are saying it simply because you feel you are putting me out, then don't," Taylor said, sipping her coffee.

"You really are the greatest," Erika said, covering her hand with her own, smiling slightly.

Dulcie ran in. "My movie is finished. What are we gonna do today, Mommy?" she said enthusiastically.

Erika looked at Taylor, smiling.

"Well, Dulcie, I think we should let mommy go shower, and we make breakfast. Then, how bout we go to the mall? We can go choose a new movie, and maybe get lunch at rainforest café as a special treat?" Taylor said.

"Yayyyyyy, I love the forest café. Can we watch the g'rillas when it goes dark?" She clapped her hands excitably.

Erika shook her head smiling, "Go choose some clothes," she said to her daughter. "She goes there far too often if she knows that much about it. I'm surprised she didn't mention Dan, maybe she's just getting used to a lack of 2 parents?" she sighed.

"Maybe she just has a good memory? She doesn't go there too often, because if she did she would be complacent about it and wouldn't have gotten that excited. Stop overthinking. You both have extremely demanding jobs, so she may just be stoked to have some time with you and has not realised it won't be the three of you. Seriously, going back to last night's conversation, we need to arrange a girl's weekend away, a spa weekend where you can de-stress, okay? Now go shower, I'll make breakfast."

"Why do you do all this, Tay?" Erika said sadly.

"Because I love you guys, and it's truly the very least I could do. Given all you have done for me," she said, hugging Erika. "C'mon, we're gonna have an awesome day today, for that little bambina. Go shower," Taylor said, kissing her cheek.

Manchester, UK

Chapter Ten

Georgia walked into the office, glued to her phone. "You look like you have a spring in your step," Georgia heard as she looked around, seeing Julia sitting on one of her team's desk, swinging her legs beneath her.

"I don't know what you mean," Georgia responded with a glint in her eye.

"Of course, you don't, you look like you've had the weekend of your life," Julia smirked.

"Well wouldn't you like to know?" she smirked back, and walked to her office.

"What was that about, Jules?"

"Who knows? Maybe she's heard about her promotion after last week's success," Julia said, walking back to her own office.

***

Julia returned back to her office and began typing an email. She smiled to herself before typing in her boss's email address, and drummed her fingers whilst she thought of a subject title. "Got it," she said to herself. 'Advice needed', perfect. Julia leaned back in her chair, smirking to herself at the recollection of Friday night. God, she was hot. She moved forward again and began typing.

Hi, I hope you had a wonderful weekend. I have a slight issue that I could use assistance with. I would like to tender a proposal to HR and think I would probably need your support. I think we should implement a 'dress code' policy.

She smiled to herself as she pressed send before grabbing her file, and leaving for the board meeting.

***

The board meeting was predominantly ran by Georgia, however Derek the CEO was up, and insisted on chairing due to the recent success of the new office. It was her objective that if she successfully opened it, and was awarded at least 2 million in business, she would get the promotion to Managing Director. So, the fact that the global board was impressed was great. She had not only met her objective but exceeded by at least 57%, and additionally, pissed all over the 2 million and strode away with a sensational 3.4 million. Georgia didn't like to blow her own trumpet, but it was also pretty great that all of the hard work and long hours had been worthwhile.

Having spent the horrendously long meeting slumped further into her chair; Georgia had been constantly embarrassed as her boss praised her, commended her, and hyped her up. She wasn't personable at all, probably more likened to a loner by most, in fact Friday night socialising was probably the most personable anyone would have ever seen her, and that was completely by default. Derek had pretty much alluded to the fact that the promotion was in the bag, however, had been oddly furtive. He confirmed that he would be back in the North West on Friday and had planned a meeting for the end of the day to go through all of the details, before leaving the meeting and allowing Georgia to continue on.

"Okay, well I guess we have covered everything. I would also like to thank you all for the excessive hours, the stress, and the nagging on the lead up to the launch. I will be sure to arrange something as soon as it's all over." She smiled, and listened to her staff all offering congratulations and well wishes in her race to the top. "Okay, okay, you're embarrassing me. Right, so I think that's all. Is there any other business from any of you?" she asked, before concluding and closing the monthly board meeting.

"Great, well if that's all then…oh, actually, there was one other thing; Julia you sent me an email this morning, I thought this would be a good forum for us to discuss it? We can broach it with HR whilst Di's in the meeting," she said, pointing to her HR Director. "So, you want to take the floor and highlight your reasoning for requiring a 'dress code' policy to be put in place?" Georgia said, smiling softly to Julia, trying desperately to ignore the flashbacks of how the night had ended on Friday. Julia was looking at Georgia concerned, and she was flustered. "Is everything okay, Julia? Are you feeling okay? You look a little peaky?" Georgia said, passing her a bottle of water.

Flustered? Seriously, of course I'm bloody flustered, Julia thought to herself. Shit how was she going to do this. She took a swig of the water Georgia had offered her and coughed a little, swearing under her breath. "No, no I'm fine," she said, smiling to all of the eyes on her and shuffling her papers. "So, basically, I was looking to impose a dress code policy. We don't have an established one, and whilst we have elements within other policies, I think it would be beneficial to address it. This given the nature of business and the route we are looking to go down moving forward," she said, praying that nobody would ask why she thought this was required. *Nope, of course not,* She squirmed in her seat, as Georgia's assistant Paul spoke up.

"But what's the reasoning? Can we not just ask HR to amplify what we already have?" he said.

"Yes, actually I think that may be an idea," said Georgia. "Has something specifically happened?"

"Well, I guess we could, I…ummm…I was just a little disappointed in the lack of commitment from certain people through the launch. And that's pretty much where it's stemmed from. It's okay, leave it with me and I'll speak to Di later. Nothing further from me," Julia finished and slumped further into her chair, wishing the ground would swallow her up.

"Okay, that's all then, guys," Georgia said, smiling at her team before leaving the office. She would go and check on Julia in a while, as she really didn't look so good.

She got back into her office and checked her phone. "Jesus Christ, I was gone a couple of bloody hours," she sighed, rubbing her temples.

"Problem boss?" Paul said, walking into her office and handing her some folders.

"No. Just no let up. Eleven missed calls. *Eleven,*" she sighed, sitting back down.

Georgia spent the next few hours returning calls and clearing her emails. She couldn't remember the last time she was actually on top of things and not just fire fighting through her weeks.

***

Julia heard a knock at her door, calling to come in. Her head was deep in her work and she was desperate to get everything finished, as it was late already and her head was killing her.

"Hey, just wondered if you were feeling any better?" Georgia said, walking in to Julia's office.

"Hi, bloody hell, this is a shocker. You out of your office?" she said, smiling and leaning back in her chair. "Come. Sit. Have a chat?" She smiled.

"Don't be cheeky, I'm still your boss, remember? And you're good, I'm okay here," she responded. "So, you feeling better? I was a little concerned earlier."

"I'm well aware of the fact you are my boss, and how you like to maintain that level of, ummm, authority…control," she smirked. "I am okay, I was… I was fine. Nothing to worry about," she said, looking away as she felt the flush rise.

"What's going on? What are you blushing for? I thought we were all good?" Georgia said, shutting her office door and going to sit down opposite Julia after all.

"I'm fine, seriously." Julia smiled. "Just me being a dick, and it backfiring."

"Why? Has something gone wrong? Look I'm sorry if I wasn't about much recently, but if we have issues then we can manage it. You just need to tell me. We can't have people taking the piss, were still a business," Georgia said seriously.

"Oh, God. George, leave it. There were no issues," she sighed, putting her head in her hands.

"What? What do you mean? I'm so confused right now," Georgia looked strangely at her.

"Oh, for fucks sake. Seriously, you can't just leave things, can you? Look, I was being coquette. I was being…I was trying to be funny. I was expecting you to come back via email. I was going to elaborate on the reason being that

I wanted a dress code to be put in, was to block people from wearing anything which could be deemed as...," she stopped, shaking her head. "God, this is so embarrassing. Which could be deemed as being too provocative. Namely the senior members of the board. I thought I was being funny and flirty, following Friday's antics. I never expected it to have backfired like this," she said, shaking her head. "I certainly never expected you would call me out in front of the rest of the board."

"*Oh*... OH," Georgia covered her mouth to stifle the laugh.

"Do not. I mean it. Do not laugh at me," Julia said, smiling herself.

"You are a loon, I can't believe you did that? What possessed you?"

"What possessed me? Oh, I don't know, maybe the fact that I shagged my beautiful boss on Friday night. Come Monday morning, she saunters in wearing an incredibly short dress and a sexy little smirk to match. I mean, you're not really playing fair. Oh God, I'm far too sober for this," she said, holding her head in her hands.

"Well you wanna change that?" Georgia smirked.

"What do you mean? Are you asking me if I want you to take your clothes off?" Julia asked, confused and a little concerned.

"What the hell?" she said. "Get your head out of the gutter woman. And no I was NOT asking that. I was asking if you wanted to change the fact you're too sober? I.e., if you fancied going for a drink after work?" Georgia said, shaking her head.

"Oh, right. Yeah that makes more sense, unfortunately." She winked. "On a Monday? You do realise that us, together, drinking, may not end well?"

"I'm sure we can maintain a level of professionalism and restrain ourselves. I mean, we're both adults," Georgia said seriously.

"Listen, the professionalism went out of the window, probably about the time you were checking my arse out, or possibly when I was screaming your apartment down," she smirked. "Yes, go on then. I'll be done in about half hour, if that's okay?"

"Sure, and you need to stop with comments like that. Wrong, you are very wrong!" Georgia said, leaving her office.

Chapter Eleven

"Hi, can I get a bottle of corona and? What would you like?" Georgia asked.

"Same is good, I'll grab a seat," Julia said, in search of a spare table in a quiet corner.

Georgia found Julia at a table hidden away. "So, how's your day been?" she said, splitting a bag of crisps down the middle and putting them in the center of the table, taking a couple.

"Amazing!" she said sarcastically. "I came in happy, made an attempt at flirting which resulted in me humiliating myself in front of the board. Shot one of my team down because of a mistake, which has taken me all afternoon to try and correct. Oh, and best of all, you'll love this," she smirked, leaning back in her chair, shaking her head. "I finally had a break because I was desperate for the bathroom. Noticed you walking down the office, couldn't take my eyes off those legs, which FYI are far too revealing in that stupidly short dress, and walked into the glass window in reception," she said pointedly.

Georgia snorted her drink out of her nose, trying to stop the beer from coming out. "Please tell me you are kidding? That's brilliant. Oh, I so wish I had seen it. I wonder if we have any cameras in the building?" she smirked. "Brilliant, *brilliant*. I love it." She slapped her hands on the table.

"Oh, very supportive, aren't you?" Julia smirked, taking some crisps. "So, how about yours? Great board meeting by the way, sounds like it's in the bag?" She smiled.

"Well I don't really want to get too excited you know? But I've smashed the objectives he set. I think I've done well, and I have the buy in of my staff. And yeah it sounded pretty positive, what he was throwing out today in the board meeting, but I don't know. There's just something niggling away at me," she said distantly.

"That's just you being nervous and apprehensive. Of course that's normal. Nobody would think any different, and when you get it you'll worry over if you can do it. They'll always be something to worry about. As you said, you smashed the targets, and the launch went incredibly. You've worked your backside off over the last 12 months and it's paid off. So sit back, relax, look at taking a holiday, and then reap the benefits. Nobody deserves this more than you Georgia, and for the record I'm not just saying that." She smiled.

"Thanks, that's sweet of you to say." Georgia smiled sincerely. "Anyways, let's leave that there, it makes me feel a bit sick. Did Glen say hi to you today?" she asked.

"Oh, God, did he not speak to you?" she said, shaking her head. "You will love this. This guy is too much," she smirked, reaching for another crisp. "First thing, like, literally *first* thing he is like, 'oh thanks so much for making me get home. I only had to wash both cars as my punishment; that's the best night I've had in around 6 years,'" she said smirking, taking a mouthful of drink. "So he's like, 'so then, Jules, you have your wicked way with our boss?'"

"Did he move his head in that wobbly way you do when asking these questions?" Georgia laughed.

"Piss off. Anyways, so then. Get this?" she said, pointing her finger to her boss. "He went on. 'Ohhh I bet she's filthy, actually I bet you're filthy.' Then he was all dreamy and distant. Obviously, sitting and thinking all sorts of shit about what we would do together." She sat back.

"Seriously, he said that? What a cheeky shit, as if I'm filthy? Oh, part of me wants to out us, just so I can wind him up," she smirked. "I'd have a ball."

"You are not wrong there; I was ever so tempted to just be like 'oh hell yeah, we were up all night long, doing things that would have turned most women gay, and gave every man the best, most explicit and descriptive tutorial ever,'" she laughed, raising her eyebrows. "He is so crude, and completely obsessed with me banging you."

"Banging? Really? Am I really that out of touch with things? And he's the crude one?" Georgia laughed.

"Oh yeah, this is the joys of being the head of marketing, they're all so young and sociable and therefore, I'm completely in touch with anything hip. This 'banging' was one of the things I was taught last week. Albeit, I'm not so sure I needed this lesson," she laughed.

"No, I wouldn't have thought so. I mean, I'm thrilled to learn that I was banged. Is that correct? Ohhh was I the bang'er' or the bang'ee'?" Georgia laughed.

"You're an idiot. I'll go grab a couple more beers, before my feet refuse to partake in any further activity from the pain of these shoes." She smiled. Taking a ten pound note from her purse, she walked to the bar, turning as she was side by side with Georgia. Julia placed a hand on her shoulder and looked down to her. "For the record, you were both the bang'er' and the bang'ee' on Friday," she smirked, leaving Georgia with the words hanging in the air.

Georgia gulped hard, this woman knew how to work it. She shouldn't be doing this, she knew it. She wasn't this person. She didn't date, but it was kind of nice for a change. And actually, it was Monday night at seven, she was forty and she was drinking beers in a bar. This was *so* not her, but bloody hell it felt good to let loose for a change.

Chapter Twelve

Julia turned around to face Georgia. "So, I guess we're equals now?" she said, pulling the cover over her.

"How do you mean?" she turned to face her.

"Well, I jumped on you on Friday. You brought me back here tonight, in what I can only detail by your actions, that it was your intention all evening to jump on me. So, were even?" she smirked.

"You know we can't continue this, don't you?" Georgia said.

"You know, the more you tell me I can't, the more it makes me want to?" She raised an eyebrow.

"I'm beginning to wonder why exactly I employed you," she laughed.

"Because you loved my wit, my humour, my innovation and most likely the fact that I flirted my arse off with you the whole time," Julia laughed.

"You did not!"

"Ohhh, I so did." She raised her eyebrow. "Anyways it's late. I should probably head home, I don't want to miss the last train, again. Least not on a Monday," she feigned a look of shock.

"Ouch, love em and leave em, ehy?" Georgia winked.

"Erm, most definitely not 'love em', it was once again… another good, couple of hours, but yeah, I need to go."

"Look, I don't want you to feel weird. Especially, given I keep saying we can't do this, but you are welcome to stay here. It's late and that."

"Ohhh, boss you sound like you're crossing the line." She winked. "Thanks for the offer, but the walk of shame is bad enough. Going to work in yesterday's clothes and undies, not so hot." She smiled, shaking her head and squishing her nose up.

"Firstly, you need to stop calling me 'boss' in that way. You have no idea what it does to me. Secondly, do you have any meetings in the morning?"

"I'll keep that info for when required. No, why's that?" she said, putting her bra back on.

"Good, well I'm imposing my seniority and instructing you to take that bra off, get that sexy arse back in this bed, and crash here tonight. You can take some gym gear of mine, go home in the morning and work from home, come back in later if you want? So, shut up and get back in bed now," Georgia demanded.

Houston, USA

Chapter Thirteen

"Knock knock?"

Erika looked up to see Vanessa in the doorway with some flowers. "Hey you, what's this?"

"Well I hear congratulations are in order, which is only right given the work we've put in these last couple of years," Vanessa said, kissing Erika on the cheek and handing her the flowers.

"You know you are tempting fate?" She smiled at her finance director, who was also one of her very good friends.

"Ahh, not at all, it's a sure thing," she winked. "So, Mike said he was calling a meeting later in the week to discuss it? You fancy going to grab a bite to eat?" she said, looking at her watch.

"Hmm, don't really have time," she said uncertainly. "Hell, I can squeeze in a very quick sandwich run ," she confirmed. "But I need to go now. We can walk and talk. You fancy the deli down the street?" she said, picking up her Coach purse. Summer was close by, which meant she would be fine in her sleeveless blouse and pencil skirt since it was warm enough, especially at this time of the day. "Yes, so Mike said he wanted to see me Friday afternoon, apparently couldn't be before that due to something to do with the meeting. It was all very strange actually; so, we'll see what happens," she said, pressing G on the skyscraper building. They currently resided on the 39th floor of a three and a half thousand-square foot floor.

"What do you mean weird? It's as good as done, lady. You have achieved all that the business set out. So, you got it, amore," Vanessa said. "We need to have a catch up outside of this place soon too. We haven't been out in forever. Or, how about you, Dan, and Dulcie come to our house for a barbecue? Next weekend maybe? The kids haven't all seen each other for a long time, and Ben is off shift that weekend," Vanessa said.

"Hmm, yeah sure," she said vacantly. "Dulcie will love that. And you're right, they haven't seen each other for a while. I will mention it to Dan," she said sombrely.

"Great, don't forget her bathing suit, they will end up in the pool." Vanessa smiled.

"Thanks, Ness. Look, I don't want to go into it right now, but Dan's been working a whole heap lately. So, it may just be the two of us, if that's okay? I'll ask though," she said seriously.

"You sure you don't wanna speak about it? Everything okay?" Vanessa said concerned.

"It's fine, and I'd really rather not, just got a whole heap of stuff going on with work, so I don't want more stress. I'll try and get Dan to come too though, okay?"

Erika had suddenly lost her appetite. But she didn't need more lectures about not eating. She would order her favourite deli sandwich. Turkey, avocado and brie. As soon as they walked through the door the smell woke her senses, and her stomach was now telling her a different story.

Chapter Fourteen

Erika put Dulcie to bed and was still waiting for Dan to come home. The food was still warming in the oven and there had been no communication at all today. She opened a beer and walked out to the back porch. It was still warm out, even though the sun was falling. *I love this view,* she thought, sighing lightly. The palm trees at the back of the yard. The pool glistening as the sky was changing. She lit the citronella candles and sat in the rocking chair, slowly rocking, allowing the tears to fall. As hard as it was, the realisation of recent absence imploded her. And the reasons why Dan had recently become so absent swam through her mind.

***

It was after 10 and there was still no sign. She locked up and threw the dinner in the trash. Checking on Dulcie, Erika listened to the slight snores of the girl she loved with every fibre. "What are we gonna do Dulcie?" she whispered to her sleeping daughter.

Erika got into bed and opened her phone to the messages and texted Dan. *Dinner in the garbage, can only you assume you don't require it!! Your daughter asked yet again for you. Maybe you can slot me in for an hour this coming week? We NEED to talk!!!*

She turned her phone off and tucked herself in. She didn't know when they had grown apart? Or when she had suddenly become a single parent. Was Vanessa, right? Was she just being paranoid and nervous over all the stuff with work? They both had such demanding jobs, but this wasn't right. Maybe she should have been a stay at home mom and not had a career after all. But Dulcie had never gone without anything. She was used to being kept up all night due to the stress of her job, but she had control over that. She had control over her company and her staff, but this seemed too far away. This seemed out of reach and she felt like everything was spiralling out of control. She felt like she had no clue what was wrong or how to fix it. Erika allowed the tears to fall once more, because she wasn't even in control of keeping the tears at bay. She couldn't even stop that? *Damn it*, she condemned herself, and that was the last thing she remembered as she cried herself to sleep.

***

Erika woke up and saw that their bed hadn't been slept in, again. The sinking feeling came once more. Sighing she picked up her phone, which revealed not a single message. Opening her messages to Taylor, Erika texted her asking if she could come over that night for dinner and a chat? It was Wednesday, which meant that Dan would be out anyhow, and she could really do with a friend right now. More importantly, she seriously needed some advice. And didn't really know who else to speak to.

Erika got up to wake Dulcie and get her ready for school, and noticed the spare room door opened. She peeked over to the bed and saw Dan sleeping. She sighed heavily and went straight back to her bedroom. She entered the en suite and got ready for work, as she could do with an early start for a change.

She grabbed her purse and walked into the spare room, shutting the door hard and disturbing Dan.

"Any reason for this?" she said pointedly.

"Well I figured I wouldn't be so welcome in our bed, following the steely message you texted."

"Is it any wonder, Dan? I just about figured as much. Well, your daughter can barely remember what you look like, so you can do the school run for a change," she said, turning and opening the door.

Dan started. "Wait, Erika I have an import…"

"Screw you, I can manage to put our daughter first over my job, you need to start doing the same," she said, slamming the door behind her and leaving their home.

Chapter Fifteen

"I'm home," Erika called out to the silent house. She had left earlier desperately trying to get home before Dulcie went to bed, after missing her that morning. She'd felt terrible. Her daughter had suffered as a consequence of her wanting to punish Dan. She couldn't do that. That wasn't her. Nor their family.

Erika could hear the shrills from the back yard, and she smiled as her daughter's laughter flowed through the house and lifted her spirits immensely. "Hey, you guys, pool party without me?"

"Mommy, Mommy," Dulcie squealed, trying desperately to get out of her donut and rush to her mom.

"S'okay, s'okay, sweetie. No, need to get out," she said, in the hope of avoiding getting wet.

"How about mommy goes and gets in her suit and joins us, Dulcie?" Taylor said.

"Yayyyyyy," her daughter screamed. "Come on Mommy, you haven't swum with me in forever," she said eagerly.

"Yeeeessss, Mommy?" Taylor winked. "Go get changed."

"Okay already," Erika said excitably. She rarely used the pool, but when Taylor was looking after Dulcie they used it a great deal, and she was glad that Dulcie wasn't one of these kids that was obsessed with electronics. She loved the pool and was happy to be in there whenever the weather allowed her to be.

Erika put a black one piece on. *Her sauna suit,* she thought. But it would suffice tonight. It was already getting late, so they wouldn't be able to spend too long before sundown and Dulcie's bedtime. She grabbed a spare towel and headed back downstairs. Stopping in the kitchen, she smiled to herself. Erika rarely let Dulcie eat junk at night, especially not through the week. But she felt guilty after this morning. Grabbing some aluminium foil, Erika split it into three individual pieces. She got three bananas and sliced them through the centres. Sprinkling choc chips and mini marshmallows she sealed the aluminium foil around the banana boats and made her way outside.

"Where have you been? We were waiting for you," Dulcie whined.

"You were? Well, I'm sorry, I guess I could leave the grilled banana boats I was making for us to eat?" she smirked.

"Really, oh they're my favourites. How come I get junk for dinner on a school night?" Dulcie asked quizzically.

"It's a one-off lady," she warned, elegantly stepping into her pool. She swam over to her daughter and twirled her in her donut. "So, what have you guys been up to today? How was kindergarten?" Erika questioned.

Dulcie entertained Erika for around 10 minutes of what had happened at school, consisting of a further pop quiz she'd had. Another borrowed tale from Taylor. Grape jello on the menu which was her '*favouritist*' in the whole wide world; she was pretty sure it had been black cherry yesterday though. And a rather confusing tale about a boy called Morgan. Who allegedly got stuck under the washbasin, whilst hiding from Miss Addison, who was trying to take his pacifier from him. To which Dulcie concluded that Morgan was far too old to have a pacifier and Miss Addison knew that. Erika couldn't help but laugh at her beautiful daughter, her big brown eyes became so animated when she was telling stories, she really could watch and listen to her for hours.

"For real? Wow, what a hectic day you had." She smiled. "Come on. Andiamo bambina," Erika said to her daughter, exiting the pool.

"Nooooo, per favore? No altri cinque minuti?" Dulcie pleaded.

"You guys, not everyone speaks Italian around here," Taylor quizzed, raising an eyebrow.

"It's time to get out," Erika smirked. And this little lady, wants 5 more minutes, puhleeeaaaasssseee?"

"I just about managed the five and please. Figured that on my own," she smirked, grabbing Dulcie from her donut.

"Come on, you, let's go get some grilled banana boats. I know I sure am hungry for them," Taylor said, holding her hand out for Dulcie to take.

***

Erika returned from putting Dulcie to bed and Taylor had opened a bottle of wine, "I figured you needed this? I hope you don't mind?" she said when Erika came back out in her robe.

"God no, you are right I needed this, thanks," she said, taking a large gulp and bringing her leg up on the chair she was sat on. "This is good. Thanks for coming over tonight, I'm sorry I wrecked your plans," she sighed.

"Hey, we're friends, you could never wreck my plans. Plus, I kinda don't got any plans at the moment, I am officially giving up on men and committing to a life of singledom." She smiled. "Cheers?"

"Well that may just well be two of us," she said softly.

"What? You and Dan have split up? What do you mean? You can't be single," she said leaning over taking Erika's hand.

"Oh, Tay, I just don't know what to do anymore," she sniffed, shaking her head. "We don't even see each other. We don't speak. I can't remember the last time we shared a bed. And don't get me started on any form of intimacy. I...I got up this morning and went to wake Dulcie and Dan was in the spare bed. After fifteen years, really?" she gulped her drink heavily.

"Well, maybe the drink wasn't such a good idea. What are you going to do?" Taylor asked.

"The drinks fine, I'm not going to do anything stupid. Honestly, I don't know. I lay in bed last night and tried to remember the last time anything in our marriage slightly represented that of a happy marriage and I couldn't even remember. What does that say? We both have busy and successful careers, I get that. I'm not sure if I should have been a stay at home mom, like it was planned? But you know the promotion came up and things just went from strength to strength and why should I be the one to give up on my career? I provide a loving, stable, comfortable life for my daughter, the problem is how will she be if that becomes a 2-way relationship and no longer the 3-way relationship?" she sighed.

"Okay, I'm kinda intrigued by one thing? At no point have you mentioned how you actually deep down feel about this? You are being a total loving and committed mom, but how do *you* actually feel? You wanna divorce? You wanna break up?" she said seriously.

"Honest answer, I don't know? I am trying to channel my inner thoughts to work that out. Honestly, I guess I'm starting to feel…," she stopped, and stared out distantly. "I guess I'm afraid, it will be more difficult to become three again. Because I sincerely think that my baby and I have just become a perfect little twosome. And I don't know how or when that happened? I can't really remember the last time it was the three of us," she said sadly.

Manchester, UK

Chapter Sixteen

"Come on. Seriously, what the hell is your problem? Please just do this for us? It's a given, George. He said it in the bloody board meeting for Christ sake. People want to celebrate, congratulate you. And well, obviously brown nose. I mean it's classic; they are actually sucking up to me too. Yesterday, that red head from accounts, I mean I don't even know her name, she cracked on to me, she actually cracked on to me. She was pretty much asking where I'm going when you become MD. I thought I'd have a little fun and said I was potentially being made redundant; you know what she did? She walked out, she literally walked out of the printing room, just like that," Paul said seriously.

"I'm completely unable to tell if that's bullshit or not," Georgia said. "Seriously, I don't have time for this."

"Well just commit to being sociable for bloody once when everyone is bugging me for this. It's dinner and a couple of beers, stop being such a mard arse."

"Fine, Paul. Fine. Get out, I don't have time for this, I have to brief for this meeting. When I'm done with Derek, I'll come and meet you for dinner and a couple of beers," she sighed.

"Thanks boss," he said, smirking at the win as he left her office.

***

"Hey, good luck, yeah. You'll be fine. How are you feeling?" Julia said, bringing her a coffee.

"Not great. Still can't shake it. I'm really nervous. I just don't know why it's all so secretive. I don't know why there's no movement on the time because it ties in with something else. Seriously, Jules, I'm shitting it, honestly," she said, cringing at her own terminology.

"Hey, come on, you're just being nervous. Be systematic about your approach. You had a plan. You had objectives and you have achieved all of those. It will be about processes, you know what this place is like. And they have processes to follow, you will learn this more than anybody in the coming months. You will be working so closely with HR after this, processes will be your middle name. Calm down though, yeah. Just relax you'll be fine, okay? And when you're out, I have, ummm, a super special way to help you celebrate," she said, leaning forward over Georgia's desk.

Georgia knew she couldn't continue with this. Someone would get hurt. But she was so sexy and had such intense sex appeal. Especially right now, as she leaned over, and allowed Georgia a full view down her blouse. Her black lace bra in sight. Yes, she was right. This most definitely took her mind off the meeting. "You need to stop being naughty, and I need to go"

"Yes, boss," Julia smirked as she oozed the word, knowing what it did to Georgia.

Georgia stood up, walking to the door. "You are in very big trouble tonight. You know what calling me boss does to me," she smirked.

"Oh, I'll be ready and waiting to be disciplined, *boss,*" Julia laughed, checking Georgia's ass out in her fitted, ivory trouser suit.

Chapter Seventeen

Georgia felt like she had been punched in the chest. Hard. She couldn't seem to remember how to breathe, and had no idea of how to deal with what she was hearing.

"Georgia, this is incredible news. You look like somebody's died. This is everything you've worked for," Derek said.

"This is *not* everything I've worked for," Georgia shouted to her CEO. She wasn't a cryer, never had been. She grew up in a well to do family, and her mother had taught her you don't cry in public. You don't let your defences down. You don't allow people to see your weaknesses. It resulted in Georgia feeling that she was a disappointment if she cried. She couldn't remember the last time she had. But at this moment, she was starting to feel like she had no control over her emotions as she acknowledged the last hour of her life. "I can't, Derek. I'm sorry, I can't do this now," she said and stood up, taking the A4 envelope that had been provided to her.

"Georgia? Georgia, you're looking at this all wrong. Take this opportunity and grab it with both hands. You will be the best MD we have, just do this?" he called behind her.

Georgia stopped, she was fuming. And knew that blowing up would potentially get her sacked. But fuck it, like it even mattered anymore? "The best MD, the *BEST* MD? Are you joking right now? Why set objectives, to go backwards when I achieved them? You get me to work like a sodding lunatic for twelve months. Batter my team. For this? Seriously, Derek. Don't, *just don't*. You have never ever insulted my intelligence as much as you have done today," she said and slammed the door behind her. "Well, there goes your career, George!" she said to herself, feeling and hearing the eyes and whispers of the receptionists.

***

Georgia looked at the message from Paul, sighing. She had sat in her office for the last 2 hours crying, and she knew what it would say.

Where are you, I look a fool? What's going on with you? Still negotiating zeros to the contract? ☺

Nope, not coming. Speak Monday!!

Wtf?!? Did you not get promoted? You can't do this to me. You promised. It can't be that bad. Come on, I'll talk you through stuff, quick bite and then we can go home. Please? ☹

Yes, I did, no I don't want to.

Don't do this please? I want to help you to celebrate, it's the least I can do.

No, I don't feel like it!

Fine, just leave it then! Thanks for making me sit in a restaurant alone for the last 2 hours. See you Monday!

God, he was like a bloody petulant child at times, but she couldn't deal with the guilt, or the hissy fits when he didn't get his own way. "For fucks sake!" she sighed loudly and left her office, heading to the restaurant in the northern quarter.

***

She really wasn't in the mood for this. She would have a starter only and a scotch and then that was it, she was going.

"Hi, I'm looking for a table for Paul?" she said to the maître D, not spotting him, excellent he may have left already.

"Yes, he's over in the back, he's been waiting for you," he smiled widely. He walked her around the divider and pointed her into the room.

"Congratulations!" was all Georgia heard as she spotted all the people. Work people, her parents, a couple of her friends, she had very few these days due to the work she'd put in. She saw the smiles, the drinks, the offers of glasses and the next thing she remembered was everything going black...

Houston, USA

Chapter Eighteen

"Good luck, sweetie," Vanessa whispered as Erika headed to the board room.

She smiled lightly and walked inside. "Hi Mike, are you ready?" she said, shutting the door behind her.

"Erika, come in please," He smiled.

She was nervous. He looked nervous. He always sat next to her at the end of the oval table. Now he sat opposite and had everything set out for her in a place on the other side. She took a seat, and waited for his fidgeting to stop, and for him to begin.

"So, I just want you to listen to what I have to say, because we have a conference set up. Firstly, I want to thank you for the exceptional work y'all have done, the launch went... incredibly. The office is fantastic. The work generated because of you and your team, namely you, is far more exceptional than we could've ever imagined, and that is all down to you. Now. As you know, we were striving for this additional business. Whilst we never doubted your abilities and your excellent work ethics, we, well I guess as a business in a somewhat difficult climate, we anticipated this was not doable. That's not saying we were setting you up to fail. That certainly wasn't the case. But you over excelled. And, well...," he stopped and started fidgeting again. "Look, Erika, the group isn't sure at this very moment in time you are ready to be the managing director.

I've assured them that isn't the case, but it's the feedback they have given me. Don't panic, they do see it. It's imminent, they know you're the one and we can all see it in our sights, I can assure you of this, Erika. You *will* be Managing Director, and then one day be in my seat. I know this to be true, because you are far more driven than I ever was, and I want you to go the whole nine yards. But just not right now," he said sadly.

Erika's head was spinning. She had worked her butt off and he didn't think she was ready? She couldn't hide the disappointment. She couldn't contain the incredible sense of disappointment of every part of her life. Why had everything come crashing down on her?

"Erika, Erika? Please, this isn't a negative, you need to take this for what it is. Just a small area and then we feel you will be in a perfect position to undertake and excel in this role, this is a big office and we have big plans for you."

"Okay, so tell me. Tell me what I suck at, Mike. Tell me what I need to achieve further than the doubling of the business? Doubling the profit? Achieving EBITDA? Keeping in the confines of the capital expenditure? So, what? *What* exactly did I not achieve? What the *hell* more could I have done, Mike?" she snapped.

"Erika, you are taking this completely out of context. Look, we can have a chat after the conference," he said, rubbing his temple.

Jesus for the positions these guys are in and all the dollars they have, none of them have the balls to deal with a difficult task or conflict! Seriously?! She was ready to walk the hell out of there. *Screw Mike. Screw them all.* She was knocked out of her thoughts as the international dial tone began.

"Hi, Mike. Hi, Erika," she heard an English voice say.

"Hey, Derek, you wanna go?" Mike said.

"Sure, Erika my name is Derek Danson. I am the CEO of the European region. Here with me I have my Area Director of the Manchester region, Georgia Carson. Like you, she has been striving to achieve a number of objectives to become the new MD of this region. Whilst Georgia is more than competent like yourself, myself and Mike have been speaking with the group board and we just feel that there is a small element missing from each of you. We have discussed you both at length and think whilst you are both at the stages we set for you. With a gentle push, you could both be far better resources. You would work incredibly well together. So, whilst you have both achieved and exceeded said objectives, we feel you need a little further steer. Now, I know this may be frustrating. Concerning. Even nerve-wracking for both of you. But I must stress this is not. I repeat, not a negative thing. This is going to take you to a whole other level. Above just being what we require of our MD's. Additionally, we appreciate that by us not standing by our words in achieving the targets set to you both. You will be incredibly reluctant to trust that we offer you the MD roles when you have done this. So, contracts of employment have been drawn up by Global HR and legal to confirm the new roles and plans. Additionally, that in twelve months' time you will both be offered the positions of Managing Directors in the regions that you were both expecting to be offered in these here meetings today. So, the proposal is that you work on a project of opening the Fort Worth, Texas office. This will be our flagship of the Americas office and we hope that it will provide ample opportunity to create kindred offices throughout the world. Erika, we would like to promote you to senior operational Director. Assisting Georgia in overseeing the office in Houston and working closely with Georgia, so you are each co-leader on Fort Worth. George, we would like you to be the managing director of the Houston office, and again work closely together for exceptional grandiose plans and opportunities. No two people are going to be able to achieve this better than you two are. I know this isn't what you wanted, nor expected. But we have to find a way to achieve this. The stakeholders and international board are pushing for this. And we have to make sure we can achieve it. I'm proud to say you two were heads and shoulders above others around the world."

Erika's head was hurting, so much. "So, you are telling me after achieving everything, you are not giving me my promotion to MD??" *What.* "I have worked my ass off for the last 8 months and you're giving it to some English woman? That's never even *visited* this office? What the hell does she know about this place?" Erika snarled.

"Excuse me. Erika, is *that* your name? This isn't exactly my idea of fun. I've worked for the biggest office in the UK for years, and equally, like you I've also worked my arse off for years. I have spent, not the last eight months, but the last twelve months working to nearly treble the revenue on the basis that today I would get MD. I also, was *not* expecting to hear that the only way I get that is to get shipped off to the other side of the bloody world. To where I'm going to take the job of someone who has likewise achieved everything. You're taking it out on the wrong person!" Georgia spat.

Erika angrily retaliated "Oh I'm so sor..."

"Ladies, ladies? This is not productive. Derek, I will leave you to discuss your end, and I will call you this evening to confer. Like Derek mentioned, Georgia, this is a positive. And I hope you will come over to bring some of your vast experience and gain more from this end. And Erika, I agree with Derek. This will be an incredible opportunity for both of you, and I believe you will make an unsurpassable duo."

And just like that, not only is my marriage in ruins, but now, so is my career, Erika thought.

Manchester, UK

Chapter Nineteen

Georgia sat on her couch, her head still spinning from the evening's meeting, being made worse as she listened to her mother going on, *and on, and on…* ever the disappointment she thought to herself.

"Seriously, this is obscene, surely they can't just do this?" her mother said, before allowing anybody an opportunity to respond. "Well of course they can, this is exactly what these high-powered execs of these big corporate chains do. Chew them up and spit them out. Make them work ridiculously, so their personal lives are in tatters, to then choose someone else better to come and pick it up. I told you, I told you this would happen one day. Didn't I? Didn't I, William, I told her? You should have gone down the route I told you. You should have gotten married and had children like everyone else your age. Now you have nothing. No marriage, no kids. Chances are it will be too late now…and..." Her mother was pacing.

"For Christ's sake, Mum. I get it okay? I'm a disappointment. I'm not like Alexandra or Joshua," she said pointing to her brother and sister standing by the floor to ceiling windows. "Okay? You're right, I should have just married and had kids. And been a stay at home mum. Had no life, no career, because hell, that's what everyone's kids at the golf club did, hey? I get it, alright. I screwed up. I screwed up everything. My life, your life...Yes, I'm a disappointment. I am gay, and can't have kids the real way. Anything else, or have we covered it all?" Georgia snapped at her mum, who looked as though she had seen a ghost.

Her mother sniffed. "I have never, *ever* had an issue with you being gay. I have never for one moment thought you were a disappointment. You have always been driven and successful. But I'm your mother. I watch you show up every year for Christmas alone and hear you discuss nothing but work, and I just worry for you. You deserve what we all have. And that's all I've ever wanted for you, Georgia. Your father worked incredibly hard to provide the best upbringing for you all. And it was our decision that whilst we would instil values in our children, we would also ensure that they would grow up *'comfortable'*. Your father put everything into his work for that reason, so our children wouldn't have to," she said solemnly.

"Yes, wel...," Georgia started.

"Whoa, George, stop," Josh said. "Mum, don't get upset. This is not so good for Georgia. You say you and dad did everything you did for *us*. Well Georgia has obviously got dad's work ethic. So, can you imagine," he said, sitting down next to his mother, lowering his voice and taking her hand. "Well, imagine that one day, all those plans, all that preparation you put into play for your children's future. Can you imagine what would have happened if the company went in to liquidation? Or dad broke both of his legs? So he couldn't work and you guys had to rely on that money? Plans don't always go in our favour. And when that happens it's devastating. Georgia knows you don't think she's a disappointment and we all know you have never had an issue with her sexuality. But equally, this is about *her* right now, and today has turned her world upside down, okay? Look, why don't you and dad go home. Alexandra and I will stay here with Georgia, we will have some time together, just the three of us," he said quietly. He smiled the smile that always won their parents over, even at forty-four he still had it.

Mrs. Carson looked defeated, so she stood up sadly and took her husband's hand that he was holding out. She stopped once more and turned to Georgia. "I have never, nor will I ever think you are a disappointment. I just desperately don't want you to wake one day and life has passed you by because of your work. I want you to experience the wonders of love and motherhood. But equally, I apologise if that's not what you want from life. You are all correct, it's not my choice to make," she said, sadly walking to the door.

Great, now she felt even shittier than she did before. "Mum," Georgia walked over to her mother. "I know you don't. I *know* you worry, but let me just get through this, and then we can go for a spa day together or go have a round of golf and discuss at length what I want and why. Then you can have your say. Like two adults; like a normal mother and daughter," she said, hugging her mother. Georgia pulled back and her mother held her face with tears in her eyes. "I love you all equally. And I know you are stubborn, but if the worst happens, you don't have to worry about money. But...," she held her hand to stop Georgia from speaking. "B*ut,* regardless of that, I can assure you whatever happens, will have happened for a reason. And maybe you should accept change every so often? And actually, listen fully to what this CEO has to say. He will have done this for the right reason. He will see in you what we all see in you. Don't run from anything without listening to everything," she said and kissed her daughter's forehead before walking out.

***

"You okay?" Alexandra said to Georgia, pulling her in for a hug.

"Amazing!" she said sarcastically.

"Right you two, mum and dad have gone. I'll go and get some fizz from the kitchen, I'm sure prissy pants has got some here. I'm going to ring Jill and say I won't be home tonight. Have you eaten today? Where's your laptop?" Josh said.

"Josh, seriously. I'm okay, I don't need you to do this. I'm a big girl now," she sighed.

"Yeah, and when was the last time us three did this? Life happened, we all drifted and got lives, so shut up and let Alex and I look after our little sister for a change and stop being so bloody stubborn. Now food? And laptop?" he demanded, causing Georgia to dejectedly laugh.

"No I haven't eaten, I don't think there's much food in there. The computer is in the study, or you can use my work laptop, it's beside my bed," she said sadly.

Alex walked over with a bottle of champagne and an ice cooler. "Okay, no more feeling sorry for yourself either. Joshie, get the laptop. We'll use that, it's comfier in here," she said, taking her shoes off and pulling her legs underneath her. "Ohhh, let's get an Indian?" she added.

"Fine, but seriously, please stop calling me Joshie, I'm not fourteen anymore," he huffed, walking in with the laptop.

"Okay, where shall we get food from, Gigi?" he smirked.

Georgia was scowling at him. "Do not even start with that?" she said, trying to continue with the sombre mood, despite the ribbing from her big brother. He was right they hadn't done this in years. "Come on then sexy, Lexi, what do you want from the Indian?" Georgia and Joshua were laughing now. He was right. This probably was the best thing for her this evening.

"Seriously, we are not doing this, I am not dealing with the 'middle child bullying' tonight. It's Alexandra thank you," she smirked and held up her drink to her siblings. "Josh was right, we have all become distant. And George don't think I'm doing a mum now, but she has a point. We're all there at Christmas with our families, and granted it may not be what you want. But maybe you shouldn't watch us all so intently and look so sad when you've had a few drinks? Maybe then you wouldn't need to defend yourself all the time. We all love you, and unlike us, mum will say what she feels. Equally, the kids love you and aside from birthdays and Christmas, we never see you. Mum and dad won't be around forever, George. And they don't want to feel you won't have anyone that you can fall upon, that's all. Anyways, that isn't what tonight's about. Let's order food, then we can concentrate on this situation in hand. Go get me a pad, pen, a menu and your phone," she said, taking more of her drink as she was getting comfortable.

Chapter Twenty

"Okay, so first we do the negatives?" Josh said. "We go through everything that you feel is a negative. Then we start a new sheet on the positives," he continued, getting on the spare couch.

"There aren't any positives!" Georgia said flatly.

"There are. And those are what we need to establish. Listen, you don't like change, I get that. But do you remember when I went and did camp America? Seriously, if I could have met a girl I would have proposed to her; just to stay there. It's an amazing place, and country. And I will tell you, a year goes damn bloody quick. So, stop being a brat, and let's get cracking. So as you're so set on being negative, let's start with those then?" He looked serious to his little sister.

"Well, it's not my job. It's not the job I have been workin…"

"Hey, George. This isn't going to work if all you do is keep going over what's happened. It has happened, we can't change it, okay? It's done, and we need to move on from that. So yeah, it's not your job. I'll put that on there, but we can't keep going over old ground," Alex said.

Georgia sighed heavily. "It's not the job I wanted *or* know," she said sardonically. "It's the other side of the world, it…"

"Geor…," Joshua started.

"No. Josh, let her talk. We will each have our chance to talk," Alex said to her brother.

"Can you tell who the psychiatrist is?" Joshua smirked, as he got up to put music on.

"Go on, love," Alex said, scowling at Josh.

"I have no friends there. I have nobody there in fact. I don't know how they work," she pleaded. "I know nothing about the office or people. Aside from the Florida holiday when I was thirteen, I have never been anywhere in the states. *And* it's Texas. They hate gays, and *I'm* gay. It's the gun capital of the world."

"It's the gun capital of the world?" Alex said concerned.

"Sod off. It's a massive bloody city. It's about five times the size of sodding England, but it is not the gun capital of the world," Josh said.

"Georgia, where did you hear that from? Do you know that for sure?"

"Well, I read it somewhere I think. It's the south where they all have guns and hate gays."

"George, you are being absurd. Texas isn't even one of the top 5 states for owning guns, *or* gun related crimes. Where the hell have you got this? Have you just watched an episode of Dallas and made your mind up?" he said accusingly.

"Okay, were digressing again. George, I have to agree with Joshua, you are clearly making your mind up without any substance to it. Remember how happy you were when you got your first job in London? You worked your backside off for months to get what you wanted, kept going on and on to us all how you were going to *'own it'* in London. You had everything sorted in your head, and no matter what anyone said you knew best. *London was great, London was amazing*. It was big and high powered; and you would have the best life ever there. And seemingly never move back home," Alex was looking at her. "Well, remember?"

"Yeeeessss," she sighed. "Point made."

"Well the point *should* be made. You assumed you knew it all and did all this research and you hated every minute of it. You hated the place, the pace, the *people*. You couldn't bear it and almost lost everything you had worked so hard for. You were proven wrong, Gigi. Texas is meant to be spectacular. Yes, you are right it's not going to be easy, because ultimately, you *are* taking over someone's job who has worked for it. Just like you have yours. But, your boss is right. This is a phenomenal opportunity. Both in terms of life and career. God, you always whine about the weather and the cold, it's hot all year there," she said.

"Yeah and that causes all sorts of 'acts of God' twisters, hurricanes, volcanic eruptions, earthquakes," she said.

"I think we are fighting a losing battle here. There's no point when she's in this mood," Josh said, standing up to go and get the food which had been buzzed up.

Alex set the dining table and served up the food. They sat quietly, infuriating Georgia even more. She just wanted to be left alone, and they knew this would make her give in. She tried her hardest to deal with the silence, but there was only one thing worse than the silence, and that was her own thoughts. "Oh, for fuck sakes, get the list again," she slammed her cutlery down.

Alex and Josh smiled and chinked their glasses. Alex picked up the pad and pen and held her hand out to Josh, as he handed her a twenty-pound note. "Easy money," she smirked.

"You bet on me? You have actually *bet* on my misfortune?" Georgia said.

"Give it a rest, Gigi. Come on, let's get this going again," Josh said, helping himself to more food.

Houston, USA

Chapter Twenty-One

Taylor poured another whiskey into a large glass, and handed it to Erika. She was still crying. She pretty much had been since she had walked through the door almost two hours earlier, and Taylor was relieved that Dulcie wasn't home.

Taylor looked at her broken friend, unsure of what to do. "Sweetie, you have to eat something," she said. "Listen, you want me to speak with Dan?" she asked sincerely. She was seriously pissed off with Dan. Erika had called and left a message outlining the day's events and there was still nothing. *Selfish dick*, she thought.

Still not able to complete a full sentence, Erika sniffed loudly. "No, I'm fine. Thanks. Look, you should go. You need to study and live your life, not babysit me. Geez, you spend most of your life babysitting either Dulcie or I," she said, lifting herself up. Erika literally walked in and didn't expect to find Taylor there when she stepped into her home, sobbing that afternoon. Dulcie was at a sleepover at her grandparents for the weekend, and truth be known, she couldn't have been happier when Taylor appeared. Taking her in her arms and allowing Erika to continue the sobbing.

The first 20 minutes were nothing other than her being a confused, blubbering mess, until Taylor finally took control and made her stop to tell her what had happened.

After Erika had lengthily explained the situation, throughout the sniffs and sobs, Taylor knew the only option was to pull out the hard liquor. "So, how was it left then?" Taylor asked, ignoring Erika's pleas for her to go home. "Did they tell you when you have to let them know? Or when this new woman is starting?" she asked.

"I have no idea, Tay. I literally walked out. I don't know what to do. I just feel like everything is falling down around me. I mean fuck, Tay. Why am I crying on your shoulder? Where the fuck is Dan? *Again*? Fucking some other dumb bitch," she scorned.

Taylor was surprised. Erika rarely swore. She turned to her friend. "You think Dan's cheating?" she stopped herself, shaking her head. "Look, let's deal with one thing at a time. What are you feeling about this job? I know you have worked your butt off for this, but ultimately, it's a minor setback. You are still keeping your job, you just have a new boss for a very short period. Alternatively, what do you do? You wanna quit your job? Really? Honestly, I don't want to make this seem unimportant, because it totally is, and I get that. But, it will feel so much worse at the moment. You do have to make a decision though, either way. Look, why don't we go away for a week? Come on. We can go down to Florida. Or Bahamas or Mexico, call your boss and say you need a couple days to think it through," she said.

Erika thought about what Taylor was saying. She was right, she needed to make a decision, but surely Mike didn't expect her to have a decision made over night. How the hell could she? "Thanks for the wonderful offer, but I don't think that's wise. You need to study. You are totally gonna flunk outta school if you don't stop picking up my shit," she said sincerely.

"Hey, you have been so helpful and supportive, it's the least I can do," she responded.

"I think you may be onto something. I may get a week off and take Dulcie to my mom's, we haven't seen her in forever. And geez, with work I never go back home, it's always her that comes here. I think you're right. I need some time out to go through things in my head, ya know? Plus, I think it gives us a good opportunity to give you some time off to concentrate on finals," she said, wiping her eyes again.

"Erika, seriously, you don't need to do that, the three of us could go. I really don't want to leave you like this."

"Sweetie, you are, and have been my best friend, and I thank you from the bottom of my heart. But I didn't pay for you to go back to school so you could flunk out. You need to have some time, too. And I will make you a deal. When I've sorted my life out and you are done with school, I'll take us all on vacation. We can do as you - say hop on a flight over to the Bahamas or Mexico, and relax. However, I genuinely think at the moment we need to each get things back on track," she said.

"Okay, okay I'll back down. You know what? I will hold you to the vacation," she said, pouring them both another drink.

Manchester, UK

Chapter Twenty-Two

Georgia had spent all day moping around in her apartment. Whilst her siblings were probably partially right, they did give her more to think about. Inclusive of the fact it wasn't the gun capital of the world, not even the states. They also weren't 'gay' haters, and actually had a big scene and an annual gay pride festival there, too. They were right that she had scrutinised it to the death without having any substance to base it on. But, regardless of anything else, she was still right in the sense she didn't know anyone there, and she didn't know how things worked over there. Yes, it was the same company, but she'd been to the London and Bristol offices and they did things differently to how she did things. She leaned her head back on the chair, closing her eyes and feeling the tears drop down once more.

'Knock knock.'

Georgia looked at the time, it was six forty on a Saturday night. It must be her parents coming to check on her. *Jesus why couldn't they just call like normal parents did?* she thought as she walked to the door. She scolded herself as she recollected her sister's words last night that they wouldn't be around forever. She opened the door and was confronted with Julia.

"Hey. I hope you don't mind me just showing up. I just heard, we were doing an exhibition in London and I was supposed to be staying down there for the weekend. When I heard, I jumped on the first train back. I have stopped off to get some necessities," she said, holding up a couple of Tesco bags.

"Jules, what did you do that for? Why? I don't need babysitting. I keep telling everybody this," she sighed.

"I didn't say you did, and I'm not here to argue. Or discuss if you don't want to, or anything else. I am here as your friend and your colleague and to help you anyway I can. Whether that be merely cooking you dinner, massaging your feet or back or sitting in silence watching a movie together." She smiled. "But either way, it's not up for discussion," she said, pushing past Georgia.

Georgia rested her head against the side of her still open door and sighed heavily…"Why can't you all just leave me alone?" she said, shutting the door.

"Because, lady. Very occasionally, situations require a friend close by," she said sincerely. "Now, stop pulling faces, go to your bathroom and run a bath. I didn't know if you had any, so pour as much as you can of this in there," she said, handing her some bubble bath.

"Bu…"

"Seriously, Georgia, I am not discussing. I've already said it, now just go," she said, pointing to the woman's bathroom. Georgia looked as though she was about to argue, but thought better of it when she saw Julia's facial expression.

***

Julia made the food she'd bought from the store. She set the dining table with candles, and an ice bucket filled at each end of the table. One with a big bottle of diet coke and the other with a bottle of pinot. She got out the throw from the spare room and threw it on the couch with a couple of the bed pillows. Julia noticed Georgia go to her room and shut the door behind her, so she walked into the bathroom and lit the candles surrounding the mass space. Opening her iPhone to the relaxing sounds app, she put on the sound of the ocean and left it in the corner loud enough to hear. Julia pulled the door over and went and knocked on Georgia's door. Opening it slightly, she saw Georgia lay on her bed with her head in her hands. Julia went over and sat beside her, pulling her hands away softly, and brushed the tears from her cheek. "Come on, Hun. If anyone can do this, you can," she said. "If you really don't want to do it then you need to tell Derek."

"Oh yeah?" she scoffed. "He made it clear I would be unemployed."

"Well, if that's really what they do, then fuck em. You will easily get a job elsewhere, and he will be fucked because he'll end up with no team when you go, as we'll all be banging down the door to come with you." She smiled.

"What am I going to do? I feel so lost and alone," she sniffed, annoyed that she was crying and upset in front of one of her staff. She hated letting her guard down.

"Which was exactly my point. I'm not here for anything other than what you need. And like I said, if that's just someone to sit on the end of the couch with so you don't feel alone, then that's fine. Come on, come with me," she said, pulling her up.

Julia walked Georgia to her bathroom and led her into the darkened room, lit only by candles. "Get yourself in there, but please don't do nothing silly," she said seriously and left, shutting the door behind her.

Julia put music on the TV. She didn't know if Georgia would be up for listening to club classics when she got out of the bath, but for now, she was happy to listen. Lighting the candles in the lounge and dining area, she finished off the last of the prepping.

Julia sat down with a bottle of beer from Georgia's fridge, remembering that she had forgot about the other bag. She put the giant tub of cookie dough ice-cream in the freezer, and put the giant bar of galaxy on the coffee table. Next to the huge, movie-sized bag of Doritos, the tub of Pringles, and the big bag of Haribo. She knocked on the door of the bathroom. "You decent?" she asked.

"Hmm," Georgia said lazily.

Julia walked in to the room. "You okay?"

"Yes. This is nice, thanks, Julia. You really shouldn't have, but I'm glad you did. I hope you know that the beach sound won't sell it to me. It's nowhere near a beach," she said seriously.

"It wasn't for that reason. I love it. It always relaxes me, so I went with that. And yes, well aware of that, approximately forty miles I think. Anyways, I didn't want to disturb, but I got you these. I wasn't really sure what was your thing. So, I got Diva, Good Housekeeping and Hello," she said, handing the three magazines to Georgia shyly. "Erm don't worry, if they aren't any good."

Georgia sighed lightly, "They're perfect, thank you. I can't honestly tell you the last time I ever stopped long enough to read a magazine. Seriously, thank you for everything." She smiled softly.

"Can you see enough with the candle light or would you like me to put the light on?" she asked.

"NO!" she scoffed. "Sorry, please don't. Just by the TV, there is a giant candle. Could you bring that in and put it here? That will be more than enough light then." She smiled.

Julia returned with the candle as requested and smiled to Georgia. As she turned to walk away, she felt the wet arm on her, and turned to look at Georgia.

"You want to join me?" she said shyly.

Julia didn't know how to respond without doing more damage. She kneeled down beside the bath and rested her arms on the side of the panel, and her head lazily on her hands smiling. "You know, there is nothing in the world, I can assure you, that I would love more right now. But I think it may complicate things a little more. And I don't want to put any more pressure on you. How about you enjoy some you time with your mags, and I leave you to it?" she said, squinting her nose slightly up at her boss.

"Yeah, I guess you're right," she said sadly.

Julia could feel the pulls and was struggling to fight it. She wanted to hug her and tell her it would all be okay, and just be with her. But the fact of the matter was, she didn't know it would be. She knew for sure it certainly wouldn't be for '*them*'; not that there was a them. But definitely, not any future possibility of it now. "You want anything else before I go?" she smiled.

"No, I'm good thanks," she said.

***

Georgia walked out of the bathroom an hour later, disturbing Julia who was laid on the sofa reading her book, and tapping her foot along to 'Girls Just Wanna Have Fun.' She got up quickly, "Hey, you okay?"

"Yeah, much better. I'm going to get changed," she said.

"Yes, I think that would be a very good idea," she smirked, causing a slight curl on Georgia's lip. "Dinner is ready. I was just waiting for you, so I'll set it up." She smiled.

"You should have come and got me."

"It's fine, just get dressed, I'll sort this," Julia finished. She went and retrieved the large candle from the bathroom and brought it back into the lounge. Then, she went into the kitchen and plated the dinners up, and set them at the dining table, just in time for Georgia to appear.

"Wow, that smells incredible. Can't say I was hungry, but I most definitely am now. It looks great. What is it?" she asked, looking over at Julia.

"Cheese and onion stuffed chicken breast, wrapped in pancetta. Boiled potatoes, and roasted veggies," she said. "I wasn't sure if you wanted a drink or not so I got some Coke and some wine?" she said in question.

"Actually, I could really do with a beer now that I've seen you drinking one. But a Coke would go down well too," she said.

"Okay, well you pour us some drinks and I'll grab you a beer," she said, going to the fridge and pulling one out. "You feeling any better?" she said awkwardly. "Sorry stupid question, dinner and a bath really isn't going to make you feel any less like your world isn't falling apart," she sighed, taking a bite of asparagus.

"Easy, it's me doing the whole sorry for myself act," she said, resting her hand on Julia's. "I am actually, the bath was perfect. I never think of having one. Certainly I never do anything like that, and it was amazing. And, FYI so is this," she said, pointing her fork to the dinner before her. "Hmm, seriously, this is too good," she said, removing her hand and digging back in.

"Thanks." She smiled. "So, you thought anymore about things? What are you planning to do? If you'd rather not talk about it, we can leave it."

"Honestly, I don't know. I feel massively backed into a corner. If I stay, they will get rid of me sooner or later, or I'll impede any opportunity I have of furthering my career. If I go, I'm going to be on the other side of the world with no friends, family, nothing. In a country where I know nothing about, a state that sounds very 'old school' and scary. And ultimately, be hated because this bitch of a woman thinks that I've stolen her job. In reality, regardless of how they sweeten it up, she's right. I don't want it, and they have given her job to me. Unless she's a complete and utter ogre, she will be no different to me. She's doing the same job, granted in a different office, but will be established and have relationships with her staff, like I have, all of whom will be indebted to her. And what will I have? Sweet FA, that's what," she sighed.

"Have you considered calling her?" Julia asked between bites.

"God no, why would I do a thing like that?"

"Because, as you say, she is in exactly the same boat as you. She's at home herself with her world crashing down too. And at least that way you can gauge how things will look if you go. I mean, I'm not trying to make things worse here, Hun. But, I don't really think you have a choice," she said sombrely.

"That's my problem," Georgia sighed, thinking about her words to potentially call this Erika woman. Maybe, when she had calmed down too, they could just work through it. Screw those idiots over, and complete the task in half the time, then she could come back home to Manchester where she belonged.

"You okay?"

"Yeah, I'm good. Look, I'm sorry I was a bit shirty earlier, but thanks for all of this, you have been an incredible friend. Which given the circumstances, speaks volumes." She smiled.

"What do you mean? Speaks volumes? What, just because we were fuck buddies for a couple of weeks and you are leaving, I can't do this? Look George, I don't know how many times I can say this. I really like you; not like that anymore. Although, if we continued and this situation hadn't have happened, that may have changed on my part. But for now, I really enjoy spending time with you. I've always liked you, you're an awesome boss, and a good laugh. So yeah, I would class you as a friend also, in which case, you help friends out in their time of need," she said seriously.

"Thanks. I can't believe you left London and a night out though," she stated.

"How come? It's London, and I'm there every bloody week, plus it's so expensive and manic, it stresses me out half the time."

"I'll drink to that, and my thoughts exactly."

"Well, one positive is that you don't have to do that for a year then." She smiled.

Georgia sighed again as the realisation hit of the situation unfolding before her.

Houston, USA

Chapter Twenty-Three

"Nonnnnnnnnn-aaaaaaa," Dulcie was screaming as she ran down the pathway into her grandmother's open arms.

"Mia preziosa," the woman said, hugging her darling granddaughter.

"Ciao, Momma," Erika said sadly.

"Mia bambina, come here, come here," she said, pulling her daughter closer. "Don't get upset in front of Dulcie, bambina. Let's get her set up and we can have some tea outside, you can tell me everything," she whispered softly, holding her daughter's cheek.

Dulcie and Erika went to their respective rooms and unpacked for the week ahead of them. Dulcie's grandmother put the TV on for her with a juice box and left her to it. She met her daughter on the front porch and handed her a mug of tea. "Dimmi? Tell me?" her mother said, and Erika was unable to control the emotions, which poured out of her.

Her mother pulled her daughter into a tight embrace, soothing her, and trying to calm her down. Erika never relied on anyone, not even Dan. She had lost her father a number of years ago, and from then she went all out to provide a solid, stable life for herself and her family. Her mother included.

Erika had bought her mom her house so she didn't need to worry about money. Her mother had never had a job, she had instead stayed at home and looked after her and her five siblings. So when her father passed, it was incredibly difficult for her mother. But she was a strong Italian woman, and very adaptable. Erika and her siblings were all still close, albeit she was the only one who had moved away from her hometown of Dallas. So, it was rare that they were all together. Even holidays were spent with Dan's family, due to them being close by.

Erika was glad that they brought Dulcie's Frozen DVD, as it gave her ample opportunity to go into detail with her mom. They had always had a close relationship, and although she was concerned coming home, she knew her mother would break her on a whole other level. She knew her mother would make her take the blindfold off and pay attention to everything unravelling before her. Which, came with the fact, she knew her life would be incredibly different upon leaving.

Leaving nothing out, Erika had shared everything with her mother, who merely listened offering tissues, tea and occasional soothing sounds. Her mother was a very wise woman and the one that all of the children came to in their search for help and advice.

***

They spent the best part of two hours, discussing in full, her marriage *and* her job. Her mother had offered her some words of wisdom, and made valid points inclusive of the fact that there was nothing she could do with the situation. So, she either accepted it and moved on, or rejected it, and become a stay at home mom, allowing Dan to support them. Erika kissed her mom, "Grazie, Mamma."

"Per cosa?" her mother said, smiling slightly.

"You know what for, Mamma. You know the whole reverse psychology will always work on me more than most. You say anything that relates to me having to rely on someone, and I'm always going to power through." She smiled. "Ti amo, Mamma," she said, kissing her mother again.

"Mommy, what are you crying for? You wanna hug?" Dulcie said, wandering out to the porch sleepily and spotting her mother.

"Ohhh, I'm okay, baby. Did your movie finish?" she said, lifting Dulcie up to her lap.

"Yup. Nonna can we make cookies today?" she said excitably.

"Well, maybe not today. We won't have anything left to do if we do it all this day," she said, stroking her granddaughter's face.

Erika looked to her ringing phone and saw Taylor's face appear. "Go to Nonna, I need to speak to Tay to let her know we arrived okay," she said, walking off, answering her cell.

"Hey you, how goes it?" she said into the phone.

Erika spent a long while on the phone to Taylor. Telling her about the three-hour journey back home and how her mother had managed within a couple hours to have made her see sense of it all. Erika detailed what her mother had said and what their plans were for the week, before ending the call and returning to her mother and daughter, who were making the evening's dinner.

Manchester, UK

Chapter Twenty-Four

Georgia hadn't been in work for almost a week, and she was feeling it. She was unable to move on and she couldn't remember the last time work hadn't dominated her life in this way. So getting out of her trackie and into work clothes, felt somewhat strange. Derek had called the day before, requesting a meeting, which she agreed to, however, caveating it with a meeting off site. She didn't want to go to work, knowing everyone would be speaking about it. But equally, she did need to do something about the situation. And after speaking in length to her family the night before, she had decided to basically go in, forget about the "whys" and just hear him out. Then she would find out what the offer was, and rather than going in with her mind made up, base the decision upon the conversation.

Georgia had agreed to meet Derek at Cloud Twenty-Three in the Hilton. Clearly, he was pulling out all the stops. Sure enough, she'd make sure she got the most expensive cocktail on the menu. The lift guard put her in the lift to the twenty-third floor, and she was taken to Derek's table.

"Hi," she said, taking a seat and putting the envelope before him.

"That's not what I think it is, is it?" Derek asked, concerned, looking down to the three-fold envelope.

"Yes, it is, Derek. However, I will give you the benefit of the doubt and at least hear you, before I decide what is the most pertinent decision for my future with the business," she said gravely.

Derek and Georgia had worked together for a very long time, and throughout that period he had been her teacher, her coach, her mentor, but most significantly her friend. Which is how she knew this was taking a toll on him also. Georgia wondered if he had genuinely been a part of this decision, or whether it was forced upon him. Either way, he looked older, as though he had not slept throughout the whole process.

Derek sighed, rubbing his temple. "What would you like, George?" he said to her.

Picking up the menu she went through the cocktails and told the waitress what she wanted.

"So, I guess it's pointless wasting any more of either of our times, so why don't you begin? I have, understandably, had plenty of time to… Now I'm not going to say accept this, but well, I guess for want of a better word, digest it. Well, I suppose as much as I'm ever going to be able to. I understand I am not going to be able to change your mind, or whoever's idea this was, and I won't push that any further. But I think the least I deserve is to be given an explanation. Additionally, I have not even opened the envelope with what I believe was the contract, etc. Again, I think I deserved more than just giving me an envelope for me to go home and sign. I mean, Jesus, I would have thought that putting me on a development plan, giving me a project to manage on the basis that if both of those things were achieved, I would be given a promotion. *Then,* achieving said objectives. Honestly, Derek. Honestly, I think the least I could have been afforded is some form of discussion. Potentially a negotiation? But clearly, I fucked up majorly along the way, or we wouldn't be sitting here now," she said, taking a sip of the drink that had just been put in front of her.

Derek sighed. "Georgia, it really isn't like that. Look, get comfortable, and I will start at the beginning, cards on the table, warts and all, and then you can make the decision. Or go away and think about it, whichever you'd prefer."

"Agreed, I would appreciate that," she said, sitting further into her seat.

Derek removed his jacket and took a small sip of his scotch and went back to the beginning.

***

An hour later, Georgia suddenly felt stranger than when she had been initially told the week before. She didn't really know how to compute the information, but equally she wasn't surprised at the turn of events. Nor Derek's involvement, or lack thereof.

"So, that's the story, beginning to end, no more no less. I'm sorry you feel so defrauded, it would have never been my intention, and I hope you know this. However, I'm going to caveat that with, George, if anyone can do this, you can. The contract you haven't looked at, incorporates this information. It is guaranteed. And hell, you want to negotiate, then go ahead. I'll get you whatever you want. You want a home with a pool? A range rover? Bloody hell, your own stables with horses? I'll do it. I do get it, Jill has had me sleeping in the spare room all week, due to how poorly I've handled this, and I just genuinely didn't." He stopped and rubbed his eyes. "I guess I can only apologise,

I've been spineless, Georgia," Derek sighed. "And given our relationship, the least you deserved was the truth."

She was annoyed that he was making her feel bad, when ultimately, she had nothing to feel bad about. But he was right, she was like his protégé, and he was like her step-father. Always had been. He always looked out for her, which is probably why Jill had now got involved. So it was difficult to be annoyed at him.

Houston, USA

Chapter Twenty-Five

"Ti amo, Mamma, Ti amo," Erika said, kissing her mother again. She didn't really know how she was going to face the situation ahead of her. But like her mom said, she needed to go home and face everything head on. She knew what she needed to do. She felt sick to her stomach, which was never ideal with a three-hour car ride ahead of them. She'd spoken to Dan the day before and said they needed to talk that night. She'd also phoned Mike to request a meeting for tomorrow at lunchtime. Erika had done exactly as her mom had suggested and had the two completed envelopes on the passenger seat alongside her. She was actually going to do this. Jesus, this could potentially change her whole life forever, and Dulcie's.

"Did you have a good week, sweetie?" Erika asked, looking into the rear-view mirror.

"Uh huh, I love going to see Nonna and my cousins. Mommy, why don't we live here too?"

"Well, because mommy had a job offer that was very good, back when you hadn't been born yet, and so I moved to Houston."

"Well, I kind of wish we lived here too, ya know?" she said seriously.

"Okay, baby. I'll bare that in mind." She smiled to her daughter. Knowing that at least if she moved back home Dulcie would be okay.

***

"Tay Tay." Dulcie was hugging her nanny tightly. "I got you a gift. Where's the gift Mommy? Mommy says I'm going to have a sleepover at your house tonight," she said, wriggling in her arms, excitably.

"You okay? You wanna come in for a coffee?" Taylor asked Erika seriously.

"No, honestly, I need to go do this. I may pop by later. I'll see how I feel. I need to get prepared for tomorrow too, and I also have a meeting with a big competitor. So, I need to get ready for that as well."

"An interview? You're quitting your job?" Taylor said surprised.

"Not an interview as such, no. And the job, well, I have a long conversation to be had with my boss tomorrow. My mom also thinks I should maybe try contacting this new woman…my new boss," she said solemnly. "Which I feel pretty weird about, but I'll see what Mike says tomorrow, and then I will let you know," she said, kissing her daughter on the cheek. "Be good for Taylor okay, sweetie?" she said, kissing her daughter and leaving them there.

Chapter Twenty-Six

Erika pulled up to the restaurant, and managed to get a parking spot right outside. She sat there for a few moments collecting her thoughts, and trying to settle her nerves. God, she needed a hard drink. She pulled her phone out to text her mom, but decided against it. She'd call her after her meeting with Mike. She just needed to grow a pair and do this. She grabbed the two envelopes and rested her head against the headrest. Closing her eyes, she said a silent prayer. Then, taking a deep breath, she left the car.

"Erika, Hi. How are you? Would you like a drink? I didn't know if you wanted to eat, so I ordered some food. Bread and meat selections, some shrimp tacos and some wings," he said.

"Odd selection. Yes, I'll have a martini with an olive," she said pointedly.

"How was your trip? Did Dulcie enjoy seeing her grandmother?" he asked shrinkingly.

"Look Mike, I can't deal with the small talk. I'm pissed, *real* pissed. And genuinely, I'm not going to lie to you, I won't be giving you an answer this morning. Not until I go to a meeting I have planned this afternoon, which could potentially sway things for me."

"You're gonna quit?" he asked concerned.

"Potentially Mike; look I'm an Area Director, I know how this works. Additionally, I know that just because I shout or scream that the business will back down and give me what I want. I get that okay? But equally, I need to do what's right for me and my family. Things aren't so great at home, so Dulcie needs to be my priority over and above," she said firmly.

"Things aren't so great with you and Dan?" he said genuinely, allowing the server to put the food down before them.

Erika's 'feed up' over the past week at her mothers, had clearly gotten her used to eating again. The aromas of the food wafted up before her, and awakened her senses. Italians loved to eat, and her mother was no different, more so on this trip, because she was convinced that Erika had not been eating, and had become 'far too skinny'.

"Not great, no. So, shoot, what exactly are the plans, and what exactly is expected of me? Am I being demoted? I've done some research and you can't just do that or change my salary. What happens with this new woman? My new *boss*? Will I be transferred to Fort Worth? Has my senior team been communicated with, that they no longer have a boss? What?" she said, grabbing a shrimp and looking up to him seriously.

"Look, Erika, I'm not going to insult you by saying that wasn't what I told you at the meeting. Because, I get it was an awful lot of information to accept and take in. However, you have misunderstood completely. So, basically, nothing changes here. You are based here and you still have the office to run, your senior team still reports to you. You are not demoted; your salary will actually increase. Nor will your position change. Well, other than you are promoted as an interim so there will be more to do. Georgia will be coming over, well that's what we hope, and she will be slightly more senior than you are. *You* will be the only one reporting to her; but I'll caveat that with, it will be with a dotted line to me. Any issues come directly to me. From what I understand of Derek, Georgia's well liked, her team respects her, and this is an opportunity for you both to develop and learn from each other. You know this office and the team, so she will need a lot of help, since the UK office runs things very differently. But she is not a permanent fixture, she is not walking into the job you were offered. That is still yours long term. When the Fort Worth office is opened, you will be going into that role, it's yours and only yours. Georgia and yourself, will be working collaboratively with the same goal, you are not competing for the same job. You are going to work together to do the same as you have both been doing, to open the new flagship office. The plans are astonishingly unlike anything we've ever done before. Hence why Derek and I really thought that you two together would surmount the tremendous difficulties and dispositions that the business is endeavouring to succeed in. I know this was never the plan, and I know you aren't happy about this, I do. Please don't think for one minute I don't. I have no doubt in my mind that this isn't easily achievable though. And additionally, you and Georgia will complement each other. We want you both to take on so much and learn from each other, then you go back to pick up the promotions you both deservedly achieved in your respective offices," he said seriously.

"Okay, one question? If the promotion is guaranteed, why could I have not been given it as always discussed and do this in addition to it?" she questioned.

"We aren't in a position at this moment to do it. The company cannot facilitate it right now, but it will happen, Erika. If there's anything you want as part of the package, I'm happy to negotiate where necessary, and issue if feasible," he confirmed. "So, have you any further questions?"

"I don't think so, I will give you an answer by the end of the day," she said seriously, taking stock of the lengthy conversation they'd had over lunch.

Chapter Twenty-Seven

Georgia felt awful. She hated long flights, and no number of magazines that Julia and Paul had brought her would have gotten her through it. Luckily, the upgrade allowed her to at least sleep for a couple of hours, and enjoy the complimentary cocktails and three course meal.

Georgia wasn't particularly afraid of flying, but she got bored easily in situations like those. And whilst she loved travelling, she always tended to stay closer to home and enjoy villas to Greece or city breaks. Another reason this whole situation was pissing her off, but she shook off the negativity. "Come on you can't be doing this again, it's too late, you're here," she said to herself.

Georgia made her way through George Bush intercontinental airport. It was huge of course, because everything was bigger in America. Following the arrows over to collect her luggage, she retrieved her two large suitcases, and made her way to the exit.

Georgia was finding it very difficult to not be incredibly negative about the whole situation. But like her parents had said to her, try it and at least you will know either way. She set herself just one month to stay without shipping her belongings, and then she could return home, if that's what she felt was best. At least that way she'd never have any regrets, and she liked that idea. It was a good outlook. Additionally, if she did stay, Julia's sister was looking for a place to rent with her boyfriend. So, if by some miracle it worked out, Julia was going to rent her apartment so she could be closer to work for the twelve months, and her sister would rent Julia's place. This would save a lot of stress for Georgia, too. Julia said she could come and visit with a friend, if she stayed. Her parents saying the same, as well as bringing the whole family out to see her.

Georgia directed her trolley to the carousel and waited for it to start moving. She couldn't believe how long it had taken to get through customs, and it still hadn't started to go around yet. She sighed, leaning up against the trolley and amending her watch to the six hours behind time zone she was currently in. She was virtually ready for bed, but it was literally the middle of the afternoon to her now. Removing her biker jacket, she realised wearing a long-sleeved shirt and a jacket to a place where it was eighty degrees outside may not have been the best idea she'd ever had.

***

Georgia made her way out, manoeuvring her trolley carefully around people who were just standing around. Ultimately, annoying her. She was tired and needed to get out of there, fast.

When she got through, she noticed a tall and slender foreign-looking woman holding a sign with the word 'Carson'. She knew she was being picked up, as Mike had emailed her so. But she was unsure if it would be an employee or someone from a specific company.

"Hi, is that for Georgia Carson?" she said to the woman.

"Well, unless there's another Carson," she said sarcastically.

"I don't know, it's a very large airport and Carson is also a first name. So, simple question? Are you here to pick *me* up? Georgia Carson?"

"Yes!" she snapped. "Are you ready? We need to go. I've been waiting for almost an hour, and the ticket will run out on the meter soon," she said pointedly.

Georgia sighed. *Amazing start*, she thought.

"So, am I going to find out who you are? Or should I consult my crystal ball?" Georgia said aggressively.

"I'm the one you stole the job from," she said, storming off ahead.

"Oh shit...and there was me thinking that they weren't arrogant arseholes here," she said to herself, trying to keep up with the woman she knew only to be Erika.

"For the record, I actually *didn't* steal your job. As I understood it, you were in exactly the same position I was; and was awaiting a promotion to Managing Director. Secondly, I don't think it is too much to ask for simple manners and courtesy, since I was not informed who would be picking me up. So, an effortless 'hi, my name is Erika,' wouldn't have been too difficult, surely?" she complained.

"Oh, I'm sorry, my job wasn't enough? Now you want me to be courteous to you? Sheesh, you Brits are arrogant," she stormed, unlocking her car.

Gobsmacked, Georgia stopped, taking in the car before her. Shit it was huge. Beautiful, but huge. As it turned out, the majority of them were. *Bollox, I hope mine isn't like this.* She didn't own a car any longer, and hadn't actually driven one for over three years. She breathed in deeply. *Chill out, it's like riding a bike. What could possibly go wrong?* she thought.

Erika made no attempt to help her. She simply got in the car and was tapping stonily on her phone. Georgia lifted her suitcases into the boot, "bollox," she cursed as she rubbed off the mark she had made on her white jeans. She shut the boot and walked around to the front of the car, realising she had walked to the driver side. Georgia tutted to herself and continued walking to the passenger side, *or* the driver's side had she been back home. She noticed the child seat in the back. She was pissed off about how rude this woman was being, but she hated confrontation and didn't want to be dealing with it. *Please god, let it only be a ten-minute car journey*, she thought.

Awkward was quite possibly the understatement of the century. They had been in the car for twenty minutes and not uttered a word to each other. Georgia thought back to when they were kids and Alex and she stopped talking; she was a forty-year old Director and was being ignored, this couldn't be a good start. More problematically, she was desperately in need of a drink. She had been drinking on the flight, against her mother's advice. Something about making you more dehydrated. Great, yet again proven wrong by her mother. But there was not a chance she was going to ask her to stop for a water, she'd probably bloody leave her there.

"How long will it take to get there, please?" Georgia asked sincerely, trying to stifle the dry cough.

"You sound like my five-year-old," she snapped, and pulled off the road hard. Erika drove into a gas station and looked at Georgia. "Around another thirty minutes, but I'm assuming it's a rest break or drink, so here you go," she said, without looking at her.

Georgia went to speak and just decided to leave it. She ran over to the store and grabbed a couple of waters. She went to the till to pay, "shit," she said to the assistant, realising she didn't have her money on her, it was in the boot. "Sorry I…," she started.

"Keep the change," she heard behind her, and looked up to see Erika handing over some notes to the assistant.

"Thanks…" But it was too late. she had walked out, ignoring her, *again.*

"Seriously, are you *all* this rude in this country?" she snapped at the assistant, who looked feared to death.

"Thank you for that, I forgot to get my money out of the boot, in the rush. Ummm, I didn't know whether you would want one," she said, placing it in the driver's holder.

"You should know you are going to confuse people saying things like 'boot'. It's 'trunk' over here. And thanks for the water, but, I'm good. Maybe you should take it. I don't know if your house will have anything in there, and the nearest store is a few miles away. You aren't going to be able to drive; if you get pulled over by the cops, you'll have a DUI before you have started work," she said.

Georgia had watched enough TV and movies to know that DUI meant 'driving under the influence'. *Amazing,* now she thought her boss was an alky! *For fucks sake, could this get any worse?*

Houston, USA

Chapter Twenty-Eight

The whole journey was silent thereafter, and Georgia was tired, which was making her feel even worse. She suddenly realised how alone she was. They turned onto a long residential road lined either side with detached houses, but there was absolutely no consistency with them. Some were white, some were brick, some were wood, some were a mixture. Nothing like back home where they would all be virtually identical. Bar the difference in windows and doors. One thing that was similar with the majority of them, was virtually everyone had an American flag at the front of it.

Erika pulled onto the drive of a big brick house, which was actually very pretty. Very suburban, which was completely new for her. Erika got out of the car and lifted the two suitcases out of the *trunk*. Throwing her bag over her shoulder, she grabbed one of the case handles and walked past Georgia up to the front of the house. She grabbed the envelope from her purse and retrieved the keys to open the door before walking in.

Georgia stepped inside, absorbing the place. It was actually incredible, but ridiculously big. Especially for one person. However, great when people came to visit. If it got to that stage, which was pretty much looking unlikely. Georgia's phone rang and she looked down at the photo of her nieces. Immediately, it hit her like a ton of bricks. She couldn't speak to Alex, not tonight. She wouldn't be able to cope, so she turned her phone over and put it on silent. Then, she looked up to Erika, who was stood staring at her.

"Umm, here are the keys to the house. Make sure you lock it up at night, too. Don't sweat it, this is a safe neighborhood. This street is like two miles long, but at the bottom there's a small seven eleven...What are you smiling at?" she said seriously, stopping her sentence.

"I've just not heard of seven elevens since I was a kid, and I didn't realise they still existed. Yes, go on," she said embarrassed.

"So, that's the nearest store, you will be able to get the basics until you are able to get to a proper grocery store. The nearest one is just a couple blocks away. If you set your navigation system to Walmart, there's a pretty big one nearby that it will take you to. Your car is in the garage, and in the envelope, are the directions and zip to the office. It takes approximately forty minutes, so I suggest you leave around 8am tomorrow morning.

"What's a zip, sorry?" Georgia stopped her.

"A Zip Code? The address to take you to the office?" she said, like Georgia was stupid.

"Ahh, a post code," she sighed.

Your phone is here, it's all set up and ready to go. So if you just use Google you will be able to find a place that delivers for dinner tonight. I'm guessing that covers everything, here is my number. I know you haven't met anyone yet, so if there is anything you need, I guess you will have to call me," she said, walking out of the house, and shutting the door behind her.

Georgia stood there quietly. This woman hated her. Which meant the staff was going to hate her. She was in suburbia, something she was completely not used to. She was expected to drive in another country when she hadn't drove in three years, and she had just been left here. Just like that. If the situation was reversed, she'd never do that. She'd never just leave someone in a foreign country with nothing but a contact number and phone to search for takeaways. Georgia had always heard that Americans were kind, caring, compassionate human beings, but in fact that was incredibly incorrect! "What have you done George? What *have* you done?" she said, putting her head in her hands and allowing the tears to fall.

***

Georgia heard her phone go. She was still laying on the floor in the hallway, having not moved past this area since arriving. She wiped her face, seeing the message from Julia.

Hey, how is it? You get there okay? What's your digs like? Hope you're ok? Xx

Georgia hovered her thumb above the keys uncertain whether to respond or not, and decided against it, well at least for the time being. She couldn't let this control her. She always knew it would be difficult, and she needed to get a grip. It's a month after all, only a month she said to herself over and over.

"You will not get beat. You're a senior director for Christ's sake. You *can* do this. Plan one, get these sodding boots off," she said, undoing them and sighing with relief.

"Plan two, go check out your digs, seriously, you have a gorgeous house. A bloody hot house as well, she said, fanning herself with the envelope. Plan three, unpack. Plan four, get showered and changed into your running gear and go to the store," she said.

"Plan five and most importantly, stop bloody talking to yourself. You are in a different house, yes. But you aren't

unaccustomed to living alone. So, sort your shit out girl."
Oh Jesus, she was even sounding like an American.

Georgia lifted herself up and dumped the envelope and
keys on the hall table. She hung her jacket up and turned
the lock on the door, looking to the staircase directly ahead
of her. Georgia stared at the double doors on her left.
Opening them she walked into the huge lounge, complete
with an open brick fireplace and a mounted TV on the wall.
She left and opened the door on the opposite side of the
entrance hallway, which lead into a large dining room. She
followed it around and walked into the extensive kitchen.
"Wooooowww," she said out loud; she walked around the
island running her finger along it, there was a double oven,
and an American fridge. She opened it and placed the bottle
of water in as she noticed the six-ft. wine fridge. These
people really did do everything bigger and better. She
turned back around, noticing the back garden, she unlocked
the door and opened the French doors. It was fully decked
the full width of the house with a wonderful built in
barbecue, complete with a fridge attached and a pizza oven
at the end of it. Bloody hell, this was immense, but the best
feature was the pool in the garden. There were three sun
loungers next to the pool, that in this moment looked
incredibly inviting, as the sun was reflecting off the water.
The garden was private, yet huge, and she wondered how
the hell you maintain a pool? She wouldn't have a bloody
clue what to do.

Georgia finally was getting excited. She walked back
inside, locking up behind her. She went to the door at the
end of the kitchen and unlocked it, but she couldn't find the
light and it was pitch black. Unlocking her iPhone and
switching on the torch, she found the hanging light switch
and pulled on it. "Holy shit," she thought, as she saw the

'assumingly' brand new electric blue Kia Sportage. She grabbed the key and went and sat inside it; it was beautiful, she thought. There was no requirement realistically to have a car when you live and work in a major city, so it was completely unnoticed that she didn't have one. The public transport was completely reliable, so why bother paying for something she would use once a fortnight for shopping. But gosh it felt good to be behind the wheel again, and it felt massive. She felt so high up, and when she switched the engine on, it felt smooth. Laughing to herself, she wondered what that even meant. This was all real? She was sitting in *her* car, in *her* garage, in *her* big house, with *her* swimming pool, listening to a radio station with Americans talking. *My gosh this is all so very surreal*, she thought. Come on, this was it, this is what she needed to focus on. *Be materialistic for a change, George, and live the highlife,* she thought.

Georgia walked upstairs and appreciated the humungous landing, noticing the large arched window on the front of the house with a built-in loveseat. She loved the idea of sitting in the window with a glass of wine, watching the world go by. But seriously, the size of it, it could have been an additional room. Georgia chose the first door and saw a double bedroom, a big one, and she wondered if this would be hers. She looked into the big walk in wardrobe, before opening the next door and walked into a bathroom, where she noticed the marbled double sink, with a toilet and shower cubicle. Walking through the symmetrical door in the bathroom, Georgia was faced with an identical room to the one she had just left. *Amazing*, she thought. A shared bathroom to co-joined bedrooms. Walking out of the second bedroom door, she left that open and arrived in the next room. She opened that to a family bathroom with a large bath, albeit a very short bath, with a large wet room style shower too. "Very nice," she said to herself, looking forward to taking a shower in that shortly. There were two doors left, so she opened the first one, and it was a study. *Good stuff,* she thought. Lastly was the master bedroom. She opened it and walked in. *That king-sized bed is far too big for my skinny little arse alone*, she thought. *Hmm, shame nobody to share it with though. It is definitely big enough to enjoy with a hot woman.* Shaking the naughty thoughts from her head. She could do this if it killed her, she wouldn't let that awful woman bully her out of her career.

***

Georgia's lungs were burning when she arrived at the store, as she had done virtually nothing since all of this had happened last month. And bloody hell did it show. She could start swimming in the pool each morning before she went to work, and run in the evening.

Georgia didn't know how the hell she was going to get back with what she needed, guessing she could get just a few small bits and then drive back later. She didn't even feel drunk; however, chances are she probably was still over the limit. And attempting to drive in a different place would only cause her to bring attention to herself. She got to the water, which was the main thing. But there were only huge five litre bottles, and she didn't even know if she could drink the water from the tap. She looked around and saw a woman stood not far from her. She debated asking, but then recalled the complete lack of assistance she had been afforded earlier in the day.

She grabbed a few bits, before making her way back home.

Georgia arrived at her front door, putting down the shopping bags and opening the door to her home for the next month, stopping to look around as she heard the shouting behind her. Georgia noticed a woman probably around her own age, maybe a little older, walking towards her. "Hi, hi," she said, quickening her pace to Georgia.

Georgia didn't know what to do, had she done something wrong? Shit, she looked like a right state, her hair would be resembling Bart Simpsons Sunday school, curtain-do right now, after that run.

"Erm hi? Is everything okay?"

"Yes, yes. I just wanted to come over and say hi, and introduce myself. I'm Emily Nottingham," she said, shaking Georgia's hand. "I understand you are here from London for a year, and I figured you wouldn't know where anything was and probably have no groceries in the house. Plus, I figured you would be real tired. So, I brought this over. It's a pot pie, it's still warm if you want it now. Otherwise, just heat it at one sixty for twenty minutes. I made you some cookies, too. Although, I don't know if you will eat anything like that from looking at you now," she said enthusiastically.

Georgia was taken aback. She had been wrong to tar all Americans with the same brush, based upon Erika's actions. "Erm…thank you, Emily. Thank you *so* much, that's ever so kind." She liked the way she had accentuated the 'H' in her surname. Back home Nottingham, was just Nottingham. More of a silent H. But Emily had pronounced it 'NottingHam.' *Note to self, remember that.*

"Ohhh, my, you have a super cool accent," she said.

"Touché," she said. "Anyways, I'm Georgia Carson, and yes, I am here for a while. However, I'm not from London, I'm from Manchester," she said, smiling kindly.

"And this right here, oh, my word, smells divine. I'm not going to lie, I don't have the slightest clue what pot pie is, but I have a feeling I'll like it. Seriously, you are now officially my new favourite person here with cookies. Yes, I like to run but I also love cookies, so it's all good." She smiled.

"You don't know what pot pie is? That's funny. Ohhh, shame y'all are from Manchester, I thought y'all may have known Prince William and Harry." She smiled softly.

Georgia smiled, unsure whether she was being serious or not. "Listen, this is so incredibly kind of you; would you like to come in for a drink? I have some beers or water," she asked.

"No, no I need to go get ready for my Pilates class, I just wanted to stop by and say hi. You need anything? I'm right across the road at twenty-one forty-two. Just there, and if you have any issues with the house, you let me know, and I'll send John over to fix it for you. We will definitely have a rain check on the beer though," she said eagerly.

"Great! Hey, Emily?"

"Yes?"

"Sorry, to be cheeky, but, would you mind if I came with you one time to your Pilates class? Well unless I have to be a member. As you can see I like fitness, but it may give me a chance to meet some people," she said embarrassed.

"Hellllll yeah, of course. If you wanna come tonight, I can wait for you."

"No, I think I may fall asleep in it tonight. I'm jet lagged to hell, plus I have a hot date with some '*pot pie*' and cookies," Georgia said, winking to Emily. She liked this woman a lot, she was very easy on the eye, too, which was always an added bonus.

"Georgia Carson, I think you and I, are gonna be really good friends," she said earnestly.

Chapter Twenty-Nine

"So, what's she like? Is she pretty? What was she wearing?" Taylor asked her, grabbing a chip from the bowl and dipping it into the salsa.

"What relevance does that even have?" Erika asked confused.

"Well, sure it does. If she turned up looking like Mary Poppins, you know she isn't gonna take no BS," she said, laughing to herself.

"You are strange, *lady*. So, how's finals?" Erika asked her.

"Fine. Stop changing the subject. So, what was she wearing? Is she nice or was she a bitch?" Taylor asked again.

"I wasn't, there's really nothing to tell. We didn't really talk. She asked who I was, and I said the woman you stole the job from," she said pointedly.

"You didn't?"

"Sure, I did," she said, ignoring Taylor and taking some more chips.

"This is your boss, you're playing with fire!"

"*And*...I don't give a hoot! And ya know what else? She's not really my boss, according to Mike. There's no real need for her to manage me, and so I'll do what I like. And *say* what I like to her."

"You think it was wise to accept it? I mean, I know you need a job and all, but with everything else that's going on? This woman is going to come over and feel like shit anyhow and then you are going to make her life hell? Surely, if that's how you feel, you maybe should have told them to stick it from the onset."

"Its fine Tay, I'm good. I'm not going to make anybody's life hell. I need the job, and I need to at least give it a try," she said sombrely.

"Alright then, so what was she wearing?"

"Why does that matter?"

"I'm just intrigued, to see if she's stylish or not. Look, my life is filled with nothing but studies, I just want some girlie gossip," she said.

"Fine already. Yes, I guess she was stylish. She had short hair, very short. Blond, styled up high on top. Ummm, a little like pink, only it was blond. She was incredibly tall, like 6 ft. maybe. Very slim, a real athletic body. She had white jeans on, high tan boots, and a dark shirt, tucked in. She clearly takes care of herself though. You could see that from her build. Enough for you?" she said, rolling her eyes at Taylor.

"Sounds stylish. Uh huh, I'm good with that information for now thanks. How about her? Was she okay though?"

"I told you already, we didn't really speak. I di…it doesn't matter."

"No tell me."

"Seriously, it doesn't matter."

"Erika, tell me?"

"Well, I do feel kinda bad. I won't even call my mom. She'll be really mad at me," she sighed. "Geez, I'm a grown ass woman, and I sound like a fifth grader!"

"How so? Seriously? Tell me already."

"I guess…she did just arrive, and had no food or drink, she smelled of liquor; I mean don't get me wrong she wasn't trashed or that, but you could smell it on her…"

"Seriously, if the roles were reversed and you got sent to the other side of the Atlantic, you are honestly telling me you wouldn't feel the need to hammer the complimentary booze? *For real*?"

"Okay, like I said she wasn't hammered, I just smelled it on her. The point was, I kinda feel bad that I did just leave her, and, do *not* be a jerk now. But I ignored her for the whole ride. Oh, and then we arrived home and she received a call, from…well, the screen saver was of two cute kids, and, well, she kinda looked pretty bummed," she said sadly.

"So, you left her? You made her feel shitty when she is all alone in our country?"

"Cut it out, Tay, seriously, don't start with me," Erika said seriously.

Chapter Thirty

Georgia lay looking at her ceiling when her phone vibrated. It was two twenty am according to her alarm. Looking at it she noticed the text from Julia.

Seriously, are you okay? I'm concerned? 🙁 *xx*

She forgot to message her back. Shit, it was late, but she was wide awake anyhow.

Hey, apologies, I didn't finish up until late and knew it would be too late. How are you? My digs are sweet, only thing though 🙁 *How are you? It's ridiculously warm here and I have a pool, it's stupid o clock and I dunno if it's the jet lag, the time difference or the stress, but I'm wide awake* 🙁 *x.*

Bloody hell, she's alive!!!

You want me to call, I'm in work. You aren't my boss anymore, so I can call the states without you worrying, he he. xx

No, it's too late, you should be doing stuff. xx

Okay, seriously, get a grip. I'm at work, and it's early, so there's not much going on right now. There's no big deal and I can sing you to sleep, haha xx

Okay.

Georgia felt the bed vibrate as she turned and saw her office number appear.

"Hey."

"Hi you, how's it going? I didn't expect your phone to be on this late."

"Don't worry it wasn't. It's on silent, but I was awake. I dunno if it's the time difference, or just the fear of what I will be walking in on tomorrow," she sighed.

"Don't panic. Seriously, they will love you, just like we do. It's completely weird with you not being here though," she said.

"Well, if they are all like the woman I'm supposed to be working with, then that's doubtful. And I will be potentially returning home in a couple of weeks."

"Wait, what? You've met her? What's she like? What do you mean by that statement?"

"Yeah, I met her. She picked me up at the airport today. She was...um...in a word, a bitch! So I get here after I've been on a flight for like twelve hours, and she's steely like you wouldn't believe. I asked who she was and she snapped that she was the woman I'd stolen the job from and left me. She dropped me off at the house, with a key and address to the office in the morning. She told me where the supermarket was, but didn't offer to stop or show me, despite implying I was a drunk. So no, it's really not looking good," she sniffed.

"Hey, George, come on. You can do this. You are ridiculously intelligent and awesome at this stuff, which is why you have been given the opportunity. Come on, she will come round. Look, it must be like two am there. Go to sleep and don't panic, and then as soon as you get a break, lunch or something, call me. You can let me know how it goes and we can chat properly?"

"Okay, thanks for the call, Jules, have a good day."

***

Georgia woke at around five-thirty am, so at least she had gotten a few hours' sleep. But in reality, it probably wasn't far off what she had back home anyways. Getting up and changing into her bikini she went to her pool. If all else in her life was shitty, this was actually pretty amazing; it certainly beat getting up and running through the rainy streets of Manchester each morning.

She really did need to find out from someone today what to do about pool maintenance though. She could probably ask Emily, since she seemed nice enough. Her house was huge, so she could only assume that Emily would definitely have a pool, too. Georgia stepped into the pool, gasping as she did so. It was fairly cold, but it wasn't completely light as yet, so it wasn't surprising. She somehow needed to make sure she didn't adjust too much to the weather, or this would be too cold before long, she was sure. It was only because the UK was so bloody cold in comparison to everywhere else in the world.

Georgia managed thirty lengths, which wasn't great, but she could still go for a run this evening. Plus, she wanted to test the car before going full steam ahead into the rush hour traffic.

Unlocking the garage, Georgia got into the car and switched the sat nav to Walmart, as that's what Erika had told her the name was. She figured she could kill two birds with one stone; have an early drive close by to get her ready and additionally, go and get some shopping in. It was still early so she would have a bit of time before having to go to work. If she was late, so what? She could blame it on the fact she was not given any assistance upon arriving yesterday.

Georgia reversed the car out of the garage and her driveway. So far so good. However, she hadn't ever actually driven an automatic, something else to add to the traumas she thought. She made her way down her road, following the sat nav; and aside from the beeps because of how slow she was going, she was actually doing okay. It said it was only 10 minutes away, so she could totally manage this. She was still pissed off to hell that someone was such a knob. Seriously, who would actually do that to another human, and to a colleague no less. But that was exactly the point. She wasn't a colleague, she was a nobody to her. This woman despised her, and she was never going to make things easy for her. She sighed loudly, before being snapped out of her thoughts by the beeping behind her. What the hell? She was at a traffic light, why were people beeping at her? Fuck, they were all doing it, the car behind her, and the car behind that. What was wrong? She looked up to the ten ft. traffic light and saw that it was still on red. What the hell was going on? "Oh no, are you kidding me?" she said to herself, as she saw the police motorbike pointing for her to pull over. The lights turned green and she turned onto the street and pulled up behind the policeman.

"Good day ma'am, can I ask what the problem was here? Why you remained stationary?" he said.

Georgia genuinely felt like she was going to cry, so she took in a deep breath trying to contain herself. "I'm sorry officer, I don't know what was wrong with those people, I was stationary because it was on red. Obviously, you couldn't see that, but that's why I wasn't moving," she sighed.

The policeman removed his helmet and glasses, smiling to her. "You're from England, right?" he said kindly.

"Yes, unfortunately."

"Unfortunately, you're from the UK? How so? I love it there."

"Oh gosh, not unfortunately that I'm from the UK. Unfortunately, I'm here instead of there now."

"Wow, and here's me thinking we were one of the nicest states here in Texas. So, what's got you so down on us here? Aside from not knowing the rules of the road?" he smirked.

"The rules of the road? What do you mean?"

"Well, I did see the light was on red, it wasn't missed," he said again. "However, over here you can go on red."

"What the hell? Sorry," she sighed, massaging her temple. "Then what's the point of having traffic lights, if you can go on red? Can you go on amber too?" she said confused.

"No no, sorry, let me explain. So, you can't go on every red, however, if you are ever in the right-hand lane, you can turn right on a red," he said smiling.

"Right, so basically, they were all pissed off with me because I was holding them up, as I was turning, right? So, I didn't actually need to wait?"

"Exactly."

"That's pretty stupid," she said, scratching her head.

"Maybe so, but it's a great deal simpler than those awful…oh, what do you guys call them again? Oh, a round-a-bout. Now that's pretty darn stoopid," he said with a long drawl.

"Not really. They're pretty easy, you give way to the right. So, am I going to get arrested or a penalty or something? Sorry to be rude, but I'm trying to find…" she stopped and looked at her sat nav again. "Walmart, to get some shopping before I have to drive to Houston to start work."

"Wow, you have moved over here."

"Well, yes, no. I don't think so. I think I may just quit it all and go home," she said sadly. "Sorry, I don't know why I just told you all of that."

"So, things really aren't so great for y'all? When did you arrive?""Yesterday," she sighed.

"Sheesh, us Texans done a real number on you, huh? Listen, it's a pretty cool place, amazing things to see and do. People are actually genuinely nice. Give it a while, don't go just yet. And in answer to your question, you won't be arrested nor will you get a ticket or penalty. However, I suggest you try this," he said, handing her a card. "Give this here number a call, you can have a few drivers ed. classes, just to give you the confidence on our roads. They are far bigger and more intense than probably what you are used to. More so if you are going to be travelling into Houston in rush hour each day."

"Thank you. Seriously, you have no idea how much that means to me." She smiled sadly.

He looked at his watch. "Look it's fairly quiet on shift, follow me. I'll take you to the grocery store and leave you there. At least that way, you can see what I do on the roads. Call it a little bit of extra help, especially if you are going to be driving into Houston this morning."

"Do you help everybody this much or just us Brits?" she questioned.

"Listen, you'll be fine, come on follow me."

She threw the card onto the passenger seat and started the car again, doing as she was told, and followed the policeman the short distance to the supermarket.

Chapter Thirty-One

Georgia walked up to the receptionist of the building, telling them she was new to the company effective today. The smiley young woman gave her a temporary pass and advised her to get a parking and building pass from her employer. Thanking the girl, Georgia got in the elevator to her new office, with a small sigh.

"Hi, um, good morning?" Georgia said to the company receptionist.

"Hey, you must be Ms. Carson, pleased to meet you. Mike has been waiting for you. If you give me a second I'll get someone to take you up," she said happily.

"Yes, um, that's me; well actually, it's Georgia, nice to meet you too. Great thanks." She smiled, taking in the surroundings. A few minutes later a young guy was in reception, "Ms Carson, follow me," he said abruptly.

The guy didn't say a single word as he marched her down the office, stomping along the way. Everyone was looking around and whispering, clearly they would have known the situation now. It still didn't make it any easier, but what annoyed her the most was normally stuff like this wouldn't matter to her in any way, shape or form; so why the hell was she bothered now?

He walked her into an office with Erika and a gentleman, whom she could only assume was Mike.

"Thanks, Tim," Erika said.

"No worries, *boss,*" he said, smiling and putting extra emphasis on the final word.

Of course, that explains it all, she thought.

"Hey, Georgia. How are you? Nice to meet you at last, I have heard great things about you," he smiled warmly. "I hope you are very happy here. I know it's not the position you wanted to be in, but I think you can do exceptional things over here, alongside Erika," he said softly. "I must say, I'm surprised you are here so early. I figured you would have wanted to get some stuff sorted this morning," he said confused, scratching his head.

"Well, when I was issued my car keys and post code last night, I was told I start work at 9am and to leave at approximately 8am to get here on time. However, on the contrary, the time difference is playing havoc with me. So, I've been up since stupid o'clock, had a swim, learnt to drive, badly, I shall say, given that I was pulled over by a policeman. However, I did also manage to go and do a large shop, so that when I return to the house this evening, I can open a very large bottle of wine, without having to worry about getting a...sorry, Erika, what was it called again? A DUI?" she said snappily, noticing the concern on Mikes face.

"You got pulled over by a cop?"

"Yes, I didn't quite have a chance to mention it yesterday, but I live and work in a major city in the UK, so I've not actually had a car for the last 3 years. Additionally, nobody forewarned me that when you are turning right at traffic lights you can go on a red light. Seemingly, the citizens of Texas aren't so happy when they are waiting to turn right and some dumb blond is stationary at the red light," she said pointedly.

"Look, Georgia, I'm so incredibly sorry. I should have..." he rubbed his temples. He reminded her of Derek, and she recalled the conversation with him, about the reason that this all came about. "Sorry, I should have come and collected you myself. I can only apologise, that you have suffered such an unwelcome arrival. I want to go through a few bits and pieces with the two of you together; however, I have now changed my mind from my initial thoughts, given the information I have just been issued. As such, I suggest we have a short meeting with the three of us now to discuss expectations and moving forward, any questions either of you may have, will be addressed this morning and in this forum. Once we are done, I will take you back Georgia and we will have our meeting in a restaurant close to your house and go through everything there; that way it will give you an opportunity to have an earlier finish and a chance to relax with that large bottle of wine. Believe it or not, there are a large number of people that are excited by your arrival," he said sincerely.

"Doubtful, but thank you that is very kind. However, I am happy to continue with your initial thoughts, I don't need special treatment."

"Believe me, this isn't special treatment. Come on, I'll give you a tour of the office, Erika, would you mind asking Tim to make some tea and coffee, and bring it into the room; we'll be back in around thirty minutes," he said, directing Georgia out of the room.

***

Georgia pulled onto her drive and quickly threw the laptop she had been issued into the house, locked the door and ran back down to Mike's waiting car.

"Thanks for this," she said as she got in, putting the folder on the floor whilst she put her seatbelt on.

"Listen to me, I'm not going to insult your intelligence by saying it's not normally like this, or it will get better. Honestly, she's pissed and I don't know it will. But equally, you are a senior director and paid a lot of money to deal with the crap; and by all accounts are a bigger ball buster than Derek. So, try not to worry, and if anyone gives you shit, you call me. Erika is a wonderful person, believe it or not, and like you she is a credit to the business. I am confident when you guys get past this, you will make a fabulous team," he said.

"You remind me of Derek. But actually, what makes you think that we are going to get through this? Because honestly, Mike, I'm truthfully thinking it was a complete waste of my time."

"Okay, hold that thought," he said, paying attention to the road, and pulling into a lone restaurant, bar and grill. He parked the car and pointed to the restaurant, "come on, this calls for some decent food and a scotch or two." He smiled.

Georgia genuinely liked Mike. He was very much like Derek, which she'd established already. But in a matter of hours only, he had taken her under his wing. The problem was, it was completely apparent that he had been the same with Erika, which could only spell disaster if she started to notice this. *Arggghhhh, why am I in this shitty situation?* she thought, as she walked through the door that Mike was opening for her.

"Hey, Mike. You're usual?" the waitress said to him.

"Normal seat. Could you give us five and then come check in? I'll have my normal, but I have a new friend today, from England no less, so let's give her a chance to look?"

"No problem, Mike. Hi, nice to meet you, I'm Amy and I'll be your server." She smiled widely.

"Wow, you're in the know ehy?"

He laughed heavily, "Yeah you could say that. I own the place," he said softly.

"Wow, bloody hell and you're CEO too?"

"Well kinda, I'm kinda semi-retired, hence why we have the likes of you 'whipper snappers' managing things pretty darn well. Anyway, enough about that. Frstly, check out the drinks and food. The wings are awesome here, if I do say so myself. Same with the burnt ends, oh and the brisket sandwich, the jus that comes with it, seriously, you won't find better around." He smiled. "So…"

"Sorry, can I just stop you a moment?"

"Yes of course, what's up?"

"What's a burnt end?"

"What's a burnt end? Honey, when you try this stuff, you aint ever gonna leave. Amy, come here," he shouted over to the waitress.

Amy arrived and placed a drink down in front of him. "One scotch on the rocks. So, what would you like?"

"Well, before we get to that, this here lady has not only never tried burnt ends, but has never heard of them," he said.

"For reeeaaal…oh boy, she sure is in for a treat."

"Yup, so while she is deciding on a drink to have, can you bring us a mixture of some of our favourites and some of the most American and/or Texan we got? We gotta show this girl how we do things in the south. Once you've placed the order, come back, and Georgia will be ready to order a drink," he said enthusiastically.

***

"I mean, I'm not even being funny. I couldn't stay just for the simple fact I'd never fit through a door again, because that was the best food ever. Albeit, I can't wait to get out for a run tonight. Bloody hell, that was amazing."

Mike laughed, leaning back in his chair. "I do love the way you Brits say, 'bloody hell', so posh," he chuckled. "Anyways, I'm glad you have enjoyed the best joint in Texas," he said, extending his arms. "Right, back to business. As I was saying earlier. Erika isn't this person you are seeing now, but equally, like you, this isn't what she was ever told was a possibility, or was ever in the cards," he sighed. "Listen, Georgia, I can't tell you not to go home, although I wish I could. I'm also not going to lie and say Derek and I didn't purposely go all out with the nice house and swimming pool, despite my learning of you not being maybe, so materialistic. But honestly, please give it a chance. For us? I won't have anyone making you feel bad, so if you are made to feel that way you let me know, and I'll be hauling their asses in quicker than you can say UK. But equally, please have some faith in us over here," he said sincerely.

"I'm not promising anything. You're right, I don't mess about, because life's too short. But I'm not about to get taken for a fool and made to feel like shit. I don't wanna be here anymore than she wants me to be here, but I don't think we're any closer to being the awesome duo that you two seemed to think we would be. If that guy was anything to go by today, they are all very much allegiant to her, so in terms of making it work? I don't really think it's me you need to be having this conversation with," she said dryly.

"I know, I know. And I will, I can assure you. I see some amazing things, so I'm not going to leave it. I'm not making excuses, and this is in the strictest confidence, but

Erika is having some problems at home. She and Dan are having some issues, potentially divorcing, which will mean that Erika will be a single mom and have a career that hasn't quite worked out as planned and a five-year-old in tow," he said seriously.

"Right okay. Well, I'll keep that in mind the next time she's being awful to me," she said, sounding like a teenager. "I will ensure that it remains confidential."

Chapter Thirty-Two

Georgia got home and showered, happy that she'd managed to avoid the rush hour traffic. It was actually not too bad this morning, but the policeman was right, she could really do with a few lessons first. Which was pretty great as Mike had arranged for someone who lived close by to give her a lift this week, so she could arrange some driving lessons hopefully this weekend.

It was quite a good afternoon actually, she had had a real heart to heart with Mike and he genuinely made her feel better. Now all she needed to do was stop overthinking about the whole Erika situation. That would be a lot easier said than done.

Georgia looked around at all the goodies she had bought that morning, and unfortunately wasn't able to unpack them, so she began with the stuff in the fridge and started compartmentalising it all. Everything was so big, there's no way she would need to shop for a good month. The portions were horrendously big, even for just one person, which meant she was able to separate and freeze them all. She would invite Emily over one night for a barbecue, or a pizza to test out her toys in the back garden too she thought.

Georgia finished sorting the food, and decided to go see Emily. She found a home for her nutribullet and fresh juicer, and looked around her huge kitchen. She was all set, she thought to herself, feeling somewhat pleased. The lunch that Mike had served was incredible, but she definitely couldn't keep eating like that. Especially as when she returned she was still too full to go for a run. She made the most of the quiet time before she was going full steam ahead again. She checked the time, realizing she still hadn't called Julia. She'd text her and if she was still up, then she'd give her a quick call.

***

Georgia got off the phone to Jules almost an hour later, having filled her in on the day's events. She was positive, and between her and Mike she was finding a little bit more of her fighting spirit lighting her up again. She could do this, if it killed her, she would not let this woman get the better of her.

Packing away the leftover chicken pie from last night, she grabbed the dishes and wine and locked up, making her way across to Emily's. As she got closer, she saw a guy playing basketball on the drive, then noticed that pretty much all the houses had basketball nets and American flags on the properties. She kind of liked the idea of getting one too. It would be another form of activity and a great stress release playing basketball after work. Not one she could necessarily play alone, but she could throw them into the basket by herself. As she walked down the drive of Emily's house, John missed the shot and it bounced off the backboard heading in her direction. Georgia reacted quickly and caught the ball with her one free hand; she had always been an avid sportsperson, thriving on the opportunity of playing any sport. She wasn't a keen onlooker, and would always opt for going out and playing tennis as opposed to watching it.

"Hey, nice catch," he said. "Go on, shoot."

"Erm, I'm not so sure that's such a good Idea, I don't think I can afford to pay for the broken windows." She smiled.

"Come on, Georgia, I have high expectations for you. I saw you run last night. Give it a shot, and I promise, if you crack a window, I will not make you pay."

Georgia smiled at who she assumed must have been John, referencing her, despite having never officially met. "John, you're on," she said, putting everything on the floor and stepping forward. "How close can I go? Bearing in mind I'm British and we don't do basketball."

"You can stand here," he pointed to her.

Georgia stepped forward and assessed the net, she threw the ball and it hit the backboard and rolled around the rim. She was convinced it was going to go in, but at the last second it rolled off the side and missed, "ahhhh, boooo, that was very close."

"Not bad, rookie," he said. "So, Georgia, nice to officially meet you," he stepped in, offering her his hand. He was a good-looking guy, salt and pepper hair, and a good build. "If you ever fancy a game, I can teach you, it's a good sport." He smiled, picking up the ball again.

Is anyone actually unattractive in this country? she thought. "You'll regret saying that. I'll be here every night, and nice to meet you too. Is Emily home? I wanted to return her Tupperware."

"You'll make my wife a very happy woman, if you come over and play ball every night," he said, returning to his lone game. "The side doors open, just go on in," he said, pointing out the door to her.

"Thanks."

Georgia knocked once and opened the door, "Hello?" she said, walking in.

"Hey, what are y'all doing here?" she said, walking over and hugging Georgia.

"Hi, how are you? I just thought I'd drop off your dishes, and I also bought you a bottle of wine to say thank you for your kindness yesterday evening," she said sincerely. "Apologies, if you don't drink it, I didn't really know what to get. But I loved the fact you do two litre bottles of wine here."

"Ohhh I love this brand. You did well. You wanna glass? Or do you have somewhere to be?"

"Um, no I don't, but surely you have better things to be doing? I don't want you to feel like you need to babysit me."

"Hey, cut it out, I told you yesterday that we would be really good friends. I have nothing to do and nowhere to be. I was just planning on relaxing with a glass and some Cougar Town." She smiled. "So, what do you mean, you were stoked because we have two litre bottles of wine? You can't get bottles of wine in England?" she said, pouring a glass for each of them.

"Oh no. Yeah we do bottles, however, we can't get two litre bottles. We can only get litre and half bottles. So yeah, I was pretty excited to see that," she smiled and thanked Emily, taking the glass from her.

"Easily pleased, huh?" she smirked.

"Well, yes, very much so. I need this, it's been a *bad* day," she sighed. "I was pulled over by a policeman," she said, shaking her head.

"You what? You got pulled over by a cop? How so? What happened?" she said.

"Yes, I was causing havoc on the road seemingly. It was a red light and I was in the right lane and was turning right. Who knew, there's actually a country out there that allows you to go through a red light," she sighed.

"Ohhh, sweetie, did you get a ticket?"

"Nope, he was actually very nice. He told me to take some driving lessons. No, *sorry*, 'go take some drivers ed," she laughed, saying with a gruff, extremely poor impersonation of an American accent.

"Cool accent, *not,*" she laughed. "Hey, John will take you out at the weekend. You will easily get away with a couple hours on Saturday and if you need it Sunday too. You'll be fine."

"No, no; its fine I got a number, work will pay for it, I'll call them."

"Don't be silly, it's fine. He will be fine seriously. I tell you what, you can have us over for dinner one night, supply the food and beer and then we are even."

"Well, I was going to do that anyhow," she said shyly, realising that she really did like this woman.

"Fine it's sorted, just let us know what time is best. So, how was your first day at work? Tell me all about it. Then we can watch some Cougar Town. It's my favourite show, and it's the only show that makes me feel like it's okay to drink as much as I do." She smiled wide eyed, and got herself comfortable.

***

Georgia finished up filling Emily in on the details; they had ordered pizza and even John had joined them. They were all united in the decision that she had been mistreated, and 'allegedly' it was a complete injustice. What they had done is gave a slightly different unrelated spin on it, and made her realise that Erika would have just been reacting in an emotional way. In reality Georgia would have been the same, but it made her feel bad and felt the need to give her the benefit of the doubt. Surely after the first few days she would ease up on her and realise they would be able to work together so they could finish this whole ordeal and get back to their respective lives. Additionally, if her and her husband were divorcing that was only going to add to the stress and difficulty. Maybe they could be friends and they would be able to work over wine, just like she was here doing with Emily and John.

"Seriously, I don't think you should worry too much. This Erika is just pissed. When she realises how awesome you are, and that actually, *you* are worse off, I'm sure everything will be perfect and you guys will work great together, period," John said.

"Ahhhh thanks so much, you guys, that's so incredibly kind. Seriously, you don't need to be this nice to me," she said sincerely.

"Don't be stupid. You are super cool, and we have never had any British friends before, let alone a neighbour. She'll see that too, just give her time. And we're just being honest with you," Emily stopped, looking at the door opening. "Hey, baby. How was track practice?" she said, looking at the teenage girl entering the house.

"Hey, Mom," the girl said, leaning down and kissing her mom. "What's for dinner? I'm starved," the girl said.

"There's some leftover pizza. I didn't know what time you would be back. This is Georgia, she's from England, and she moved in across the street yesterday," Emily said.

"And, I think we may be able to grab a new person to play ball with Torr," John said. "Georgia this is our daughter Torrance."

"Hey." The athletic girl looked to be around sixteen said. "Sorry to be rude, you guys, but I have a few tests coming up. I'll take the pizza and go study. Nice meeting you, Georgia."

"You too." She smiled.

"Sorry about that, she's completely absorbed in track, which means that school and '*us*' have to maintain a level of, how do you say….Oh *blackmail,*" she laughed. "That's to ensure she keeps her grades up," Emily said, smirking.

"Hey, nothing to apologise for. My nieces are half her age and they are interested in me for about an hour, and then the novelty wears off." She smiled. "It's great that she's so motivated."

"Ahhhh, don't be fooled by that. She is incredibly intelligent, but all she's interested in, is making a career of track. She could do far better on studies, but she literally pulls out the grades she needs to keep everyone off her back and that's it. She'll do the studying she needs and then she'll be all over Facebook, Instagram, and Twitter, whatever new form of social media is trending this week. You get the point?" Emily said, rolling her eyes.

"Ouch, sucks to be a parent," Georgia laughed.

John laughed at the woman, before nudging his wife. "Heeeeyyyy, baby, she sounds like an American already. So, have you seen this show? It's so funny, and this one here thinks that it permits her to drink every night because of it," John said, starting the TV show.

"I do not drink that much." She slapped her husband's arm playfully.

They were a gorgeous couple. Georgia thought back to the many films and TV shows that she had watched with characters that are the high school prom king and queen and stay together and get married. She was wondering if it was not actually stereotypical after all. These two completely sold that story she thought as she looked around the room at the pictures of them both barely much older than Torrance.

Chapter Thirty-Three

Georgia felt worse today than she had yesterday, and albeit the lack of sleep and the heavy and large amounts of food yesterday hadn't really helped her. She was well aware it was the nerves from firstly another day at work, but secondly the whole *lift* situation. In reality, the only person nice to her yesterday was the receptionist. Worse still, she was probably a little fuelled by the beer she'd had at lunch when she agreed to this, and she should have just faced the rush hour roads again.

"Too late now," she said to herself, finishing styling her hair. The swims each morning were seriously amazing. And if she left in a month, this would completely be the biggest thing she'd miss. She should really look into that. She didn't need a massive house, but if she relocated out of the city centre when she moved back home, she may be able to get a smaller house with more land that she could get planning permission to build an indoor pool. *Hmm worth a look*, she thought.

Georgia heard the car beep outside. Grabbing her belongings and coffee cup before leaving her home, she awkwardly walked into who knew what with this person.

She was suddenly scared of what she was going to walk in to. And it annoyed her that she was letting this whole situation take control of her, this was not the person she was. Fuck she was a senior director. She controlled an office for a multibillion pound global company, she needed to sort her shit out.

"Hi, sorry to keep you waiting."

"Hey daaaarlin, not to worry. I only just arrived. Nice to meet you, we haven't officially met yet. I'm Anne," said the older woman, holding her hand out. "I hear things weren't so great for you yesterday."

Phew, Georgia thought relieved. She seemed lovely and nice, causing her to instantly relax and start chatting.

***

Georgia was impressed by the front of the Americans, holy hell, they did *not* hold back. She had been in the heads of department meeting for the last hour and a half. Mike was chairing it and had outlined that this would be 'allegedly' for this and *only* this meeting. Moving forward it would be on a roster basis between Georgia and Erika. Great, they all fucking hated her! Jesus, she needed to stop swearing so much, her mum would not be happy if she was swearing like this when she went home.

They went around the table and introduced themselves, with about as much interest in doing so as a fish being introduced to a sand pit. Interestingly, whilst Erika was not being so much of a cow, her smarmy, shitty little PA was smirking to every single person that was an arse. Funnily enough, he was driving her a little more and more with every arsehole move he was making. The only way and probably the most appropriate way to assimilate him, was that awful guy, the PA one in ugly Betty, she thought. Albeit she didn't actually know if Tim was gay. Unlikely she thought, he was acting like a little prick, just like the character did though.

Georgia didn't know what had come over her, but seriously, she was actually getting off on it almost. She scrolled over her phone and sent an emoji of a questioning face and a fist to Julia. Straight away she received an emoji filled response of giggly faces and streamers back, with 'you go girl!!' Georgia smirked and was actually relatively happy when she looked up and noticed Tim and Erika catching her smirking into her phone. *Screw it, screw you all,* she thought to herself. She would do this, if it killed her. And she would stand her ground, she was the boss after all. If they thought they would take her on, bring it on, it would be easy enough to fire their arses.

Chapter Thirty-Four

Erika walked out of the boardroom annoyed. Mike had totally made her feel incapable, and had completely undermined her. He was acting like his loyalties were all with Georgia, and not her. They had worked together for so many years, and he spun her this tale that this situation would be great for her. But now he was making her feel like she was worthless, and like she had been demoted after all.

A short while after the meeting, Vanessa walked into her office. "How you holding up, sweetie?" she said to Erika, who was looking off distantly.

"Hey, yeah it all kinda sucks, you know?" she said sombrely.

"Is Dulcie back home? The meeting wasn't exactly great, was it? You wanna come over for dinner this evening?"

"You know what, I'll take a rain check. I want a night with my girl, cuddle up, watch Frozen, maybe get a Luigi's. I dunno, bake some cookies maybe. Chill in the pool. But thanks, I dunno what Mike's playing at, but honestly, I'm just about ready to quit."

"Come on, don't do that. You are just in a crappy place right now. Go see Mike and talk to him, or ask for a couple days off to clear your head."

"I can't do that. This chick just got here. Plus, I only just got back from my mom's. It's fine, seriously, I'm good. I just need some time with Dulcie."

"How's things with you guys?"

"Yeah, ya know?" she said sadly. "Look, I need to do this report for her ladyship, you mind if we catch up later? I just wanna get this settled and then head off home to my baby girl."

"Yes of course, if you need anything you know where I am right?"

"I know, I know," she said, attempting a smile.

***

Erika couldn't concentrate at all. Her head was in a million and one other places, and the last thing she was able to do was finalize this darn report. She could feel herself getting more and more frustrated, equally making the process considerably harder. What wasn't helping further was the fact that she was getting upset and angry about the whole thing. She could normally do this with her eyes closed, but at this moment in time she was completely unmotivated, and she was disengaged. Erika sighed loudly, slamming her pen down. She picked up her phone and walked to the window dialling the number, and looked out over the busy city.

Erika listened to the dial tone, as she heard it connect, "Ciao bambino come stai?" she heard the soothing voice of her mother.

"Ciao, Mamma. Not… so good, Mamma," she said, allowing the tears to fall.

"Baby, what's the matter? Hey, come on, you're scaring me. Are you okay? Is Dulcie okay? Erika please?"

Erika controlled her breathing, "I'm fine, I'm sorry for worrying you, Mom. I'm just having a pretty bad day, well week," she scoffed. "Month actually."

"Baby, I know things aren't great at the moment, but you have a beautiful daughter. You are both healthy. I am, well, I believe I am healthy. You have a loving famiglia, this will be a little setback. You need to not let this takeover you. We need to focus on the positive energy, bambina."

Erika heard a knock and a hello, so she turned around to face the door. She quickly wiped her tears as she stood in front of Georgia, which really was all she needed right now. "Mamma, I need to go, call you later, ciao," she said, hanging up before her mother had a chance to respond.

"Hey, what's up? Is everything okay?" Georgia said, rushing over to Erika and shutting the door behind her, which unfortunately, was a little too heavy and resulted in it slamming.

"I'm fine," she snapped.

Georgia stopped herself from being reactive, and inwardly counted to three. She breathed in deep. "Well, clearly you aren't," she said quietly. "Look, why don't you go home? Take the report, and do it there? You can email me it tomorrow. Go spend some time with your family."

Erika was mad, who the hell did she think she was? It was up to her to send people home? She could feel herself boiling.

Georgia could read that Erika was pissed off, something else to add to the list she thought. Jesus this woman hated her. "I hope that didn't come across like I was trying to domineer, because that wasn't my intention. I will cover for you with Mike and say you have gone to do the report as you were being interrupted, if I need to?"

Erika looked at Georgia blankly, "I don't need cover with Mike. But I *will* go; I'll have it in your inbox before the end of the night," she stated.

"Seriously, I can wait until tomorrow. If it's easier. Either way, the options there," Georgia said, walking off before Erika had an opportunity to dismiss her further.

***

"Hi Georgia, do you have a minute?" Mike said, coming into her office and shutting the door behind him.

"Yes of course, is everything okay?" she asked, concerned at the look on Mike's face.

"Um, yes. Well, no, actually. I was wondering if you could tell me what happened today please."

"Today? When today?" she said confused.

"With Erika? What happened between you two?"

"Oh, right. Sure, I wanted to ask her for some information, so I went to her office and walked in and she was on the phone. She turned around and was crying. I said to her why didn't she go home and that I could wait for the report until tomorrow. She said no, she'd have it to me before the end of the night and I left. Why's that?"

"So, you didn't storm into her office and slam the door and make her cry?"

"*What?*" she spat incredulously. "Are you joking? Of course I didn't. I'm not going to lie, I shut the door when I saw her crying and rushed over to her, and it did slam, but that was nothing to do with her per se. I was concerned, she was clearly very upset. But no, I wasn't the one to make her cry," she couldn't believe this. Erika had completely screwed her over, *again.* She genuinely thought she was doing a good thing. She was livid, and she had a good mind to go to Erika's house and bawl her out over it, but what was the point? She was seriously fighting a losing battle in this place. Plus, seriously, if anyone had ever done that in front of her nieces she'd go mental. It wasn't fair to do that in front of her child.

"Right, okay, simple misunderstanding then, I guess," Mike said. "I'll leave you to get on with things," he said, making his way to the door, clearly stressed as he sighed loudly walking out.

"Actually, Mike. Suddenly I'm not feeling so great, would you mind if I left? I'll do what I need to from home, but I could do with some time alone."

"Yes, that's fine," he sighed again, leaving her office.

Geez, he didn't even try to talk her out of it. Or try to make her feel better. She couldn't do this. She needed to get home, and speak to someone. She didn't quite know who yet, but she just felt the need to leave.

***

Georgia spent nearly a hundred dollars on the taxi, which was pretty stupid, truth be known. But she was fuming, and she could not believe this was happening. She knew it would be hard, especially in the first week, but she really thought she was being genuinely kind to her when she was upset. And she goes and pulls a stunt like this? This woman was horrific. Who would be so nasty?

"Hey there, rookie. You okay?" she heard, turning around to see John jogging over with his basketball in his hand.

"Hi," she said sadly; and disappointed that she had not managed to get in her house before she was seen. She really wasn't in the mood to see anybody right now.

"Hey, what's the matter? What's happened?" he asked concerned.

Georgia could feel her eyes fill up. Shit, this was not her. But it was too late, John was grabbing her in a big man, bear hug.

"Hey, rookie, come here?" he said, squeezing her tight. It had been a very long time since she'd hugged a guy outside of her family. But at this moment, it was all she wanted and needed. And as a result, couldn't stop the tears from coming.

A few moments passed and Georgia had managed to contain herself. "I'm sorry, John. I am not this person," she said embarrassed.

"Hey, you don't apologize. We have your back, buddy. Come take a seat," he said, tapping her front door step. "What's going on?"

"Thanks, John. You have both been so incredibly kind in the short time I've known you. It doesn't matter what happened, seriously, I'm good," she said.

"Rookie, sit your butt down now!" he snapped. The kindness in his eyes spoke volumes and she genuinely didn't feel alone right now.

She didn't know what relevance it had, but she just oddly felt like John knew about her sexuality. She was concerned in case Texans really were homophobic and these incredibly kind people she'd made friends with turned her back on her because of it. "You know I'm gay, don't you?"

"Yeah I kinda figured. Although, my wife thinks I'm stupid," he smiled kindly. "Although I dunno what relevance that has? Hey, do not tell me that's what's up. Has someone said something because of your sexuality?" he jumped up, livid.

"Woah, easy tiger." She smiled, holding out her hand to him, dragging him back down to the seat. "No, it's nothing to do with that. I dunno, I just felt like I knew you knew, and was just curious I guess. Nope, I have been royally screwed over by the woman that I'm here to work with, *again.* I just can't believe anyone could be so deceptive and poisonous. But seriously, I really don't want to talk about it. I think I need a run. I just don't feel ready to talk about it right now. I'm sorry," she said sombrely.

"Nothing to apologize for," he said, holding up his hand to her. "How about you ditch the run, get in your sweats and come play ball with me? I'll teach you to play. Which will take your mind off of it, and it's still gonna give you a great workout. It's a great stress release," he said. "If you're lucky, I'll teach you a finger spin," he said, picking up the ball and spinning it around on his finger, nudging her shoulder and smiling.

"John, seriously you don…"

"Ohhh, Rookie, if you're gonna go down the '*you don't have to do this,*'" he said in a great British, lady voice, causing her to giggle. "BS, then Imma seriously kick your ass," he said, looking down at her. "Now go change, I'll meet you out front in ten. Don't be late, rookie, you'll get a punishment. Like 'twenny' squats," he said, jogging back over to his house.

"Yeeeessss, sir," she saluted him, as she watched him running backwards laughing at her.

Randomly she felt somewhat better already. She still couldn't believe the days turn of events, but maybe a game of basketball would help her work through this, if she even could. Seriously, could she really leave less than a week after arriving? Did she want to? Well that was stupid, she one hundred per cent wanted to. What would she do? She didn't know if they would make her redundant? Pay her off? Demote her or just sack her? God this was all so messed up. She sighed heavily. She was so completely stressed out and felt helpless.

Georgia changed into a racer back sports vest, an oversized Nike vest over the top and some running shorts. She tied her laces and grabbed a couple bottles of water for them both.

Meeting him at his house as requested, John was fishing about in a giant cool box. *Seriously, is anything normal size in this country,* she thought?

John took the waters from her and gave her a bottle of beer. He unscrewed his cap and held it out to her, "Cheers. Here's to basketball, beer and buddies. Oh, and to forget about nasty broads," he said winking.

"You are too good to me."

"I'm allowed to be. I got a twenty riding on you being gay, easy money," he said, laughing and putting the beer down. "Come on, rookie, lets teach you some basketball."

"You bet on me? Charming," she laughed. "Okay, shoot. No pun intended."

***

Georgia was sweating like a bitch. She loved this game, and this was exactly what she needed. John was great, and incredibly good at it, and incredibly fit. She was leaning her arms on her legs, watching the sweat drip from her head onto the ground.

"It's far too hot to be playing this," she said, downing half of her third beer, feeling the effects already.

"This isn't hot, rookie, wait until summer," he said smirking.

"I don't think I can cope with summer," she said, opening another beer. "I owe you some beers, I feel pissed," she said.

"You look it. You'll love summer here. Come with me," he said, stealing himself another beer and walking round back. Georgia was fit, and she loved exercising. And albeit the last few weeks had been somewhat non-existent, she *was* still fit. But John didn't look like he had sweat one bit.

Georgia followed him to the back garden, which was huge, even bigger than hers. The size of the properties over here was insane. The garden was perfectly done, filled with a number of palm trees and a giant pool situated in the middle of the garden. "Oh my God, you haven't?" she said as she stopped, looking before her.

"Yes, ma'am," he said, looking proud of himself. "So, you can't leave just yet," he smirked.

Georgia was walking around the pool looking at the basketball nets on either side of it. "So, in summer when it gets too hot, you play water basketball?" she asked, shaking her head, feeling her hair flopping around from the damp of her sweat.

"Yup, sure do. Or water volleyball," he said, holding up a net in his hands before returning it back to where it belonged.

Georgia whistled impressed. "Wow, I should have just rented a room from you guys," she said, smiling. "I'm not gonna lie, that's amazing," she said. "You mind?" she said, pointing to the pool.

"Sure."

Georgia sat down on the side of the pool, dangling her feet into it, "It's all very surreal for me; *this*. You know?" she said seriously.

"I can't begin to imagine," he said, joining her on the edge of the pool.

"It's like a weird dream. It's like bittersweet. I love my apartment and love being in the city centre and stuff, but… well, I guess I did, before I came out here. But this has just made me think differently. I love my new home, I love having a car, I love my pool and the heat, and you guys. But then the situation at work is awful. So today I thought I was helping the woman who thinks I've shafted her. I was being kind to her, and she went and told the CEO I made her cry and she had to leave. He was so pissed off with me John, and I literally didn't do anything. She was crying before I got there, so I said go home and spend some time with her daughter, and that I didn't need the work she was doing until tomorrow. Jesus, I even said to her I'd cover with our boss. And she did that? I am so upset that someone did something like that. They were all pretty mean in the meeting too. I don't know how to deal with this. I'm not used to it. I'm likeable, I always have been. My friends, my staff they all like me, *a lot*; so, I don't know how to deal with these people being so nasty to me. And it's not even like I can win them over. They all *do*, and *will* only ever see me as the woman who has shafted their boss. *Their* friend, who they all love too," she said, putting her head in her hands. "I just don't know what to do. I genuinely am liking this place, and she was such a bitch when I arrived I was actually quite happy thinking it would make the decision so much easier. Ya know? If everyone was arseholes? But then Emily came over with dinner and cookies, as a welcome for me. And you guys were really kind. The policeman I met was nice and kind too. Jesus, even Anne, who is my lift this week, was lovely, the only one in the office that's being nice to me as well. So I'm torn on what to do. Honestly, I don't think I'm strong enough to stay and fight this battle, John. What am I going to do?" she said, laying down and looking up to the blue sky.

John copied her, "Do you think you can deliver what they are asking?"

"Well, if I wasn't being terrorized, maybe so."

"Okay, forget about the people and what they are doing to you. Can you deliver it alone?"

"Doubtful, we haven't both been given separate projects to work on, because we really need to work collaboratively. Plus, I know nothing about the states, the laws, the business, work styles, and I have no relationships built up. So, in reality, I guess no," she said sadly.

"Right, what about what you can do without her? Can you be working on stuff without her? Let them all know you ain't about to be pushed around? You're a tough cookie I can see that, but equally, letting these bosses of yours know *you* are trying; *you* are getting on with it. You are essentially gonna be rising above it, right?"

"Hmm, well maybe," she said, watching and following the few clouds passing across the sky.

"You said you came to open up an office or something, right? I mean, you could even go to him and say you wanna know where the office is, as you wanna go up there and acquaint yourself; learn more, arrange some meetings. They will soon realize, that this woman is digging her heels in and being problematic, and they will have no option but to deal with it ya know?"

"I suppose, but what if they take her off the project or get rid of her? I will be screwed, because she has all the knowledge." She turned her head to look at him. "Plus, he told me she is having problems with her husband and she has a small child. Additionally, when I caught her crying today she said, '*ciao momma*', so what if she has problems with her parents? I don't want her to lose her job."

"Well, that's not really your problem. Plus, given the size and importance of the company, they ain't ever gonna do that, they ain't gonna put no global firm in jeopardy. They'll get someone else with a high level of experience and knowledge, or maybe the CEO will transfer what he can to you. They'll be someone, I can assure you of that."

"But she has a daughter. I'd feel terrible if they got rid of her."

"Once again, not your problem. She's the one acting like a school ground bully here, right?" he said.

Georgia sat quietly, digesting the information, which was certainly food for thought. He was right, she should just crack on, at least with what she knew. Ultimately, she could get the client details from Mike and start making contact. Like John said, even if she went up to Fort Worth and 'wined and dined' them. She had always been exceptional at networking and relationship building, so she could easily get them on her side. If she had a relationship with the key stakeholders, she would be well on the right track, she would be able to liaise, communicate and potentially get everything she needed.

"What are you thinking?"

"Just considering what you said. I think, you just may have a point."

"Hey, there y'all are," they heard, looking up to see Emily walking in. "What are you doing here?" she said, smiling and kissing her husband.

"Sorry I hope you don't mind...I..."

"Hell no, of course I don't. It's great to see you. I see you have been leading my husband astray," she said, taking a gulp of his beer. "So, I'm guessing basketball, from looking at you," she said, moving her pointed finger the length of her body.

"Bad day, again. John kinda forced me to ditch running in order to learn basketball as a way to de-stress. He was right, but I'll be killing tomorrow." She smiled.

"Oh, no, sweetie. Are you okay?"

"She's good, we've been balling and chatting. I am not just a pretty face, and apparently, I can give some good ass advice too. Ain't that right, rookie? Oh, and you owe me twenty bucks."

"That's right, he's been an amazing agony aun…sorry uncle. And yes, he's right about that too. I'm gay, so you owe him twenty bucks," she said smiling to her friends.

"You told her we bet on her sexuality? Shit, John, like she isn't having a rough enough time already out here," she snapped at her husband.

"Oh, seriously, that's the least of my problems; but actually, I was kinda flattered. I'm honestly not bothered." She smiled. "But, on that note, I should probably get going," she said, making her way up.

"Hey, rookie," John grabbed her hand. "You ain't going nowhere. When you were changing, I got some good ole Texan barbecue meat out. When Torrance gets home, we'll light the barbecue and you are staying here for dinner. We'll show you how y'all should really barbecue," he said, smiling to her.

"What's with the rookie, honey?" Emily asked.

"Because the day I met her she caught the basketball with one hand. Your dishes and wine were in the other. Then she took a shot, and for a 'rookie' it was pretty darn awesome. Hence where 'rookie' came from," he said, taking more beer.

"I actually kinda like it," Georgia said, smiling to them both.

Chapter Thirty-Five

Erika and Dulcie were making cupcakes, which was actually the best thing she could have done. She was more relaxed than she had been for days. Being with her daughter, who was trying to put everything from the pantry into the unbaked cake mix, was amusing her immensely. "Mommy can we put choc chits in there?" she pointed.

"Choc *chips*? Well I don't know, sweetie. I don't really think it will go."

"How so? I think it would be awesome," she said, eating a choc chip. "Can we try? Puhleeeaaaasssseee?" she said, grinning and holding some over the mixture.

"Baby, I don't think it's gonna work; I think it may just melt."

"Well we could try."

"Do it. Only in one mixture though, and that will be your cake. Okay?" she said, moving her daughter out of the way, so she could put them in the oven. She rarely gave in to Dulcie, but at the moment, she was overjoyed to be with her baby and forgetting about all the junk going on in her life.

"You wanna watch a movie with me, Mommy?" Dulcie said, her big brown eyes wide. Erika's heart melted. She was obviously biased, but damn she was a cutie, she thought.

"Well, why don't you go put something on in the second living room. Mommy needs to just do some work first and then I'll come watch with you."

"Okay," she said, running off with her new stuffed toy.

***

Erika had been staring at the screen for the last ten minutes. She had done more than she had managed at work, but she really was just struggling. Additionally, she was pissed at herself for considering purposely destroying it, in a bid to screw Georgia over. She needed to speak to her mom again, and she would soon put her in her place. This wasn't her, she'd never done stuff like this before. If someone was treating her daughter like this, she'd kill them she thought. So, why was it acceptable for her to behave in such an atrocious way?

Erika sighed out loud, and pushed on with the report. She would ensure she completed it tonight if it killed her, at least that way she wouldn't owe Georgia anything. She was thinking about today again. Georgia had been nice to her; why couldn't she just be a cow? She'd even said that she'd cover with Mike. Granted she didn't need that, but Georgia wasn't to know that.

Erika heard her phone ring and saw it was Taylor. She picked it up, opting for an opportunity to procrastinate as oppose to working once more.

"Hi, how are you?" Erika said into the phone.

"Yes, fine what's up? I called you at work and they said you went home as you were unwell. What's up? You want me to come over and take Dulcie off you, so you can rest?"

"I'm fine; and no were good, it's the exact cure I need right about now. How's things with you, how was the date last night?"

"Seriously, I officially give up. You want a little more company? I could come over and see you," she said.

Erika was quiet for a moment.

"Hey, don't worry if not, I just want to make sure you're okay."

"I'm fine, seriously. If you wanna, yeah for sure. I guess I could use a friend right about now. However, I do have a report to do for Georgia. I was supposed to come home and do it, but we were baking instead. So, can you leave it a couple hours?"

"Yes sure. I'll tell you what, I'll grab some takeout and come over when Dulcie's gone to bed, give you two some alone time."

"Thanks, Tay, you're awesome."

"Hmmm, shame we can't find any decent guys who think so," she giggled, before hanging up.

***

A little after seven, Erika heard the front door go, "Hey, I'm in the study," she quietly called out.

"Hey, are you not finished yet?" Taylor asked, kissing her cheek.

"I'm done, I just need to spell check and send to her. I'm not going all out, screw it," she said.

"Ummm, okay then," Taylor said questioningly.

"Don't say it like that. I am not doing it to be vindictive. It's just I don't know the woman, or the style she likes, and until I do, I'm not messing around with a ton of effort for her to throw it back in my face and say it's garbage. When I learn more about how she wants things done, then I can go into a higher level of detail geared to her way," she said sombrely. "Why don't you go and open a bottle and I'll send this. I'll be there in five," she said, turning back to her pc.

Erika finished up and sent the email over to Georgia, happy she'd gotten it done earlier than expected. She quickly texted her mom and told her Taylor was over, so she'd check in tomorrow. She knew she'd be worried after today's call.

"Hey, sorry about that. Ohhh, is this for me?" she said, picking up the glass of wine. "So, what happened with last night's guy?" she asked, laughing.

"Don't ask," she sighed, putting out some pasta for them both.

"How so? Come on, you gotta tell me, that's why I called you over. I need this," she laughed.

"Why? What happened today? How come you left?"

Erika sighed heavily. "Honestly, I don't want to talk about it right now; I just kinda feel like I need a night off you know?"

"Yeah, I do. But equally, you keep trying to deal with all this shit alone, you're gonna walk yourself into a breakdown. Did you speak to your mom about any of it? Georgia? Dan? Dulcie? The more you keep hiding from it the harder you're gonna make it for yourself. You're going to just keep getting pissed over the shit and stress yourself out more, you know? I don't mean to lecture Erika, but seriously, you are not gonna be able to do all this alone. I'm not in school right now, so I'm here to be a friend, a support mechanism. Jesus a permanent nanny if you need. But, seriously, you can't shut everyone out."

"You're already a full-time nanny," she laughed.

"Well, I actually meant if you wanted to have some time to get back on track I could take Dulcie, or I could move in and help out whilst all this is going on. I'm not looking for responses, so please don't feel the need to do that. But, dude seriously, you gotta sort your shit out," she said, rubbing her friend's shoulder.

"God you're worse than my mom."

"Yeah, I know, you tell me frequently, but that's why you love me. Ya know for an Italian you sure do cuss a lot."

"Whatever. Tell me about the date last night, and then if you make me laugh, and relax me enough, maybe I'll talk," she smirked.

"Ohhh, goodie. I love it when I'm tasked with getting you drunk. It's so fricking easy." She smiled.

"Get lost. C'mon already."

"Okay. So, he was nice, he was cute, super cute actually…"

"But that always unnerves you."

"Yes, I know, right? So, anyways he was cute, nice, opened the doors, pulled the chairs out, insisted on paying, walked me home, and didn't even try to come up," she said, eating.

"So then, what's the problem?" she asked confused.

"He's Greek."

"*And*?" asking again, confused.

"Have you never seen the movie my big fat Greek wedding?"

"Ha ha," she said sarcastically. "Yes funny. Okay, you did it!" Erika said shaking her head.

"Huh? What you mean?"

"Well, you're poking fun at me, to get me to relax and make me spill."

"No, this is for real."

"*Shut up*. And you say I have problems? Firstly, my big fat Greek wedding is about a female Greek. Women are the ones who have the overbearing parents, not guys. Take me for example," Erika smirked. "Secondly, it was a freaking movie, Tay. What the hell is up with you? Are you just a serial dater? You don't actually wanna meet someone for real? Sheesh kiddo, you need to get a grip. Call him, ask him out again," she said, shaking her head.

"Whatever. I am an independent woman. I don't want to get pushed into having thirty kids and a house full of Windex. Ok, I'll call him, if you fill me in?"

"Dude, you are killing me right now. Why are you so hell bent on me talking?"

"Seriously, I'm worried. You're my best friend and I have never seen you like this. I'm concerned, okay?"

Taylor watched Erika walk out sighing. She lay her head against the back of the sofa. She shouldn't push her, she should just let her get on with it. She's a grown ass woman after all. A few moments later Erika walked back in with a couple tumblers and a bottle. "Wow, you got the hard stuff out, huh?"

"I don't know what you want from me. But equally I don't know what anyone wants from me anymore. I just broke down today in the office, I had to call mom, and I'm so confused. I just feel completely numb, and I cannot move past this situation. More importantly I don't know if I want to. I have been thinking about stuff and honestly I don't know what I want anymore. I know it would go down like a ton of bricks, but I'm considering moving back home to Dallas," she said quietly.

"WOW, I completely didn't see that coming. Look, Erika, I'm not gonna pretend this is awesome and everything's okay, because I know crap has gone down for y'all, on a massive level. But you can't run forever. You're gonna have to learn to deal with that, not by quitting but by facing it head on. I mean, are you really prepared to throw out everything you've worked so hard for? Move Dulcie away from her family, her friends, Jesus her nanny?" she said pleadingly.

"Her nanny will be leaving school soon, and walking into a big hot shot law firm, which is why I am not considering that."

"*Whatever.* Regardless of me getting a job, I love you guys and I would still have wanted to see you on weekends and evenings. How can I do that when you're on the other side of the state? And then what? You just walk away from your job? What about Dan's folks? You think that's fair taking their grandbaby away from them?"

"*Hey*, my mom is that exact same distance away from my daughter," she retorted.

"I know, Erika, but you're not going home for your mom, you're running from your marriage and your job, and more importantly, this whole situation. Look, I know you're having a real rough time with it right about now, but seriously, is it not better that it all happens at once, rather than all at separate stages?"

"I'm not running from anything, and no I don't agree with that theory. I just hate all this shit. I hate everything that's happening. I hate Mike for doing this to me. I hate Georgia for coming here and fucking this all up. She can go screw herself, they all can!" she said pointedly.

"For the woman that doesn't usually cuss, your cussing is telling me otherwise."

"Look, she can take the job and take the business to where they want it to be. Me on the other hand, I'm tired. I'm tired of it all. I have too much other stuff going on."

"You know what I think? I think you are being stubborn. You don't want to like her or work with her just out of bullheadedness to the company. To Mike."

"Oh, you do, huh?" Erika said simply.

They stayed there in silence for a long while, each sipping the liquor slowly. Taylor knew this was how her mom would deal with it. Sit quietly and let her ponder on it all. Her thoughts would get the better of her and make the guilt kick in eventually. Erika was a kind, caring and compassionate person, which was what everyone loved about her. So she wouldn't be able to cope with the realisation that she had been mistreating someone the way she had.

***

Erika and Taylor spent the remainder of the night talking about everything but her earlier disclosure. Her head was still up in the air and she probably should have spent some time talking with Taylor properly rather than beating her down, but she just couldn't face it today.

"So look, I'm sorry about earlier," Erika said coyly.

"Come here you goofball. You are one of my very best friends, and there is no need to apologize. I know you know where I am when you need to talk, and it's only because I know you and know how you think and worry and stuff. You *can* do this, ya know you can. And I'll be there every step of the way. I think if you continue, and give it a shot, then you might feel better about it."

"Well, I can't feel worse, can I? So I don't really feel up to talking as you have clearly already guessed, but do you think you'd be game for a little pool party Saturday afternoon? Just the three of us, barbecue, cocktails, my gal putting her demands in? And I guess I will open up a little. It'll give me an opportunity to have a few days of gathering my thoughts," she said seriously.

"Sounds awesome. We'll get through this you know? All of it," she said to Erika earnestly.

Chapter Thirty-Six

Georgia woke up ridiculously early again, unable to get her body onto this time zone. She was cringing as the previous evenings events flashed through her mind. Oh god, she was steaming, and she was crying to John and Emily. She wasn't even 'crying', she was actually more inclined to say she was sobbing. She barely even knew them and yesterday's events had got her that insane that she must have seemed like a flipping lunatic. Amazing, she'd probably lost the only friends she'd actually made here. Georgia was interrupted from her thoughts by the loud knock on her door. What the hell, it was just after five. And still dark. She threw her robe around her and rushed downstairs. She looked out the window and saw Emily. "Hey, what's up? You ok?" she said, as she opened the door.

"Yes, more to the point, are you?" she said, handing her some tablets and a bottle of water.

"Yes, but what's up? Thanks, I need this," she said, taking the water and tablets from her.

"Well, you said you wanted to join me on my early morning Pilate's class, to get you through the day. So, I was coming to check if you were up to it? However, from the look on your face right now, I'm guessing you don't recall that conversation," she smirked at her.

"No, no. I Erm… yeah I totally remember, when do we need to go?" she said confused.

"You totally did not. I'll be leaving in fifteen, that cool with you?"

Georgia was laughing, "Whatever; yeah, I'll see you in fifteen," she said, walking back indoors.

***

"I don't know if that was the best or worst idea I've ever had," Georgia said, splashing her face with water in the bathrooms.

"Well, I can't believe it made you sick. I'm guessing that may make you feel a bit better," she said, giggling. "Here. Have some water, we should get going."

"Arggghhhh God," Georgia said. "Why do I do it to myself?" she finished.

Emily was laughing at Georgia, "Ohhh you poor thing," she said sincerely, rubbing Georgia's leg.

"I'm sweating like a bitch. It's disgusting," she said, feeling her wet clothes.

"Hmmm, now there was an over-share," Emily laughed. "So, what are you going to do today? Do you feel any differently?" Emily asked concerned.

"Nah, not really. I'm annoyed that I didn't even manage to get through a week," she said sombrely.

"Look, I know I don't know you too well, and you can totally tell me to mind my own business, but I stand by what I said last night. I totally think you should talk to this woman and tell her you're leaving before you actually do. She's clearly having some issues of her own and maybe she isn't aware that you're being made to feel this way. Equally, I think you haven't given it sufficient time, you're going to *literally* leave your company? This opportunity, seriously, in a month you could have no job, you could be

176

having to give up your apartment and for what? Because, there's a bunch of folks who don't like what you're doing here?"

Georgia sighed lightly, "I know what you're saying, but, really Em, outside of you and John, there is nothing for me here. After she did that yesterday, seriously, how can I contend with that? I have never experienced anything like that. I'm seriously flabbergasted, I can't move past that, and I don't want to. I don't want anything to do with that, and I don't want to associate myself with people like that. Additionally, I will never ever be able to work and have a trusting and respectful relationship with someone who behaves in such a manor," she added.

"Right, well I'm not happy. I only just met you and I don't want you to leave. But I guess I can understand where you're coming from. John's upset, he thinks you're his new buddy and was stoked at the prospect of you guys playing water basketball in summer. When will you leave? I'm assuming as you only just arrived you don't gotta do a notice period?"

"Honestly, I dunno. It's Friday, so I'm not gonna do anything today and then I'll call my boss back home over the weekend and find out what happens now. I mean, I don't know if it means I'm actually completely out of a job or whether I can go back to what I was doing, or demoted, you know? So we'll see what he has to say. He may want me to stay on for a bit whilst he speaks to the group. I really don't know," she sighed, looking out of the window.

"Well, promise me we get to do something before you leave."

"Yes, of course. You know I'm really happy I met you guys, and I can't thank you enough for your hospitality. If you ever fancy coming to the UK, you have totes got a place to stay at mine," she said sincerely.

"Ohhh that's awesome, we've always wanted to go. You can't forget about us, you must come back and visit us some time. After all you '*totes*' have a place to stay with us," she said, giggling at her.

Chapter Thirty-Seven

Georgia felt bad, she'd said very little on the car journey to work that morning. Anne had tried to coax her into conversations with little success. She would go out at lunchtime and get her a little gift to thank her for the rides.

Georgia looked up as she heard the knock at her door. "Hi, Mike. Are you ok?" she said as her boss walked into her office.

"Yes, how are you? I was wondering if you completed the report. I only ask as Erika won't be at work today, she will be working from home."

"Oh, right okay. Yes, I have just finished it now, I just need to catch up with marketing in her absence. Would you like me to do that and send it to you?" she asked him.

"Yes, please if you wouldn't mind. I am going to need to head up to the office next week, so I will run it past the investors there," he said. "Thanks, Georgia."

She felt rubbish. She knew it would be hard, but now he was thinking that she was doing stuff to Erika. When actually, in reality, Georgia was the one being treated like crap. She'd never been made to feel this way, and she wondered if this would be construed as bullying. She'd always been popular and likable and never been in this kind of situation before, and truth be known she didn't know of any other way to deal with it, bar this way.

***

Georgia went and found the marketing team, but she wished she could just send it to Julia and get her to do it the way she always did. She'd heard that the marketing head was called Amber, so she hoped that it would be an easy enough task and that Amber would assist her without it being a big drama. But clearly, that was wishful thinking. Amber couldn't have actually been any more unhelpful, to the extent that Georgia actually had to tell her that it was Erika's work, and she was just helping her out as she wasn't in work that day. However, Amber had all but told her it was the lowest of her priorities and she would get around to it when she was able to.

Georgia walked off frustrated and annoyed. Fucking amazing, Mike was going to be even more pissed off with her now. Seriously, she could do with going home herself and hiding from all this ridiculousness. At least it was nearly lunchtime, and she'd be able to nip out and get away from this hell hole, she thought.

Georgia looked onto her phone screen feeling it vibrate in her pocket. Smiling as she answered it, "Hey you're up? Bloody hell you have impeccable timing, you can't even let me have a wee in peace now?" she laughed into the phone to Julia.

Julia was laughing back. "Shit sorry, I can call you back," she said.

"Don't be silly, I'm done. How goes it?"

"Yeah ok, I'm a little drunk. It's Friday and we're out. How are you?"

"Shit, to be honest. So, you know how I said I'd give it a month and see how it panned out? Well, I'm done. I've gave it a week, and I can't do it no more. I'm calling Derek this weekend and saying I'm out."

"Fuck. What? Why? What the hell? What's happened? George, you really think this is the right thing to do?"

Georgia washed her hands and left the bathroom, "I'm sure. Hopefully, I'll be home this time next week. Listen, I'm going to lunch shortly, I just need to sort a couple of bits out. Can I call you back when I've left the office? If you can't speak I'll catch up with you in the morning," she said.

"No, no that's fine. Call me when you're out and we can have a proper chat. Keep smiling lovely," Julia said.

***

"And you're sure that's what she said," Tim said to Jane as she sat on the edge of his desk.

"Yup, certain. I was in the bathroom with her. That's exactly what she said."

"Hmm. This is good. So, all we really need to do, is, just…tip her over the edge this afternoon, so she doesn't bail on calling back home," he said, smirking.

"Exactly. Better still, I was speaking to Amber, and she said that Georgia's asked her for her help on something quite pressing for Mike. She needs the office report and plans this afternoon. I've told *her* what's been said too, so Amber's not going to do it. Or likely lose it, basically one way or another she's going to screw her over the way she has Erika," Jane said vindictively.

"Excellent. She'll be so proud of us. I think we should call her and tell her," Tim said, plotting.

"No, no. Let's leave it as a surprise for her," she responded. "With everything going on at home, she'll be super stoked to return to work and her arch nemesis has left the building," she said destructively.

Chapter Thirty-Eight

Georgia walked back into the office at the end of her dinner hour. She literally couldn't remember the last time she had taken an hour for lunch other than when she was entertaining clients. She was very pleased with herself for the gift she had found for Anne too. Anne had mentioned that she enjoyed knitting, and that one of her children was having a child. She was trying to make some booties and some cardigans for it. Georgia had found a lovely knitting and crocheting book, with loads of ideas and a beautiful silver picture frame. She got some wrapping paper and a card, and would give it to her that night on the way home. Maybe she would forewarn her of the situation too, she had been so lovely to Georgia, and she didn't want her to be told by someone else.

Georgia had walked past a number of desks, noticing the whispers and dirty looks. God, she couldn't wait to get the hell out of this place. She stopped off at Tim's desk and asked him if he would be able to do a few bits for her. She hadn't really been given an assistant, and Mike had just said to her whilst they were getting everything sorted, to utilise Tim. The problem being, he hated her, and had absolutely no qualms with making that completely obvious.

Tim's response was no surprise. Basically saying to her that he was too busy, doing things for Erika, who was his *actual* boss. She was all but ready to go down the HR route with him, but seriously, she couldn't be bothered with this little demon anymore. "Fine, Tim. Don't worry, I'll do it myself. And I'll remember to give that feedback to Mike, so he can consider that when it comes to pay reviews," she stomped off.

Georgia's next stop was Amber. "Hi, how long will it be? Mike needs it this afternoon. He needs to run it past the investors," she said stroppy.

"I don't know, as I told you before I'm incredibly busy, and this is not my priority at the moment. My boss is Erika, and she has given me a large project to complete before the end of the month, and at the moment that needs to take precedence," she said, not even looking up from her computer screen.

"So, middle of the month and a project which doesn't need to be completed until the end is more pressing than, plans, development designs and business reports for the CEO which is required by the end of the day because he needs it to take to the investors? How exactly is that more important?" she stormed.

"Look, Georgia, I appreciate your request, but you aren't my boss, and I report into Erika. So, when she asks me to do something, that is my priority."

"*Unbelievable,*" Georgia said, dumbfounded.

"Stupid bitch," Amber muttered under her breath, but loud enough for Georgia to question if she had just actually heard correctly.

"Goddamit," she made a fist with her hand, walking into the kitchen. She couldn't do this, it was seriously going from bad to worse. She grabbed a mug and put some coffee in the mug as she waited for the kettle to boil. She was furious, her breathing was sharp and deep, and she needed to calm down. Turning around hearing footsteps behind her, she saw Jane. God, all she needed. Another office arsehole she thought and turned back around.

"Excuse me," Jane said to Georgia, reaching over for a glass.

Full of manners, are the people in this place, she thought.

Jane poured herself a pint of milk, before smirking at Georgia and walking out.

Georgia was pissed off. These people were unbelievable. Georgia poured the water into the cup and went to the fridge for the milk. She looked all over the fridge, "un-fucking-believable," she muttered to herself.

"Wow, big words, are you ok?" Georgia turned around to see Anne before her.

"No, she's just watched me waiting to make a coffee and poured a pint of milk purposely, so there was none left for me," Georgia said, visibly upset.

"Hey, come on. You can have some of mine. I buy my own as I have lactose free. You can have some if you like? Come on, don't let them win. They will soon get bored," she said, rubbing Georgia's arm.

Georgia poured the milk in and thanked Anne before leaving the kitchen and returning back to her office.

***

Mike came in late in the day, "Hi Georgia, I'm really sorry to have to nag, but have you got the report done? I really need to pull it together with my information and go through it all before I go there next week," he said.

"Hi, erm, yes. I'm sorry. I am not really great with marketing, so I'm just trying to pull it together now. I don't think I will get it done before we finish today, but I can work on it at home this evening, and send it over tonight," she said.

"Georgia, why are you doing it yourself? We have a marketing team. They should be doing this not you. You should really be making a start on the development."

"Yes, I get that. But unfortunately, marketing is too busy doing the projects that Erika has set and she couldn't assist, so I'm doing it myself," she sighed.

"What?" he barked, grabbing the landline and heavily poking the phone buttons.

"Amber, can you come to Georgia's office. Now!" he said, slamming down the phone.

Moments later Amber walked into the office, "Hi, sir. How can I help?"

"Amber, what are you working on at the moment?" he asked sternly.

"Erm, the state project that Erika asked me to do?"

"The state project for the end of the month?"

"Yes, sir."

"So, why is that more important than the plans for the new office?"

"Erm, I'm sorry, sir? What do you mean the plans for the new office?"

"The project that I am in dire need of. The one to review and go through pre-meeting with the investors next week up in Fort Worth," he said, clearly agitated.

"Well, nothing would be *more* important than that, sir. However, I have not been asked for it."

"*What?*" Georgia bellowed, shocked by her response.

"Ummm, I'm sorry, Georgia. If you asked me to do this, I could have spent the afternoon on it. But if you don't tell me, I can't get the team to help," she said seriously.

Fucking hell, this woman was the best liar she'd ever met. Holy hell. Georgia started talking and then just gave up. Seriously, she is not doing this anymore. *This* was insane.

Mike turned to face Georgia, "Geor..." he stopped talking. Georgia could feel her face burning, and she was livid. "That's all Amber," he said, shutting the door behind her.

He paused looking at Georgia, paying attention to the clear agitation of her demeanour. "So, you asked her huh?" he said sincerely.

"I can't do it, Mike. I don't give up on things easily. But this is obscene, this wasn't my doing and I've had the shittiest week of my life. Yeah, I asked her. Of course, I did," she said, feeling the tears drop.

"Please? Come on, Georgia, don't get upset," he said, handing her his handkerchief. Mike picked up the phone, "Hi, how busy are you? Great, can it wait until Monday? Ok, pack up please, Georgia needs to leave."

"Go home, forget about the report, have some time off, I'll get Amber to do it," he said walking off.

"Actually, I'm almost done now, I may as well finish it at home and submit it, then you can get her to change it to your style and amend where necessary. It's far too late in the day now, she'll never get it completed starting from scratch. So, I'll just finish it, I'm almost done."

Mike turned around at the last moment. "Georgia," he said, looking genuinely sad and concerned.

"Yeah?" she looked up from her bag that she was packing up, pissed off that she'd spent so much of the week crying.

"I'm sorry, Georgia. I'm genuinely sorry. We never anticipated a situation such as this," and just like that he was gone.

186

Chapter Thirty-Nine

Georgia got out of the pool. She'd had a great weekend, but it was over far too quickly. She had spoken to Derek and, well understandably, he was seriously pissed off with her. Unfortunately, that was the downside to getting on well with your manager. They were never phased by making you see, hear and feel the disappointment in their voices. Her parents weren't much better. Her dad was passionate, driven and very competitive, so being bullied was not really a viable excuse for him. Which pissed her off immensely. Seriously, being told to toughen up from her parents really hurt. She was forty years old and her parents had no concept of being stranded on the other side of the world where everything you worked your arse off was being taken from you. She genuinely didn't know what else she could have done.

Georgia picked up her phone and re-read the email from Derek. *Flights booked for Wednesday*, and that's all he wrote. He'd sent it yesterday and she was well aware by the tone that he was so annoyed at her. She was still unclear if there was a job waiting for her back home. She wasn't even sure she wanted there to be, so she'd spent all day yesterday sharpening her CV and sent it over for a few jobs already. At least she had some idea as to what was out there.

Looking at the phone vibrating to alert her of a message, Georgia saw the text from Mike on her phone and opened it. She was nervous, and she hadn't spoken to him since Friday afternoon when she left. She breathed in deeply, wiping the pool water dripping from her head. She looked at the message and read the words.

Please do not come to work today, meet me at my restaurant at one pm, Mike.

Ouch, Georgia thought. "Sod it," she said to herself, she was going anyways. Realistically, what could he say or do? She dumped her towel and got back into the pool. She may as well make the most of it before she left. A while later, Georgia left the pool and made her way back inside to start packing.

***

Georgia pulled up at the restaurant. She'd not driven since that first morning, and luckily the roads were quiet, as she followed her sat nav the short distance to Mike's restaurant. She was nervous as hell at what was waiting ahead of her. The conversations with her parents' and Derek were bad enough, but all she wanted in the world was to get shouted at. Seriously, she could easily deal with him having a go at her, but she could not deal with him having that same sense of disappointment in her that everyone else had. Jesus, she was even getting it from Emily and John. Bloody hell, even Torrance had jumped on the band wagon at one point, and she was young enough to be Georgia's kid. She took a deep breath and walked into the restaurant.

"Hi, can I help you?"

"Hi, I'm here to meet Mike... he is..."

"Sure thing, ma'am, follow me," the waitress said, smiling to her.

Georgia followed her around to a separate cordoned off area of the restaurant. God it was like walking the plank. She entered the room and saw Erika and Mike sat down, and she stopped unknowingly. Mike stood instantly, "Georgia, please?" he said, pointing to the chair.

Genuinely, Georgia didn't think she could have felt any worse about today, and actually she now realised that she did. Making her way to the table she took a seat next to Erika and Mike. "Hi," she said quietly. She hadn't seen Erika since she'd fucked her over with the lies to Mike, and now suddenly she realised the reason for the meeting.

"Hi Georgia, thanks for coming. What can I get you to drink?"

"I'll just have a water thanks."

"Georgia, this isn't going to be a quick meeting. Doubtful it'll be pleasant either, as I've just advised Erika. You may want something stronger. She is having a wine, and I'm having a scotch. Whilst I'm not trying to influence you into drinking, I'm merely wanting to point out, it may assist with matters. Still want a water?"

"I'll have a large red please," she said nervously.

They heard the door go and looked around, "Oh dear God," Georgia found herself saying, as she felt like her knees were about to buckle. She tried her hardest to control the emotions as Derek walked towards them. He leant over and kissed Georgia on the cheek. "Hey, lady," he said to her warmly. She could see and hear Jill in him, and she could just imagine her raging at him for putting her in this situation, and making him jump on the first flight to deal with it. However, he looked happy and relaxed, kissing Erika on the cheek, offering pleasantries about being happy to meet her. "Nice place you got here" he said, shaking Mike's hand.

There was a complete awkwardness as Mike and Derek exchanged discussions of the restaurant and location whilst they were waiting for the drinks, as Erika and Georgia sat there fiddling with phones, glasses and cutlery.

As they thanked the waitress for the drinks and waited for her to leave, Derek began. "Okay, let's get down to business. So, as I said nice to meet you, Erika. I'm sorry it has to be in these circumstances. Clearly it hasn't worked since we're in this situation," he said, holding out his hands to the surroundings, and sighing heavily. "We are disappointed that..."

Erika coughed a little. "Look, how about I make this slightly easier on all of you. I'm resigning. It isn't what I worked towards, and she can have it. Too much is going on in my life, so I've decided it makes more sense for me to move back home."

"I don't want the job, I have already quit, that's why we're here. I fly home the day after tomorrow," Georgia shot back to Erika.

"What? *You're leaving*? When did this happen?" she snapped at Mike.

"Right, enough, already! Seriously, you two are acting worse than my teenage granddaughters. This was a fantastic opportunity for you both, and it's been a week? A *god damn* week? I thought we may have had a little bit of...well, competitor activity between y'all, but I'm pretty darn sure that Derek's feeling exactly the same as me. In the respect of you are not the women that we portrayed. Erika, I appreciate you have some personal issues going on, but I've never known you to be like this. Jesus, you are virtually the same people, I can't believe we're here. I am indeed staggered that this wondrous opportunity has turned into some of the most powerful women in the business, turning into," he stopped, shaking and scratching his head in disbelief.

"Into childish playground bullies," Derek finished.

"Yes, thank you, Derek. I'm not going to lie, I'm completely stunned and genuinely…well I'm hurt, and I feel let down," Mike said disappointedly.

Erika rubbed her head. *Seriously? The guilt tripping?* She uses this on Dulcie for Christ's sake.

"Sorry, can I just interrupt here?" Georgia said. "Firstly, I apologise to both of you, for well, for clearly disappointing you both. However, I'm not so happy to have my reputation tarnished and be called a bully. I'm forty years old, I'm likeable; well I was," she scoffed. "I've left my family, my friends, my colleagues, my job, my career, my country, Jesus the person I was seeing…"

"You met someone? Why didn't you tell me?" Derek said immediately.

"Well, I didn't… oh I don't know, that's the least of it all. The point I'm trying to make is, I have at no point bullied anyone. I've tried to make an effort. I was insulted and left in a foreign country, with no clue on how to drive. Given I haven't driven a car for the last three years made it somewhat harder, then was treated like shit by everyone in the office. People were rude, ignored me, refused to help me with work and then lied to my face in front of the CEO about me ever asking for it. For Christ's sake, they came and poured pints of milk for themselves in front of me so I couldn't even make a brew. So seriously, when exactly was *I* a bully?" she said accusingly.

"Ok. Well, I agree you've been put through the mill, and I apologise about that, more so for Friday with Amber. But I just don't think you should leave. We can sort all of that, we can come down on the staff, *hard!*"

"What happened with Amber?" Erika snapped.

"Georgia?" Mike said, pointing to her. "While I'm sure my assumptions were correct, you're probably best suited to explain the situation."

Georgia was really struggling with all of this. Seeing Derek was making her feel more homesick, and she was sure that whatever was discussed would be front page news tomorrow. But screw it, she was out of here the day after next anyhow, it's not like she would see any of them again. "I received your report, thank you. It was fantastic," she said, feeling the pain as she said so. "I asked Tim for some help and he said no, he was too busy doing stuff for you, which you'd told him was too important to leave. And as '*you*' are his boss, which he felt the need to keep pointing out, he didn't need to help me at all. His words, not mine. Then I asked Amber to amend some parts and, basically, do what we needed to have it ready for Mike to take. She said she had a project for you to do, so I went back and asked her later and she reiterated this fact. Then she told me it was for the end of the month, and I advised the importance of getting this done, not for me, but for Mike. I even explained it was your work thinking she may actually do it. Oh, and I then stated that it was the middle of the month, so clearly it wasn't as pressing as the CEO needing something to take on his visit in a mere few days, *and* to the investors. Anyways, Mike came and saw me later in the afternoon, and asked where it was," Georgia stopped, sighing lightly. She felt stupid, she couldn't believe this is what her life had resorted to. "Anyways, I explained the situation to him, he called Amber and she came down to the office, and said that I'd not actually asked her, nobody had mentioned anything to her."

Mike finished his drink, "It was pretty obvious that was the situation, I could see the hurt in Georgia's eyes. And while I'm sure she, like you, is a tough cookie, I also can't stand by and watch someone be mentally abused, by my own staff. *Your* staff," he said pointedly.

"Georgia, I can assure you I didn't know anything about this," Erika said somewhat difficultly.

"Well, I'd hardly expect you to admit it," she said sharply.

"What's that supposed to mean?" Erika said.

"Well, I offer you support when I see you visibly upset, tell you to go home. Jesus, I even said I'd stick up for you with Mike if you needed me to. And you go rushing to the CEO to say I stormed into your office, bullied you, made you cry and so you haven't been in since? I'm sure it's all a ploy, quickest and easiest way to get rid of the British *bitch*," she snapped.

"*What* are you...?"

"Wait, Erika?" Mike stopped her. "Georgia, where did you get that Erika came *running* to me about you?"

"You told me," Georgia confirmed.

"What? I didn't, when?" Mike responded.

"You came in and asked what had happened? You said she went home sick because I made her cry."

"Yes, I did, bu..."

"You did?" Erika questioned. "What did you do that for?"

"Because Tim told me. That didn't happen?"

"No," Erika said.

Georgia turned to Mike. "What I told you is correct," she said quietly.

"Okay, okay. I'm sorry to step in here, Mike. But, I think as I'm the only one not directly involved, we may need to back up a bit. Clearly, Georgia has not been exaggerating, but equally, I get that Erika has not been involved in this... conspiracy theory. How about we order some food and start from scratch?" he said.

Chapter Forty

"Holy hell, that's pretty darn bad huh? So what are you going to do?" Taylor asked.

"Nothing, I'll decide whether I retract my resignation over the next couple days, and I'll discuss with Dan tonight, then I guess go from there," Erika said squarely.

"Right," she nodded her head.

"What's that mean?" Erika snapped.

"Nothing. So you fancy taking Dulcie the movies?" she said.

"Don't do that to me. What do you want from me? Honestly, I don't actually know if I fancy it, could we go for dinner? I just kinda feel like I need to spend a little time with her and then an early night."

"Well, I can leave you guys. It's no biggie."

"No," Erika jumped in. She grabbed her hand, "Seriously, I just need a friend, and I'd really like it if we all went for dinner, if you got the time?"

"Of course. I best make the most of our time together, before you leave," she said sadly.

"Mommy, what's Taylor mean? Are we leaving?" she said sadly.

Taylor looked at Erika apologetically. "Ummm, come here, munchkin. You need to stop eerie earwigging with these little things," she said, wiggling her tiny little ears. "I just meant before she needed to go back to work, you know? Cause she's been spending some time at home with us," Taylor explained to Dulcie.

"Ohhh, I know, I don't like it when you work, Mommy. I like staying at home and baking choc chip cakes." She smiled.

Erika stroked her daughter's face softly. So, y'all wanna eat out, then get dessert after?" she said animatedly, trying to not over think what this could do to her baby girl.

"Yayyyyyy, can we go to forest café?" she said, jumping up and down on Taylors lap.

"Not tonight baby, it's too far for night time. We need to just go someplace local. And then we can go there one weekend. Go get your jacket on, okay?"

"Okay, Mommy."

"Sorry about that," Taylor said apologetically.

"Don't worry about it, it's fine. I'm gonna have to tell her sooner or later. I guess I should just talk to the family first," she said sombrely.

***

Erika got seated at the restaurant and ordered their food. Dulcie was happily coloring with some crayons and papers the server had given her. She and Taylor and she were chatting quietly about the situation.

Erika stopped talking and began focussing in ahead of her.

"What's up, who have you seen? Is it Dan?" she said concerned, turning her head around to see what Erika was looking at.

"No, it's her."

"Who her?" she said, trying to have a look.

"Don't look," she said, grabbing her arm.

"Well, you can't say to someone '*it's her*' and then not expect them to look. Who is it?"

Shit, too late. Erika quickly turned away.

Chapter Forty-One

"Damn, it's her," Georgia whispered to Emily.

"What? Who?"

"It's Erika. Over there a couple of tables away, two women and a child, the dark haired one."

"Is she gay?"

"*What*?" Georgia spat. "No, why?" Georgia turned back to her.

"Is who gay?" John asked.

"Nobody," they both turned around and snapped at him.

"Sheesh, eaaaassssyyy. I was just asking," he said confused.

"Sorry, baby," Emily said to her husband. "That's Erika over there," she pointed out to John.

"And she's gay?" he said, looking at the family of three.

"God! No, she's married with a kid, clearly, the little one there," she said.

"Well, you need to go say hi. I know you don't want to, but clearly you have both seen each other, and that's not good to just ignore it. Essentially, you are the more senior person, plus you're leaving tomorrow, so I think you should go over," John said sincerely.

"Seriously, I couldn't just meet some immoral folk, could I?" she sighed.

"Honey, he is right. Like you keep saying, you're forty years old and are more mature than the rubbish at work, so be the bigger person," Emily said to her.

"Ya know what, I'm retracting the invite to my house," she said to them, shaking her head as she walked over to Erika's table.

***

"Hi," Georgia said nervously. "I thought I should come over and say hi. Figured it would be rude not to. Shit." Shit she swore in front of the child, and she immediately covered her mouth. "Sugar, I'm so sorry," looking down to the little girl. "I'm sorry for swearing, and I'm sorry if that sounded like a dig, it wasn't at all."

Taylor felt incredibly awkward, the poor woman was reaching out an olive branch. "Hi, I'm Taylor, I'm guessing you must be Georgia?" she said warmly.

"Ouch, never a good thing, when people are aware of you, without meeting," Georgia said awkwardly. "Anyways, I just wanted to say hey, and, well I'm sorry about yesterday *and* sorry things got as awful as they did. But as I won't see you again, I guess all the best for the future whatever you decide," Georgia said, smiling kindly.

Erika was about to say something, before she was beaten to it.

"Who are you? I'm Dulcie. That's Taylor, she's my nanny. Are you a nanny too?" Dulcie asked inquisitively.

"Well, hi, Dulcie. That's a cool name. I'm Georgia, nice to meet you," she said, shaking her hand. "And no, I'm not a nanny. What you doing there?" she asked, showing an interest in the little girl, and ignoring the look from Taylor over to Erika.

"It's a coloring, ya want it?" she asked.

Georgia couldn't help but smile at her. She was absolutely adorable, and it made her realise how much she missed her own nieces and nephews. "Um, that's incredibly kind, but maybe you should give it to your mum or your nanny," she said.

"Why do you speak funny, Georgia?"

"Dulcie, that's rude," her mom reprimanded her, causing Georgia to desperately remain tight lipped.

"It's ok," Georgia smiled. "I think you're confused. I don't speak funny. It's you that speaks funny," she said seriously.

Dulcie was laughing hysterically, "No, I don't, you do. Doesn't she, Tay?" she asked.

"Erm, maybe she does, I can't quite work it out," she said, tickling Dulcie

"Anyways, it was very nice to meet you, Dulcie. I'm gonna head back to my friends," Georgia said.

"Bye, Georgia," she said, waving enthusiastically.

Georgia smiled widely, "She's a beautiful, incredibly infectious, little girl," she said to Erika. "Nice to meet you, Taylor, good luck," she said, smiling and leaving the table.

Chapter Forty-Two

Erika put Dulcie to bed and joined Taylor, pouring them both a glass of wine. "Do you think we have a drinking problem?" Erika said.

"No, I think we are working through a difficult time," Taylor said, laying further into the couch.

"Cool, I'll go with that. Okay, c'mon then?"

"C'mon what?" Taylor asked confused.

"Don't pull that with me. I know you've been desperate to say something all night. Just get it off your chest already."

"Seriously, there's nothing. I was surprised by her. I didn't expect her to be like that, she was good with Dulcie, and I bet she got homesick. She was nice, and I have to give her dues, she was gutsy coming over like that, is all," she said.

"Yeah, I guess so."

"It's a shame it went the way it did, I think you would have gotten along well with her, ya know?"

"Yup, well everything happens for a reason. There's nothing I can do now," she said.

"Hmmm," she said.

"What, Tay? *What*? What exactly could I do? I mean, I'm still not sure I'm staying yet."

"Hmmm, yeah I guess," Taylor said.

"Okay, so what would you suggest then, if you were me what would you do?"

"Stop her. And try to work it out…oh, and sort your staff out," she said.

"Stop her? Jesus, this isn't some freaking love story where I run after her at the airport and beg her to stay. We work together, she's a colleague," she said.

"Okay, no need to be sarcastic," she said. "I didn't literally mean go and run through the airport, jumping over boarding gates and beg her to stay, you ass. I mean call her up, ask her for a coffee in the morning and see if she wants to give it a proper shot, work together, collaboratively. Be a team and try to make this work. Geez, it's twelve months, if that?" she said. "Listen, Dulcie is amazing, she just emanates beauty, kindness, generosity. That's you guys that have instilled that in her. In most part, you. If she behaved like that, seriously dude, you'd kick her ass."

"Hmm, well I think it's probably too little, too late for that right now. I think we have half way killed Derek and Mike, ya know?" she said seriously.

"All the more reason, to show them you are professional and serious!"

Taylor and Erika spent the remainder of the night discussing everything down to a T. More so since the pool party hadn't gone as planned on Saturday, so they hadn't really spoken since last week. Taylor was definitely pulling her mom's and Mike's card out on her, and the whole guilt trip BS was driving her insane.

Chapter Forty-Three

Georgia finished packing and was relaxing until Derek came to pick her up that afternoon due to booking on the same flight. She still had hours to go though, and still needed to go and buy something for Emily and John, and Torrance too. She was a good kid, so completely motivated and driven, and Georgia saw a lot of herself in her. She had passed a sport shop when she drove to Mike's on Monday, so she wanted to see if she could get anything from there.

Georgia grabbed her car keys and pushed her phone into her back pocket. God she would miss this weather so much she thought to herself. Taking in her white jeans, flip flops and sleeveless denim shirt, Georgia grabbed her purse, opened the door, and bumped straight into Erika.

"Erm, hi?" Georgia said, looking down at her watch, checking the time.

"Oh, sorry, you are on your way out?" Erika said.

"Erm, yeah, I was just going to try and find a sport shop that I think I saw the other day, for a present. Err, what are you doing here?" she said confused.

"Do you have time to talk, or do you need to go to the store now?"

"Well, I have a fair few hours before Derek's picking me up, so I suppose? Do you want to come in or do you want to go somewhere?" Georgia said.

"Here's fine, well, if you are prepared to invite me in?"

Georgia sighed lightly, "Come in. We can sit in the back garden, it's nice out there."

Georgia opened the door for Erika to come in, trying to assess the sombre look on Erika's face as she noticed the packed cases by the front door.

"I guess somewhat different to back home huh? I got this for you, it's nothing, just a bit of a peace offering," Erika said, handing her a six pack of beer.

"You sure about that, I mean it's not really going to help with alcoholism, is it?" she said, unlocking the door and allowing Erika to go outside.

"Ok, I deserved that."

Georgia opened her beer and took a long swig. Seriously, there really was no better feeling than an ice-cold bottle of beer in the sun by the pool, she thought nostalgically.

"So, what's up? What are you here for?" Georgia questioned.

"Well, I came to apologize. And, yes, I know it's too late in the day. I didn't know my team would behave that way, and my personal situations are in no way an excuse, but I apologize for my behavior. Believe it or not, Mike was right on Monday, my behavior has been completely unacceptable, and I should have welcomed you in as the woman who was going through the exact situation I was. I should have been more professional in front of my staff and maybe not been so emotionally reactive about you, without first understanding the situation. And lastly, I should have never made anyone feel this way. If anyone did that to Dulcie, I'd kill them. And you, like you say, have been thrown through the mill, actually, in a much worse position than I have. I'm not going to beg you for forgiveness or to stay, but what I will say is, I'm not too ashamed and proud to say I was a dumbass and it took my nanny to make me realise that. If I could do it over, it would have been done very differently. Starting with taking you out for a beer on the way home rather than beating your ass down and insinuating you were a drunk. Which, FYI, as my nanny also pointed out, I would have done exactly the same thing as you had the situations been reversed with the drink on the flight over here," she said.

Georgia was taken aback by what she was hearing, and she had to give it to Erika for apologising. Although, she was wondering if it was just another set up.

"I'm sorry. Like I said, I didn't expect you to just start jumping up and down and accept the way I behaved, but I couldn't let you leave thinking that's me. I'm not looking for acceptance, nor forgiveness, but you pretty much walked into my life as it hit destruction. You didn't deserve to be the one that got beaten down because of that. I took out my marriage and job issues all on you," she said sadly "But look, that's all I came to tell you," she said, standing and walking away.

"Erika?" Georgia said, standing.

"Yes?" Georgia could see by the look of fear and hope in her face, that she wasn't here to screw her over again. God, she wished she wasn't such a soft touch. "How bad do you want to make it up to me?"

Erika raised her eyebrow. "Well, I suppose it depends on what you want," she said nervously.

"Chill out," rolling her eyes. "So, funny story. I got a pretty amazing car in the garage. However, I have never driven in the states. Pre-coming here I hadn't driven back home for three years either. Nor had I ever driven an automatic. So when I arrived I got..." she shook her head sarcastically. "Like, ditched. Was called an alcoholic. Basically, leaving me no option but to attempt to drive again and then got pulled over by a cop. So, as you can imagine, I'm somewhat nervy about driving at present," she said seriously. "I'm thinking you've apologised, and if you really want to make it up to me, and if you have time? Then how about taking me to a place I can buy a sports top. I need to buy a Texas Pacers top."

"Okay, okay already, I get it I'm a bitch. Sure I can, but I don't think I have time," she said seriously.

Ouch, Georgia thought. She suddenly felt like an idiot, and she really shouldn't have bothered. "Oh okay, not to worry I can do it, I'm sure," she said embarrassed.

Erika was smiling at Georgia, "I can take you, for sure. The problem is, we may have to travel the entire US to find a Texas Pacers jersey," she said.

"Really? Are they that important? Why are you laughing at me?" she asked inquisitively.

"No, they aren't that important, they are, that non-existent. The Pacers are Indiana's team."

"What?"

"It's the Indiana Pacers, not the Texas Pacers," she laughed. "Come on."

"Is Indiana not an actual place? Why would you support a team that isn't where you come from?" Georgia said confused.

"Not much into sports then huh?" Erika laughed.

Chapter Forty-Four

"You sure you wanna do this?" Erika asked again.

"Well, I think it's too late to back out now, it's done," Georgia said to the woman.

"I guess we better go then," Erika said.

A short while later, Erika and Georgia were sat in front of their respective bosses.

"So, what's this about, ladies?" Mike asked seriously.

"You wanna go?" Erika said to Georgia.

"Yes, sure. Ok, well I guess we've stressed you both out enough, which we would both like to apologise for. But to cut a long story short, Erika visited me this morning and apologised, we both did. I'm not gonna say we both acted like idiots, because I genuinely don't think we did, but equally, we didn't really do great with the situation. We have decided to give it a go. A *proper* go this time. I'm not saying it's going to work, I'm not saying we are happy about any of it still. Nor are we going to be best buds, but we will maintain an element of professionalism and try it. I will go back to my original plan of giving it a month and then if Erika's happy to do so, I'd like us two to have a meeting and discuss how we both feel."

"I am happy to do that," Erika said confidently.

The table was deathly silent as the two men took in the details, before Derek finally spoke.

"Thanks, George," he said. "I know it's hard, and has been hard, but I think you're doing the right thing. And thank you, Erika. That was incredibly courageous and shows such integrity, now I can see what Mike meant about you. I would love to sort these fine details, but it looks like I have a flight to catch alone, so I should get off. I will leave this with you Mike?" Derek questioned.

"Thanks Derek. And thanks for coming over. I actually have a meeting to attend, however, I have a plan for you two. You say you are going to try this, so you need to know more about everything. *Both* of you. So when I leave I'm going to contact the investors and rearrange the meeting until next week. I want you guys to go up there, spend some time getting to know it, and you can deliver the presentation to them. It's your baby, so it really shouldn't be me doing it," he said.

"Mike, it really isn't as easy as that. I have a child. If Dan can't have time off work I won't be able to just take off in a couple days."

"I'm sorry, Erika, but that's for you to sort out," he said, walking out just like that. He was still clearly pissed with her.

Chapter Forty-Five

Georgia knocked and waited patiently for the door to open.

"Hey. Dang, we thought you had just left without saying goodbye," Emily said, pulling her into a hug.

"Don't be silly, of course I wouldn't. When do you have to leave?"

"In about forty minutes. I just wanted to come over and say thanks and give some thank you gifts," she said seriously.

"Oh, you didn't need to do that. Come on in," she said.

Georgia accepted the coffee that Emily had offered her and was happy that all three of them were there.

"So, I have a gift for each of you. A thank you for your friendship and kindness towards me. So Torrance, for you," she said, watching her open it.

"Oh man, you got me a Pacers jersey? Thank you so much. I'm so bummed you're leaving," she said, hugging Georgia. "I was totally hoping we could start running together and kick dad's butt at basketball," she said sincerely. "Thanks so much for this, it's totally awesome."

"For you, Emily," she said, handing her the workout water bottle with insightful words written on it. "Sorry, it's pretty rubbish, but I only went to the sport shop," she said.

"Don't be silly, you really shouldn't have. And actually, I needed a new one. I go through these so quick," she smiled easily.

"And last but not least for you, John," she said.

John opened his basketball, "Hey, this is awesome! You can never have too many basketballs," he said. "But you know you really shouldn't have. That jersey alone is far too expensive, you really shouldn't have," he said sincerely.

"Guys, you have absolutely no idea how your hospitality has kept me grounded and sane. If it wasn't for you guys, there's no way I would have been able to cope. It really is the least I could do," she said sadly, before continuing on to them.

Georgia smiled to her friends, incredibly grateful that she had met them. "And seriously, you guys got pretty naff presents in comparison to Torr. More so because I was kind of selfish and got the basketball for you, albeit, I figured we could use that one for water basketball when summer comes," she said.

"Huh?" John said surprised, looking between her and his wife.

"What do you mean? I thought you weren't here for summer? Are you gonna come back and visit? *Or,* oh my gosh, say it ain't so. You're not leaving?" Emily said, shooting up over to her new friend instantly.

"Correct!"

"For real? How? When? Why?" Emily said, clearly confused by everything.

Georgia laughed before telling them the days events as she threw her bag in to her car. She was glad John had spent a couple of hours over the weekend with her driving. She completely felt at ease and confident driving again. Entering the postcode, she followed the directions on the sat nav on the twenty-minute journey to Erika's place.

Georgia pulled up on the driveway of Erika's house, and it was very much how she expected. It was a gorgeous property, with bikes and toys visible in the garage. Georgia walked up and knocked on the door waiting for it to open. Inside she could hear Dulcie crying. *Oh dear God, what's happening?* she thought to herself, wondering what an earth was going on?

Erika opened the door with such anger, she practically ripped it off the hinges. "I knew this was impossible, I said so," she confirmed. "I'm sorry, you will have to go alone. I suggest you keep that quiet for a couple of days, because Mike is sure to fire my ass when he finds out, and you will have nobody that will be able to help you. Dulcie, will you please cut it out for just a minute?" she snapped, rubbing her head.

Georgia was completely confused. She didn't know what was going on, and more importantly, she didn't know how she was supposed to react or what she was supposed to say to her. They weren't friends. She didn't know her really, and she didn't know how to broach it without getting her head snapped off.

"What's the matter? What's happened?" asking the only thing she could think of.

"*What's happened*? I told you what would happen? I told him on…"

"Ok, stop a moment, and calm down. Do you mind if I come in?" she said, walking in before Erika had a chance to respond. "Hi, Dulcie, pleased to see you again. How come you're crying? What's the matter, sweetie?" she asked the little girl as she was sobbing uncontrollably, and leaving Erika to deal with her apparent anger issues.

Georgia had somehow managed to calm down Erika, who in turn had managed to calm down Dulcie. They were sitting down at the breakfast bar discussing what the problem was. It seemed she wouldn't find it easy to just get up and go, like she had highlighted to Mike. Either way Georgia was concerned as they needed to make a move.

"I'm sorry about being rude to you. I didn't mean to. Again, you seem to keep taking the hit for my crap. I did explain this, didn't I? It's too short notice. Dan can't get the time off work, and Dulcie's grandparents are on vacation, so what the hell am I supposed to do?"

"What about your nanny?"

"I can't ask Taylor. She just finished school, she needs to have some time alone, plus she's away visiting some friends. I can't go, Georgia. It's as simple as that," she said bluntly.

"Well, I can't go without you. I know nothing about this place, the way you work out here, nothing. Can we realistically do it remotely?"

"What choice do we have?"

"How hard is it over here to take kids out of school?" Georgia asked.

"What do you mean? Taylor's just finished school."

"No, not Taylor, Dulcie. So back home, if my sister wants to take my nieces out of school when it's not half term, the parents get fined. Do they do the same here? If not, why can't we just take her?"

"You spend absolutely no time with your nieces, do you?"

"Erm, no, not so much. Why, what's that got to do with anything?"

"Well, she is five. What, will she be doing? Sitting at the head of the table talking to the investors about the future plans?"

Georgia rolled her eyes. "No need for sarcasm. All I mean is, at least if we're there we can sort something out. Girls love kids, they can watch her whilst she colours."

"Who exactly? We're opening an office. Nobody's there yet."

"Shit yeah, forgot about that point. My heads all over the place. Right. Ok, well you said last week you were resigning and moving home. Mike said that you could still do this from back home, so why not do that? Can't we take her to your parents to look after her the days we have meetings? Where possibly you can keep her with you. If she's anything like my nieces and nephews, you just take an iPad or some videos, she'll be happy to chill doing that."

"Videos? Please tell me that reference is because you don't watch much TV and it's not because the UK is not as advanced as DVD's?" she said, shocked.

"We have DVD's *and* blu ray's. I just still call them videos," shaking her head. "Look are we going to do this or not? Because we need to crack on either way."

"Why are you doing this? Why are you going all out to help me? When…when I did what I did? Or is it a ploy, are you going to go back to Mike and say how unprofessional I am, and that I took my kid?"

"Seriously, I'm forty years old. Life's too short for holding grudges. I said I forgave you and I do. I've moved on. Now, this," she stopped, pointing to them both. "Well, I can't do it without you, I need assistance from the person who knows all there is to know. You seemingly have had a pretty rubbish time of late, and I can't imagine having to just dash off and leave your daughter for a week is going to assist matters. Equally, it's probably been a difficult time for her, so I don't want any more stress on her either. So the way I see it, this is our only option. If you need to stay at your parents' and I just go in, then that's fine. Or, if you want me to change the hotel to somewhere closer to them, we can do that too. I'm easy," she said seriously.

"Gimme a sec?" Erika said, rushing off in a different direction, leaving Georgia where she was.

***

"Okay, it seems like we're on. I hope you know what you have let yourself in for. Hey, Georgia," Erika said sheepishly. "Firstly, thank you. Secondly, I know you owe me nothing, but can we keep this from Mike? I mean, I'm not asking you to lie for me, but…"

"It's fine. Enough said, I won't say nought," she said quickly.

"Hey, Dulcie?" Erika called out.

"Uh huh?" Dulcie walked out holding her teddy bear, still red eyed from the excessive crying.

"You fancy going on a little road trip and visiting Nonna?"

Dulcie was giving Erika a questioning look, as though she was trying to trick her. "When?"

"Right now. Georgia's coming too. Well, not to Nonna's, but on the road trip."

"You are?" she said quietly.

"Ummm, if that's ok with you," Georgia said, unsure of what else to say or do.

"I like that idea a whole lot," she said, smiling the faintest of smiles with a couple of sniffles.

"Right, ok. I will literally be ten minutes, I promise. Thank you, Georgia. Hey, why don't you make us some coffees for the journey while I pack?"

"Well, chances are I may need to just buy us one, as I can't actually work out how to use my own properly yet. But, I'll have a go," she said.

Twenty minutes later, they were in the car and on their way to Fort Worth. Dulcie had more stuff than both of the women put together, but as Erika had highlighted, they needed to make sure she had stuff to keep her entertained through the week.

"Mommy, can we put Frozen music on please?"

Erika sighed and rested her head against the headrest. She mouthed sorry to Georgia.

Georgia was confused about what she was saying sorry for, but turned to face the window and take in the views on the journey.

"Baby, I will put it on, but Georgia will not want to listen to 'Let it Go' for the next four hours, so we listen to it once, and then shut it off, K?"

Dulcie sighed heavily, "Okay, but we'll just see because Frozen maybe is Georgia's favourite too?"

Georgia couldn't help but giggle. She turned further in her chair, being aware that Josh and Alex always told her off when she was laughing at her nieces and nephews, usually resulting in them 'playing up' more for the attention.

***

There had been a difficult silence for the first part of the drive, feeling somewhat forced. Understandably so given the very surreal circumstances and tremendous change to the dynamics. They were both clearly unsure of how to deal with the situation, and had obviously both wanted to make an effort following the previous week. However, they just couldn't find any common ground.

Simply put, they were nothing alike, regardless of what Mike thought.

Georgia looked back behind her, noticing the quietness in the back seat. "Oh, thank god," she whispered, noticing that Dulcie was asleep, switching the CD off.

Erika was laughing at her. "Welcome to parenthood," she said, immediately feeling a blush appear. "Um, sorry, I didn't mean…" she stopped.

"It's okay, don't worry, I know what you meant. My brother and sister say it to me all the time," she smirked. "I didn't think you were insinuating that we were going to start co-parenting."

Erika looked confused. "Actually, I thought you may think I was insinuating that you would be an in-house babysitter for me this week because of the situation we are in. Although, I don't think my daughter's kindergarten would be too impressed with her teaching her class so many cuss words," she smirked over to Georgia who was looking sheepish.

"I'm really sorry," she whispered. "Interestingly, I'm not normally this bad. I keep having words with myself, as my mum will kill me if I swore like this in front of her," she squirmed. "I am more aware though, I just keeping forgetting because I'm putting so much pressure on myself," she said seriously.

Erika was giggling to her, "Hey, don't worry. She's kinda tuned in to right and wrong. So it's doubtful she would then think it's funny to start repeating it. Anyways, more importantly, you have been 'having words with yourself'? What the actual hell?" she was laughing.

"What?" she said.

"What is that even? You talk to yourself?"

"No, well yes. How do you not know this?" Georgia said evenly. "So, clearly it's British terminology. You do something wrong you have to tell yourself off," she continued.

"Tell yourself off?" Erika was paying more attention to Georgia's face, which was unreadable.

"Yeah. So, if I'm doing something wrong I go in to the corner for a few minutes, and tell myself off for doing wrong. I reprimand myself," she said seriously. "You know, a bit like the naughty step but for adults?" she continued.

Erika was looking at her seriously. "Like…is that a British thing? I mean that super nanny does that with the kids, puts them on the naughty step or in the naughty corner. But you're telling me you do it for grownups too?" she asked mortified.

"Well yeah, but it's not just for kids. We need to do it too, even as adults if we've been bad," she said. She was trying so hard but couldn't help the pull on the corner of her lip.

"Oh no, you're totally fucking with me. You are evil," she said, laughing loudly.

"And you say about my swearing?" Georgia asked. "Anyways, sssshhhh, your kid's adorable, but I cannot listen to 'Let it Go' another four hundred times," she said, smiling.

"Ahhhh, you wait till we get to the hotel. I'll warn you now the movie will be on auto play," she giggled.

"Dear god. Mike did book us two separate rooms, didn't he?" she asked animatedly concerned.

"Actually, I have no idea what he booked, did he tell you?"

"Erm, you're clearly asking the wrong person, he hates me," she smirked.

"He does not. He was way more pissed with me than you. And on the contrary, he told me on a number of occasions how amazing you were," she said quietly.

"What can I say? They all do," she smirked.

Erika looked at Georgia and rolled her eyes.

"And then they get to know me," she laughed.

Erika was shaking her head at Georgia, glad that it had become somewhat more relaxed. Her back was starting to cramp already and her neck and shoulders were tight. The stress of late was certainly doing a big number on her. She would need a spa day with Taylor like she had mentioned when she returned for sure.

"Are you okay?" Georgia asked, pointing to her neck.

"Yeah, just getting old. My neck and shoulders are just cramping up. Why, are you offering to massage me?" she quipped, smirking.

"I'm not that nice!" she laughed. "Actually, I saw a service sign a little while ago. I was going to say, I could do with going to the bathroom, and we could swap. I'll take the wheel and you could chill out for a bit, lay the chair back and sleep. I've had some driving lessons now, I'm a pro, what can I say?" She smiled sincerely.

"You want me to wake Dulcie, and grab a bite for lunch?" Erika asked her.

Georgia was quiet for a few moments. "Look, Erika, I have nieces and nephews, but I see them a couple of times a year, at Christmas and birthdays only. I don't really interact…well, with anyone actually, I just work. But least not with kids. So asking me questions like that, is almost like asking me to order a burger in Russian. I don't know? I'm assuming your daughter has routines, so if you need to wake her to eat so she sleeps tonight or doesn't miss her feeding time, etc. Sorry, that really made her sound like an animal." She grinned. "Clearly, as you can see I'm not very good at this. The point I was trying to make is, I'm honestly easy. She's a good kid and very entertaining, and due to her being here, I'm quite happy to be led by you guys. I don't want to upset anyone's routines, so long story short, if you need to wake her to eat then yes. I can eat. I rarely do, but I always can. If not, I will grab some crisps from the store when we stop for the bathroom and we can eat when the little un' wakes up," she said sincerely.

"Georgia?"

"Yes?" she said looking at her.

"While that was kinda nice, bar you referring to my daughter like she was some kind of monkey at the zoo that people come watch at 'feeding times'. Do you always over speak? Is it a British thing? That was so long winded," she said, shaking her head.

Erika pulled into the service station, checking her gas. She looked up at the restaurant chain turning her nose up. "Hey," she whispered. "Let's stop somewhere better when she wakes up, I'm not eating here," she said.

"Ohhh, you're such a snob. Yeah, I'm easy. That's fine, but do you mind if I go first? I'm desperate," she said.

"Sure go. Oh, and Georgia?"

"Yeah?"

"I know you said you don't really do much but work, but if and when you do, you really should stop saying to everybody that you're easy. Guys will take that as the green light over here," she said, smirking.

Georgia went to say something, but stopped. It wasn't really appropriate. She shook her head and grabbed her purse, running across to the toilets.

***

Georgia had been driving for a while, and they were very tedious roads here. Luckily, she had found a great radio station in Erika's car with lots of great old eighties' and nineties' tunes. It was unfortunate that she wasn't able to turn it up loud and sing her heart out. Very difficult, with two snoozers in the car with her. She was humming along to a song quietly, tapping along to the wheel and eating a Twizzler.

"When did you start driving, Georgia? You weren't driving before. Watcha eating? Is that candy? Can I have some please? Can we put Frozen music on please?" she said all in one breath.

Oh shit, Georgia thought to herself. She looked over to Erika, who was sleeping in the chair with her earphones in. *Bollox*, she thought. She didn't know the answer to these questions. Was she allowed sweets? And dear god, she really couldn't cope with anymore Frozen. Erika was right, this kid was obsessed. Okay, she could do this. Maybe? Hopefully. Josh always said that kids were fickle, so maybe that would work.

"Hey, you?" she said, looking into the rear-view mirror. "How was your sleep? You okay? We need to speak quiet, your mummy's asleep," she said. Did you have good dreams?" She wondered if kids her age actually even had dreams.

"Yuh huh. I dreamt that I was a mermaid and swimming with the dolflins?" she said eagerly. "Georgia, can I have some candy please? I'm hungry," she said.

"The '*dolflins*' ehy? Wow, I'd love to swim with them 'dolphins' too," she smirked. "Hey, Dulcie, are you allowed to eat sweets?"

"What's sweets?"

"Candy."

"Yep, my momma lets me eat it when I want to. I love the red pencils, but my favouritist is the blues ones, or the spotty ones that make my tongue feel funny," she said.

Georgia found that hard to believe with how Erika came across. But she seemed to know an awful lot about Twizzlers, so she'd just hope for the best, and handed her one.

"Umm, be careful with how you eat it okay?" she said concerned. Desperately willing Erika to wake up now, in case she had done something wrong.

A new song came on. A song that took her back to her childhood. Late summer evenings playing out late with her brother and sister. Georgia was very reactive to the song, enjoying the reminiscing and dancing along to the sounds.

"Is this your favourite song? What's it called? You dance funny," Dulcie said.

"I don't dance funny, I'm restricted because I'm driving," she said, looking back to her. It's called 'Summer of Sixty-Nine', and it's a great song. It reminds me of being outside late with my brother and sister playing games," she said enthusiastically.

"I wish I had brothers and sisters. I don't got any," she said sadly.

"Well, it's not always great ya know? Plus, you're still only young, maybe you will have some one day."

"I doubt it. My momma moved out. But, we are going to Nonna's house. And there I have lots of cousins; cousins are mommy's brothers' and sisters' children's. I got lots of those, because mommy has lots of brothers and sisters," she said lengthily.

"Right okay," she said concerned by the child's words. No wonder Erika was so stressed. If she's moved out of her house and left her husband she does need this job. Clearly that's why she wanted to move back home. "So, are you excited to go and see your cousins?"

"Yep, my mommy said that I needed to go to Nonna's while she has to work and then I can see all my cousins and then my Nonna too. We can bake cookies and play games. I love my Nonna," she said lovingly.

Georgia couldn't help but be drawn to the little girl. She had barely spent this much time with her own nieces, but Dulcie certainly was entertaining. "Wow, how exciting. I wish I could come do that."

"Well you can. We have enough cookies. My Nonna would let you," she confirmed.

Georgia and Dulcie spent a short while dancing along to the music and eating sweets together, before Erika eventually woke up.

"Hey," Erika said embarrassed. "Sorry, I didn't mean to sleep that long. You should have woken me when she woke up," she said seriously.

"It's fine. We've been getting to know each other, plus your daughter is now fully acquainted with '*real*' music. We've gone back to the eighties' and nineties', haven't we, Dulcie?" Georgia responded.

"Yep. And we've been eating candy too," she said.

"Well, I hope you weren't fibbing to me, when you said you are allowed to eat candy all the time, or you've just totally dobbed me in," Georgia said questioningly.

Dulcie was laughing hysterically, causing a sense of confusion to both Erika and Georgia. "Your daughter is crazy," Georgia told Erika.

"I think that's actually your fault. You have put her in a sugar induced crazy state," Erika said.

"She talks so funny, it just creases me up," Dulcie was laughing loudly, hitting her leg.

Georgia rarely spent time with kids, and she was completely magnetized by her energy and how full of personality she was at such a young age. Georgia couldn't help but laugh at her.

"You know, we've already discussed this? It's not me that speaks funny, it's you," she said.

"Nuh uh, it's totally you. My mommy says grandma's been drinking when she speaks funny."

"Dulcie!" Erika scolded.

"*What* you do?" Dulcie said simply.

Georgia was trying to contain the laugh.

"I'm sorry," she said to Georgia. "Lady, I think you forgot your manners back in Houston. So, you hungry, or you all full up on candy?"

"It's okay. And I can assure you, little one, I have not consumed any wine or beer for… well," she looked at her watch. "Like at least an hour," she smiled goofily to a giggling Dulcie.

"Can I please have some lunch? I'm kinda hungry now."

"No way. Clearly the fifteen Twizzlers didn't fill the gap?" Georgia said, shaking her head. "You have some appetite kiddo."

"She did not have fifteen," Erika said seriously.

"Nooooo. But in my defence, firstly, I have no experience with kids. And secondly, in her words, "Momma lets me eat it all the time". And, to the extent she pretty much named nine different types of the stuff, it was clear she wasn't making it up. But apologies if I gave it to her before lunch. Alex would have battered me if I'd done that, but I didn't want to wake you," Georgia said.

Erika went to say something but stopped herself. "Oh, she knows about candy alright, it's fine. Come off at the next turn and we will find somewhere in the next town, rather than eating in some service dive. I'll enter it into the navigation system and it can direct us someplace," she instructed Georgia. "So is Alex your brother?" she asked.

Georgia paid attention to the road as she steered off and followed the sat nav in a different direction. "No, my sister. Alexandra." She smiled. "My brother is Josh, Joshua."

Chapter Forty-Six

Georgia pulled the car into a cute little lone restaurant. The car park was full, which always alluded to a decent place in her opinion.

The three of them got seated and ordered food. It was an odd dynamic and an even odder concept for Georgia to understand. It was bizarre to be sat at a table in a restaurant with a five-year-old and her mother whom she barely knew. But equally, Erika and she would have to work quite closely to make this project successful.

"Not really your idea of fun, huh?" Erika asked Georgia, referring to the situation.

"Excuse me? Sorry I was miles away. No, not at all. I was just thinking about a conversation I had with my mum before I left. It wasn't a particularly great situation and this…*this* situation, kinda made me think back to it," she said quietly.

"Look. I know this isn't great for either of us, and I appreciate you're not a 'kid' person. Which when we get to Fort Worth will be fine. But you are all the way over here, and I'm sure, as a mother myself, regardless of whether you have the best or worst relationship with your folks, you shouldn't ignore it. Additionally, regardless of your age, they'll still be worried about you over here alone. Seriously, I know parents can get…somewhat, *'difficult'* when they get older, but it's only because they love you. Take it from someone who knows, if you leave it too late, you have to live with that for the rest of your life," she said sadly.

"Wow. There's a wakeup call if ever there was one," Georgia said. "Thanks, I'm sorry to have made you feel that you needed to say all that. Additionally, I have no issue with this. And I'm guessing you have lost a parent? Sorry, to hear that. And apologies, that's kind of a personal question."

"It's okay. Yes, I did. My father. But how about we change the subject, young ears and such conversations, aren't really the greatest."

Erika and Georgia looked down at the ringing mobile, noticing Julia's name. Georgia said she'd call her back, she didn't think it was right to do that just now.

"If you want to take that, it's fine. I'll ask them to keep your food warm," Erika said.

"Who was that? Why aren't you speaking with them?" Dulcie asked, looking up from her picture.

"Baby, where did you get your nosiness from? You're as bad as your Nonna. Stop asking questions that are none of your little button noses concern," Erika said, tapping her daughter's nose.

"It was my friend from back home. And I'm not speaking to her because unlike you, I didn't eat 37 trillion liquorice's. So actually, I'm quite hungry and looking forward to my lunch," Georgia said, smiling.

"I did not eat 37 trillion, I only had this many," she said, holding up four fingers spread apart widely.

"Do you always talk back this much?" Georgia asked, giggling.

Erika and Dulcie responded in unison, with their varying answers.

The food was brought over to the table and Erika was right, coming off into a town had provided much better food than a petrol station would have ever offered.

Georgia quickly picked up her phone and started a text to Julia to tell her that she would call her back later, she was just in the middle of it when Dulcie grassed on her.

"Ohhh, Mommy, she has her phone out. That's naughty. There aren't no phones allowed at the dinner table," Dulcie said.

Erika looked apologetic, "Hey, Dulcie, those are our rul…" but before she could finish Georgia had already responded.

"I'm very sorry, I didn't know those rules. It's gone, look? No more," she said, putting it into her back pocket and picking up her knife and fork.

Erika leaned over and whispered to her. "You didn't need to do that."

"Look, if you are bringing your child up with manners and discipline, then I am certainly not about to throw a spanner in your works. It's fine. Come on, let's eat. It looks delicious."

***

They finished their food, all suitably impressed and stuffed, and made their way back to the car to get on their way again.

Dulcie was in the car for a maximum of two minutes before she was already asking to put Frozen back on again. "Baby, I told you, we are not going to listen the whole way. Georgia doesn't want to listen anymore."

Dulcie was visibly upset, her little lip coming out. Georgia turned around to look at her properly, "I thought you and I were going to dance now that mummy is driving? We have to have the music up really loud and dance together," she said seriously.

"But I don't know the music," she sniffed for added effect. God this kid was good.

"You don't need to," Georgia said back to her, finding the station she was listening to before and turning it up loud. The next song came on and Erika was laughing, "I love this song," she said.

"I know! So, this is an amazing song called 'Nothings Gonna Stop Us Now'. And this is brilliant," Georgia said, dancing animatedly in her seat, making Dulcie and Erika laugh, before Dulcie followed suit.

Erika was impressed that this woman who was so completely, *not* 'kid friendly' and didn't appear to seem or want to be personable initially, would be so impressionable on her daughter. She was glad. Dulcie had so much instability in her life now and she didn't want any more upheaval for her.

Georgia and Dulcie spent a solid twenty minutes dancing and singing at the top of their voices, before the station changed and the news came on. It literally took a matter of seconds before Dulcie was on the case to put her Frozen CD back on again.

"Shall we play a game instead?" Georgia said, turning around in her seat.

"Yes, I love games. What shall we play? What games do you play in the car? We usually play I spy," she said excitably.

"Well, I rarely go in a car. But when I do, we play 'mini, no returns'. I don't think we can play that here," she said, smiling to herself.

"What's that?" she asked inquisitively.

"Not something we can play over here. I haven't seen one mini since driving, and the cars are all humongous." She smiled to the little girl. "I'll tell you some other time.

Hmm, let me think. I have a good game, how about you pay me money every time you make me listen to Frozen?" she laughed. "I think that's a good one to start," she winked, laughing to Dulcie.

"No way, I'm not playing that game," she said sternly.

Georgia was laughing. "Ok, do you get pocket money?" she asked.

Erika looked at Georgia seriously. "Please tell me you aren't about to teach my daughter to gamble."

"Nahhhh, I'll save that for tonight," she laughed, raising her eyebrows to Erika.

"Uh huh? Why? I'm not giving it to you though! And I'm not gonna give you money just to listen to my favourite song," she said pointedly.

Georgia laughed at her. "Oh okay, my bad. Right, ok, so how much?"

"How much what?"

"How much pocket money do you get?" She needed to think on her feet, she had no idea what game she was going to play.

"Watcha mean? All my money goes in my pockets," she said seriously.

Erika laughed at her daughter's innocence, "She calls it an allowance, not pocket money," she said to Georgia.

"Oooh, right. Okay that makes more sense. She is *too* funny."

"Okay, Dulcie, how much allowance do you get?"

"I get one dollar a week, but my friends get more, though," she said defiantly.

"Well, I'm sure if you helped your parents you could earn some. You don't just *get* money. You have to earn it. We had to. I'm sure if you did some housework for your mum, like help wash up, or tidy away your toys and clothes you could earn some more."

"See, I told you," Erika said, looking at her daughter in the mirror. "If you do some chores you can get more."

"But the other kids don't gotta," she said triumphantly. "My mommy says if I do a couple chores around the house each week, I can get extra bucks, but my friends don't. We're just kids," she said, crossing her arms across her chest.

Georgia had to turn back around in her seat to stop Dulcie from seeing her laughing, because the personality on this little girl was incredible. She loved her nieces and nephews, but she couldn't remember any of them being this way. Maybe if she spent more time with them she would realise they were.

"Cut it out," Erika told Georgia, shaking her head.

Georgia turned back around to Dulcie, "But I bet they grow up and have to marry rich guys to buy them all the things they want. If you work hard you can be just like your mum and you won't need a guy to do that. I know what I would prefer. I don't want no man having to pay for me, I want to go out and buy it all myself."

"What you mean, like an Elsa?"

Georgia looked over to Erika confused.

"Well I think that's maybe a different conversation for your mummy to have with you when you get older, but why not? Dream big kid," Georgia said.

"Really? *Really*?" Erika said aghast. "So you teach my daughter it's okay to buy women by day and gamble at night? Sheesh, my kids gonna learn all sorts of bad habits from you," she said, shaking her head.

"What? She won't remember that they'll be something new and better for her to use her one dollar a week on,"

Georgia smirked. She stopped herself from making any remark about 'buying women'. It was certainly not good with a child listening and was inappropriate. Especially because they have had a mere twenty minutes only being nice and having a laugh together, she thought.

Erika laughed. "You have *no* idea," she said, laughing. Shaking her head at Georgia's innocence on not realising that kids will take everything literally, "You really need to watch what you say to a five-year-old," she said questioningly. "Just saying!"

"What? She could buy a lot worse. Okay, I'm kidding," she said, holding her hands up in mock defence. "I think you are having a different conversation than your daughter and I are having. You're okay, you don't have nowt to worry about," she said simply.

"Nowt? What the heck is '*nowt*'"? she said, pulling a face.

"Nothing, it means nothing. You have 'nowt' or 'nothing' to worry about. Okay, let's just get Frozen back on," she said in defeat, smiling over to Dulcie and rolling her eyes.

Chapter Forty-Seven

They arrived at the hotel at a little after two thirty, which was good going, considering they had stopped a couple of times. It looked like a nice place to stay, and Erika was overly relieved and impressed that it had a pool and spa facilities, which meant that both her and Dulcie could be entertained through the week. She most definitely needed to get a day in the spa, thinking she could get her mom to look after her, for sure.

They checked in and were issued room keys and directions to their rooms. They had been booked interconnecting rooms, which Erika was not happy about. All she needed was Dulcie thinking it was okay to just wander into Georgia's room when she felt like it, but she could keep that locked. Georgia didn't seem concerned, unless she was just very good at not showing her pain.

Each woman went into their respective rooms. Erika figured she would leave Georgia alone, since she had spent the last five hours with her daughter. If her friends and family were anything to go by, she would now be going to bed with a couple Tylenol and maybe a very large bottle of wine.

Georgia unpacked her case and hung up everything, annoyed she didn't bring her bikini. She could have got up and enjoyed the pool and spa every morning before work. She would have loved to have done that. Picking up her phone, she Googled to see where the nearest shop was that would sell them. A big Debenhams or John Lewis type store or a sports shop would suffice.

Georgia found what she needed and could get there by foot. It was still early, and she didn't want to just sit in a room and do nothing for the next three hours. She went to the interconnecting room and didn't know whether to knock on that or whether to go to the main door. She leaned her head against it listening…to what exactly, she didn't know. "Well that aint weird at all, you freak," she mumbled to herself, as she listened to Dulcie chattering away in the room. She knocked quietly on the interconnecting door, and within a few seconds Erika stood there with the door open, a frown on her face. Dulcie rushed to her side, stupefied by the door and Georgia. That was it, she was in and going through Georgia's room.

"Erm, I'm sorry I didn't know whether to knock, apologies," Georgia said embarrassed.

"Don't apologise to me, I was just trying to avoid this," she said, pointing to her daughter and the distance between the doors. "Good luck is all I can say to you; I am taking absolutely no responsibility for this. Even if she is my kid," she said, shaking her head.

"It's fine," Georgia said. "I just wondered if you wanted anything from the shops, or if you wanna come. I don't know if Dulcie has a sleep or what?"

"Shops? Why? Where *are,* you going?" Erika asked inquisitively.

"Just to a couple of shops. I want a bikini. I want a swim and sauna, and it means I can enjoy the pool each morning before I go to work," she said enthusiastically.

"Yayyyyyy, I wanna go swimming with Georgia," Dulcie was saying excitably, coming over to the women. "Can we, Mommy? Puhleeeaaaasssseee?"

Georgia was feeling incredibly awkward, looking at Erika, unsure of what to do.

"Now, look what you've started. You are going to have to learn to start speaking quieter through the week. Dulcie, how about you and I go and have a swim now and let Georgia have some time alone? Some grownups need some time out, baby. We may see you as we crossover for a short while," she said with a faint smile.

As they said their goodbyes and returned to their respective rooms with a disappointed Dulcie, Georgia left the hotel in her search for swimwear.

Chapter Forty-Eight

Erika plonked Dulcie watching the TV as she quickly checked in with Taylor.

"Hey? How goes it? How was the ride?" Taylor asked.

"Hi. Yes, it was okay. Dulcie made a new best friend. We got here like thirty minutes ago, and Georgia just knocked and said she was going out to look for a bikini, since the hotel has a sauna and pool and stuff. Lady here heard, and so now we're going to the pool," she sighed lightly.

"Hmm," she laughed.

"Don't hmmm me. We aren't going with her. Dulcie and I are going now, and she's gone out to find a swimsuit first. We need to be getting a grip on the work stuff, but for today she has spent enough time with us."

"Wow, sounds like you have it all figured out."

"Hardly, but it's only a week. Anyhow, I should probably get Dulcie to the pool. I'll check in, in a few days. Lemme know if you find the man of your dreams in the meantime," she laughed as she hung up on Taylor.

***

"Come on, sweetie. Let's go swimming," Erika said, making their way down to the pool.

A short walk later, they had filled a couple of sun loungers with their belongings and made their way to the steps of the indoor pool. Over on the corner of the pool was an attached Jacuzzi. She planned to make use of that and the other facilities when Dulcie was with her mom. She could use it right now. Within seconds Dulcie had jumped in and Erika was apologising to the few guests around, who were looking at her like she had no control over a 'bratty' child. She shook her head to herself, wondering if they should leave already.

"Hey, Dulcie, you gotta be careful okay? People are here to swim. It's not like back home okay?"

"Okay, Mommy," she said politely. "Can I swim up to the top?"

God, she loved her daughter more than anything on this planet, "Sure, sweetie. I'll swim right behind you," Erika said, following her daughter as she swam up to the end of the pool. It was always Dan who had wanted the massive house and a pool. She had lived a somewhat different upbringing to Dan, and while her parents weren't necessarily short of cash, they didn't live in the big fancy houses with pools and stuff. But Dan was adamant, more so for the pool, so that they could teach Dulcie to swim from a young age, which she was now glad for. The child could certainly hold her own in the water. Erika was of course like any parent, maybe overprotective a little, but she didn't like the idea of leaving Dulcie to swim by herself. She was only five, regardless of how well she swam.

They both reached the end of the pool and Dulcie was up wiping her face of the water. "I beat you, Mommy," she said excitably. She certainly was like a fish in water. She adored the water and just hoped that that love would maintain and she didn't end up just being addicted to technology like so many other kids.

"You sure did, baby," she said, noticing the glares of the elderly women and men who were now leaving the pool, and making her feel like it was all her fault for bringing a child there.

"Blimey, who did you annoy?" Erika heard, nearly going under as she turned one eighty to see Georgia standing before her in her new two piece. You could tell she worked out, more importantly you could tell she didn't have any kids. Erika suddenly felt more insecure than ever, rubbing her tummy over her bathing suit. She worked out, always had, and always had taken pride in herself. But this woman had an incredible physique, and height that only accentuated it.

"Georgia, you came. Are you coming in? It's real nice. I just beat mommy at a swimming race. You wanna race me?"

"Okay, okay, one question at a time. Do all kids do this, or is it just you that's mastered the art of asking seventy-four questions in one breath?" she said, sitting down on the side of the pool next to Dulcie.

"All kids, but she is particularly good at it. Baby, how about you give Georgia a moment to settle in. Why don't you show her how you swim?" Erika said, trying to get Dulcie to give Georgia some breathing space.

"Okay, watch me, Georgia?"

"I'm watching, kiddo," she said, laughing at the little girl.

"I'm sorry about this. If it's any consolation, she's very fickle, and you'll be forgotten about when Frozen gets mentioned or some toys and stuff," Erika said, without even looking up as she watched her daughter.

"Nothing to apologise for. It's all a bit strange, but I'm not going to lie, I'm not used to this. I suppose none of this is normal, so I may as well make the most of it, for the next nine months. So, what was the crack with the golden oldies? Geez, if looks could kill, you'd be dead several times over," Georgia laughed.

"Nine months?"

"Yeah. I figured, if we are as amazing as what they both keep alluding to, then we'll have this done and dusted in nine months."

"Ahhhh, right, good way of thinking!" she said. "Ummm, yeah, I guess they don't like kids so much. Apparently, I wrecked their world by bringing a child into a communal pool," she sighed, shaking her head.

Georgia checked that Dulcie couldn't hear. "Bollox to em. They can deal with it. I wish I had been here, I would have done my very best, 'new swimmer' swim, to piss them off even more," she said, lowering herself into the water.

Erika couldn't help but notice her muscular arms and core. Jesus, she was in good shape, making Erika feel insecure all over again. "You're what?" she said, laughing.

"My 'new swimmer' swim," she reiterated. "Watch," she laughed, before engaging Dulcie in a race and proceeded to swim with all arms and legs flailing and splashing about into the water, making more water come out of the pool than was staying in. Erika couldn't control the fits of laughter as she watched her daughter, confused by the comical scene going on around her.

Chapter Forty-Nine

They spent over an hour in the pool. Georgia was even kind enough to entertain Dulcie for a while to allow Erika to enjoy some time in the Jacuzzi, which was incredibly peaceful. As she enjoyed that time, Georgia and Dulcie sat at the edge of the Jacuzzi and were talking over the separator to her.

Dulcie had always been full of personality and very outgoing, so it was no surprise that she'd found a new best friend in Georgia and wanted to spend as much time as possible with her. Which was fine for Georgia, but was making Erika feel increasingly more uncomfortable. A week ago, this woman was about to leave the country on the basis that Erika was making her feel *bullied*. Now, she was probably thinking what a useless mom she was and pissed that there was a five-year-old on a week-long work trip. A five-year-old who was now imposing on her perfect, little, single life. She was probably hoping that both Erika and Dulcie would shove off so she could enjoy some swim, spa and Jacuzzi time, then go out and hit the town.

Fort Worth was kind of a decent place to hang out. She would be able to meet people, and if she hit up a couple bars or clubs, she'd get plenty of attention and could get almost a free night out. Instead, her five-year-old daughter was making plans for every minute of every day, resulting in her having to keep reigning Dulcie in.

They walked up to their rooms together and Dulcie was hyperactively filling them in on her favourite parts of the 'pool fun' today.

"Do you actually ever come up for air, missy?" Georgia asked, laughing at Dulcie. "So, do you want to eat together tonight? If you don't want to or have plans then that's fine, I thought I should ask."

Erika was taken aback by the question. "I don't want you to feel like you have to spend every second with us, Georgia. If you would rather go out and enjoy the sights, Fort Worth is pretty awesome. They have Sundance square with some pretty cool restaurants and bars," Erika said.

"To be honest, I'm not too fussed on going out, it's not really my thing. I very much tend to steer away from stuff like that. However, if you would prefer some time to yourselves, I get that," Georgia said quietly as they arrived at Erika's room.

"No, not at all. I figured you would just want some peace and quiet. If you're sure, and you don't mind an early dinner, we could head over there now and grab a bite, so you can at least say you've seen it. I'll drive so you can have a drink, but I kind of need to go fairly soon-ish to get Dulcie to bed on time."

"Excellent, that's a plan Stan."

"Mommy, who's Stan?" Dulcie said, suddenly aware of what was going on.

"I'm Stan," Georgia said.

"No, you're Georgia," she giggled.

Georgia laughed at Dulcie, "Ok, how long will it take you two to get ready? And I'll knock on," she continued.

They agreed to meet in half an hour. Georgia got into her room and put the radio on through the TV, dancing around the room enjoying the music as she got ready. She couldn't help but think about how surreal the situation was. She could have been, she *should* have been at home now, in her own apartment, possibly without a job. But here she was in a hotel in Texas, with the woman who contributed to making her life difficult, plus her daughter, getting ready to go out for dinner with them. She didn't do kids, nor going out, and yet here she was. It was random and she picked up her phone and text her mum to let her know she was ok and things were improving slightly. Georgia knew her mum would be keeping Alexandra and Joshua in the loop, too. After styling her hair and doing her makeup, she searched for something to wear. Unsure of what type of clothes she should be wearing, she figured if a five-year-old was going with them then it wouldn't be anything too smart, so she decided on a casual look.

A short while later, Georgia had opted for some heeled sandals, black jeans and a sleeveless coral and grey blouse with buttons down the back, which stopped half way down, allowing visibility of her lower back. It was one of her favourite tops, and luckily the weather in Texas allowed for it. Georgia was messing with her hair and clothes, unsure why she was so bothered about what she looked like. It's not like she was going to a gay bar or something, but equally, she didn't know that there wouldn't be a gorgeous waitress or customer nearby. She heard the soft knock at the door, and assumed it was Dulcie. Spraying perfume on herself, she made her way over to the door and opened it up to the sweet little girl. "Hey up, kiddo. You're looking beautiful," Georgia said to Dulcie, who had a little pair of sandals on and a cute little dress with a cardi over the top.

"Thank you, you look very pretty," she said coyly. "Look, you got shoes like mine," she said more enthusiastically.

"So, I do." She smiled.

"Sorry about the little lady, she was being too impatient," Georgia heard from inside the room. She stepped in, following the voice. "Hey, no worries, I was just faffing anyway," she said as she spotted Erika at the mirror. She took another glance and shook her thoughts away. She was wearing heels and a wraparound lime dress that accentuated her dark skin tone and defined body. Given the fact this woman had had a baby, you certainly wouldn't have ever known from looking at her.

Erika smirked at Georgia's words, making fun of more sayings that nobody had ever heard of before.

"So, you ready?" Erika asked her.

"Sure am," she said, grabbing her bag and locking the door behind them.

Chapter Fifty

"You're right, this place is stunning," Georgia said, animatedly taking it in.

"Very easily pleased, huh?"

"No, not at all. Well maybe, but this is amazing," she responded.

"Sorry, I didn't mean to poke fun at you. I guess it's just difficult for me, because I grew up close by, so I'm used to these types of areas. Although, it has evolved incredibly now though."

"Yeah, I bet. Look, thanks for this. I'm sorry I keep crashing time with you guys, I guess it must be pretty important right now, so I really appreciate it."

"You've gotta be kidding, I love my daughter more than anything, but a week with no adults is a bit of a killer. I'm completely grateful, and you may just become my sanity."

Georgia was laughing as she drank some of her speciality cocktail. "God, you can tell you don't know me. I can assure you, I'm nothing close to sane," she said.

"Georgia, what does sane mean?" Dulcie asked.

"It means you're not crazy," Georgia said simply.

"So, you're not crazy?"

"Nooooo, I'm very, very crazy," she said, shaking her head energetically in front of Dulcie, causing her to laugh uncontrollably.

"Hmmm, yes I see your point," Erika stated, as she moved her arms out of the way so the server could put the food down.

The conversation was limited throughout the dinner, aside from the numerous appreciative grumbles. Erika was right, this place was gorgeous. She felt like she was on holiday. The smells of food wafting through the street, the outside seating, the sun still burning through, the flow of cocktails and alcohol amongst other things. It was actually her best night here, even topping the nights that Emily and John had given her. The extraordinary thing was she didn't expect that a night with her arch nemesis and a child was partially the reason for it.

Chapter Fifty-One

"Do you want to come in and play a game or watch Frozen with me?" Dulcie asked.

"Baby, ya know how I explained before about this not being a vacation? Georgia is not here to be with you and I, okay? We just need to remember that. Tomorrow you're going to Nonna's and we must work," Erika explained softly.

"So, I don't get to see her no more?" she said sadly.

"Baby..." Before Erika had a chance to speak, Georgia was kneeling beside the little girl.

"Hey, come on. We are gonna see each other again and get to play in the pool another time before we leave. We will make sure we have a little bit more fun. But your mum's right, it's late now, we all need to go to bed. I'm completely wrecked because you've worn me out," she said face to face with the little girl. "Is that okay?"

"Okay, I guess," she said quietly.

"You sleep well okay? And dream big, kiddo," she said, looking down at her.

"Goodnight, Georgia," she said, grabbing her mom's hand.

***

Georgia got changed into some trackie bottoms and a hoodie. It was far from cold, but it had always been one of her favourite things to do, lounging in comfies. She logged on to her computer, suddenly engaging with the relaxing flow of alcohol through her body. Wanting more, she got back up and grabbed her purse and room key. Unsure of whether to ask Erika, Georgia waited outside the woman's door, debating whether she should stop and ask if she wanted anything. Obviously, Dulcie would be in bed now, which would mean she couldn't get out. Georgia recalled the comments about her insinuating she was some kind of drunk and decided against it.

Georgia was pretty sure the bar staff must have thought she was having a party, by what she had bought. She had no intention of drinking them all, but she was a creature of variety.

Getting comfortable with a glass of red wine and the TV on in the background, she sent a couple of emails back home and continued with some work. It had been a weird couple of weeks, and she had never done so little. Jesus, even when she went on holiday she felt like she did more work than what she was doing now. Either way, things were moving in the right direction now and ultimately, she needed to get on top of stuff again, or she really would end up out the door. Maybe that was Erika's plan. Maybe she was pretending to be nice in a bid to set her up royally? *That was unfair,* she thought to herself, but she couldn't help having her guard up, especially after her arrival. She was dreading going back into the office. Nobody knew what had happened, and that was how the four Directors decided to play it. Just leave them all guessing and then when Erika and Georgia returned they would stand united as the two levelled bosses. She sighed inwardly at the thought of going through that hell all over again.

Georgia heard a faint knock on her interconnecting door. Moving closer she listened before opening it and was faced with Erika, still in the clothes from dinner that evening.

"Wow, you didn't take long," Erika said, pointing down.

Here we go again she thought, lifting the glass of wine up, "Well, you've already accused me of being a drunk, so why disappoint?" she said with an edge to it.

Erika shook her head. "No, the clothes. We didn't even get back an hour ago, and already you are in slacks."

"Oh? *OH*, right sorry," she said apologetically. "Yeah, it's pretty much my favourite pastime.

"*Really?* That surprises me," she said. "Um, sorry to interrupt, I have just been getting several emails from you, so figured you were working…and well, I wondered if you needed a hand? Or wanted to focus on something together? I mean, if you don't want to, I get that," she said.

"Why are you surprised that I like my comfies? I have no issue, but I figured you would want some peace and quiet. I'm guessing Dulcie is asleep, so I didn't want to disturb you. I assumed you would want some…*you* time?"

"Nope. She's sleeping, so I was also going to do some work. Honestly, I don't know what else to do with myself when Dulcie goes to sleep. So, I predominantly just work, more so these days," she said.

Georgia didn't want to pry, so she pointed in to the room to come in. "Would you like a drink? I have red, white, rose or beer. I guess it's the least I can do, as you were the designated driver, allowing me to drink," she said.

"You're really going all out on proving you have a drink problem, huh?" she laughed. "I would love some blush," she said.

"Come again? Some what?"

"Blush? The pink one? Unless you don't wanna open that, I can grab a beer, or the red, whatever."

"Bloody hell, are you always this indecisive? Rose for you," she smirked.

"Thanks. And no, not normally. Just recently, I guess," she said curtly. "And, further to earlier comments, I just think you look like someone that would not dare be in clothing like that, let alone be seen in it. I guess you look incredibly put together each time I've seen you, not like a mom at all." She smiled. "And apologies, if any part of that sounds like an insult, it genuinely wasn't meant to."

Georgia laughed, shaking her head at Erika, "Just comes so naturally ehy? Joke. So, you're calling me a chav?"

"Excuse me? A what?" she said confused.

"A chav? Someone that looks like…a scruff? A chav? It's a British word, clearly. Wearing skanky clothes, fake designer brands and just looks, hmmm how do I put this? Well I guess a bit 'yucky,'" she laughed.

"I did not say you looked like a *chav*, but oh my gosh, I have literally heard a multitude of words that I have never heard in my life just then. The only insult that could have been formed from what I said was that you were too perfectly put together. Not a hair out of place, not a mark on your clothing, even after 15 hours of travelling in white jeans." She pointed out.

"Ahhhh, right! Okay, I've been told that before, so I'll take that on the chin, but no, you are completely wrong. If I finish work early, I love getting into comfies. And to be fair, even weekends are spent with mornings in the gym and afternoons in my comfies, working or watching TV," she said seriously.

"Well as I said, I stand corrected. Cheers?" Erika said cautiously.

Chapter Fifty-Two

"Oh, my God, that was mind blowing. Dontcha think?" Erika asked as they walked back to the car. They had spent the last 3 hours doing a presentation to the investors for the new site. They had gotten so much done the night before, and seemingly worked incredibly well together. Especially after a few bottles of wine, but they had paid for that today.

"It actually really was. I thought we had screwed it majorly when we started, but we nailed it. We actually just went in and smashed the arse off it," Georgia said.

"That we did. Listen, how about I call mom and ask her to take Dulcie for the night? I kind of owe you a big ass drink."

"Seriously, we pulled it off together. This wasn't you *or* me, this was *us,* okay? You really don't need to buy me a beer."

"Well, what if I wanna?" she said, immediately regretting the words. She sounded like some desperate kid begging for a friend at recess.

"Well, how about you don't buy me a drink, because I haven't earned you *buying* me a drink. But *we* deserve a drink after that. If you are okay with not seeing Dulcie tonight, then yes of course, I'd love to."

"Okay, well I'm down with that," she said excitably, with the adrenaline running through her veins.

***

Georgia checked the time and said goodbye to her sister, ignoring her jibes and equal concern. It was six o'clock, the time they'd arranged to leave. She knocked on the interconnecting door whilst she was looking through the emails on her phone. Erika opened the door.

"Hey, you good to go?" Erika said to Georgia.

"Ye…" Georgia stopped as she looked up to Erika. "Wow, you're going all out."

"What do you mean?" Erika said, looking down at herself, feeling diffident.

"Erika, calm down. You look incredible. I feel suitably underdressed is what I meant. I wasn't looking to offend, on the contrary, I was just merely looking to compliment." This woman was stunning and even more so now. Wearing her long black hair down and straightened, heels, ripped jeans which she wore incredibly well and a black chiffon halter neck with a long silver dress necklace and matching earrings. And yet, she was the most insecure person Georgia had ever met.

Erika didn't know how to react, because she couldn't remember the last time she had received a compliment. Well, least not personally as opposed to professionally anyhow. And now she was completely thankful that she'd made a point of arranging to go out for a drink. Erika didn't go out, since she was either at work or at home with Dulcie. So actually, having a night out where she could try and spend a normal evening with someone out drinking, dancing maybe, and getting just one night off was awesome. She loved her life and her daughter and wouldn't change it for the world. But after the last couple months and the adrenaline rush filled day they'd shared; she was completely ready for this. "Well thanks, I guess. You look good, too. Come on, let's head on out," she said.

***

Erika and Georgia had spent a long time talking about the day's events. The more drink they consumed, the more excitable they both got about the success of the presentation.

"You wanna get some food? We could get some bar snacks. I think I may end up in bed crying tomorrow if I don't eat with all this drink," Erika said into her glass.

"*Why*? Are you *okay*? We can go home if you like," Georgia said seriously.

"Hell no…I'm loving this, I don't ever do this. I can cuss, openly. I can openly cuss. Fuck, fuck, fuck, balls, dickhead. Okay, that's not really as much fun as I expected it would be," she smirked. "But the point is," she said, pointing to her British colleague. "I'm actually kind of liking just being a normal thirty-eight-year-old woman for a moment."

"What do you mean? Do you regret having kids?"

"Hell no. No, I love my daughter more than anything. But for just one night, I can go out and get drunk with someone my own age, who has no links to me in that life. I can drink away the stress of the *job* situation, the *home* situation, of everything. Ya know? Just one night, to be normal and not the woman that lays awake all night wondering about the impact of my troubled marriage, and what it is going to have on my daughter. The potential damage it will do if I leave Houston and move back home. Taking Dulcie away from her family. *Sheesh,* having to tell them that. Being a divorced woman. Losing my job. What will I do? Can I do anything else? Do I wanna do anything else? So yeah, for tonight I just totally wanna forget it all, and be a normal woman on a girl's night out," she said soberly.

"*Wow,* I didn't see that one coming," she said, concerned. "Look…"

"*Don't*, George. Please don't. I'm sorry I darkened it. That wasn't my intention. The point is, that's exactly what's going on outside of here…*now*…anyways. So yeah, just for one little night, I want my stress to be that I'm dancing like an idiot, or that I'm mixing my drinks, or…*or* whatever, but just none of that stuff, okay?"

"Okay. But then I say we need shots." She smiled widely.

"Oh, I can't do shots."

"Nobody can do shots. Unless their 18 years old. That's the point. I'll get some bar snacks too," she said.

"Hey, cool accent you got there."

Georgia and Erika looked around to see the guy standing next to them, directing the statement to Georgia.

"Ummm, thanks,"

"I'm Mark, can I buy you a drink?"

"Wow, just like that? You guys are fast workers," Georgia smirked over to him.

"Life's too short to not take risks."

"This is true." She looked back to Erika who was grinning at her.

"So, what can I get you?" he said again.

"Ummm, actually, I'm okay thanks. I'm here with my friend so thanks, but no thanks."

"Come on, I'll buy you both a drink, it's no biggie. Lemme buy you a drink? It's not every day a guy gets to buy a beautiful British woman a drink," he said, giving his best *winning* smile.

"Well, I don't really think it's fair to waste your time, because I'm not interested. So, I'm going to respectfully decline your offer," she said again.

"Come on, one drink? Get to know me? You may just learn to love me, and we can ride off into the sunset together," he said, rolling his arm out in the distance for extra effect.

"Mark, you seem lovely and I'm sure there's a load of women that are queuing up to meet you and *'ride off into the sunset with you'*. But really, this is never going to happen, you are *really* not my type."

"Well, try something different for once. Variety is the spice of life and all that." He winked.

"Listen, if it was a case of I go for blondes and not brunettes, yeah I'd totally give it a go. If not for anything else, because of the fact you're so committed. Unfortunately, you are *too* much variety, so much variety that I left that variety back in the nineties," she said openly.

"Huh?" he said confused. "Oh, *oh!* Shit man, you're gay?" he said, clearly disappointed.

Erika choked on her drink, causing them both to look around "Apologies, an ice slipped down the back of my throat," she said, cringing.

"Ding ding ding, jackpot." She winked.

"Damn man, what a waste," he said, whistling loudly.

"Well, I'll maybe have to call a few women and find out about that. I've not had any complaints historically though," she responded sharply.

"Good comeback. I'm sorry, you are super cute. Hey, can I buy *you* a drink?" he said, leaning over and looking at Erika.

"Dude, you just hit on my friend. You really think I need some guy to buy me a drink that is evidently marking me as second best? Come *on,* man," Erika said, shaking her head. She really didn't need this now. She felt good when she came out, and she thought she looked pretty good too. And clearly, she wasn't worth a second glance. She couldn't blame him; Georgia was very attractive. She had the cool accent, *and* the confidence. She could just hear her mom now, telling her that if she feels and acts negative then that will pour out of her and that's why people will be apprehensive around her. It didn't matter though, she had no control over the negativity surrounding her now.

"Story of my life, man. Seriously, I come into a bar with the two hottest women I've seen in a while, and I hit on the gay one. This is Soooo not good for my rep," he said, shaking his head, smiling. "Yo, Frankie, give these two beautiful women whatever they want on me. Y'all have a wonderful evening ladies, it was nice speaking with you," he said and left them to it.

"Are you ok?" Georgia said to Erika, noticing a sudden change in her.

"Yeah fine. So, what shall we have on that douchebag?" she said without looking at her, and trying to change the subject.

Georgia didn't want to press Erika. She may have just drank too much, but additionally, it could be the whole gay thing. She ordered them both a couple more drinks and some shots and decided to leave it. She'd dealt with it before; it was a way of life now.

***

They had been in three different bars and had been out drinking for over five hours. They were both wasted, and work would not be productive tomorrow morning by any means. Erika seemed to pick up a little bit more, which relaxed Georgia a bit. Having to work so closely with someone who had an issue with her sexuality would have been difficult for sure, because it bared no relevance on the job she did.

"So, do you like dancing?"

"Ummm, I'm not really much into it if I'm being honest. I'm more of an observer."

"Oh right," Erika said quietly.

"Can I ask you something personal?"

"Sure, go ahead," Erika said, looking at her concerned.

"What's going on? You got weird and quiet with me earlier around the time I'd said I was gay. You did it when you asked to go out for a drink, and now with the dancing? Do you have an issue with me still? I thought we were over that," she said.

Erika shook her head "Ya know, I used to be…*so*," she leaned her head back and looked up to the ceiling. "I used to be so normal. I was confident, I was happy, outgoing, and now I've just become this shell of a person I used to be. Honestly, I dunno what's happened. I just feel so incredibly insecure and crappy about everything. I'm sorry, you must think I'm bat-shit crazy. I just feel pretty shitty, I guess. I just wanted to get made up tonight, make an effort, feel good about myself for a while. But I couldn't even do that right," she said sadly.

"Okay, new rule. No more feeling sorry for yourself, okay? We're going to get you through all this stuff and make you see how incredibly hot and amazing you are," she said. "Come on," Georgia said, grabbing her hand and pulling her up. "Oops," she said, falling backwards.

"What? Where are we going?"

"To dance. You wanted to dance, so dance we shall," she said, smiling and feeling sorry for all the shit Erika was going through right now. Whilst Georgia wasn't over the moon by this situation, in the grand scheme of things she has twelve months of sunshine, a cool house, a cooler car, amazing friends across the road from her *and* a swimming pool. And she had actually built a bridge with the woman that was causing her some big-time issues. So in reality, things weren't as bad as originally thought.

"Yeah, but you don't like it."

"Yeah, because I'm shit at it, and I don't like being shit at things. But I don't care, I'm too drunk, so I'm gonna help you have a good night," she said, walking onto the dance floor and dancing, trying not to think about how out of her comfort zone she actually was.

Erika looked at her intently as they danced freely and animatedly to Wilson Philips, *Hold On*. God knows how they ended up in a bar with this kind of music on, but it was a good place. Very lively, and filled with people of a similar age range to them. One corner had guys playing pool and the other was the makeshift dance floor which was where they were currently residing.

"Why you looking at me like that? You're now making me insecure. I know I'm a shit dancer, but you need to stop making me feel like it," Georgia said loudly into her ear over the music.

"You are not a shit dancer. Why do you keep doing all these nice things for me? What did I ever do to you, other than be a bitch? And you're just making me uncomfortable by being nice. I don't know how to deal with it."

"Fine, I'll be a bitch," she said seriously. "Erika, I can't keep going over this, I'm too old to fuck about holding grudges. We're over it, okay? I'm being nice to you

257

because I like you. And just so you know, just because I'm gay doesn't mean I fancy every pretty girl that comes along. I mean I don't like you in that way, so don't worry. You're amazing at your job, a great mum, funny, have great taste in music, and I'm kind of liking being up here. And well, in fact, the states. *Who knew*? But, as you are aware, initially I wasn't."

"Oh, don't worry. I know you don't fancy me," she said quietly. "Come on, let's go back, I'm done with dancing."

"Seriously, stop with this self-loathing bullshit," she shouted at Erika, causing her to stop and take stock. "Come on, this is horrendous. You are bloody gorgeous, so I don't know what or where you're looking in the mornings getting ready, but it clearly isn't a mirror. Your husband is an idiot, end of. And a prick if he's made you think this lowly of yourself. And FYI, if things weren't the way they were and you weren't straight, I'd totally fancy you. And yeah, I'm drunk. But equally, I'm not blind, nor am I stupid," she snapped. "You looked beautiful when you opened the door tonight, and completely caught me off guard. Don't let anyone do this to you, but certainly not the person that should be the one making you feel like you're the most beautiful woman in the world."

Erika went to say something and stopped herself, knowing she was far too drunk to get into this now. She smiled slightly. "Thanks, that's the first time in a long time someone's said that. And I'm even going to stop my 'self-loathing' self from saying that I don't believe you," she smirked. "Come on, I think I need to go to bed," she said. "Shit, I um didn…"

"Shut up, idiot. I didn't think you were offering," Georgia laughed, linking her arm through Erika's as they began their staggered journey back to the hotel.

***

"Thanks again for tonight, I actually really enjoyed it. And seriously, if any of my family come over don't you dare tell them I danced, I will shoot you," Georgia said, smiling to Erika, who was leaning against her door, looking very drunk. "A*nd* I can do that. We're in Texas, the all singing, all dancing, gun slinging state," she said, movingly pointing to Erika.

"Only family? Not your girlfriend?" she asked seriously.

"I'm single, I don't have a girlfriend," she said seriously.

"Oh, it's just you said that you did to Mike and Derek when we had that first meeting at the restaurant."

"No, I said I was seeing someone. It was an exaggeration of course, due to the situation. But no, I was just, well, you know. We just had a little bit of fun for a very, *very* short time, when this all happened. And I mean like a couple of weeks, short time. I don't know why I'm feeling the need to over explain this," Georgia confirmed.

"Ahhhh, I see. Well you have yourself a good night's sleep, lady. Thank you again," she said, opening her door.

"No, no, no, don't do that. Don't '*ahhhh I see*' me. You don't see. You think because I'm a forty-year-old, single, lesbian I just slag it about, and I don't. I don't know if something would have come of it had I not came over here as I said it was about two weeks, but equally I hadn't even so much as kissed a woman since my last relationship

259

which ended three years ago. So please don't assume," she said seriously. Georgia was drunk and she probably shouldn't have jumped on Erika like this, but she had a real issue with the whole stereotypical gay thing. You *have* to fancy every woman because she's a woman; you're a slag; you're out to change every straight woman. It annoyed the hell out of her.

"Okay, already. I was only busting your chops. Interestingly; I didn't get that impression at all. You don't seem like the type of woman to just 'fuck em and fuck off,'" Erika said, looking at her intently.

Georgia suddenly couldn't control herself and knew she needed to go. "Right, I...I," she coughed lightly, "I should go...to bed," she finished quietly, pointing her way to her bedroom.

"I guess if that's what you need to do, then that's what you need to do," she said confidently, with those big brown eyes on Georgia's.

"You need to stop looking at me with those eyes that way," she said, still standing in front of her.

"I don't know what you mean," she said, feeling the nerves rising in her tummy. She couldn't believe she was doing this. *Her*? Doing this?

"You know full well what I mean, stop it. You need to go inside, it's late," Georgia confirmed.

"I'm fully aware what time it is. I learned how to tell the time a long ass time ago. I'll go inside in a moment, but you said you were going, and yet you're still standing here, so I'm kind of just trying to work out what the reason is for," she questioned.

"For someone that's so insecure, you get awfully confident when you've had a drink," Georgia said, returning the deep glare.

"I have no idea what you mean. I'm just merely waiting to make sure you get home okay. I'm a mom, I have that deep rooted, caring streak," she smirked.

"You think you're really clever, don't you?"

"Once again, I don't know what you mean, Ms. Carson," she smirked.

"Okay, okay. Well, I should leave before we do something we regret whilst we are both heavily intoxicated?" Georgia said more as a question.

"If that's what you want."

"I think you know the answer to that. But I'm losing self-control whilst I'm this drunk, and we both know this will be a bad idea."

"I don't know the answer to anything. I was just hoping you'd kiss me already," Erika confirmed.

Georgia choked a little, completely stunned by the words. "Wow, you guys are forward when intoxicated," she said, suddenly very aware and nervous of what to do next. Truth be known, she was desperate to kiss her. She had been since she'd opened the door tonight in that outfit. She took a step forward maintaining eye contact. "You know when you act all confident and shit, you're ten times hotter than you already are?"

"I didn't, but thanks, I guess," she said quietly.

"You're gonna regret this in the morning," Georgia said, closing the gap between them.

"Maybe I will, maybe I won't. But I guess you will, too," she said confidently.

"I'm a lesbian, about to kiss a beautiful woman, I'm pretty sure I won't," she smirked.

"Do you always talk this much when you're about to make out?"

"I was just making sure you had an opportunity to bail should you wish, but since you keep throwing shit back at me, well, you're out of time," she said, putting her hand on Erika's back. Georgia gasped as she recalled the lack of material at the back of her top. Georgia put her other hand on her cheek and laced her fingers through her thick, silky hair. She looked down at Erika's glistening lips. *This is so wrong,* was all she kept thinking, but genuinely, she was way too drunk to have any kind of control over herself right now. Georgia closed the gap entirely, placing her lips on Erika's, pushing her against the door, as she deepened the kiss.

Erika couldn't remember the last time she had kissed someone with such passion and vigour, it was like a drug that she couldn't get enough of.

Georgia's concerns went out the window as soon as she felt Erika relax into the kiss, god she was hot, and a bloody good kisser, so she had no control over it. Their tongues exploring, dancing, becoming versed together.

Erika wrapped her arms around Georgia's neck, pulling her closer into the kiss and biting her lower lip just ever so slightly. Suddenly it was too much for Georgia, her knees felt as though they were about to buckle, and she had no option but to cut the kiss short, breathing far too deeply.

Erika looked shocked and disappointed. "Hey…err…um…sorry, I'm sorry about that, I shouldn't have done that. I said you'd regret it." She felt completely exposed at this moment and reached for the door.

"Hey, hey, stop? Please, stop?" Georgia said, suddenly feeling very sober. "Listen, I don't regret that at all, and I'll put all the money in the world on the fact that I won't tomorrow either, okay? I'm not saying I won't be suffering from a bout of 'teenage awkwardness,' but I won't regret it.

I stopped because I have had too much to drink to be able to control myself. I want nothing more than to walk in there right now and finish what we started. Seriously, Erika. You have *no* idea how much I want that. But, you have too much going on and I can't do that to you. And that isn't a cop out, *at* all. Just so you know. But I'm pretty sure if I continue this kiss I'm not going to be held accountable for my actions," Georgia said seriously. "Don't doubt your self-worth, because my word you're gorgeous," she said, walking away and slowly releasing Erika's hand from her own.

Chapter Fifty-Three

Erika walked into her room feeling embarrassed and suddenly very sober. Georgia was right, that she'd regret it. Checking the interconnecting, she slowly lowered herself down the door, pulling her knees up to her chest and resting her head in her hands. Erika knew Georgia was right, but it had left her feeling worse. She instigated it. She was married and she wanted it and she instigated it. Only for someone else to reject her. Erika lifted her head as she felt the door behind her move a crack, and turned her ear towards it. "Fuck, fuck, George, what are you doing?" she heard on the other side of the door. Erika didn't know whether she should say anything, so she listened a little while longer, before she heard three short bangs on the door around the level of her own head.

"Are you knocking on my door or are you smashing your head against the door because you fucked up so much?"

"*Oh*, you're there? I didn't *fuck* up," she heard Georgia say.

"Yeah, I'm here."

"I was smashing my head against the door."

"Right, go to bed, Georgia. We'll just forget about it, okay?" Erika said sadly.

"If I could forget about it, do you think I'd have been smashing my head against the door?"

Erika went silent. She didn't know how to respond to that. Was she not regretting it? Did she enjoy it as much as

Erika had? A small smile formed on her lips. Yeah, technically she was still married, and yes, this was horribly wrong. But she felt good for tonight, and seemingly somewhat good about herself for a bit.

"You still there?" Georgia asked.

"Yup," she said back.

"I don't regret it you know? Not at all. I regret stopping it. Just a little."

Erika smiled as she heard the words. "Yeah?"

"Hm hmm. So, you're a pretty great kisser."

Erika could hear the smile in her voice and lightly rested her head back against the door. "Backatcha signora."

"What's that mean?" Georgia asked her through the door.

"It means same to you," she smirked.

"Shut up you idiot, I know that part. What's signora mean?"

"What? You asked I told. It means lady, in Italian," she giggled.

"Ahhhh yes I forgot, you're Italian. Explains a lot. Hmm two things off my bucket list."

"Oh yeah? What's that then?"

"Ahhhh, now that would be telling," she said, laughing. "Good night, Erika. Thank you for a…an *interesting* night," Georgia smirked.

"Tell me?" she said. "Georgia?" she barked.

"Good night, signora. I'll see you in the morning," she laughed.

"Buona notte," she whispered, getting up and shaking her head.

Chapter Fifty-Four

Georgia woke at five thirty am, her head was banging, and she desperately needed some tablets and coffee. She lay in bed thinking about the previous night's occurrences, causing her mind to run away with her. Regardless of anything else, Erika *was* gorgeous. She was completely off limits, but gorgeous all the same. The problem was Georgia was bright, intelligent and normally totally sensible, and this was not good. She would never be stupid enough to go after someone that she shouldn't. She wasn't into games and would never normally take a second glance at someone with so many crosses against her. "Why, oh why?" she said to herself, wondering if being homesick and alone out here was influencing her judgement.

Getting up, Georgia put her bikini on and threw on some joggers and her hoodie, making her way down to the steam room. A good steam was always the best thing for a bad head. More so for sweating out all the alcohol from her body she thought. Georgia put her towel and clothes on a sun lounger close to the entrance door of the steam room. Opening the door, she felt the steam hit her full on. God this maybe wasn't the best idea she'd ever had. She stopped in her tracks as she saw Erika laid out on the marble seats.

"Hey? *Hi,* what are you doing here?" she said, immediately getting up and putting her arms around her waist in a bid to cover herself.

"I'm assuming the same as you, trying to clear my head and trying to sweat out the alcohol and hangover. I can leave if you want and just go in to the sauna or pool?" she asked apprehensively.

"No, no, its fine. It's not mine, and I suppose it's better I share it with you than the oldies who hate me," she smiled shyly.

"Well this is true," Georgia said, laying down on the long marble seat, feeling the burn under her skin from the heat on the marble. I love the smell in these places. I normally hate lavender, but they reckon they are predominantly filled with lavender for relaxation, don't they?" Georgia grimaced, confused why the hell she was sat there making conversations about lavender!

"Um, actually, no idea," Erika said awkwardly.

"You know, it kind of defeats the purpose of a relaxed environment, when you're all twisted and seemingly far from relaxed," Georgia said. "Seriously, I don't mind leaving. I don't want you to feel uncomfortable in here."

"No, it's fine, it's a free country after all."

Georgia ignored the comment and went for a different approach. "Excellent. I must say I would have been devastated to have left this view behind," she smirked, looking up to Erika.

"Screw you."

Georgia started to speak, then raised her eyebrows to Erika and covered her mouth, causing them both to laugh. "At last she relaxes," Georgia said with a lop-sided grin.

"Shut up," she scorned her. "So, is this you're coping mechanism, Ms Carson? Sarcasm?"

"Sarcasm?" she spat. "I'll have you know its wit, and nothing less. On the contrary, I don't think I need anything to cope with," she said seriously. "Other than the pounding in my head. Even my hair hurts. Do you get that ever?"

"No, and no I guess not. Making out with the woman who bullied your sad ass last week, whom you now you have to work with. And have to see all day every day. That's awesome," she confirmed.

"Ahhhh, so you're a glass half empty kind of woman. I on the other hand am a glass half full. The way I look at it, nothing happened last week. As I've previously mentioned, I am working with someone seemingly incredibly creative, intelligent and driven, which is awesome for me. Best of all, I got to kiss a super sexy Italian American last night. I mean seriously, what part of any of this is bad?" she said pointedly to Erika. "The problem I have is, I came down here to try and behave and shake off the thoughts I have been having this morning and am faced with you. Half-naked, hot, and sweaty. Now, you see, *there,*" she pointed to the floor. "That right there is a problem," she said dramatically.

"You're busting my balls," she said quietly.

Georgia stood up, walked closer to Erika, and gently moved her hand from where it was covering her tummy. "I thought you realised last night. I don't like balls. Stop hiding yourself!" she said confidently as she gently placed her hand back over her stomach. Georgia sat back down facing away from Erika this time. Leaning back, she closed her eyes so she could enjoy the relaxation around her.

***

Twenty minutes of silence later, Erika got up. "Right, I officially am melting, so I need to head on out. What do you want to do about work today? I need to get Dulcie later, so I was wondering if you wanted to hang out here today and just go through some stuff, then I can head over to my ma's to collect her mid-afternoon?" she asked Georgia.

"Yep, fine by me. You want a coffee first? I'm going to get one now before I go to get dressed," she said, following Erika out the room.

"Yes, please, coffee and cream, no sugar," she said, leaving Erika behind.

Georgia got back upstairs and knocked on the door. As it opened she took in Erika with a towel wrapped around her, and her long black hair dripping onto her bare shoulders. "Really? *Really?*" she asked.

"What? You were so long I figured you'd forgot about me, so I showered."

"You are *killing* me right now!" she stated. "Coffee for you." She said nothing else, shaking her head and walking back to her own room.

Georgia took a quick shower and lay on her bed, sipping her coffee. She picked up her phone and typed a message out.

Hey, so you know how you gave me your number to call if I had any issues? Gimme a shout when you can talk. Gx

She put her phone back down and switched the TV on, trying to forget about the headache that was still niggling away. She couldn't remember going out and drinking that much in about ten years, and suddenly she'd done it twice in a couple of months. How things change, she thought to herself.

Georgia's phone started ringing, picking it up she looked at the caller ID seeing Emily's name. She smiled and pressed the answer button.

"Hey you? How goes it?" Georgia asked Emily.

"Hey, how are you? We're all good here, how's Fort Worth treating y'all?" she asked.

"Yeah, I like it. Reminds me of being on holiday. Thanks for calling me, I didn't know who else to speak to. Can you talk?"

"Sure, of course. What's going on? Are you ok?"

"Yes…no. You may need coffee and biscuits for this," Georgia said.

"You know what biscuits are over here right? We don't dunk *scones* in our coffees," she laughed.

"Whatever. Just call me back when you have got yourself comfy and have a drink," she said.

"It's okay, I'm good. I have got everything I need right here. So, what's been going on? Has she been a bitch again?" Emily asked concerned.

"No! So, I kissed her last night."

Georgia listened to Emily spit out whatever she was drinking. "You did *what*?"

"I kissed her," she said nonchalantly.

"Umm, okay? Is this normal for a lesbian to do? So, did y'all do anything else? Do you like her? Do you think it's a good idea to get involved with someone who…umm, how do I say this?" she said.

"With everything wrong? Work together? Hated me? Straight? Married? Got a kid? To name a few."

"So, what happened, fill me in."

***

Georgia felt better after talking to Emily. She knew it wasn't the best idea she'd ever had, but nobody else was there. And granted, Georgia had never had much self-control when it came to sexy women. In her defence, she never really put herself in that position either. But it was more than that last night. Erika seemed so sad and low, and although Georgia didn't know her from Adam, she could tell that wasn't her. It felt good to make her feel good about herself if only for a moment. And she wasn't doing it to be saintly, but it did feel good. Truthfully, it felt good to kiss her. But that was under the influence and today...today she was sober, and needing to be sensible.

Georgia got changed and did her hair. They were only staying in the hotel so she figured she would go casual. At least that way she would look like she had tried. She threw on some flip flops, a pair of jeans and a plain racer back vest. Grabbing her laptop bag and phone, she left the room and made her way down to the bar area.

Erika was already sitting there, looking uncomfortable. She was fidgeting, a lot. Her hair, her pen, her purse, her hair again. Georgia was realising very fast that last night was going to cause them a lot of problems, problems she could do without right now.

"Hey up? You ok?" Georgia said, sitting down and watching Erika's reaction as she looked her up and down in surprise.

"What's up? Am I not allowed to wear casual clothing when we are just staying here?" she said to Erika, who immediately looked embarrassed.

"I'm sorry," she whispered.

"Why?"

"Huh?"

"Why are you sorry?"

"For being rude."

"And why were you rude?"

"Huh?"

"Why...were...you...rude?" she spelled out.

"Because I made you feel uncomfortable."

"And how exactly did you do that?"

"Why are you asking these questions?"

"Because, it's the only way I can see possible, that I can break down this uncomfortableness. This barrier. So, why do you think you made me feel uncomfortable?"

"This is dumb. I am not uncomfortable nor do I have barriers around you."

"Uh uh uh... au contraire, I think you're sorely mistaken. You looked me up and down, you looked confused, shocked, and then you couldn't look me in the eye," she said. "Now, the way I see it, we got over all this difficulty this morning. We steamed together, I bought you coffee, I had to look at you virtually naked. So, by my reckoning, if anyone was going to feel uncomfortable, that should be me. So, do you have some issues with me? Our kiss? Us working together? My attire? Just tell me. Let's discuss it and move forward, okay?"

Erika started to speak and stopped herself, before giving in and nodding slightly.

"That? That right there, I can't deal with. Talk to me. We cannot have a good working relationship if you do that all the time."

Erika felt self-conscious but strangely comforted. "I was just thinking that was actually quite nice that you cared so much, to try and make me feel better," she said shyly.

"Good, well believe it or not, I can be quite a caring and considerate person occasionally. Now, do I need to change or are you happy to associate with me looking like a scruff?" she asked, amusing herself following their conversation a few nights earlier.

"You may be kind and considerate, but you're also a jerk," Erika said, pulling all the paperwork out between them.

"Yup, but a cute one," she smirked.

"Okay, new rule. No flirting," Erika said.

"What? Moi? I'm insulted you think I would do such a thing," she smirked again.

"Are you always like this?" Erika questioned.

Georgia started and stopped. "See, I was going to be evil then and wind you up. Tell you I had something wrong with me that made me like it, *but...* I will be kind. I am pretty much like that all the time, yes. As I keep telling you, life's too short to waste time, Erika. I like having fun with you, without sounding like a bully now. Oh, *wait* that's you." She winked. "Without sounding like a bully, it's too easy, and too much fun. But most likely only going to result in problems for me," she said. "Right, anyways, stop flirting, Georgia, back to business. What we starting on?"

Erika tried to hide the smile from listening to the reference that someone was flirting with her. "What do you mean by that? What problems? And I wasn't the one who bullied you, and nor will I. I just didn't help matters when you felt that way, and didn't control my staff," she said.

"Don't worry, it doesn't matter. Come on let's get started."

Chapter Fifty-Five

Georgia was singing along to the music in the car, and tapping her knee. "So, for the record, I normally get a lot further than just a kiss before I meet the parents."

Erika rolled her eyes, tapping along on the steering wheel. "I knew I should have stopped you from drinking."

"Whoa, easy tiger. Don't you start controlling me already," she laughed to herself. "I'm just messing with you. I figured it would make more sense to get it all out before I meet your family." She smiled.

"Georgia, for the last time, you are not meeting my family. We are literally going to collect Dulcie, and my mom wants to make us a good, hearty Italian dinner. For the record, it will be for my benefit not yours, just so she can throw it back in my face that I wasn't brought up to mistreat folk," she said, sighing.

"Amazing! Oh, I'm gonna have so much fun with this. I'm going to tell her all about how you bullied my little arse and made me nearly leave."

"You do, I'll bully you for real."

"Oh…" Georgia stopped herself. "Never mind," she said, smirking.

"Do you ever get your head out of the gutter?"

"Yes, twenty-three point five hours of a day, normally. But I guess the sunshine and cute gals reverses it," she laughed. "Okay, okay, I will stop. I told you it's only because I know it makes you uncomfortable. I will behave though, seriously. And I'll apologise, I only do it as a form of sarcasm. It's a bit like an escape route. I use it like a comfort blanket, a way to protect myself."

"What do you need to protect yourself for?" Erika asked inquisitively.

"Nothing to worry yourself about. So, how long will it take us to get there?" she said.

Erika eyed her suspiciously. "Two minutes," she said, not forcing the position any further.

***

"Were here, kiddo," Erika said, pulling onto her mom's drive.

"Kiddo? Kiddo? You know that I'm older than you?"

"Yup, but you been acting like my five-year-old. Are we there yet, are we there yet?" she laughed.

"Piss off. On a serious note, do I need to know or do anything? Other than the Italians in Italy I have never met any Italians before," she said eagerly.

Erika was smiling at her. "Seriously, you *are* comical. No, my ma is awesome! She is an older version of Dulcie, and she will literally love you. Unfortunately, that will not go in my favour. In actuality, massively against me," she said concerned.

"Erika, don't panic, I won't get you in shit, okay?"

Before she had a chance to answer she could hear her daughter screaming down the drive. "Mommy, mommy," Erika jumped out of the car and picked up her daughter.

"Hey, baby! How are you? Did you have a great time with Nonna?"

"Uh huh. Hey, Georgia. We baked cookies, I made you a special one." She grinned widely. "How come you're here, Georgia? Are we going swimming later? Are you eating dinner with us? My Nonna said she thought you sounded real nice," she said all in one go to both Erika and Georgia.

"Bambina tranquillo?" the elder woman said, following her down the path.

"Hey, Ma, ciao. You know she won't ever quiet. Come stai?"

"No, just as you didn't. I'm well, a little tired," she said, stroking Erika's face.

"You are? How so? What's up, Ma?"

"Erika, relax. I am an old lady now, looking after a five-year-old for long time. Of course, I'm tired. Anyway, introduzione?" she scorned her daughter.

"Scusate Momma. This is Georgia, the woman from work."

"Do they always speak in different languages?" Georgia whispered to Dulcie, who was giggling to her.

"Si," she giggled, running off into a different room.

"Amazing, even the child is speaking a different language to me now," she whispered to herself.

"Hello, Georgia. I'm sorry we are being disrespectful in speaking when you are not understanding. As I know, this is not the only mistreatment you have suffered from this familigia, and for that, I apologise. I did not bring my children up this way," she said seriously.

Georgia looked at Erika, who suddenly looked like a small child, being told off by her mum, and she suddenly felt the need to step in.

"Actually, Mrs. Conte, I think your daughter has most likely portrayed it as far worse than it is. Which as my parents always taught me, was a true reflection of a good, disciplined and well manned upbringing. Your daughter didn't make me feel that way, it was the staff. Who were only behaving in that way because of their respect and loyalties to your daughter. I can't honestly say my staff wouldn't have behaved in exactly the same manner. So please, your daughter, as soon as she was made aware of this fact, came to apologise and offer us the chance to work together," Georgia said sincerely.

"Grazie, thank you, Georgia. This is kind. I work hard to bring my children up respectful and loving. This makes me happy. Now, come, we eat?" she said. "You like pasta?"

"Do I ever?" she said, linking arms in the elderly woman's. She turned around to Erika, who mouthed '*thank you*' to her.

Chapter Fifty-Six

"Mrs…I'm sorry Antonia," Georgia stopped herself, recalling the numerous warnings to call her by her first name. "Thank you, that was seriously the best meal I've ever had in my life. It was a true pleasure to meet you, and I feel very honoured. And I was not joking earlier, I will be in touch first thing. I would love for you to come down and spend our final night with us, well that's truly presumptuous. If your daughter and granddaughter are happy to spend it with me. But I will get a room for you, we can go anywhere you guys want and then we can drop you off before we drive back to Houston? I know you have plied me with wine, but seriously, I'm not joking," she said, kissing the woman, who then kissed her other cheek. She felt like she was back in Italy or Spain.

The ride home was quiet, and Erika didn't know how to broach the conversation with Georgia. She had saved her ass tonight, and then she had made her mom's and her daughter's nights. Probably her own, too. She couldn't remember a time someone was so thoughtful and considerate to do something like this. She remembered something her brother Gianni said when he visited the UK years ago. That although London was awesome and stunning, the further north you went, that's where the true hidden treasures were. The beautiful greenery and the beautiful people. He was a huge advocator of the northern hospitality. She wondered if that's why someone as strong as Georgia felt so mistreated. *Or maybe it was because she was* she thought. Sooner or later though, Erika knew she needed to thank her. She looked in her rear-view and saw that Dulcie was sleeping.

"So hey, that was pretty awesome back there. I don't know how to thank you. But I guess I should probably start by the simplicity of a *thank you,*" she hesitated.

"Can I tell you something?"

"Sure, shoot?"

"You may not like it, but just do me a favour and please just listen until I've finished?"

"Um okay?" she said warily.

"I came here, apprehensive as hell. Interestingly, my brother and sister, who I speak to probably three times a year talked me into it. Then I arrived, spending twelve hours on a flight convincing myself it would be okay. But then you…now, don't react. You were awful, and suddenly I figured that basically, Americans were arseholes. I went for a run straight after you left me, hating you all. But I got home and heard this woman's voice and there was this woman from across the road giving me food cause I'd just moved in. FYI, said woman, has become my closest friend here. So much so, that I called her this morning to talk. Anyways, apologies, I'm digressing. The point is, these last few days have made me question everything. But tonight? *Wow,* just wow. I feel truly touched, and your mother is an exceptional woman. I didn't do that for you, well I did obviously. But I didn't, I did that for her. For that belief that she never failed as a parent because, you know what? She didn't. She raised a wonderful daughter, who equally, has raised her own wonderful daughter. Apologies, your mum has basically got me a little inebriated. But seriously, Erika, I genuinely have never felt more part of something than I have tonight…us Brits? We don't do this shit. We're too hard, we don't do the softly shit. But this, wow. Just...*wow,"* she said seriously.

"See, you're a softie at heart. FYI, Italians are the same. We don't either, but since my father passed, my mom has really tried. More so with us as we are the only ones who live outta town," she said sadly.

"Well, I am genuinely grateful for you allowing me to be part of that. Anyways, I think we've done way too much '*soft*' rubbish now, so we will leave it there," Georgia said, turning to look out of the window.

Erika didn't want to push Georgia. She was a tough cookie for sure, and hid her feelings particularly well behind sarcasm. But she could feel the fact that she was out of her comfort zone right now. So, leaving her to enjoy some peace and quiet was definitely the best bet.

***

"You want me to stop anywhere? We're nearly back."

"No, I'm good, thanks. Thank you for driving, a bit unfair that you weren't able to drink when it was your family," she said sadly.

"George, I have a five-year-old remember? I drink after she's crashed. It was nice. It was nice for my Ma to have someone else to speak to other than the same people. She liked you a lot. I could tell. Plus, she told me so." She smiled.

"She did? That's amazing, I really liked her too. I hope she didn't think I was a drunken bum and chatting shit about offering to get her a room to come and spend our last night with us?" Georgia asked concerned.

"Hell no. She's stoked. She couldn't believe how incredibly kind and thoughtful you were. Especially considering the circumstances between you and I. Which FYI, gave her another opportunity to kick my butt," she said, smirking as she pulled into the hotel car park.

Erika grabbed her daughter from the car seat, desperately trying not to wake her.

They walked the short walk from the car park to their rooms, as Erika manoeuvred her bag and child.

"You need a hand?" Georgia whispered.

Erika looked at her seriously and paused before she began speaking, "I'm fine, thank you for the offer though."

Georgia took Erika's bag from her, "Here, let me help," she said, getting the key card and opening the door for her. "You need owt else?"

Erika smiled at her "No, I don't need *owt* else," smiling at the terminology, before entering her room. "Bye, Georgia."

"Goodnight, Erika," Georgia said quietly.

Chapter Fifty-Seven

Georgia heard a faint knock at the door, switched the volume down and heard the tap again, before opening. "Hi, you okay?" Georgia asked Erika.

Erika looked her up and down and shook her head smiling.

"What?"

"Nothing. Hey. So…would you mind doing me a humongous favour?" Erika asked.

"Of course, if you tell me why you're shaking your head, looking me up and down?" she said, leaning against the door with a lop-sided grin.

Erika couldn't help but notice how cute she looked when she was in her slacks. Seriously, she pulled off just about every outfit, but the 'lounging' look, was her personal favourite. "You just make me laugh how quick you change into your sweats. Would you mind watching Dulcie, for like five minutes please? That's all. She's sleeping and it's incredibly doubtful that she will wake up. But certainly, not while I just run downstairs?" she asked.

"Yes of course, I can nip down there if you want? Do you need something from your car?"

"No, I just figured it was maybe my time to have a drink, ya know? Catch up from some others?" she smirked, eyeing Georgia's beer. "Thanks for this, I'll be five is all."

"Well that's fine, I don't mind at all. However, I have got a bottle of white, a few beers, half a bottle of red and half a bottle of pink. Sorry *blush,"* she smirked. "You can have these if you like, saving you buying any?"

"No, I couldn't possibly," she said.

"Why not? I'm offering."

"Are you sure? I can get some cash," she said, walking back into her room.

Georgia grabbed her hand and pulled her back. "I don't need nor want your money," she said as her face was close to her own. "I would like to give you a drink," holding her hands up, "no strings, no expectations," she said. "I tell you what. I'll even throw in a movie if you fancy it? If not, just take what you like and go back to yours. Help yourself," Georgia said, turning her back to Erika and grabbing another beer, trying her damnedest to not sound weird and desperate.

"Well, I wouldn't want to intrude. You seem kind of chill here."

"As long as you don't talk through my movie of...boy meets girl, boy falls in love with girl, boy fucks up, boy gets sense, boy declares his undying love for said girl, boy gets girl. Then I'm more than happy to allow you to share this special moment with me," she smirked. "What do you want to drink?"

"Do you mind if I continue with the blush? I'm just gonna go change into my sweats. I don't like being stuck in this, while you're in your sweats already."

Georgia poured a drink for Erika and put it on the bedside table across from the side she was sitting. She lay back down sipping her beer. She desperately tried to have words with herself over the way she was acting.

A few minutes later, Erika returned with her hair pulled in a high ponytail, a pair of cotton shorts and a zip up hoodie. "Hey, is this mine"? she said, picking up the glass and settling on the bed.

"Nah, it's for the little girl next door, when she wakes up," she smirked, trying desperately to ignore the exceptionally long…bare legs." *This wasn't good. How the hell has this happened? We've literally been speaking for about a week,* she thought to herself, and here was Georgia having thoughts like this. This wasn't good.

"You always this sarcastic? Or just when you're nervous?"

"I'm not nervous at all. I am always naturally sarcastic," she smiled sarcastically.

"Hmmm, sure you are."

"Whatever. Anyhow, sssshhhh, I love this movie."

"Yeah me too. Can't beat a good ole fashion love story," she said.

"Wouldn't have put you down as the romantic movie type."

"How so?"

"Don't know. I guess because you keep going all shy and embarrassed around me after our kiss last night."

"You can't stop bringing it up, can you?" Erika smiled.

"Yep, I sure can," she said, mocking her with a gesture of zipping her mouth shut, taking more of her beer.

The pair lay quietly watching the TV together, every so often each sneaking a glance to the other. Erika got up. "You want another?" she said, pouring herself the remainder of the blush.

"Yeah, while you're up, you may as well make yourself useful," she laughed.

"You're a jerk you know that?" she said, throwing an ice cube at Georgia, who squealed as the cold, cube hit her.

"Screw you," Georgia said, putting the ice cube in the bin.

"You wish, honey," Erika said in a long southern drawl, handing Georgia the beer as she climbed back onto the bed again.

"Ohhh, check out little miss confident, now she's had a drink."

Erika leaned in close to Georgia's face, "I don't need booze to be confident, nor do I need to hide behind sarcasm," she smirked, taking a sip of her wine and returning to the position she was in on the bed.

Georgia was lost for words. This woman had got her nervous and it was pissing her off. "Hmmm, whatever."

"Whatever *all* you want. It's true. I can do all I want without booze, if I *wanted* to."

"Well, you couldn't last night. You wanted to kiss me, but you got me to do it. You didn't have the confidence to take the lead," she smirked.

"Maybe it's because I wasn't bothered about kissing you. Maybe the booze was why I didn't take the lead," Erika laughed back.

Georgia went to say something but didn't know how to respond to it. *Shit.* How the hell was this woman getting under her skin so much?

Erika hadn't known Georgia to go quiet once since they had been spending time together, and suddenly felt kind of shitty. Unfortunately, Georgia was right, she didn't have the confidence anymore. She wasn't the bold, brash woman she used to be. Which was annoying her to no end. Because as the alcohol was flowing freely through her body, all she wanted to do right now was kiss her again. Although she knew being here on her bed, probably wasn't the greatest idea she'd ever had. Albeit, she knew that was the reason she had purposely knocked on Georgia's door to ask her to look after Dulcie. In the hope, she would have done exactly this.

Erika turned to look at Georgia who was watching the TV intently. "But I guess you know I'm lying about that," she said in response to the comment about not wanting to kiss her. She looked over at Georgia to see if there was any change to her demeanour.

Georgia sipped her beer and looked over to her. "Who knows, you were fucked. Could have just been a chance opportunity, try something new? Forget the pain, ya know?" she said harshly, pissed off at herself for being so reactive when they were just messing about with each other.

"I deserved that, I guess. But the issue remains. I was trashed, yes. But I did want to kiss you, desperately. I just didn't have the courage to do so, more so because I didn't know if you wanted to kiss me. I thought you might have, but I couldn't be so sure. That was the reason I put it on you. *Just saying,*" she said seriously.

"I wanted to from the moment you opened the door," Georgia said, still looking at the TV. "Also, *just saying,*" she smirked, not looking at Erika and keeping her eyes on the TV.

"You did, huh?" she raised an eyebrow.

Georgia shook her head at the woman, "You, *lady,* are painful."

"What? I have no idea what you mean."

"Hmmm. Sure, you don't. Just like you don't think I don't know that you gain a bit more confidence with every drink you have. And now that you know I wanted to kiss you, then maybe you need to return the favour."

"Return the favour?"

"Yeah, you owe me one," she said, laughing as she got up. "You want another drink, or do you need to stop after two, in order to control yourself?" she smirked, looking over her shoulder to Erika.

"You're gonna get your ass whooped if you keep up this ball busting."

"Promises, promises."

Georgia got back on the bed and handed Erika a glass of white. "One glass of white, with a side of confidence," she said, unable to control the laughing.

"You really are a pain in the butt. You know that, right?"

"Yup, fully aware. Which only makes me want to do it more."

"Hmmm, yeah I can imagine. Loving it, huh?"

"Yeah, I really am. I mean, I have debated just kissing you on several occasions this evening, but I think I'll enjoy it even more by pressuring you into it. To see if you have actually got the bottle."

"Well, maybe I don't wanna kiss ya no more. Maybe I realised after last night, that…ya know it's not all that good. Maybe like a five, or if I'm in a generous mood, a six?" she smirked, sipping her wine without looking at Georgia.

"Sod off, I'm a great kisser. I've been told loads. Cheeky cow."

"Well maybe you are to Brits, but ever thought that they are shit kissers, too? I mean, I'm just saying. I'm Italian, the language of love, romance, and passion." She couldn't help but laugh at the ridiculousness of what was coming out of her mouth.

Georgia picked up her pillow and threw it to Erika.

"Heeeey, the drink man," she said, wiping her arm of the drips that had fallen, and putting it on the side. Erika rolled over on her side moving closer to Georgia. "So, you have a real thing over me kissing you, huh?" she said, smiling.

"I don't have a real thing! I just think it's amusing that someone like you, doesn't have the bottle to kiss me, when it's so apparent that you want to," she said, stifling the grin and copying Erika's position.

"Wow, you're so full of yourself," she laughed.

"Interestingly, I'm not," she said, moving closer to Erika. "But you do seem to have a weird effect on me. Or this place does," she said doubtfully.

"Oh yeah? How so?"

"Well, I know you won't believe this, but I am never like this. I don't know whether it's this place…well not this place per se. But the whole being away. Maybe it's making me take a different look at my life *and* me. Who I am?" she said seriously. "Or maybe it's just because you are so uptight at times, and I love taking the piss. Honestly, I don't know. I think historically, girls came after me. *Oh, my God* that sounded so arrogant. I didn't mean it to sound that way. I don't have time for women, so I tend to not get involved. As you've already seen." She stopped, and pointed down to her bright coral pineapple dance trackies. "I love my comfies and chill out time, so I don't even go the village and do what normal singletons do, get wasted and then go home with countless women. I work hard, then go home and try to rest hard. So, for that reason the very rare occasions I've been near anyone, it was all instigated by them. I guess to put it simply, being around someone, a *lot,* that's more oblivious and less confident than even I am, is almost giving me this…I dunno…like booster. More confidence, ownership…it's making me want to make you realise you shouldn't lack such confidence, and you should have some fun and enjoy life. Ok, well I don't know who this is talking but certainly isn't me," she said, pulling a confused face.

"Well, personally I dunno what you have to lack confidence for, but that's my view."

"Touché."

"So, it seems your little speech worked?" she said, maintaining eye contact.

"Yeah, *how so?*" she winked at the play on Erika's terminology.

"Well, whether it was true or not, it's given me that extra boost of confidence you said you had."

"I don't lie, Erika. I don't see the point," Georgia said seriously.

"And strangely, again. I believe that," she said as she leaned in and gently ran her index finger down the side of her face, causing her to gasp. Erika leaned in and met Georgia's lips with her own. She pushed her fingers to the back of her short hair, feeling the soft spikes at the bottom of her head, from the short crop cut.

Georgia couldn't control the feeling inside of her. She was shocked that Erika had the bottle to pull it off, but by god this woman could kiss. Georgia moved in closer, deepening the kiss, and pulled Erika to her and found her tongue with her own.

Georgia thought she heard a giggle. She pushed past it, figuring she had heard wrong. But she hadn't, that was definitely it again. She continued the kiss before giving in and realising it was a no go. "Ok, so laughing into a kiss, is not the best thing for a girl's confidence," she said, pulling back, looking at Erika.

"I'm sorry, sorry. Honestly, I'm so sorry. It isn't you…"

"Oh, my God. Do not *dare* say it's not you, it's me," Georgia spat.

"Shut up. It's not a break up here. It isn't you. I am thirty-eight, gone back to fifteen. That's what's giving me hysterics."

"What do you mean?"

"I mean, I'm making out with someone on a bed that isn't my own and that I'm not dating. Seriously, I feel like a freaking teenager, and it was just making me giggle. I'm sorry. It wasn't you, *or* the kiss, I can *assure* you. It just feels kind of weird, you know?"

"Yeah, I get it," she said sombrely, but she kept kicking herself for pissing about with A. someone so off limits and B. a straight? Seriously, she got this shit out of her system twenty years ago. She wasn't one for thinking that she could change straight girls, Jesus they had far too much baggage. She didn't want to be dealing with that, but there was something about Erika she liked, and she knew there was so many things wrong with that.

"I've offended you?"

"No, no you haven't. Honestly, just all a bit weird and a bit of a mess, I suppose."

"Ouch, yet again I get ditched. You are awesome for my self-confidence, lady," Erika said coolly.

"You need to stop overthinking everything I say and listen to me when I talk to you...last night, and possibly tonight. I'm not going to be able to control myself, and I'm already thinking this is going to be so messy. So, with me not being able to control myself, yeah, I think it's a bit of a worry. But God, you are looking at it all the wrong way. You are looking at it that I keep stopping and starting. I want you, then I change my mind. That isn't the case, that's never been the case. The fact of the matter is, you're fucking gorgeous, who gets me completely engulfed with each kiss we have that I *don't* want to stop. I don't want the kiss to stop, in fact I want nothing more than to spend all night long, kissing you longer, harder, deeper, and more importantly all over," she said, looking deeply into Erika's surprised eyes.

Erika couldn't breathe. She'd never fully understood when people spoke of being at a crossroads when there was a decision for you to make there and then. Suddenly, for the first time ever, she was invested in that decision. She couldn't think of what to do though, because she always over analysed everything. That was just her. That was what she did. So, for now, she was just going to go for it and deal with the consequences later.

And that she did. Erika pushed Georgia back, grabbing her hands by the wrists. The expression on her face gave everything that Erika needed to continue what she was doing. "How about you stop talking and realise that I'm a grown ass woman. And how about I be the decider of that?" she said, before kissing her deeply once again.

Georgia felt like she was chained to the bed, and although Erika had said herself about being a *'big girl'*, she didn't want to push it too far. But God, that was the most difficult task ever right now. And one she didn't know if she could achieve. She genuinely didn't think she had the self-control over this woman. Georgia heard a faint groan and didn't know if it was her or Erika. It was only when it happened the second time that she realised it was neither of them.

"Shoot!" Erika stopped and pulled away, listening to the grumblings of her daughter in the next room. It was quiet for a moment before the crying began. Erika rolled over onto her back and smashed her head against the pillow

groaning loudly. "I'm sorry," she said sincerely. "I'm really, *really* sorry," she said, getting up and going to her daughter.

"Don't be. Go and make sure Dulcie is okay." She smiled kindly, watching Erika leave.

***

Erika was feeling uncertain of what to do, and she wished she'd just shut the door behind her when she left to get Dulcie. Now it had been over thirty minutes since she left and the door was still open, leaving her with the dilemma of whether she should go back or just stay here. Did Georgia want her to go back? Was she awake still? Equally, she didn't want to appear presumptuous. *Come on, pull yourself together, you're a grown ass woman.*

"Hey, you still up?" Erika poked her head around the connecting door, looking at Georgia. "I didn't know if I should come back or not."

"Yeah, I don't think I'm going to be able to sleep for a while after that," she said. "I didn't know if you'd come back either, or if you wanted to." She smiled at Erika.

"I didn't know if I should, or if *you* wanted me to. My daughter has impeccable timing," she sighed. "But, maybe it was a blessing in disguise?" she questioned.

"I don't want to sound like I regret that, because it isn't the case, you are sexy as hell..."

"But?"

Georgia squirmed "Unfair! *But*, as much as that was probably the most passion I've experienced in a bloody long time, I can honestly say I have never ever, had so little self-control, and it's killing me. But equally, I just don't want you to get hurt, and I think you are going through a somewhat difficult time. Getting pissed and shagging someone, who in fact was your arch nemesis last week, leaves me thinking that you will wake up feeling shit, beat yourself up, and live to regret it forever. Which in turn will make me feel rubbish because I'm pretty sure I'll have had one of the best nights of my life, but will then feel incredibly guilty and bad over making you feel this way. Additionally, the only way you will be able to deal with the guilt attached to bedding me would be to become distant, and then that will result in more issues at work, and potentially Mike kicking both of our arses," she sighed.

"Wow, you really have thought all that out, huh?"

"Well, I've spent the last half hour praying you'd come, praying you wouldn't…that was no pun intended," she looked at Erika, who was sitting on the edge of the bed.

"You're a goofball," she laughed.

"I know, but I do it so well. You have an incredible smile; *for the record,*"

"For the record, flirting with me is not going to help when it comes to trying to steer clear of each other. So, how did it fall when I came in?"

"What do you mean?"

"Well, you said you were praying I would come back, then I wouldn't etc. I figured you were doing this like a bit of a 'he loves me, he loves me not' method, so when I arrived back at your door, was it on come or don't come?"

"You really need to stop saying that, it's doing things to me that are going to result in those problems I was just mentioning. It fell on do come."

"I think you have your head in the gutter, *again.*" She took some more of the wine she was drinking earlier and lay back down on the bed, ensuring she was as close to the edge as she could be without falling off."

Georgia moved closer to Erika, laying face to face with Erika she could feel her breath on her face. Her heart quickened, causing her breathing to increase. "I can't get my head out the gutter when you look like that. You have the world's shortest shorts on. You have the sexiest legs on the planet. They are so tanned and toned, causing me to try desperately hard not to run my fingers all the way up those long, tanned, bare legs," she said seductively. "Instead, I'll be having some wickedly dirty dreams tonight," she whispered to her, noticing the heavy breaths she was taking.

"You are so, *so* bad," Erika said back, holding her own with the eye contact.

"You have *no* idea," she said. "But, I'm back to losing everything again, so I am going to kiss you now, and then…and dear God this will be the biggest regret I'll make in my life, but then I think we should call it a night and go to sleep."

Erika liked the positive impact Georgia had on her when she spoke to her and maintained eye contact. She made her feel that she really did want to be with her, which in turn made her feel very *wanted,* which was something she hadn't experienced in a while. Equally, it meant she could have some fun with her too. "Well, aren't we the polite one? Forewarning me of the kiss," she said, smirking. "I must say you are very sensible. I on the other hand, am not so. However, I will respectfully do as told and go and get myself a cold shower," she said with a lop-sided grin.

"You had to say that, didn't you? So, now not only do I have that to contend with this," she said, pointing at Erika's bare legs. "Now, I'm faced with visions of you in the shower," she said, shaking her head defiantly.

"Gutter head. Well I have a way that will help that, and no, it doesn't involve me touching you in any way shape or form."

"Well, that's most disappointing," Georgia smirked. "Okay, okay, my bad. Cool let's do it?" she said.

Erika was loving this, and control was the biggest turn on to her. Moving closer to Georgia, her face mere millimetres from her own, looking serious and composed herself. "Simple. I'm going to remove myself from this situation," she smirked. "I will go next door, get myself undressed, which as you mentioned doesn't involve a lot due to the lack of clothing I'm currently wearing," she said, running her long fingers up over her knee, up her thigh, intently watching Georgia's eyes following her finger. She reached the bottom of her shorts and lifted them slightly, giving Georgia a little more skin visibility at the top of her leg. "Then, that shower I mentioned. A cold one, real cold," she whispered. "And, well, as you can imagine, you know what the cold does to a woman's…b…body," Erika leaned into Georgia's ear and softened her voice. "Cold water running down my naked body? Ya know, right? Hard…erect… But then, maybe when I'm a little more, hmm…Como posso?" she said seductively. "How do I explain? A little more composed, I'll adjust the shower to heat, and allow my mind and body to explore. Explore thoughts of had we not stopped." The whole time she was seductively whispering these words to Georgia, her eyes looked as though they were about to pop out of her head. Erika leaned in again. "What would have happened. *How* it would have happened, before I allow my, *long* fingers, to move down below." She was loving this, and Georgia looked as though she was about to pass out. "My fingers paying particular attention to the part of my body that I'm sure you would have paid much attention to had we not stopped. I'll be thinking about exactly what we would have done to each other," she said quietly. Erika smirked a little and leaned in to Georgia, who was apparently speechless and dumbfounded. Erika pushed her lips against Georgia's and gently bit her lower lip, pulling away and meeting Georgia's eyes. "Good night, Georgia," she said and got up, leaving the room and shutting the door behind her.

"Fuck, *fuck,*" Georgia said loudly. This woman was sexy as hell, and was driving her in-fucking-sane.

Chapter Fifty-Eight

Erika couldn't put into words the way she felt at that moment. Wow, it had been a long time since she felt in control, felt sexually attractive, and sheesh, felt sexually aroused. Georgia was sexy as hell, and for some reason, she seemed to be attracted to Erika. Georgia was being considerate to her situation and trying to stop her from getting caught up in a web of deceit, pain and trouble. Yet, Erika was going all out to see how far she could push her in a bid to make her unable to resist. The problem was Erika did want to push her. It was a long time since anyone had paid her any attention, and it was even longer since she felt like this, felt alive again. Alive in her own self. She wanted to push her, she wanted to be with her, find out what it would be like to be with her in a sexual way. More importantly, she just wanted to feel again and feel wanted, to be aware of those sensations that someone was desperately trying to resist her, and they couldn't. Someone wanted *her* that much? She was trying to control her breathing, what she had just said to Georgia was new to her. She'd never done anything like that before. Least not to someone she didn't know. But by God had it turned her on, as she sat on the bed thinking about what would have happened had Dulcie not woken up. Would they still be there, being intimate together right now? Would one of them have pulled away and thought better of it? Her mind was running away with her, and she couldn't help but feel a sense of ecstasy, by the fire it was igniting inside of her.

Erika felt the bed vibrate, and she picked up her phone to see a message come through from Georgia. She immediately experienced that excitement and nerves in her stomach as she opened it.

For someone who allegedly suffers from a lack of confidence, you have certainly made me regret being sensible. You are fucking hot and don't let nobody tell you different. I am the biggest dumbass on the planet, and FYI, if I hear your shower turn on I'm breaking down the door and going to come and pounce on your arse, just saying! Good night, sexy lady, sweet dreams, I know I will be!! ;) xx

My God you even talk a lot in your texts, dude. I'd love to tell you what I'll be dreaming bout, but as you've text me from a work cell to a work cell, I don't think that would be so appropriate!! ;) But I'll assure you I'll be dreaming sweet ☺ xx

Erika smirked at her response, enjoying fucking with Georgia. The problem was she couldn't help wishing it was for real. She heard the vibration again and smirked as she grabbed her cell, but was disappointed to see the unknown number instead of Georgia's name appear. She threw the phone back down on the bed and switched the shower on. As funny as it was winding Georgia up, the fact of the matter was she did feel the need to have a cold shower.

***

Erika got out of the shower a short while later, allowing her long hair to lay wet around her shoulders. Putting on the hotel robe, she went back to her room and checked on her daughter. Dulcie was the best thing that had ever happened to her, and she was so concerned over what was going to happen between her and Dan. It would tear

Dulcie apart, but Taylor had made a valid point, it was probably best it happened now than later down the line. Additionally, it would only cause more damage if they stayed together when it was like this. But Dan didn't appear to want to do anything to make it better. Jesus, Erika couldn't even remember the last time they did anything as a family. "Come on, Erika, you were delirious a little while ago," she whispered. Smiling to herself, she thought of Taylor. She would call her and fill her in, knowing she could trust Taylor implicitly. And by the way she had been speaking about Dan of late, she knew she'd love this new revelation.

She opened her phone and saw three messages from the unknown number, and opened the messages to read before she sent a text to Tay.

TELL ME TEASE? Gxx

Seriously, I can hear your shower. You best not be misbehaving in there. ☺ xx

OMG you are not a tease, you are a bloody NIGHTMARE, you can't do that. You cannot tease the arse off someone and then go silent...payback is a bitch darling!! Xx

Shit, she didn't think for a second that the number would be Georgia's, so she had left them. Here she was, talking like Erika was desirable. Like she was worthy of being a tease. Like she was bothered by Erika being a tease. She knew she shouldn't be doing this, but for the first time in a long time, she went against her better judgment and decided to put herself first for a change. Erika typed the new number in her cell and updated it to Georgia's contact, then responded.

Hey, good looking ;) Sorry, I didn't recognise the number so I pretty much decided to go and entertain myself.

Would I misbehave? And a tease? Really? Me? ☺ Xx She pressed send, and within seconds saw the grey dots appear to notify her that a response was being done immediately.

What ya got cooking? You are bad, and you are going to get taught a lesson next time you wanna 'make out' ;) Yes you would misbehave! Yes, you are a tease! And yes…you…really!! Xx

Huh? Cooking? I'm in a hotel. And we ate already. Did you continue partying without me? ;) Xx

Nooooo, it's a saying. "Hey good looking, what you got cooking?" Forget it ☹ Nope I didn't continue partying, but more than happy to do so if you want to now? ;) xx

You are SO bad. But as much as I'd love to, I think I need to have some "me" time ;) I'll be sure to think about you lots though haha. Good night, Georgia, sweet dreams ☺ xx

Georgia read the message, exacerbated by the response… "Oh, I'll kick your beautiful little arse, bitch," she said, rolling over and screaming with frustration into the pillow before she rolled on to her back and chuckled to herself.

Chapter Fifty-Nine

Georgia was up stupidly early, and in reality, she could understand why. Erika had stirred far too many of her senses last night, which had resulted in several very inappropriate dreams. Unfortunately, amongst the *interesting* ones, there was the very, very uncomfortable one. The one where she set her up. The office and Erika were against her, albeit in a very sexy naughty teacher type dress up. *She* was leading it, leading them, and it was worse than before. Georgia sighed. This wasn't good. She was feeling out of her comfort zone and apprehensive all over again. What did it mean? Was it her head telling her to stop? She knew it was the effects of the drink, and the fact that she could feel like she was losing control when it came to this woman. Which was annoying as she didn't know what it was. But she'd always had a protective streak. Her dad used to tell her she was the most kind-hearted person ever, because if anyone was upset or being unfairly treated she'd always stick up for them, no matter who it was. She would do anything and everything to make sure those people believed again, felt better again, were happy again.

Sighing heavily, this was all too much. She got into her bikini and made her way downstairs to the sauna and pool. She knew she would enjoy some time there, and it would hopefully get rid of all these thoughts and help her to get back on top of things.

***

Erika woke with the knocking at her door, adjusting to her surroundings and recalling the previous night's events. Suddenly getting nervous at the prospect of soberly seeing Georgia following her actions and behaviour last night, she heard the knock again and the faint calling of Georgia's name.

Erika rolled over, "Baby, what are you doing?" she said, facing her daughter and rubbing her eyes. "Dulcie, why are you in your bathing suit?"

"Hey, Mommy," she said, quickly walking over to her mom's bed. "I wanted to swim, and I didn't want to wake you so I tried to wake Georgia to ask her to take me," she said seriously.

Erika felt her stomach tighten, "Baby, come on up here. We need a talk, huh?" Kissing her daughter's cheek, she smiled. "I love you, baby."

"I love you too, Mommy. I love swimming, too. I didn't mean to wake Georgia. Am I in trouble?"

"Nooooo, baby, not at all. But ya know, Georgia and I are going to be working together, real close for a little while okay? Things changed a little, and now Georgia and mommy are both the bosses. That means you may see her some, but you shouldn't really be here ok? But that's fine cause I'm pretty sure Georgia likes you, baby, a whole lot. You can't just go wake her, she doesn't have kids. She doesn't have to be up early, and she isn't used to spending a whole lotta time around kids, ya know? So, we just need to let her be a grown up." She smiled.

Erika's heartstrings pulled as she could see her daughter's heart breaking. She was too young to understand this, and all she was hearing was that someone didn't wanna be with her. Otherwise translated to, Georgia didn't like her. And that was not what Erika intended to do at all. Sighing heavily, "How about I take you swimming?"

"No, it's ok. I don't wanna no more," she said sadly.

Erika picked up her phone, quickly Googling, before finding what she was looking for. Reaching over to Dulcie's favourite stuffed toy, she put it to the side of the little girl, and with her very best cuddly toy voice she danced him up and down. "Hey, Dulcie, Mommy said we could go to Lego world and forest café. You wanna? You wanna? Ohhh I know, I wanna," she said, jumping the bear up and down on the bed next to Dulcie, watching her silent daughter, seemingly trying to digest the previous words about Georgia.

"You don't wanna go, baby? I was kinda hoping you would enjoy it. Then we can go get Nonna and bring her back and we could take her swimming." She had no idea how the fuck she was going to handle the whole work and Georgia situation, but for now, she had to be focused on her kid.

"Can we see the g'rillas when they shout?" she said, a little more excited.

"Sure we can, baby. How about we get showered and dressed?"

***

Erika and Dulcie left the room, excitably discussing her favourite place to go. She didn't know what the attraction was with the place. She didn't love going to the zoo this much, so it confused the hell out of her where it had ever come from.

"Hey, you guys," Georgia said, hair wet from her morning swim. "How's it going?" she asked, smiling to them both, and focussing more on Dulcie than Erika.

"Yes, I'm really sorry. I may need to get you to hold the fort today? We have project 'cheer up' day, if that's okay? I will catch up this afternoon, before I go get my mom though, if that's alright by you?"

"Project 'cheer up'"? Georgia said concerned.

"Yes, we're good, we're gonna have some quality time together."

"Ah right, I see. Well yeah, I can do the work side. You have a good day. I hope you enjoy your day, Dulcie," she said, walking away a bit concerned.

"Yeah, we're going there because I was sad, cause you couldn't take me swimming," Dulcie said.

Georgia turned around looking confused, noticing Erika's eyes close and her head shaking, "Dontcha just love kids," she said sighing. "Baby, we…"

Georgia was there before Erika had a chance to finish her sentence. "Dulcie, I didn't know I was supposed to be taking you for a swim. If I did I would have come got you. I'm very, very sorry, I promise I didn't know," she said to the little girl.

"I knocked, but I couldn't knock too hard as mommy was sleeping, so I wanted for you to take me swimming, but you didn't answer me," she said innocently.

Georgia unfortunately didn't spend enough time with her family to know the innocence of a child and the pain when they hurt them. "Sweetie, I didn't not answer you. I wasn't there. I had a lot of things on my mind, so I got up, well, when it was still dark outside. It was still night-time," she said exaggeratedly, "but if I knew you wanted to come down with me, I would have waited."

"It's ok, she figured she'd come get you on that magical door you introduced her to," she said.

"So, it wasn't that you didn't want to take me?" Dulcie asked seriously.

"No, sweetie. God no, not at all," Georgia said sadly, feeling her very own heart breaking, and making a mental note to pay more attention and have more involvement with her very own family.

"Well, you could come the 'forest' café today with us, if you wanna?"

"Erm, I should probably stay...and...um work. But, you have a good day, okay? And I best get a present," Georgia smiled to Dulcie, avoiding Erika's glare.

Erika grabbed her arm. "Come with us? I know it's not your idea of fun, but why not? We can do a couple of hours tonight working or something, together," she said apprehensively.

Georgia suddenly felt a lot more at ease seeing that Erika was okay with her. She did need to talk to this woman and set some ground rules, because this was like Groundhog Day. The pair of them wondering if they were back to 'week one'. "Well, as much fun as that sounds..." Georgia stopped, looking at Dulcie. "Phenomenal, your mums coming over to spend the night remember? So, how about you pair go and have some fun alone for a change. Don't be long though." She winked. "I'll do some work, then when you guys get back, maybe the three of us can grab some ice cream, go pick up your grandma, come back, go swimming, have a nice dinner out and the grownups can have a nice bottle of Italian wine or two and then, we go back home tomorrow?" Georgia said, smiling.

Erika was disappointed she wasn't coming, but she was right. And it was very kind that she was allowing her the opportunity to have some time off while she went gallivanting. "If you're sure?"

"Yes, I'm sure you can make it up to me for being so kind and considerate," Georgia said, smirking and glad that the euphemisms were going over Dulcie's head.

"I'm pretty sure that can be arranged. You'll have to have a little think on what you'd like. Sure, you can be trusted alone?"

"No, but you can't have it all." She smiled.

Chapter Sixty

Georgia was in her room getting ready for the night ahead and thinking back to the day she'd had. It had been quite a productive one. Incredibly, she'd learned that a couple of inappropriate texts to Erika was a booster for productivity. Even if she had been suitably reprimanded with a few choice words. Her nightly '*talks to herself*' regarding said situation, were failing miserably and each day she woke up, she managed about ten minutes without going back on her own word.

Georgia finished styling her hair, ready for the evening ahead, still feeling unsure on the outfit. She'd not seen Erika since that morning and was now quite excited at the prospect of seeing her, and had very clearly made a huge effort because of that fact. God, she needed a drink. She was craving a nice glass of red and a decent meal, maybe a good steak. She'd still not had one, and that was her parting words from her brother, *best steaks in the world, sis!*

***

Georgia sprayed some perfume and checked herself in the mirror one final time, breathing in deeply. She'd never missed having friends, but seriously, in this moment she wished she had someone to bounce some stuff off. She had a great idea and smiled to herself. Georgia grabbed her phone and took a picture of herself in the black sleeveless jumpsuit she was wearing and her six-inch heels, giving her already incredible height an even bigger push. She posed a little in the mirror with her finger to her mouth in a questioning manner, before typing *too much? Xx*

Georgia waited impatiently tapping her fingers for the response to come in. She wanted to see if it really was too much before she left and made her way to reception. Looking down at her phone as she felt it vibrate, and Georgia smiled seeing Emily's name on the screen.

"Hey you," Georgia said.

"Oh my gosh *and* oh my gosh, all over again, girlfriend! I have John here with me, and he believes you are the cutest real life lesbian he ever did see in that outfit," she said, laughing. "Heeeeyyyy girl, you looking goooood," he piped up.

"Ahhhh thanks, you guys. I strangely miss you both. I'll be home tomorrow, hope to see you this weekend? Anyways, answer please? Do I look like I'm trying too hard?" she added. "I have to leave."

"You look phenomenal. You go and knock her dead. And hell yeah, we'll see you this weekend. I want ALL the details," Emily finished. "Enjoy tonight and be good," she laughed, hanging up.

Georgia still couldn't quite get her head around the fact that no Americans seemed to say bye and just hung up on you. Feeling the nerves slowly begin to disappear, she put on her long silver dress necklace and made her way downstairs. It was infuriating how anxious she was right now. But after last night, and then not actually seeing Erika at all today, it was messing with her completely. And the fact that she would have to be super behaved tonight in front of the woman's mother was stressing her even more. Still though, the thing that was messing with her above everything else, was the fact she was bothered at all by seeing her. Shaking her head of the thoughts that were now rushing around her head, she walked into the bar, surprised to see they were already there. Georgia first noticed Dulcie and her grandma at a table at the far end of the bar, then noticed Erika standing and being served at the bar as she strode over towards her.

"You're early," she said, bumping her shoulder, noticing too late her sipping a glass of wine, immediately feeling embarrassed.

Erika turned incredulously, she looked Georgia up and down. Unfortunately, still with her glass to her mouth. So, upon seeing Georgia in that outfit, it was too late to control herself from choking on her wine and dribbling some of it down her chin, before quickly wiping it away. "Well, that was probably the least attractive thing I have ever done," she said embarrassed. "Wow, you have made me feel completely underdressed," she said, looking down at her own attire. "But, you look incredible, like…" she stopped and turned to look at her mom and daughter, who were still unaware that Georgia had even arrived. "Like, holy hell. Incredible. Molto bella," she said.

"You have no clue what it does to me when you speak to me in Italian," Georgia said seriously.

"Good to know. Seriously, you thought this was appropriate attire? After last night and when my *mom's* here? Geez, man," she said, shaking her head.

"I told you payback was a bitch," she whispered, leaving Erika at the bar, captivated and desiring of the bare back on show. This left Erika very little option but to acknowledge the thoughts of desperately wanting to touch her and feel her bare skin. Erika instantly craved at some point in the evening to walk behind Georgia and escort her through a door, just so she would have ample opportunity to place her hand on her exposed lower back. She was shaken from her thoughts as the bar tender coughed, looking at her in disgust, as he had clearly caught her watching Georgia longingly.

***

They had had a fabulous meal, and Josh was most certainly right. The steaks in Texas were amazing. After arguing over who would pay the bill, Georgia had no alternative but to give in. The argument being that she had paid for the room for Erika's mum, before the four of them made their way back to the hotel for a nightcap and to put Dulcie to bed.

When arriving, Dulcie was giving her strongest argument for why she should have ice cream. Much to Erika's dissatisfaction, knowing full well she would be on a sugar high going to bed, but it wasn't really helping that her grandma was on board with it.

"Please, Mommy? How bout we just share one, between us all, and then I just have a little?" she said, making Erika realise there was no winning this one. "What do *you* think, Georgia? You think I should get some, don't you?" the little girl said.

"Woah, keep me out of this one, kiddo. You got me in trouble last time, saying your mum allowed you to eat sweets, and when she woke up, she told me different," Georgia laughed, poking her tongue out to Dulcie.

"You told her that?" Erika said to Dulcie surprised.

"Nuh huh, I told her momma let me have it," Dulcie said nonchalantly.

Erika could feel her heart race as she was suddenly aware of what was unfolding before her. She looked to her mom concerned and noticed her mom's confusion, before she looked over to Georgia, who looked more confused than anyone. *Shit, shit* she said inwardly.

Georgia was smiling confused, "What do you mean your momma?" she asked Dulcie.

"It's only my momma that allows me to eat candy. Not my mommy," she said, swinging her legs, unaware to the situation.

"Erm, what?" Georgia said confused, looking between all three people before her.

"That's my mommy," she said, pointing to Erika. "She don't so often. I'm a special kid, cause I gots two mommies," she said, spreading her two little fingers widely for Georgia to see.

Georgia's head was spinning. She wasn't normally attracted to straight women, but Erika as a whole, had just felt different. But she certainly hadn't seen her being gay, and didn't she refer to a husband? Why had she told her she had a husband? Had she? Shit, why couldn't Georgia remember? She didn't know if she had, or not. She always referred to a partner whose name was Dan, and even Mike had only said Dan. Equally, she had lied to Georgia, having had at least two opportunities this week alone. Georgia looked over to Erika, who was looking nervous and apologetic. She didn't want to raise it, not now in front of Dulcie and her mum. But Georgia was pissed off. She could just about deal with the fact that there was so much wrong. Like she was a straight woman, that was *actually* married, and as far as she actually knew still together with her…partner. She knew all of it was wrong but couldn't stop it. But she hated lies. It was only Dulcie that had alerted her to Erika having moved out, wasn't it Erika? What did Dulcie say? She said 'momma' not 'mommy,' therefore, it wasn't Erika that had moved out after all. It was Dan, whoever the fuck Dan was. How did she not pick up on this? In reality, why the hell would she? English kids flitted between mum and mummy all the time. Why would she think that a child saying mommy and momma would be the difference between two different women? Shit, she couldn't deal with this, but before she could do anything, she was pulled out of her racing mind.

"Um, I'll take Dulcie to bed," Erika's mom said to her, much to Dulcie's disappointment.

"Nooooo, I want some ice cream," she said, getting upset.

"Do not get upset, baby. You don't cry to get your own way, you are tired," her grandma said. "Come, we take you some ice cream to bed," she said. "Come, we will leave mamma and Georgia, to have one final drink? Bambina, I take Dulcie to my room," the elderly woman said, taking Dulcie and leaving.

Chapter Sixty-One

"Georgia, please allow me to explain? But please, can we go to one of our rooms, I don't want to do this down here. I don't want to cause a scene, or you to. And at least that way you can scream at me as much as you like."

Georgia was still struggling with it all. "I…I don't…sorry, I just…I can't. I found it hard enough liking someone as much as I do…I did, who was straight and someone who was still technically married, but having had the opportunity to tell me you were gay and then not? You lied? I can't do lying. People think that lying by omission isn't lying. Well it is to me!" she said, placing twenty dollars on the table and leaving.

"Georgia please?" Erika ran after her. "I know you feel betrayed, but I never lied to you…granted, I didn't tell you. But that wasn't me lying, that was me…delaying, *delaying* the truth. Truly, I didn't do this to hurt you. I just didn't want anything else getting in the way," she said as they got in the elevator with other people and so remained silent.

They exited the elevator and started walking back to their respective rooms. "You didn't want anything else getting in the way? What the hell does that even mean? You know what? I've been lucky enough to not have had any backlash with my sexuality. *And that's great*, but if you were to stand here before me and say I'm not ready to come out yet, that Texas can be still quite homophobic. And if that's the case, then maybe, just maybe I could get it. But you have been with a woman for…shit, God knows how long? Years…*and* have a five-year-old daughter with her. You're openly gay, and you're telling me you didn't want you being gay getting in the way? What the fuck does that even mean?" she said, opening the door to her room. "You know what? Don't answer that. I don't care. I'm pulling out before it goes any further. It doesn't matter why you did what you did, the fact of the matter is, you bare faced lie to me," Georgia said, walking inside her room.

Erika pushed the door and stopped Georgia from shutting it. "Do not shut me out. I don't know what's happening with any of it. I know it's wrong, but it equally feels right. And I can't deal with that. Hell, I'm still married. I haven't even had the conversation with my wife past anything further than a trial separation. So, should I be doing this? Hell, no. But do I wanna do this? Hell, yeah. I haven't felt more alive in…you know what, Georgia; I don't know I ever have. And that's the truth. But, in my head I just think…if that night in the bar when you declared you were gay I then said, FYI me too, the dynamics would have changed. Honestly, I don't know if I was being selfish because it would have been for the…well, I don't know if it would have been for the worse or the better? But maybe I was worried that you would have taken stock of the situation and taken a step back from me. And at that point you were already making me feel more alive than I'd ever felt. Or maybe it was because I was worried I was not in a good place. Me telling you I was gay, equally, would have made you push more. I don't know. I don't know why I did it. I have no excuse, but please do not feel like I betrayed you, that wasn't ever my intention. Please, Georgia," she said pleadingly.

"I…Erika, we both knew we shouldn't have gone there. I'm just glad we could stop it before we did anything we'd regret. I can deal with a lot of things, but I can't deal with lies," she said again.

Erika felt like she'd been sucker punched. She stepped backwards, feeling the pain of Georgia's words. "For the record," she stopped and shook her head, breathing in deeply. "For the record, if you're referring to *'being together'*? *Intimately?* I wouldn't have regretted that, but I guess the single life allows you to detach yourself from your feelings. I'm sorry, Georgia, I never thought I was lying to you. I just didn't tell you, because…hell, I don't even know why. But I'll leave you, you're right. But at least you didn't make a mistake by fucking me, huh?" she said, opening the door.

"Do not dare. Do not even fucking dare, turn this around on me," pushing her arm out over Erika's shoulder and slamming the door shut before she could leave. Erika turned around stunned. "How dare you? You did this. *You, not me, you.* I never lied, or, what did you call it *'delayed the truth?'* So, don't come in here and talk to me like I'm some dyke that slags it about. I told you I don't do that. I told you that I don't have time, nor have interest in doing that. I'm forty fucking years old. So, do I think it was good that we didn't sleep together? Yeah, because it would have just lead us into a whole world of difficulties, and I don't know if I could have handled being more into you and then finding out you lied. I had no intention of 'fucking' you as you so *crassly* put it," she spat. "I genuinely was trying everything I could to not do what my body was so desperate to do, because I knew it was wrong. But ultimately, I was *desperate* to physically be with you," she spat. "But I guess that's irrelevant now. We go back to Houston and we work professionally, and leave *this*…" She pointed to them both. "Leave this here!" She was furious and needed to calm down. "Look, you should go, this isn't getting us anywhere. It's late," she said, looking for the first time up to Erika, who looked as though she was desperately trying to hold back the tears.

Erika was defeated. She could see in Georgia's eyes that she was over it. Why had she done this? What was the possible reason for it? Why the hell did she not just tell her in the first place? What would it have even mattered? But it was done, she'd done it and there was nothing she could do to take it back. Erika felt shitty all over again, and all she wanted was to be held, but she certainly wasn't going to get that here, "Good night, Georgia. I know I have said it already, but..." She stopped. "I'm sorry, you have no idea," she said, leaving her there and closing the door behind her.

***

Erika got into her room and allowed the tears to flow freely. Seriously, what the hell? She met her a couple weeks back, when she was married. S*eparated* granted, but married with a wife. A partner of fifteen years, and a daughter, a beautiful, wonderful five-year-old daughter. Furthermore, she had hated this woman a week ago, so why the hell was she so bothered now? Why did she have such an effect on her? She felt her phone vibrate in her back pocket and rushed to get it, desperately hoping it would be a message from Georgia, only to be disappointed to see it was from her mom.

Are you okay? If you need to speak, come to me. Dulcie is sleeping, I love you, Bambina x

Erika cried a little more. She didn't want to tell her mom what was going on, since she was already disappointed that the marriage was in difficult times. So, telling her that she was developing feelings for another woman when she was still married, would…sheesh, she'd kick her butt.

I'm fine, Momma, I'm gonna get some sleep, I'll come get you for breakfast in the morning. Exx

Ok.

Her mom always felt the need to have the last word, even if she did waste a text on 'OK'. Erika got undressed and slipped under the duvet, allowing the stress of everything once again to crumble around her. She wondered if that was the reason she'd lied? Jeez, she *hadn't* lied! She wondered if that was the reason that she'd not told her she was gay, too? Because for just a short while, she would actually be able to hide the fact that her life was falling apart around her. She picked up her phone and started typing.

I don't know why I did it. I wish I did. But I certainly never did it to lie, and I'm incredibly sorry that you would ever feel that way. That night at the bar, we'd had such a blast at work that day, and as I explained, I just wanted one night away from all the shit that was going down around me and just be 'normal' for a night. I'm not saying I don't feel normal being gay, but I just wanted to hide away from it all, and in my defence, I did tell you that. Maybe that's why I didn't tell you? Then the next day we'd made out already and I didn't want to risk losing that way you made me feel. I can't remember feeling that good, or alive, or wanted. Shit, that attractive. So, when you said what you to me about my husband, I didn't want to correct you, in case it made you stop. Stupidly, as I write this, I can see/hear/read how dumb that sounds, a gay woman may go off a straight woman if she thought she was actually gay!! It is dumb and I don't know what's going on in my head anymore. What I do know is this sucks!! It sucks I hurt you, it sucks you feel I lied, it sucks that I'm here alone, crying when all I want is to lay with you. Most of all, it sucks that I did all this to prevent you from pushing me away, when in fact that's all I've done. I'm sorry, and I deeply regret not being with you intimately, because all night long that's all I've thought about. You looked incredible tonight, and I just thought you should know that. G'Night. Erika XXX

Erika hovered over the send button for a long while and re-read the message, which was far from a message. It was war and peace but, it was her explanation. All there in black and white. And if that didn't work, then nothing was going to she thought, pressing send and putting her phone under her pillow.

Chapter Sixty-Two

Erika woke up feeling groggy. She was immediately hit with the recollections of the previous night. Her head was hurting real bad and her eyes felt raw. She felt as though she'd been punched. Checking her phone, there were no messages on there, which just made her feel crappy all over again. She needed to get up and get packed, as they needed to drop her mom off before they left. She was not looking forward to the long ass journey back home, trying to entertain a five-year-old, as well as having a forty-year-old who wasn't speaking to her. Not exactly her idea of fun, *but she needed to face it sooner or later* she guessed, making her way up to start.

On her way to the bathroom Erika noticed the hotel paper that had been pushed under her door, picking it up she read the note.

Hi, I didn't want to wake you. I have left, as I didn't really feel up for the journey back. I've rented a car from reception. Please say thanks to your mum for dinner, and that it was lovely to meet her. I'll see you in work on Monday, have a safe trip back. G

Erika stood there dumbfounded. How the hell had this gone so wrong? She couldn't believe she had just left. What the hell was she supposed to tell her mom now?

***

Erika had finished putting everything in the trunk before making her way back up to her mom's room with Dulcie's clothes to change into. She prepared herself for the lecture, which she *so* wasn't ready for, knocking on the door and waiting for them to open it.

"Hey, Mommy. Are we going swimming? Where's Georgia? Is she still sleeping? Nonna's not got a door to Georgia's room like we got," she said.

"Hey, baby. No swimming today, but we can go in the pool and have a barbecue this afternoon, okay? Georgia had to leave already, she needed to get back home. Here's your clothes, how bout you go change? We have a long day ahead, so we need to get on the road soon."

"Mommy, will momma be at home when we get there?"

Erika sighed heavily. "I think she'll be working baby," she said, trying to sound as bright as she could about it.

"Stai bene?" her mother asked. "What's happening, Erika?"

"Nothing mamma, don't worry. I'll go help Dulcie."

"Bambina, don't shut me out, not again. She didn't know you were gay, but why did that matter? Please tell me you have not cheated on your wife with this woman? She is nice and kind woman, and she likes you a lot and Dulcie a lot, this is clear. But this...is no good, you are married, Erika."

"Mom, please just leave it. I am not cheating on my wife, and no she didn't know I was gay. I guess she was just a little pissed that we were friends and I didn't tell her, after everything that happened last week. It's fine."

"No cussing. So, why she left?" her mother asked, walking off, with a disapproving shake of the head, and not giving her an opportunity to reply.

Chapter Sixty-Three

"Hi, sorry I'm late," Dana said, kissing Erika on the cheek and sitting down.

"It's fine, how was work?" It amazed her that you spend most of your adult life with someone and have a child with them, to then be sitting in front of them in such an awkward manner.

"Yes, stressful but I guess you know that more than most. How was Fort Worth, and the new boss? Did you get everything you needed done?" Dana asked in between looking at the menu, making it completely evident she didn't have any interest in the questions *or* the answers. Erika thought about Georgia and the interest she paid when having a conversation, before recalling their last words and being immediately saddened.

"Yes, it was good and your daughter loved it. Plus, we got to see mom. So, that helped me out, considering I was there for work and all," she said sarcastically.

"Great!" she slammed. "You're still pissed I couldn't take her?" she said, nodding her head behind the menu.

Erika snatched the menu from her hand, forcing Dan to look up at her. "Honestly Dan, I don't think we'll be here long enough to eat..." she started.

"*You* invited me for dinner," she said sarcastically.

"Just listen for once, huh? You won't need that. No, I'm not pissed. Yeah, I was. She's *your* daughter, too, not like you act like it!" she spat. "But it's always so one sided. I'm not the stay at home mom. We both have challenging

321

and esteemed careers, but the difference is nothing will ever come above my daughter. And as for you, well nothing will ever come above your job," she yelled. Calming herself down a little, she started again. "I think we both know it's over. I don't want to waste any more time, Dan. I'm done, I'm over it and I'm past caring or getting upset any more. We haven't spent the night together in well over a year. Geez, I can't even bring myself to say the words 'make love to you'. We haven't kissed, held hands, or been affectionate in any way. We're rarely even in the same house at the same time. And honestly, do I think we can work on it? *No*, I don't. I thought I could and I thought you moving out would totally be the perfect opportunity for us to realise what we were doing and get back on track. But seriously, it's made me realise a lot more is wrong than is...*fixable*. Maybe if we tried to stop or manage it, *like* a year ago, it would have been different, who knows? I don't know if you've met someone else," Erika held her hand up to stop Dan from talking until she'd finished her point. "Honestly, I don't wanna know. Seriously, I'm pretty sure I don't care. But for what it's worth, I never gave up so easily. What I want is for us not to have a damaged child. What I want is *our* child to have a stable, loving upbringing rather than settling for second best. Or doing herself out of being in love, and somebody *wholly* loving her back, just because she has two moms who don't love each other anymore. I would rather her have two separated parents than that. I want a divorce, Dan. I'm sorry it's come to this, but really, there is no alternative."

"Wow, great speech," she said sardonically. "I...I think you're right, things have changed for us both. I don't know when or how, but it has, so I agree. We can file, and I don't want to have a messy battle. You can have Dulcie full time and we can arrange amongst ourselves a set time she comes to me, and we'll sort out the house and belongings like adults. I'll stay with my folks until I find a place of my own," she said, as if the last fifteen years meant nothing; as if it was as simple as picking up the groceries.

Erika knew wholeheartedly what she was doing was for the best, but she never expected her wife to be so nonchalant about it, leaving her somewhat unbalanced. She didn't expect for her to break down in tears, but she never expected to be so blasé about it either. In that moment after listening to Dan's response, she would have bet everything she had on the fact that Dana had already moved on and that's why it had come to this. Either way, she *couldn't* know. She didn't want to know either.

"Okay, well how about you have her this weekend? She hasn't seen you in a few weeks and was asking this morning for you."

"Oh, um, well…I hav…"

"Lemme guess. You have plans? I tell you what, Dan, forget it. Don't blame me when your daughter starts feeling the same way I did. Like you're second best. Call me when you have time for her, K?" she snapped, before getting up and leaving her wife alone in the restaurant, and walking out of her life, *'their'* life forever!

Chapter Sixty-Four

"Ohhh honey, I'm sorry. Things are not going so smoothly at *all* over here, are they?" Emily said to Georgia after she'd filled her in on the whole trip.

"Nah, not really," she rolled her eyes. "I'm just annoyed. It's like...I don't even know. It's like she is, devaluing being gay. I know that's stupid as she *is* gay, but I just don't know why you would do it?" she added, sipping her beer.

"I don't think she's done that, sweetie. I just think she's in a pretty rough place and probably just wanted for one night to not have any label, ya know? Like, not a mom, not a boss, not a lesbian, not a wife. Just a normal woman out for a normal drink with a colleague, doing what so many take for granted."

"You don't think she's done anything wrong?" she said astounded.

"No, no, I'm not saying that. What I'm saying is, I can appreciate why she felt the need to do it, but she should have told you the next time for sure. She screwed up on that front," she said back to Georgia, almost trying to backtrack.

"*But*, she had a hot ass blonde paying her some attention...which it doesn't sound like she got too much of for a long ass time," John said, waving the barbecue tongs around. "Why would she? As a guy who likes women...correction, woman," John winked to Emily. "If it was me, and I'm pretty sure numerous amounts of other dumb guys, if you don't tell the first time it's a mishap. So, you go and correct that the following morning. If you don't, it becomes...well, it becomes difficult. She's now getting some interest, and if she tells, she faces losing that. She probably feels pretty crappy over the failing marriage, so it's a catch twenty-two. You tell her, she stops chasing you. You don't, you have gotten sucked into a world of lies. I know it's not what you wanna hear, but if I was feeling so crappy, I probably wouldn't have been able to tell you either. But that's why us guys get into all kinds of crap with lies," he said from the barbecue.

"Okay, so you guys both think I've overreacted," she said quietly. She was feeling somewhat annoyed that her only friends didn't really see her point on this, and more annoyed that she was feeling this way about them. Why was she caught up like this?

"No, we're not saying that at all, you're misinterpreting us. We agree it's wrong to withhold the truth, especially when you are spending time together and have got acquainted on a different level, on a sexual level," Emily said seriously.

"Wait, I didn't sleep with her," Georgia said shocked.

"No, but you kissed and you wouldn't be this pissed if you didn't like her. But as a mom, there's been times when I've been desperate for just one night to be someone else. And it's great, but the next morning you wake up and you deal with life. Then yeah, you tell the truth," Emily reiterated.

Maybe they were right? She wasn't a parent, and maybe she genuinely did do it for that reason. Regardless of that, she found it *that* easy to lie to Georgia numerous times after that. And that she *couldn't* get over, she could not deal with liars, she hated it. She'd been burned in the past by them, so she wouldn't put herself in that situation again.

Chapter Sixty-Five

Georgia had been sitting in the car for almost twenty minutes. She'd not seen nor spoken to Erika since Thursday night when they argued. And she hadn't been back here, seen or spoken to anyone in this place since she walked out and left. Equally, they had all thought she had left and gone back to the UK. So, when she walked in all hell would break loose...all over again. She knew this was going to be bad, and was annoyed at herself for getting involved where she shouldn't have. They were getting on so well, and she would have totally been able to do this had it stayed platonic, just the way it was. But instead, she had to go and get blindsided by a beautiful woman! Georgia thought back to last week, the night Erika opened the door with the black halter on, recalling later in the evening as she got up to go to the bar when Georgia noticed for the first time that it was backless. Her first view of the smooth dark skin beneath her top. She could remember the slightest piece of material on the top around her neckline and then a thin tie across the centre and that was is it, the rest was exposed. Her tanned, perfect, naked back. It had caused a stir inside her, and it was that moment she knew she was playing with fire. Georgia stopped and scolded herself for letting her thoughts wander back to the incredible woman.

Georgia knew she had to do it at some point. It was five to nine and according to Erika's email to the heads of departments last night, there would be a meeting at nine am. Basically it was now or never. An inopportune moment for her to walk in on the meeting and surprise them all, *just what she'd always dreamed of,* she thought sarcastically!

Georgia arrived at the office and was met immediately by Mike. "Hey Georgia, how you doing?" he said seriously.

"Amazing!" she responded pointedly, trying to ignore the looks and whispers from the two receptionists.

"Come on, if anyone can pull this off y'all can. I'll quickly check and see they are ready for ya," he said.

Mike returned a couple of seconds later, "All set, united front, remember?" he pointed his finger at her.

***

Georgia walked into the room, feeling incredibly uncomfortable. More so because the person she needed to have an alliance with to help her get through this with, was Erika. Not the best of plans given the situation at present and their parting words to each other. Keeping her eyes on Erika, she noticed her eyes were warm and apologetic, allowing her to relax a little in the situation unfolding before her. Additionally, it allowed her to block out all the gasps and confusion from them all, as she concentrated on the beautiful face.

"Hi, Georgia. Please come in and sit?" Erika said warmly.

"Okay y'all, thanks for your time this morning. As you saw last night/this morning, I needed to have a meeting with y'all. As you can now see, this is the reason why," she stopped and pointed to Georgia. "Georgia is back! For those of you that have been discussing the fact that she had returned to the UK and left, that's obviously incorrect. And now you will realise why I didn't text you back about it, for those of you who were texting," she said, looking around

327

the room, disappointed at her team and the sheepish looks they were wearing. "So, to bring y'all up to speed, Georgia never left, nor would I have let her. We were both up in Fort Worth last week, starting on the new office. We purposely refrained from messaging any of y'all, so we could focus on what we have both been brought in to do. And Mike and Derek, the UK version of him, were right. We make a great team and this will be an incredible opportunity for us both to work together and improve our knowledge and experiences. As well as utilising each other's skills." She stopped and looked at Georgia, smiling. "Lastly, what happened before is *over*. I get y'all wanna have my back, and you maybe don't like change, but we don't do that here," she rebuked. "If I hear people talking, or refusing to help and do their jobs, or be unkind in any way whatsoever, I'll be down on you so hard you won't know what hit you. As I said, I get that you were all being loyal to me, and I appreciate that. But we don't operate like that. I will not have anyone screwing this up. It's not ideal, but remember Georgia didn't come after this. This *wasn't* her idea, and so you either work with *us,* or there's the door," she said seriously, pointing to the boardroom door.

Everyone was silent, and Georgia was impressed with her impetuousness. She gave it to them hard and they didn't look like they were about to take her on at all.

"Any questions?" Erika asked. The silence was deafening.

"Good, okay. So, for information purposes, Georgia *is* the new boss, yes. However, I will be the one reporting to her and you guys report to me still. We have one aim and twelve months to do it in. It's no different to the others, but ultimately, this will be the global flag ship. So, if we are going to exceed and excel at anything, it *has* to be this.

Bonuses will ride on this! Georgia, you want to add anything?"

"Well, I guess my main thing as we discussed last week is, I don't know this place. The way it works, the clients or well anything. So, although, they have sent me over to be above you, I don't work that way. And I don't want to under the circumstances. For me, I would like you and I to work collaboratively to pull this through, and I would like all of you guys to be part of that so we achieve it, *together*. We can't do it without all of you. You people are the experts, and we need your expertise to make that work. So, as Erika said you have two choices. So, who's in?" she asked.

Erika turned to her, "Bring it, I can't wait to…What did you call it? *Smash the arse out of this thing?*" she said, smiling at Georgia, as she repeated the words Georgia had used last week.

Georgia laughed back to Erika at her teasing, glad they could remain professional in front of the staff. "Nice," she said, looking at the room, taking in the quiet grumblings of 'count me in' around the table.

***

Georgia and Erika watched everyone leave when they finished the meeting. When the last person left, Georgia sank in her chair and sighed heavily, "Thank God that's over," she said, raising her eyebrows. "Erm, thank you for that," she said politely. "And thank you for your support. I don't know if it will work, we shall see. But thank you all the same," she said seriously, getting up to leave.

"Don't go!" Erika said, suddenly embarrassed. "It was the least I could do. And they will," she said optimistically.

"If they don't I'll fire their asses," she said seriously. "Listen, Georgia. I'm sorry again about last week. I was dreading this morning. If you'd come, or how you would be with me? I never meant to hurt you, or lie. I would never have lied to you or anyone, that isn't what I'm about. I *am* a coward, but I'm not a liar. I would never have intentionally done that. I have spent all weekend regretting it, and I didn't do it to you…for you or…because of you. It was something that I needed in that moment for *me,* just because of everything that was/*is* happening in my life. If I could take it back, I would in a flash. I would have just told you and taken the risk of you backing off, I…" she stopped, as they were interrupted by the knock on the door. Erika was the one to sigh heavily now. "Come in," she said unhappily.

"Heeeeyyyy," she heard as a woman Erika had never seen before walked into the room.

"Julia?" Georgia scoffed. "What are you doing here?" Georgia asked sheepishly, looking back to Erika.

"Well, I figured you needed a friend with everything that had been going on. So, I got Derek to give me a week off so I could come over and surprise you." She smiled, rushing over to Georgia and giving her a hug. "I guess you must be Erika?" she said, holding out her hand.

"Hi," Erika said rigidly. "Umm, I'll leave you guys to it since we're finished with the meeting. Nice to meet you…um?"

"Sorry," Georgia said awkwardly. "Erika, this is Julia, the marketing director from my office. Jules, as you've just worked out…this is Erika," she added, feeling weird. She had no idea that Julia was coming, nor why. And she could feel the tension, but more importantly, she could see the sadness in Erika's eyes. It couldn't have happened at a worse time. Georgia turned to Erika as she was leaving.

"Erm, I'll come find you this afternoon and we can finish off?"

"It's okay, you go and enjoy some time together. I'd finished what I needed to say," she said and walked out of the door.

Fuck. Georgia thought as she watched the woman leave.

"So, how's it going? Hope you don't mind me coming. FYI, I am not here as the trademark bunny boiler!" she stated. "I have literally come as a friend. I was worried about you, and then when Derek returned and told me what had been going on, I figured you needed one right now? I haven't booked anywhere to stay, it…well it was all a bit last minute. But you said when you arrived I could crash in one of your spare rooms when I came over? If that invitation is still open, I would like to take it up. If um…well there isn't going to be any issue. Just that that seemed somewhat awkward," she finished, pointing to the door where Erika had just left.

Georgia wondered what she meant. "Yes, that's fine. But I can't get out to take you back, and it's quite far, so I don't really know…"

"George, George, its fine. I know you're working and I don't need babysitting. I've booked into a spa for the day. I figured what better way to start my holiday than a relaxing day of pampering. Hopefully, by a hot American." She winked.

"Right," Georgia giggled. "Got it all planned out, haven't you?" She smiled. "Thanks for coming to check on me, Jules. That's very kind. Last week made things much better," she said sadly, only lying a little.

"Excellent, I'm glad for that. I was worried about you. Okay, if I'm alright leaving this case in your office, I'll come back. What around six?" Julia asked.

"Yeah, that's fine. Come on, I'll take you up to my office, you can dump it there."

***

"Hey. You got a minute?" Georgia asked, knocking on Erika's door.

"Sure…Erm, sorry yeah, come in. So, the girlfriend came out, huh?" Georgia went to speak and before she had a chance, Erika stopped her. "I'm sorry. That was idiotic and childish. Clearly, I'm shit at all forms of well, everything. I'm sorry I was out of line for saying that, it's none of my business," she said, avoiding eye contact and inwardly shaking herself for her own stupidity. "Look, I was serious earlier. I'd finished. I just wanted to tell you again I was sorry. I just wanted to say I hope you knew I had and will forever regret it. Regardless of what you think or feel but it's done, there's nothing I can do to change it. The only thing further I would have said was my mom said to say thanks for the room and she enjoyed spending some time with you. She thought you were lovely," Erika finished. "Anyways, if you need to go be with your, um…Julia, it's fine. I can pick up here. It's gone well as anticipated, deathly silent with them all," she added, smiling a small smile.

"That's nice, I really liked her too. And she does do the best pasta. For the record, I have said and I will say again, I am not in a relationship. Not with Julia, not with anyone. I'm single, and I don't know why she came over. She said she was concerned after speaking to me a couple weeks back, and then Derek when he returned. But I didn't speak to her at all last week, so maybe she was concerned things got worse? I don't honestly know. But she is just a concerned friend. That's all, *not* because we're together."

"Well maybe she wants to be, maybe that's why she's here. She's cute, you should do it. Like you said, had this whole moving to the other side of the Atlantic BS not happened, you don't know where things would have ended up. She could be the one. Twelve…" she stopped, looking up to Georgia for the first time, forcing a smile. "Sorry, nine months, ain't a long time at all, and absence makes the heart grow fonder, after all," she said, trying to force a smile again, looking away from Georgia again.

Georgia went to say something and stopped herself, rubbing her eyes. "Thanks for your time and this morning, the meeting I mean. I'll catch up with you in a bit," she said, admitting defeat and leaving.

"You *idiot,*" Erika said quietly to herself when Georgia had left. *Seriously, what was that*? she thought as she hit her head with her hand. Why the hell had she done that? She was so lame.

Chapter Sixty-Six

"My God, George, this place is immense! Shit," Julia said, looking around with Georgia. "Which room do you want me to put my case in?" she asked, stopping and spinning around. "Sorry, I didn't mean that like insinuating spare or yours. I didn't. As I said, it's not why I'm here. I meant which spare room?" she said.

"Chill...the...hell...out! I didn't think you meant that. They are both spare, so take your pick." She smiled. "So, you fancy a pool party and barbecue with some beers?"

"Shit yeah, Manc was raining when I left. Although, I'm jet lagged to hell, I managed to sleep half the day in the spa," she said, eyes gleaming.

"You are as loopy as ever. Come on, let's go and party in the pool." She smiled wide.

Georgia picked up her phone, hearing it vibrate on the side, laughing as she read the message from Emily asking who the woman was?

"Hot bit of stuff," Julia said looking at the phone.

"*Shut up*! My neighbour inquiring as to whom the mystery woman was?" she laughed, raising her eyes.

"Wow, nosey here ehy?" she laughed.

Georgia took Julia outside and lit the barbecue. They both got in the pool with their beers and enjoyed the early evening sun, discussing everything that had been going on back at home.

"Seriously, I'm starting to think I should have thrown myself at you earlier. I could happily live this lifestyle."

"Shut up," Georgia splashed her friend.

***

The last of the sun was just disappearing in the distance. "I know I keep saying it," Julia slurred. "But, seriously this is incredible."

"Yeah, yeah I know. You've told me at least four times."

"I'm sorry, it's the jet lag. It's got me drunker than what I would normally be. Oh, *and* the drinking in the sun. It always gets me pissed quicker. But check this out, look at my tan line," she leaned back, lowering her bikini bottom at the waistband ever so slightly. "I'm glad I came to check on you, so I can get a week of this," she said pointing to the fading sun. "With a pool to myself whilst you're at work every day, happy days!" she said seriously.

"Yeah, alright for some ehy? I've not even had a chance to chill out around the pool yet, but this weekend I have the perfect excuse now," she said, pushing Julia playfully.

"Or you could always take a sickie?" she hiccupped.

"Erm, yeah my first proper day without no disasters. I think I need to get my arse into gear with this working project, so you'll have to entertain yourself," she laughed.

"Hmmm, that's a shame." She winked. "Right, I am feeling very intoxicated, and seeing you lay there half naked and clearly, um…cold," she giggled. "I think I should go to bed, before I try to jump your bones," she said, looking at Georgia.

Georgia covered her breasts with her hands, feigning shock. She was drunk herself and knew it wasn't a good idea to go back there, least of all not now. "Yes, well, now that you've virtually professed your undying love just to get into my cool new home, I think it will only end up in disaster for sure," she giggled.

"Undying love my arse, I was merely talking about a fuck buddy for the week. Just like before you left," she said bluntly, causing Georgia to spit her drink out.

"You are *so* bad," she said, walking to her phone to see who was texting her now.

Hi, didn't want to call, figured you'd be busy entertaining. Could we have the afternoon together tomorrow? I have an idea for Fort Worth, and think your expertise will be perfect. Apologies for disturbing you, have a good evening! Thanks, Erika.

Georgia read the message a couple of times, shaking her head at the…*professionalism* to it.

"Everything okay? Who's the text from? It certainly looks to have sobered you up?" Julia questioned.

"Oh, it's nobody, just work. So, where were we? Fuck buddy eh?" Georgia smirked, knowing full well she was about to make a big mistake. She pushed Erika to the back of her mind and kissed Julia regardless.

Chapter Sixty-Seven

Erika was kicking herself for being such an idiot and sending the message. She hadn't been lying, she'd had an amazing idea which she did think was great. In reality, it could have waited until tomorrow to discuss. All because she couldn't stand the idea of Georgia with that woman, but it wasn't her place to say anything. She was single after all. Jesus, they had a couple of kisses for goodness sake. She'd known the woman a couple of weeks and hated her the first week. She rested her head against the back of her couch and closed her eyes tight, wondering if this what it had come to. A single, thirty-eight-year-old mom, who jumps on every lesbian that shows her a little bit of interest or takes a second glance at her? She couldn't be that person. She had never needed to be in a relationship, and she wasn't afraid to be single, as she never had been. She'd always been a strong, independent woman. So why the fuck was she acting so dumb over this one?

Picking up her phone she looked at the message. She could see it had been read over ten minutes ago, so she was clearly otherwise engaged, Erika thought sadly. *Great, now you're acting like a stalker,* she thought to herself.

Erika felt so lonely. Her daughter was in bed and she now had nobody else left. She picked up her phone and typed a message to Taylor, asking if she'd like to come over for dinner the following day, because she hated feeling alone. She did need to consider the prospect of moving back home closer to her family. She was Italian. They didn't do alone, and they did big families.

Taylor responded, straight away confirming, and asking if Erika was okay. Apparently, she hadn't sounded it. It amazed her that Taylor could tell if she was down even over a text. She wasn't about to text telling her she wasn't. So, she responded with fine and they'd talk tomorrow. Feeling deflated and beaten, she gave up and decided to just go to bed. It wasn't particularly late, but she wasn't up for sitting and dwelling on things that were now out of her control. She grabbed some water and used her phone to search local things to do. She decided then and there she needed to start going out a little more. If she could get a couple activities to do through the week, she would be able to meet new people. Not for dating purposes, but maybe she could meet some more friends. She was always so preoccupied with work or her daughter that she'd never had any time for anything else. But it was time she made some changes to her life. Erika made a pact with herself that she was going to do stuff, start living a little, and make the most of this new life she had.

Chapter Sixty-Eight

Georgia was laid on her bed, looking at the ceiling in the dark room. She felt shit. No, she felt worse than shit. She didn't fuck about and play games with people. So why the hell did she decide to start tonight? And more so, faking? *Really*? She couldn't remember the last time she'd faked an orgasm. She looked over to Julia, quietly sleeping naked next to her. At least she hadn't been selfish and had seemingly gave her a good time. The problem was, her mind was in other places. And unfortunately, when it came to Julia wanting to repay the favour, she couldn't do it. She closed her eyes and saw Erika, which was turning her on immensely. But then she'd think better of it, and open her eyes and see Julia and she didn't want that either. Why did this woman have such an effect on her? This wasn't good, and the more she knew she couldn't, the more it compounded the situation. Georgia thought back to the night they went out, and she couldn't help but recall the feeling when she looked up from her phone to see Erika stood in front of her. There was no denying the woman was incredibly beautiful, stunning in fact. She recalled leaving the hotel, walking out in the cool evening air with the slightest breeze blowing her long, black, straight hair to one side. She remembered thinking then she could have been off some bloody L'Oréal advert. Georgia virtually had to hold onto the rail to keep her legs from giving way. Yet incredulously, this incredibly beautiful woman didn't see what she saw. She had so little confidence, and that ate

Georgia up inside, because to her she was the most perfect being she had ever met. Recalling the end of the night stood outside her room. Georgia thought back to her words *kiss me already*. Erika had taken complete control then, and she knew it. Her words and the *way* she spoke them. Her accent, *god that accent* she thought, and then the feel of her bare back. Shit, she wished she'd had a chance to appreciate that body. Georgia could feel her senses stirring, and knew it was wrong. Why was this happening to her? Why couldn't she have just kept it professional? Not gotten with Julia? Anything would have been better than this.

She picked up her phone and read the message again. Georgia began typing, and then stopped. This woman was getting under her skin, and she just couldn't stop thinking about her. She stopped herself, knowing it was wrong and deleted the words. Looking over at Julia again, she was embroiled in the guilt she was feeling. She'd never felt guilt about having sex before, and she never slept with anybody that there could be issues or dramas with. Well not for the last twenty years. She had enough stress in her professional life, and the last thing she needed was it in her personal life too. Georgia picked up her phone again, knowing she just had to bite the bullet. She wasn't going to get any sleep whilst she kept thinking of Erika and feeling guilty.

Hey up, you could have called. You wouldn't have been disturbing me. We just had barbecue and enjoyed the weather and pool, us Brits aren't as lucky as you guys. Sounds interesting, can't wait to hear it. Yes, I have all day free, so I'm all yours ☺ G

Too nicey *nicey*, she thought. Unquestionably guilt ridden too. Too flirty…'all yours'? but she couldn't just ignore it all anymore. Despite how royally she may have fucked up tonight.

It was bizarre, the whole situation was. Three weeks ago, she didn't know the woman. Two weeks ago, was being bullied by the woman. A week ago, kissing the woman. Now, lying next to a woman who up until a month ago, she'd been happily sleeping with. And was now feeling guilty going back there because of the reason for doing it. *Jesus, she was one nonstop soap opera.* Georgia had prostituted herself. That *was* it. She'd shagged Julia in a bid to stop thinking about Erika, and ultimately made her think about her more and was now feeling guilty towards both women. Great, this was a new one even for her. *I'm a bloody prostitute!* she thought, shaking her head to herself. Georgia was out of order for what she'd done to Julia, and they couldn't drink again. It wasn't fair, but maybe she wouldn't care. She said she wanted a fuck buddy after all. Surely fuck buddies didn't only have one fuck buddy? Otherwise it would have just been a relationship, wouldn't it? Shit, this was doing her own head in now. Georgia noticed the grey dots appear and couldn't help but feel nervous as she waited patiently for the response.

***

Erika didn't know how to read the message. She was being flat yet jovial, yet she couldn't help but feel jealous over the fact that Julia was sitting there with Georgia. That incredible body in a bikini, she sighed, thinking back to the first day at Fort Worth when she spotted her in the bikini. God, she had an incredible body. Then when she was doing that stupid swim for Dulcie's benefit. And how the bottoms had raised slightly, giving Erika a little more flesh to look at, that amazing ass. She could feel herself getting aroused. She read the last part again. Was *she* flirting? *I'm all yours.*

Was it a euphemism? What was she doing? Was she drunk and flirting with her? Had she forgiven her? Or was she just merely saying that she could have that time tomorrow? *Stop acting like a kid*, she scolded herself.

Erika began typing, before deleting it and rewriting. This happened at least four times before she finally knew what to write.

Well as I said, I didn't want to disturb, out of work time and all that!! Glad you enjoyed the weather, it was a lovely evening for it. I think you'll like the idea actually☺. Honestly, if you didn't have company, I'd be tempted to call you regarding it. All mine? I guess I should feel privileged. You should get back to your friend and stop texting me. E

Very noble of you ;) I told you to call! However, now I'm intrigued and excitably awaiting tomorrow afternoon. It was a lovely evening and I made some beautiful grilled lamb kebabs with pitta. Hmmm. ☺ I was very impressed with my little self. You should feel privileged indeed. It's ok, she's in bed, jet lag. Gx

Wore her out, huh? ;)

Georgia read the message that was back within milliseconds, sighing. Why the hell had she done it? If she told her, it would go bad, and Erika wouldn't have wanted to know her at all. But if she didn't then she was lying to her, doing exactly what she was pissed with her for. And she hated lies.

Sorry, I'm an ass ☹

Yes, you are! But a cute one ;) and have a very cute one actually x

Hmmm you think ,huh? Nicely avoided. ;) X

You wanna know exactly what we did tonight? I will tell you if that's what you want. And yes, I do, very much so. Which is pissing me off ☹x

No, I'm feeling kind of shitty tonight, pretty low. So, I don't think it would be wise for me to know ☻ why pissing you off? X

You ok? Can I do anything? You want to talk? I can call you. I dunno, I guess because I'm not a drama kind of woman. I'm simple. I like simple things, and there's a hundred reasons why I shouldn't fancy you and then I think about you in a bikini. your soft skin against my fingers. How beautiful you are. Your loud, croaky sexy as hell laugh, and most of all the way you kiss me, then those reasons go out the window again x

Wow you been doing a lot of thinking? Simple huh ;) X

Shut up! Yup, you have got in my head! ☻ X

Ditto x

So why you feeling down? X

Just shitty I guess. feel bad for my baby, I feel bad that I couldn't make my marriage work. Pretty sure my wife has been cheating for God knows how long, and I feel guilty that I made you feel I lied to you. I feel guilty that I'm having completely inappropriate thoughts about you when I'm married, and I feel guilty that I cheated on my wife with you. Albeit we were separated and we haven't kissed for a real long time, and over all the guilt I feel, the biggest guilt I feel is that even after all that, regardless of anything else, I regret having not spent the night with you! There I said it!! X

Georgia read the words, surprised by what she was reading. She got out of bed and threw a shirt on. She couldn't stay in here laid next to a naked woman she had just slept with, when all the time the person she wanted to sleep with was the person on the other end of the phone. Slipping into the spare bed, Georgia picked up her phone and dialled the number, unsure of whether she would actually answer.

After the second ring tone, Georgia heard the soft American voice.

"Hey."

"Hi."

Silence.

"You ok?" Erika asked concerned.

"Not really, I'm pissed off at myself and I'm concerned about you."

"Don't worry about me, I'm okay. I'm always okay," she sighed. "So why you pissed off?" she asked, thinking she already knew the answer.

"Look, I don't do this. Never, and I can't deal with people that do. But equally, I was pissed at you for keeping something from me, so I needed to do this," she sighed heavily. "Will you make me a promise?"

"Well it depends what it is."

"Promise not to hang up until I've finished speaking?"

Erika sighed, knowing what was coming, and she felt her tummy tighten and felt sick to her stomach.

"Sure," she said almost silently.

"I slept with her," she sighed. "I'm sorry. And I don't know why, but I am. She tried it on when she was pissed, then I got your message and saw what you had put, or more how you had put it and it got my back up. So, I thought I'd prove that things were fine and you were just some woman and it didn't matter. But I couldn't do it, because every time I shut my eyes I kept thinking of you. I wanted to be making love to you and when I opened my eyes, it wasn't you. I don't know why this is happening. You're married, and strangely I never do shit like that either. I just wanted to prove to myself I didn't like you, that you were just a sexy

Italian American that I kissed a couple of times and that was it," she finished.

Georgia listened to the silence, the only give away that she was still there were the soft breaths she could hear.

"That's um…probably more information than I needed to hear," she said ever so softly.

"I'm sorry. I just needed to tell you. How could I not after everything I said and did to you last week?"

"So…what? I have nothing on you, you are a big girl and I can't say or do anything."

"I regret it, and I want you to say something. I want you to tell me I fucked up. I was a fucking idiot and I shouldn't have done it. Instead of being silent, I know I'm an idiot and I do like you and I can't change that and I should just deal with it and move on. I want you to tell me you're pissed at me. Just like I did to you, Erika. I want you to say it, because you like me too, and I shouldn't have slept with someone else. Certainly, not in a bid to convince myself I don't like you," she said to Erika.

"I'm pissed that it's affecting me. I'm pissed that its making me feel sick. I'm pissed that I have to deal with her being with you for a whole week. I'm pissed she got to be with you," Erika sighed loudly.

"I'm sorry, Erika," Georgia whispered.

"Yeah me too, Georgia. Look it's late, I should probably," Erika said, before hanging up on her.

Georgia stayed on the line for a few moments, feeling shitty all over again. She needed to be truthful to her, but then it backfired anyway. She knew she had done right in telling her. What the fuck was she doing? Georgia looked back to six months ago, when none of this was on the cards. She worked, and there were no women in her life. Her job was guaranteed, and then this major turn of events. But interestingly out of all of it, she missed the feelings that had started to creep in. She missed being silly, laughing, feeling the stirs when a beautiful woman comes into the room. She'd been single for three years and honestly, she didn't think she would ever get with anyone again. When a relationship breaks down over work and those dynamics don't change, then how do you ever get past that? Georgia thought sombrely. Katie had cheated on her because she didn't pay her enough attention. The ease of having a second life because she spent so much of her life at work. So why would she ever consider getting into another relationship? Why would she put herself through all of that again?

***

Erika lay there in silence, listening to the nocturnal noises from outside the window. Should she have ended the call that way? She had no rights to Georgia, but hearing her say the words made her realise the situation she was potentially getting herself into. She was married, and she was about to start a process of divorce. Plus, she had a five-year-old daughter, and she was chasing after someone. For what, because she felt she missed out on sleeping with her? Because she paid her some attention? Surely, she'd just screw her and that would be it, done. So why would she put herself through the agony? Yeah, she enjoyed the feelings of someone wanting her and looking at her with desire, but she was a grown ass woman; a mom, an area director. She needed to start behaving like one.

Chapter Sixty-Nine

"I'm sorry again," Georgia said.

"Please stop saying sorry. It's fine."

"It isn't though, it really isn't. That's not who I am."

"Yeah, and I know that, George. I'm not going to lie, if all of this hadn't happened I wonder what would have happened between us. But equally, you don't know what's around the corner. A year is a long time for anyone to put their lives on hold. But seriously, you aren't a bad person. Granted, you made a bit of stupid judgement on Monday. But equally, consider the way I was coming on to you and offering you 'free shags', *and* the circumstances. Your attraction to this woman, I can get it. I was in this place a few years back with you remember? I shagged anything that moved in a bid to get over you, but it doesn't work that way. Honestly, when you are a decent person, it makes it ten times worse as you have to deal with the way it leaves you feeling. But for what it's worth, I don't think you should lose out on this. If something's there, I think you should go for it. Think about that TV series we were watching the other night...The Bachelor. People spend their whole lives searching for love. If you have one iota that is interested in this woman, don't risk losing it, for all you know she could be the one."

"You are such a lesbian. You *sure* you don't want to transfer here? I could do with a friend," Georgia said, cuddling Julia one last time. "Text me when you get home, yeah?"

"I don't think Erika would be too happy with that, babes, but I think she seems pretty cool from what you've told me. I think…and this is probably the stupidest thing I've ever said to you, but…it is my belief that there *is* one true love for everyone out there. I'm not saying that it's her *or* that it isn't, but I'm a firm believer that everything happens for a reason. So, don't hold back, George. You're a good woman with a lot to offer. Stop overthinking everything and follow your heart."

"Wow, that was all a bit deep. You're talking like we've known each other months and I'm in love with her or something. Follow your heart? *Blimey*. Seriously, she's a sexy woman, and I've never had an American. It's just my body being naughty craving what it can't have."

Julia stopped looking at her. "Keep telling yourself that darling! As I said, stop overthinking. You are purposely putting barriers in the way, because you *know* it is more than just a 'sexy American you can't have'. Just remember," she said seriously. "Where do lesbians go for their second date?" she laughed.

"Shut up, you dick. Get on that plane. Thanks, and sorry again," she said, hugging Julia one last time.

"What? They go to the estate agents," she giggled. "Yeah, we may move fast as a general stereotype, but if you are into someone, why the hell would you waste any time? And if you think you're into someone, why would you waste time focussing on what could go wrong? Why not put your heart on the line and enjoy it for what it is and see what happens? It may blossom, it may end horribly, or it may end with just a little bit of fun." She shoved her shoulder. "But life's too short to waste time, and if it doesn't work out, then I guess at least you can have some fun over the next year. But I do have to go. Have fun and come see us soon, yeah?" she said, kissing Georgia on the cheek and leaving.

Georgia felt all the worse now. She had used her friend and colleague to sleep with her, and now she was talking to her like she'd met the love of her life. She was a horrible person, who didn't act this way normally, and *that* was the harsh reality of it.

***

Georgia thought about what Julia had said on the drive over. She hadn't spoken to Erika at all other than anything work related, since their call this time last week. She had been honest with Julia, and despite it being driven by Georgia, Julia had revealed that she was completely aware that Georgia had faked it. *Just what any single woman wants to admit,* she thought. Admittedly, Julia had confirmed that she could see something behind Georgia's smile and eyes about this woman, was that right? Georgia didn't know. What she did know is that when she was at work and saw Erika, or in a meeting with her she felt different. She felt...happy, happy just to see her. When she didn't see her she just wanted to see her, speak to her about nothing in particular. Merely to be close to her and listen to her laugh, her voice. But the fact of the matter was, it was all wrong. She was married. She had a kid, and they were two complete opposite ends of scale from each other. They were chalk and cheese, so why the fuck was she even thinking about any of this? What was it about Erika that was making her feel this way?

Chapter Seventy

Georgia's alarm went off at five forty-five am. She'd slept quite well, and was thankful for a night off the booze. She got into her gym gear and grabbed some water before making her way to Emily's house.

***

They arrived at the Pilates class, which Emily was sure would be what she needed to clean up her head. Emily had told her she needed something mentally stimulating, given she thought it was acceptable and appropriate to sleep with a woman to get another woman out of her head. She was not happy and was making it very clear, and Georgia liked that about her. She wasn't pussy footing around her. Their friendship, which had been very quickly established, allowed Emily to make it clear exactly what she thought, feeling confident enough to let her see her disappointment. It was like being with her mum all over again. But she wouldn't change it for the world. This woman was the best friend she had had for a bloody long time.

"So, you coming to Torr's meet on Friday? I thought we could maybe go out. Have a girl's night after? Maybe go for dinner and dancing?" Emily asked.

"Yeah, sounds fantastic. I'm definitely up for that. I've never been to a 'meet' before," she said. "And like I said I don't dance, but I will happily watch you and drink," she added, laughing at Emily.

"Ohhh, but maybe if I was a hot ass, Italian, American lesbian you would, huh? Typical, you lesbians are no different to guys." She winked, looking back to Georgia. Emily had told her she'd never met any gay people before. She wasn't homophobic at all, but Texas was a state where they were probably a little behind the times. Especially compared to some other states. Either way, Georgia was happy that she didn't seem to have a problem with her. If it wasn't for her and John, there's no way she would have lasted.

"Shut up. Come on, let's go and see if Pilates stimulates my mind enough to make me stop misbehaving," Georgia laughed, getting out of the car.

"Not funny, Georgia, *not* funny!"

***

The class was harder than she expected. She was fit and always keen to maintain that, but Emily was right, it was more about focussing your mind on your core. It made her stop thinking and focus, which had been Emily's point. As they were getting ready to leave, Georgia noticed Erika's nanny in the class. She looked around to see if Erika was there too, but was disappointed to find she wasn't. Taylor looked up and spotted Georgia, looking as though she was trying to place where she knew her from.

Georgia turned to Emily, "I'll be two minutes," she said, walking over to the woman.

"Hi, its Taylor, isn't it?"

"Hey, Georgia, right? I couldn't quite place you when I saw you then, but the accent gave it away." She smiled softly. "How are you?"

"Yeah, seemingly not as fit as I thought I was, but outside of this class I'm okay. How's things? Pilates is the de-stress for looking after kids I see." She smiled.

"Yeah for sure. That and law school. You look pretty fit to me." She smiled. "So, I hear Fort Worth went well. I'm glad you guys sorted things out. I know it's not my place to say, and I hope you don't mind an American's directness. But we spoke, and honestly, Erika isn't like that. She was just in a bad place with everything that was going on at home, and like you, at work," she said.

"Wow, you are a nanny *and* training to be a lawyer. Jesus you're a glutton for punishment. Well, I just hope that things work out for Erika. I know it can't be good to be separated when you have a kid, too," she said, trying to be as diplomatic as possible so it didn't look like she was snooping.

"Oh, she's sorted everything out now, and she's in a much better place, too," she said seriously, watching Georgia a little too intensely.

"Oh right," she said, trying to hide her disappointment. "I'm glad for her. Well, I guess I should get back, before she kicks my arse for being late." She smiled. "Nice to see you again, Taylor."

"She likes you, ya know," Georgia heard Taylor blurt out. "She doesn't know how to deal with that. She was with Dana for fifteen years and has a child with her, but Dan doesn't really give a hoot. Not about either of them. But one thing's for sure, she likes you. A whole lot. I know her better than anyone, and no matter how much she ignores it, it isn't going to go away," she said seriously.

"*Was* with? You just said she had sorted everything out with her wife now," Georgia said confused.

"She has sorted the situation. The day you guys got back from Fort Worth, Erika told Dan it was over and she wanted a divorce. She is single, Georgia, or in the process of being. Look, I should go. I have to go pick up Dulcie. Have a good day at work. And Georgia? Please don't mention this conversation to Erika. You don't wanna make an Italian American mad," she smirked as she strolled off.

***

"Was that the girl with Erika?" Emily said, walking out to the car.

"Yeah," Georgia said quietly, taking in the words.

"What were y'all discussing?"

"Erm, nothing she was just saying hi," Georgia said distantly.

"Liar. But you don't wanna discuss it, so I won't push. You know we got your back right? You wanna talk, you know where I am."

"She's divorcing her wife. She told her the day we got home."

"For real?" she squealed. "So watcha gonna do?"

"What do you mean? I do nothing. Why would I? She has been in a relationship for fifteen years, Em. Has a kid and is now getting divorced, what the hell am I supposed to do?"

"Well for starters, think why you're snapping at me. Because if you didn't wanna do nothing, then you wouldn't be getting pissed at me, now would you? Seriously, are all you Brits this uptight over love? Heck, no wonder y'all get married so late," she said.

Georgia was looking at Emily shaking her head. "Sorry, just surprised I suppose," Georgia said.

Chapter Seventy-One

Georgia was probably the least productive or functional she had ever been in work today, following the conversations with Emily, Julia, and Taylor in the last twenty-four hours. It all seemed to be influencing the direction of her thoughts, and it especially wasn't helping that Erika looked beautiful again today. They had spent the most part of the day in meetings together, alone. Georgia finished the salad she had gotten for lunch and grabbed the documents, before making her way back up to Erika's office to continue with their brain storming session. She could already smell her perfume coming from the room as she knocked on the door and walked in, stopping as she heard Erika's voice raised. Georgia stepped back, trying to ignore the conversation.

"No way, Dan! Fuck you. She's your daughter too, and I'm not having you ignore her…yes, I know she loves spending time with your folks, but she needs her mom. She needs reassurance through this, you're just being a selfish bitch is all."

Quiet. Clearly she's listening to whatever Dan was saying in response, Georgia thought. She was feeling uncomfortable at listening to the conversation.

"Screw you, Dan! I guess I was right all along, clearly you were screwing around and now that doesn't fit with the life you have, the life *you* fucking wanted. Screw you, I'm not letting my daughter spend a whole weekend without seeing her mom. Either you arrange for something for the two of you to do or you aren't seeing her."

"Arggghhhh, fuck! Fuck you, you dumb bitch," Georgia heard along with a loud bang. Unsure of whether to go in, Georgia knocked again and popped her head around the door. "Hi, would you like me to come back?"

Erika spun around, surprised. "Oh hey, I'm sorry. I wasn't aware you were standing there," she sighed. "Come in," she said embarrassed. "You have a nice lunch?" she asked, trying to avoid the elephant in the room and any form of eye contact.

Georgia smiled softly. "Do you think we will be here for the remainder of the day, doing this?" she pointed to the work before them.

"Um, I dunno? If you need to leave we can reconvene tomorrow," she said surprised.

"Actually, I thought *we* could leave? If you haven't got anything else on, how about we get out of here, and go to a bar and have the meeting there? You look like you could do with a drink or two. And whilst I don't regularly go and have meetings in bars, getting inebriated, I think it may be a little more productive. Because the way I see it, you're going to stay here and get more and more pissed off thinking about whatever's going on at home, and we aren't going to get anything done," Georgia said seriously. She admitted that, if it weren't for Erika, they would have gotten nothing done anyways, thanks to her mind wondering off to things it shouldn't be around her.

***

A short while later, they were in a bar with their laptops and paperwork surrounding them. Georgia had insisted on going close to Erika's house because of Dulcie, and they were now sitting with a bottle of red before them. Erika had already become a little more relaxed, but it was apparent she was still clearly pissed off.

"Thank you, again. It seems you just keep coming to my rescue," Erika said sadly.

"I think you are overthinking it. I just think if I was in your position, the last thing I'd want is to be in an office where people could keep interrupting and ultimately, have zero productivity because you keep reliving the conversation you had. I always find a drink helps in these situations. I mean, don't get me wrong, I'm not talking let's get hammered. That would make you feel far worse. But interestingly, when I was going through a difficult break up a number of years ago, this…" she stopped and pointed between the two of them. "This is what Derek did for me. Sometimes it's just nice to know that people would like to help," she offered.

"I know this is getting tired, but thank you. I still don't know why you keep being nice to me," she said, sipping her drink.

"Yes, it is getting tired. Because I'm not perfect, and I make mistakes like the rest. But I'm not a nasty person, nor would I actively set out to hurt or mistreat someone. You're nice, and I like you. Maybe more than what I should, and I don't want to see anyone upset or hurt, least not you," she said seriously.

"What did your friend say about it all?" Erika asked seriously.

"About what?"

"About being here? The situation, you two?"

"There is no *us* two. I told her everything."

"Huh? What do you mean?" she said concerned.

"Literally everything. You. Me. My feelings. The fact I faked it and felt terrible," she said, noticing Erika's flinch.

"Wow, that must be what every woman wants to hear," she said sarcastically. "So, what did she say?"

Georgia smirked, thinking back to the conversation.

"What?" Erika asked concerned.

"She said, stop wasting your life worrying what might go wrong and why you like someone after two weeks. She also said 'where do lesbians go on their second date?' Don't worry, I don't rush things. But I think the point she was making was, stop over thinking it all. Life's too short. So, follow your heart. She somehow knew that I think it's all somewhat 'fairy-tale like' and not very realistic. I mean we've known each other two weeks. It's a bit of a full-on statement to make, follow your heart!"

"Wow. That's surprising…" she said, shocked. Erika was looking at her intently as she took a sip of her drink. "Okay, then, I'll be blissfully ignorant and forget about that last statement. And ask what's your heart saying?" she questioned.

"That you need to stop drinking your drink seductively and talking in that way." She smiled sarcastically.

"You're an idiot, you know, that, right?"

"I wasn't aware until I met you, but now that you have offered that information like, twenty-five times, I'm fully aware. What I also think, is that after the day you've had today you need a friend *only* right now," she said seriously.

"Wow, the only time I need you to misbehave is the time you go all straight with me?" she said.

"Straight?"

"Yeah…responsible."

"Ahh, I know, but you'll thank me one day."

"Oh, you think? I'm not so sure. I was hoping you were going to call in the debt that I owed you."

"Seriously, Erika, you need to behave," she said, raising an eyebrow to her.

"How so? Watcha gonna do? Punish me?" she smirked.

"Stop now! I am going to take you home if you don't."

"*Really?* You do a full circle? Tell me that you want to be good, then say you're gonna take my ass home. Wow, that's all it took? I have a while before my daughter gets home, plenty of time to have some fun," she said, smirking to Georgia.

"Erika, stop it. I am not as strong as you are giving me credit for. Stop it!"

"Alright already," she said, smiling and pulling out the paperwork between them both to start focussing on the reason they were there.

Chapter Seventy-Two

Georgia had been in the shower for around half an hour, and she still couldn't stop thinking about the afternoon. Erika was playing hardball and was loving teasing her, and she was glad that she hadn't been drinking. Had she been, she was pretty certain that she would have caved.

Making her way downstairs, she made a coffee and was thinking about what people had been saying. She didn't know what to do. She liked her, but was she walking out to her own execution? Was it too messy? Or was Julia right, was she just overthinking everything? It may be nothing, and they may realise they aren't sexually compatible she thought.

Picking up her phone, Georgia wanted to text Erika to make sure that she was okay after the meeting and that awful argument. She was hoping that she helped her feel better, even if it was just a little.

Hey you, hope you're ok. And you didn't have more arguments. You were very distracting today, however, I liked it. We are very productive in a pub it seems, and I prefer that format of working ;) Drink plenty of water, or your head will hurt otherwise. xx

Hearing the response, Georgia opened the message from her to immediately be faced with a picture of Erika taking a sip of a very large glass of wine. "S*hit,*" Georgia said out loud. The picture was probably the worst thing she could have seen. It's not too hard to control yourself when you are not around people, you can talk yourself in and out of certain things. However, having seen that picture made it all the harder. She was incredibly beautiful, and Georgia couldn't help but stare at the picture. "What are you doing to me lady?" she said to herself.

You just can't stop yourself, can you? And really? More to drink? You needed more? Xx

Yeah figured I'd drown my sorrows. I was kind of hoping a kiss would have been on the cards to cheer me up. ☹ Xx

Are you always like this? You could've kissed me. It shouldn't always be on me. Xx

Yes, I'm always like this ☺ you don't like it? I can stop. We left it with you being mad at me, why would I think to kiss you? You may have whooped my ass. xx

Georgia considered her response carefully. Should she try to reign her in? Or would she be fighting a losing battle?

Seriously, you are so bad! I bet if I began flirting back you'd stop then. Xx

Try it, I betcha I won't. Xx

What would you like to bet? Xx

I'll bet ANYTHING you want honey. The world is your oyster. ;) Watcha fancy? Xx

You!!! As well you know!! Xx

Backatcha lady. xx

So, are you gutted you didn't get a kiss ehy? ;) xx

I am so. Maybe you should drive over and you can gimme one now. ;) xx

You want me to drive over and give you one? Wowzers you Americans sure are forward, aren't you? Xx

And I'M the one who's bad? Xx

You are very, very bad. Xx

But you love it, don't lie. Xx

I wanna say I don't. But I guess I kind of do. You have this incredible ability to make me forget what I'm worrying about with you. That both scares and thrills me, but I can't help but want more. And when you send me sexy pics it doesn't help matters. xx

Ohhh honey, that wasn't a sexy pic ;) xx

Erika Conte-Thomason don't you dare. Xx

It's just Erika Conte now. And I don't know what you mean? ;) Anyhow, send me a pic of you. xx

I'll remember that, and you know full well what I mean. I best not open another message that's going to make me drive over there and slap your arse. xx and no, I will not send you a pic. xx

Spoil sport! Slap my ass? And you say that I am forward? You like slapping asses, Georgia? Is that your thing? Xx

Maybe! Guess you'll never know. ;) xx

Oh, I'll find out, believe me. Xx

Kind of sure of yourself, aren't you? Xx

You have no idea how wrong you are with that. However, on this occasion, I'm not gonna lie, I think the pull is too much for us both to fight. So, I'd like to think that I'm right on this occasion. So, ass slapping.

If you found out it was my thing would it scare, you? Xx

So, it is your thing. I knew it. Told you I'd find out. ;) xx

On the contrary, I was merely asking a question. I wasn't offering any form of information as to what I may or may not like sexually. xx

I imagine you like control, so you would like the spanking. Xx

You are entering very, very dangerous territory, Erika. Xx

I am, how so? Xx

You know how so!! And you're wrong. Well, not about the control thing, I do kind of like being in control. But I'm not so much into spanking, personally. Whatever floats your boat, I guess. xx

So, serious question. What floats your boat? Xx

Hmmm I dunno. xx

Yeh you do, c'mon tell me, I wanna know. Xx

Why? Xx

Because I just do. Please? ☹ Xx

Confidence, sexiness, a great kisser, someone that fights for the control. I love that. I find that an incredible turn on. ☺ xx

So, if we were together, like together, together, and you were doing stuff to me, and I stopped you and took the lead and rolled you over, got on top of you, straddled you, and pushed you back hard and changed course, you'd like that, huh? Xx

OMG :/... You're such a tease. xx

Answer my question. Xx

Why, what you gonna do if I don't? xx

I'll come over and kick your ass. xx

You won't because you have a child in bed. ;) xx

Ok fair point, but I'll make you regret fucking with me. ;) xx

Ahhhh, baby I've not even began to start fucking with you yet. Xx

Tell me, last chance. Xx

See, now you are making me not want to just to see what exactly you could do. Lol. xx

Georgia watched the grey dots appear, smirking to herself. She was ignoring the 'should she, shouldn't she's' going around her head and just went with the flow. She couldn't resist, and she was having fun. But then the dots disappeared and didn't reappear. She waited for a while, starting to worry that she wasn't going to reply? She threw the phone on the bed, wondering if she should text her back, but before she had a chance to, the bed started vibrating with another message coming in. Georgia saw Erika's name on the phone as she smiled widely.

"You little shit," she said out loud. "You absolute little shit," she pressed call, waiting for the dialling tone to begin.

"Yeeeessss?" she heard down the phone with a giggly slur.

"You think you're funny, don't you?"

"No, I actually think I'm freaking hilarious. I thought you'd like them, honey? You seemed to like them last week," she purred.

"Seriously, I'm going to kick your arse."

"Is that a promise, Georgia? Because the more you keep saying it the more I can't stop thinking of your sexy ass. And, well as you know, I'm kind of just sitting around in my shorts and bra."

Georgia sighed heavily as she looked back to the photo of Erika in the mirror with those long-tanned legs, in the short shorts she'd worn last week when they were getting it on. The problem was, this time it wasn't with a hoodie but just her bra. In reality it was not any different to seeing her in a bikini, but it *was* a different look. She was confident, and she *wasn't* insecure. Maybe it was the booze, but God she looked hot.

"You still there?" Erika said quietly.

"Come out with me Saturday night," Georgia said before she could control her loose lips. "Shit, I'm sorry. I don't know where that came from."

"Why? Did you not mean it?" Erika asked seriously.

Georgia didn't know how to respond. She wouldn't have said it if she didn't mean it. She needed to not do this, but she'd done it already. So, did she really want to take it back now?

I guess not, huh," Erika said sadly.

Georgia sighed. "Will you come on a date with me on Saturday? No, should 'we' or shouldn't 'we's'? No overthinking, just you and me, two grown...*gay* women, going on a date," she said again.

"Was that a dig?" Erika said.

"Would I? So, you going to make an already embarrassed and nervous woman worse by not answering?" Georgia said shyly.

"I'm sorry, I didn't mean to. I can't believe you're the type to get nervous or embarrassed though. I will go out with you on Saturday," she said.

"Well as I keep saying, I don't do this. Okay, well I'm going to go before I make this situation any more awkward and weird. Especially as I'm now the epitome of a teenager who just got asked out for the first time."

"What do you mean? You need to? So, you can go scream into your pillow?" Erika laughed.

"Good night, Erika."

"Really, you're gonna ask me out and then leave me hanging? Shit, I hope you never ask me to go steady," she giggled. "What are we going to do?"

"We are going to hang up, I have a date to plan."

"Whatever, man. Good night, and thanks. For today, and tonight, for being concerned. You are pretty awesome."

"You too, pretty lady. I'll see you Saturday then yeah?"

"Honey, its Tuesday. Are you not intending to come to work for the remainder of the week?" She smiled.

"Maybe not, depends how easy it is to plan a date in this place."

"Well, why don't I just come over to your place, and you can cook? We don't have to do anything special."

"Hmmm, not really how I roll, but maybe leave it with me? Look, I should go. I'll see you tomorrow though," Georgia said quietly. "Oh, and Erika.." She stopped. "On a serious note, if it's too soon or you have a change of heart from the booze, then just text me in the morning okay?"

"Good night, George, I can't wait to see you tomorrow, but more so Saturday," she stated matter of factly.

***

Good morning you. FYI, I still wanna go on a date with you on Saturday. Just saying. xx ps. You were right, my head hurts. ☹ xx I could do with sexy snuggles with a hot Brit to make me feel better. ;)

Georgia read the message and smiled to herself. She ignored the nerves and the alarm bells and figured she would do exactly what Julia had told her to do, and just go with it.

Chapter Seventy-Three

Saturday came around fast and Georgia still didn't know what to do. She had tried to book tickets to a show or concert, but without knowing what she liked, she had no idea what to do. She needed to go see Emily. She needed advice on what to do, or at this rate she would have to invite her over, which was a shit date. *And a dangerous date*, she thought.

Georgia was about to go to Emily's when she saw Erika was calling her.

"Hello?"

"Hey, Georgia, I'm so sorry, like really sorry."

"You've changed your mind?"

"God no, but my B I T C H of an ex-wife, has just called to say she has to work so she can't have Dulcie. I know I'm being a stubborn ass, but I refuse to leave her with her grandparents if her mother cannot be bothered to look after her, and Taylor is out of town. I'm sorry, Georgia. I was really looking forward to it, like *really* looking forward to it. Can we please rain check? I mean if you still wanna go out with me?"

"Get ready."

"Huh?"

"Erika, get ready. Get you and Dulcie ready, pack or wear swimwear, and some comfy clothes. Maybe a spare set of clothes, and I'll do the rest. I'll pick you up in an hour?"

"Georgia, you don't have to do this. We can rain check and do it another night, when I have a sitter."

"Erika, for Christ's sake, just do as you're bloody told for once. You're wasting time, and I'll be there in an hour," she said, hanging up on her. She'd seen something the other day when she was looking at things and didn't think it was a good idea, but now…now it was the perfect idea. She made the call and booked some tickets before getting herself ready.

***

Georgia grabbed the cool box and filled it with fruit, sandwiches, water and some twizzlers. She checked herself in the mirror, making sure that the outfit was ok. Wearing a pair of denim shorts, her favourite pair of tom's pumps, and a light blue shirt with the sleeves rolled up, she put her sunnies on and left, trying not to over think everything all over again.

Twenty minutes later, Georgia pulled into Erika's driveway. She got out of the car and jogged up to the front door, hearing Dulcie excitably squealing inside. She knocked on the door and waited for them to answer.

"Hey," Erika said, opening the door, checking Georgia out. "Wow, you look amazing. Sorry," she said embarrassed. "That was lame."

"No, it wasn't, it was lovely. And same goes to you. Come on, I promise, no fear. I don't want you to feel uncomfortable, so if you need to back out, that's fine."

"No, don't be silly, it's fine," she breathed in heavily.

Georgia looked her over. Erika was wearing linen shorts and an oversized vest, which gave an incredible view to her bikini top. "You really *do* look incredible," she said.

Dulcie came running out in her little sun dress, "Hi, Georgia. Mommy said you're taking us out. Where ya taking us?" she said excitably.

"Well that's a surprise, but it's kind of far, so we need to get moving soon. Also, I have something for you in the car for the journey."

"You do?" she said wide eyed.

"Yep."

"Where's your car keys? I'll go put her car seat in the car," Erika said.

***

Ten minutes later, they were all in the car with Georgia being tight-lipped about where they were going. "Ahhhh, I forgot, this is for you," she said, handing Dulcie an iPod pre-loaded with the frozen album on it. "Put the headphones on," she said, pressing play and watching Dulcie's eyes widen as she listened intently.

"Wow, you thought of everything, huh? I'm really sorry your day got ruined, Georgia," she said.

"I don't really think I can call spending a day with one of the most beautiful women I've seen in my life, a *ruined* day. I think it's actually worked out better." She smiled sincerely, noticing Erika blush.

"Smooth! That's kind. So, what are we doing?"

"It's a surprise, for now. You have some time to kick back and relax." She smiled again, turning the music up.

"Ohhh, how very American."

"I know, I just heard it on MTV." She smiled, singing along to the music on the journey.

"You nervous?" Erika asked seriously.

"Interestingly, not anymore. I was, I really was actually." She stopped, looking into the rear-view to check Dulcie was listening to her music before continuing. "I was shitting myself, but now that Dulcie's here I feel strangely calm," she said, looking around to Erika smiling. "Why, are you?"

Erika looked out the window distantly. "Shitting myself," she said.

"*Really*? I'm sorry. Shit, the Dulcie thing wasn't an excuse, was it? I kind of railroaded you into this," Georgia said concerned.

"No, God no, don't be stupid. I'll be fine. It's just, well it's just been a while. And honestly, I'd be fine if it was just you and I. We could drink, since I am better with booze as you know," she smirked.

"You are, but that was why I was nervous. I don't think I would have been able to stop myself from jumping on you," she said seriously.

"And that's so bad?" she smirked.

"Yes, now kick back and relax." She smiled.

***

"You've brought us to the coast?" Erika said, smiling.

"If by that you mean have I brought you to the beach, then yes. But also, no." She smiled with a glint in her eye.

"You really are a big kid at heart aren't ya?"

"Ohhh, you have *no* idea."

Erika got Dulcie out of the car, listening to her excitably chatting about the beach that she was desperate to go to and build castles on.

"I can't believe you brought us out to Galveston," she said, bumping shoulders with her. "That's sweet."

"Get out of here, you're making me sound like a right boring S H I T," she said. "See, see what I did there? I remembered to *not* swear," she gloated.

"Can we go there?" Dulcie was asking, as she pointed out a space on the beach.

"Hey, Dulcie, we will be going to the beach. But not just yet, okay? First we have something much cooler to do."

"But I wanna go the beach first."

"Baby, that's rude. Now Georgia has organised something, and if she says we go here later, then we do that okay?"

"Okay," she said solemnly.

They arrived at the Baywatch tours desk. "You brought us dolphin and whale watching?" Erika said surprised.

"I did."

"Oh my gosh, Dulcie, we're going to see whales and dolphins," she said.

"We *are*? Coooooool!"

"Woah, easy tigers. It isn't guaranteed, okay? Hopefully we will, but it isn't guaranteed," she said seriously.

***

Georgia was thrilled that the day was going great so far. They hadn't seen any whales, but saw many dolphins, which Dulcie seemed impressed with. Following that, they had gone down to build sandcastles, which again, thrilled Dulcie. Georgia had run back to the car and got the cool box with the picnic to Erika's surprise. "You really shouldn't have gone to all this trouble, I don't think anybody has ever done something so thoughtful for me. For us. I'm stunned. Overwhelmed, really"

"Well, it isn't over just yet," she said, smiling widely.

"Thanks, Georgia, seriously," she said.

They finally finished the castle making. Dulcie was starting to wind down now. It was a long day and she didn't know if she would be able to hold out. But they both seemed to enjoy the day so far, which was great. Georgia told them to wait so she could take the cool box back to the car. She was shattered herself and craving a large glass of wine. But she wanted to try and see the last part out, thinking that Erika would really like it. Georgia spotted a large smooth grey pebble in the sand as she walked back to the car. Picking it up, she ran her thumb over it softly and put it in the cool box, smiling to herself.

***

"So, last part of the day guys, you fancy going to the funfair?" she pointed to pleasure pier. A place she'd read about, but she was uncertain with Erika if it seemed pathetic. But now that Dulcie was here, it seemed quite fitting.

"Woah," Dulcie squealed excitably. "Are we going up there?" she said, pointing to it.

"We sure are, kiddo, come on! I'll race you!" Georgia said, running off and leaving them behind.

Erika watched Georgia as she became the most competitive person on the planet, in a bid to win Dulcie stuffed toys. She kept telling her it didn't matter, but she wouldn't give up. Not until she'd won her something. And when she finally did, she was happy to move on. "You wanna go on that ride, Dulcie?" Georgia asked her.

"I'm kinda tired," she said sleepily. "Can we go home now?" she said, holding tightly on to the stuffed toys.

Erika looked to Georgia, who was looking concerned at her watch. "You ok? What's up?"

"Oh nothing," she said disappointed.

"What's up? Did you have something else planned?"

"No, it's fine honestly." She smiled.

"George talk to me? Please?" she turned to her pleadingly.

"It's just, I thought it'd be nice to watch the sunset over the pier. But I guess it has been a long day. I didn't think that through I guess," she said sadly.

"Listen, you have given me...*us* the best day ever. Unfortunately, yeah, it's a long and busy day for her. So, we do need to go home, otherwise she'll be a terror tonight." She smiled bashfully. "But...I spoke to Dan's folks earlier, and they will take Dulcie for the night. If you want to we could go back to yours? I'll cook for you, maybe mom's pasta recipe and have a '*grown up*' night?" she said softly.

"I don't want to make you feel you have to do that. I know how you felt about her going to her grandparents'."

"No, they are lovely. They are loving, adoring and wonderful grandparents. I just didn't want them to be babysitters, when her mom should be looking after her. I have no issue with her going there, they love seeing her and vice versa. Plus, I was kind of hoping you may have wanted to spend some *alone* time with me. Unless you're done after today," she said seriously.

"You sure?" Georgia said, trying to contain the slight smile starting to form. "I know you don't believe this, but I don't do this. So, I'm not so sure doing stuff on the first date is the right thing?"

Erika stopped and looked at her daughter, watching the ride go around. "You have no idea, how much that speech just reaffirmed exactly how sure I am," she said, kissing her lips softly. "Come on, let's get outta here," she said, grabbing Dulcie and making their way back home.

Chapter Seventy-Four

"Thank you for today, you have no idea how beautiful and thoughtful that all was. Seriously, it was the best date of my life," Erika said, dropping the cool box on the kitchen floor.

Georgia laughed. "Well, that's a bit of an exaggeration, but thank you for saying it," she said.

Erika turned around to face Georgia. "Please don't disregard my comments, Georgia, I'm not exaggerating at all. I'm stating the facts," she said seriously. "Now, how about you open a bottle and we go and enjoy the sunset in the yard?"

Georgia opened the bottle and put it in an ice bucket to take outside. She sat on the edge of the pool with her legs dangling in as she poured them both a drink, waiting for Erika to return. She put her hand in her jeans pocket, feeling the area and smiling softly. It had been a perfect day. *And now what a perfect ending* she thought, as she looked out to the sun setting before her, illuminating the sky with pinks and purples. It was the most perfect setting, and in this moment, she didn't care about everything that was stacked against them.

"Hey you," Erika said, coming to the pool to join her. She lifted her legs over one of Georgia's so they were dangling in the water between hers. "How you doing?"

"Honestly? I couldn't be better," she said. "I've had the best date ever with an amazing and beautiful woman. I'm now sat in my back garden, watching an incredible sunset with said woman, realising just how incredibly lucky I am," she said, leaning in and kissing her softly.

Georgia took her glass from her hand, continuing the kiss, before dropping herself into the pool.

"Are you mad? Its freezing!"

She put her hands on either side of Erika and pulled herself up to be level with her. She was smirking a little as she kissed her lips briefly.

Erika was mesmerised by the woman's toned arms, and she found them sexy as hell. "My God those arms," she mumbled, leaning her head down to kiss Georgia again.

Georgia put her hands under her bottom, and lifted her in to the water, noticing the slight gasp from Erika. "I have a feeling you'll warm up very quickly," she said, kissing her deeply once more.

Georgia heard Erika groan into the kiss. She laced her fingers through her long hair, feeling the soft curls, as she pulled her closer into the kiss. Erika couldn't feel the cold any longer. Georgia was right, she was getting warmer in this moment and she wanted more. Deepening the kiss, she found Georgia's tongue with her own, moving together slowly. She could feel the heat and softness of her tongue, and taste the light remnants of the pink champagne they were drinking. God, she was sexy, even now as they were both fully clothed in the pool. She couldn't remember a time she was more turned on.

Erika could feel her breathing increasing and was struggling to compose herself. This woman was too much, and for some reason she had complete control over Erika. Which was both terrifying and exhilarating all at the same time. She pulled away from the kiss and looked intently at Georgia, watching her. She stepped back an inch and pulled her top off over her head, feeling the chilly effects around her.

Georgia breathed in deeply, unable to take her eyes from Erika. She continued and removed her bikini top. Georgia gasped loudly as she was looking at her beautiful naked upper body. "Erika, you don't…"

"Shhh. I've waited long enough for this. I can't wait any longer. I'm ready if you are?" she asked nervously.

"You have no idea how incredible you are. It stuns me that you don't realise this. I am desperate to show you how much," Georgia said, pushing Erika against the side of the pool and kissing her soft and deep.

Erika kissed her deeper, adding more force and passion. She felt like she had waited forever for this. It had been *forever* since she had been intimate with someone, and she'd been desperate to be with Georgia since their celebratory night that they'd ended up kissing. She was desperate to feel her, caress her, enjoy every minute of being with her.

Georgia grabbed Erika's hair and pulled her head backwards slightly. She was glad of the privacy in this moment, because the scene was perfect. The *moment* was perfect, and more importantly, the woman was perfect. She kissed her way down her jaw line, moving down her neck and making her way down to Erika's erect nipple. They both gasped as her mouth met the sensitive area. She gently flicked it with her tongue, and bit ever so slightly, causing Erika to groan loudly again. God, she was turned on, and she didn't know how long she would be able to last with this woman. Georgia could feel the night drawing in and the temperature lowering. She played a little more with Erika's nipple, feeling the effects it was having on her. She knew she wouldn't be able to wait. The temptation was too much for her. Georgia lowered her hands, gently scraping down her stomach until she reached the waistband of her shorts, undoing the button with one hand, and still using the other to pull her head back. Erika was gasping, knowing what was coming. She pushed Georgia's head further into her breast, forcing her to be a little rougher. Georgia looked up and watched the woman basking in the fulfilment she was enduring. Georgia pushed her hand beneath the waistband and into her bikini bottoms, hearing Erika cry out. She pushed her finger inside her and lifted her leg up around her, allowing her better access. She pulled her closer to her, sliding her fingers deep inside, as she continued to bite and suck her nipple. Her arousal was off the charts. And although the water was getting cooler, she couldn't be denied the unmistakable heat emanating from Erika, causing her to tighten around her fingers. Georgia was flicking her tongue over Erika's nipple hard and fast now, and pushing her fingers deeper inside her. She could hear both of their breathing quickening as her pace increased. Erika was pulling her closer in and could feel she was on the edge. It had been a ridiculously long time since anyone had made love to her, and the fact she had been so desperate to be with Georgia last week, it was no surprise that she was on the cusp after so little time. Erika could feel her body tighten around Georgia, as she grabbed tightly onto Georgia's back. Her leg tightly wrapped around her waist, she delighted in the impact the angle was having on her. Georgia continued to get faster and deeper, and in no time at all, her legs had buckled as she hit the highest state of euphoria. She wrapped her arms around Georgia, suddenly embarrassed in the moment and desperate not to look at her.

Georgia moved back, forcing Erika to look at her, attentive to her avoidance. "Hey, hey? What's wrong? *I'm sorry*, did you not want to?" she said, looking scared.

"Yes, *yes*. I'm fine."

"No, Erika, you're not. What have I done?"

"Georgia, you haven't done anything I swear. It's just me."

"But why? I clearly have, you're scaring me."

"*Seriously,*" she urged, noticing the concern in Georgia's eyes. She hadn't realised that she would make her feel this way. More importantly, she *wasn't* used to that kind of consideration. "Sweetie, you haven't done anything, it's just been a while, like a real long time. And I guess I just felt a bit... I dunno, um, silly. Embarrassed, I guess."

Georgia put her arms around her and held her tight, shaking her head. She pulled back and looked deeply into her eyes, "Erika," she scoffed. "You...I don't even know what to say," she said sadly, feeling frustrated as her emotions were running high.

"Hey don't, it's just me being dumb. Come on, what's up?" she said seriously.

"You have no idea. Honestly, you have no idea. Look at you. You are the most incredible woman I think I've ever met. You are beyond stunning, and you make me feel inferior to your beauty when I'm around you. You have no idea how wonderfully amazing you are, Erika Conte. I wish you could see what I see," she said sadly. "You do things to me that nobody has ever done before, babe..." she paused, letting the term of endearment linger for a moment. "Please don't feel embarrassed. I have dreamed about making love to you. For me, that couldn't have been more perfect," she said seriously.

Erika could see everything she needed in Georgia's eyes. She wasn't lying. Her eyes. Her face. Her expression. Everything was communicating to Erika exactly how she felt and how she saw her.

"I'm sorry, I didn't mean to upset you. I guess the mixture of emotions just took me by surprise," she said sombrely. "Come on. It's cold out. We need to get back on track with this mood. Let's take the bottle up to bed please?"

Georgia looked at her seriously. "Of course, but how about we just relax, watch a movie together and enjoy some cuddling."

"*Cuddling?* That's just *so* British. I'm sorry but I'm not making no promises. I genuinely don't think I can resist that body all night," she said seriously. "From the day I saw you at the pool I've been desperate to touch you."

"Well you best try," she said, pulling her out of the pool.

***

Georgia was lying in bed, waiting for Erika to finish in the shower. She had put the TV on and was blowing on the pebble, pouring them both a little more to drink. Georgia assessed the room, appreciating the glow and scent of the candles she'd lit.

"Hey, girl done good," Erika said, coming out of the shower with just a shirt on. "It's perfect. You are *too* much, lady," she said seriously.

"No, I'm just a bit of a hopeless romantic, apparently," she said softly. "But there is one last thing," she said, smiling.

"Something else? Wow, I don't think I've ever felt so special," she said, crawling up on the bed towards her. "Okay, what?"

Georgia got closer to Erika, pulling the candle over to allow her to see. "This is for you," she said, holding her hand out closed.

Erika looked at her confused, before opening her hand up and seeing the smooth grey pebble lay there. Georgia flipped it over, allowing Erika to see. Picking it up she saw the words written on it, '*you're beautiful,*' with the date and their initials. "It's kind of stupid but…"

"Don't you dare…" she stopped, stunned by the action. "I love it. It's amazing. A memory from our first ever date," she said. Putting it on the side table, Erika rolled back over and looked into Georgia's eyes. "You are so incredibly beautiful, and I can't wait to make love to you all night long," she said seriously, pushing Georgia back and kissing her passionately.

Chapter Seventy-Five

Georgia woke and realised that Erika was not lying when she said she wanted to make love to her all-night long. She was lucky if they'd even had an hour's sleep. But by God it was worth it. She looked down to the woman before her and all her fears seemed to fade. She didn't know if it would go perfectly or if it would end in disaster. One thing was for sure, she didn't feel like she had any further doubts in her mind right now. This woman was simply spectacular.

Georgia debated laying and watching her or making breakfast, opting for the latter. She gently eased her way out of bed and threw on an oversized shirt, and quietly made her way downstairs.

Having no idea what the woman liked, she decided she would make a mixture of things. That was certainly something she had noticed over here. They mixed their foods together between sweet and savoury, like melon and bacon, or orange and scrambled eggs. Odd and definitely *not* for her, but she was happy to make a few different things.

***

Georgia walked back into the room a short while later, "Heeeey there you are," Erika said sleepily.

"What you missing me?" She smiled to her, walking over with the tray. "I thought I'd make you breakfast in bed."

"Wow. You *did*? I thought you'd had second thoughts," she said, still coming around. She sat up slightly, pulling the cover over her embarrassedly.

"You're kidding," Georgia said, pulling the blanket down to where it was originally. "Please don't hide yourself from me, I *want* to see you. I love looking at you," she said seriously.

"Me too," Erika said shyly. "So, what do I got here?"

***

Erika had managed to get Dan's parents to look after Dulcie for the rest of the weekend. Which resulted in the day being spent in bed, watching back to back movies. Well, maybe *not* watching. They were on in the background as the women were enjoying…getting to *know* each other's bodies. Erika couldn't remember if anyone had ever made her feel so alive. Her body would hit a full state of ecstasy and then mere moments later, she was craving Georgia's touch once more.

It was almost six pm when they finally decided they needed to get up and eat, having realised that nothing had passed their lips since breakfast in the morning. While they were reluctant to leave the comfort of the bedroom, it was going to end up with them getting bed sores. So, they agreed they would get up to eat and then return to bed. After all, an early night was required when they were back in work in the morning.

***

Georgia couldn't remember feeling like this, being like this, or behaving like this, in…well, forever. She felt giddy, and she wanted to make everything perfect. Have everything perfect, and allow this beautifully incredible woman to realise how perfect she was. They were lying in bed, naked once more. Georgia one way and Erika resting her head on her tummy another way, as they quietly watched the pinks and purples of the sun set fill the room. The soft sounds of Sarah McLachlan love songs were playing in the background. *It really has been a perfect weekend,* she thought, feeling the fear of this odd and idiosyncratic situation.

"George?"

"Yeah?"

"Thank you…*seriously*, thank you for everything. You have truly given me the most incredible weekend," she said.

"Me too. I've loved every minute of it. I wish we could stay like this forever," she said, softly twisting her fingers through her long silky hair.

"Forever huh? Forever's a long time," she said seriously.

"Well, forever's not long enough in my opinion."

"You are such a softy. *I*... I love it," she said.

"Interestingly, I'm really not. I'm a worker. I work and don't get involved. It's new to me. I can't explain it, but you…you appear to bring something out of me. Something I've never experienced before," she said.

Erika turned around onto her side to face her. "Do you mean that?" she asked seriously.

"I've never been more serious in my life," gently tapping the tip of her index finger on her nose.

"You wanna hear something weird?" Erika said.

"Sure? Crack on."

"I've never been so sex obsessed with anyone before." She smiled wide eyed.

"You have got to be kidding. You wouldn't bloody think it." She smiled.

"Nope," Erika smirked, raising her eyebrows.

"Erika, seriously you've gotta be kidding me. I can't take any more," she said, as she watched Erika slowly making small kisses down her tummy, gasping deeply.

Erika made her way up the bed and faced Georgia, her long black hair falling over her face. "Well that's kind of a shame. Because I'm ready for dessert, and I'm completely hungry for you."

"God, you are insatiable. I don't think I have ever met anyone as beautiful as you," she said, meaning every word as she looked deeply into her eyes.

"Nobody's ever made me feel as beautiful as you make me feel. I love that. I love…" she sighed. "I love being like this, I love how you make me feel," she said sadly.

"So, if you love it so much, why do you look so sad?"

"It's nothing," she said, allowing the fear and concern of how she was feeling to fill her body.

"Don't shut me out, please? Talk to me, it's me and you now. Well and Dulcie. Just the three of us," she said seriously. "Well, if you want it to be," she added. "I'm falling in love with you, Erika Conte," she said finally.

Erika suddenly felt overwhelmed at the words, and knew in that moment that Georgia wasn't Dan. "Really?"

"Yes."

"But why? The way it started, the way I treated you…"

"Erika, we can't keep doing this. It's done and now…well I don't know; I've not done this before. I work and don't play. I don't have a social aspect because everything is about business. But I can't deny how I feel. And I don't know how the bloody hell its happened. But maybe it was just meant to," she said incredulously. "I feel I need to just maybe stop being afraid and just let go," Georgia said, terrified. Especially how rapidly it was happening, but she couldn't not.

Erika's eyes went wide as she kissed her way down Georgia's trim body, to make love to her once again.

Ten months later

Epilogue

"Are you kidding?"

"Nope, you were the ones who caused all of this. What was it you said? You will get on cracking together? Umm, was it? You're so much alike," Georgia said seriously.

"So what happens now?" Mike looked between Derek and the women sitting before him.

"Well realistically we don't know, we figured it would probably be best if I leave," Erika said.

"Wait? *What*? Jesus, I'm not having that."

"Well, in that case then, just as you asked us to give it a go and have faith in the situation, we will put our faith in you once more, and ask you to do what you need to do to make something happen. Georgia can't leave. She won't get another job because she isn't a citizen. But for now, we have a spouse green card meeting," Erika said, smiling widely and grabbing her girlfriend's hand.

"So, you're actually not planning on coming home?" Derek asked her seriously.

"I'm really hoping not, Derek. I love her and I want to spend the rest of my life with her. So, I need you guys to help make that happen."

"And what about the MD job in Manchester? You know the one you were working towards?" he added.

"It left me the day I met Erika," she said seriously, getting up and leaving the restaurant hand in hand.

"Are you sure you wanna do this? It's kind of a big deal," Erika said seriously.

"Unless you've changed your mind. I love you and want to be here with you and Dulcie. Forever."

"I love you too, baby girl, let's go kick some government butt." She smiled, kissing her girlfriend softly.

***

"*Mommy,*" Dulcie said excitably. "Look what we're doing," she called out from the kitchen.

"Georgia, this one's for you," she said, pointing to the cookie she'd made for her.

"It is? *Wowzers,* that's awesome," she said, kissing the little girls head. "Tay, thanks for today."

"Hey, no worries, how did it go?"

"Who knows!" she said concerned. "Hey, kiddo, how about we make some hand cookies?"

"What are they?" she said seriously, looking up to Georgia from the chair she was standing on.

"You don't know what hand cookies are? Wow, you haven't lived until you've made them," she said. "Okay, so we need to wash our hands first." They returned to the cookie mixture and pressed Dulcie's little hand into the mixture. She used the knife to cut around her hand and did one of her own.

"Hey, baby, this is Sharon Lopez," Erika said, walking into the kitchen with a short Hispanic woman following her.

"Hi, nice to meet you," she said, wiping her hand. "Apologies, hand cookies." She smiled, holding up her hand. "Okay, kiddo, you finish these with Tay and we'll decorate them together in a, while right?" she said, leaving the kitchen to face the woman who was going to be involved in the process of hopefully making Georgia an American citizen.

Georgia followed them into the second sitting room and sat down. "So, how does this work then?" she said nervously.

"Today's meeting is just about you guys. We just go through a heap of paperwork and some questions to prove that you are really a couple and are together." She smiled widely.

"Okay," Georgia said apprehensively. She felt the squeeze of her girlfriend's hand, as she looked over to her. "I love you, angel," she whispered as they both looked up to Sharon who had caught them, and was smiling at them both widely.

"This will be fine, ladies. *You* will be fine," she said back to the couple, before issuing them the documentation to begin the process for citizenship.

S.L. Gape

About the Author

S.L. Gape is 36 years old and enjoys writing, cooking, travelling and photography. She lives in Cheshire with her partner Jen, and currently splits her time between writing and her day job as a Regional HR advisor.

She gets a lot of inspiration from travelling and her experience as a holiday rep for seven years, where she was lucky enough to have lived and worked in Spain, Greece, Bahamas, Egypt and Lapland. Whilst she has only been writing for a year, she find it a tremendous stress release for her job, and loves to live through the escapism.

Follow her on Twitter: @louise_7uk and Facebook: S.L. Gape

Other Titles Available From
Triplicity Publishing

Boone Creek (Law & Order Series book 1) by Graysen Morgen. Jessie Henry is looking for a new life. She's unknown in the town of Boone Creek when she arrives, and wants to keep it that way. When she's offered the job of Town Marshal, she takes it, believing that protecting others and upholding the law is the penance for her past. Ellie Fray is a widowed, shopkeeper. She generally keeps to herself, but the mysterious new Town Marshal both intrigues and infuriates her. She believes the last thing the town needs is someone stirring up trouble with the outlaws who have taken over.

Blue Ice Landing by KA Moll. Coy is a beautiful blonde with a southern accent and a successful practice as a physician assistant. She has a comfortable home, good friends, and a loving family. She's also a widow, carrying a burden of responsibility for her wife's untimely death. Coby is a woman with secrets. She's estranged from her family, a recovering alcoholic, and alone because she's convinced that she's unlovable. When she loses her job as a heavy equipment operator, she'll accept one that'll force her to step way outside her comfort zone. When Coy quits her job to accept a position in Antarctica, her path will cross with Coby's. Their attraction to one another will be immediate, and despite their differences, it won't be long before they fall in love. But for these two, with all their baggage, will love be enough?

Never Quit (Never Series book2) by Graysen Morgen. Two years after stepping away from the action as a Coast Guard Rescue Swimmer to become an instructor, Finley finds herself in charge of the most difficult class of cadets she's ever faced, while also juggling the taxing demands of having a home life with her partner Nicole, and their fifteen year old daughter. Jordy Ross gave up everything, dropping out of college, and leaving her family behind, to join the Coast Guard and become a rescue swimmer cadet. The extreme training tests her fitness level, pushing her mentally and physically further than she's ever been in her life, but it's the aggressive competition between her and another female cadet that proves to be the most challenging.

For a Moment's Indiscretion by KA Moll. With ten years of marriage under their belt, Zane and Jaina are coasting. The little things they used to do for one another have fallen by the wayside. They've gotten busy with life. They've forgotten to nurture their love and relationship. Even soul mates can stumble on hard times and have marital difficulties. Enter Amelia, a new faculty member in Jaina's building. She's new in town, young, and very pretty. When an argument with Zane causes Jaina to storm out angry, she reaches out to Amelia. Of course, she seizes the opportunity. And for a moment of indiscretion, Jaina could lose everything.

Never Let Go (Never Series book 1) by Graysen Morgen. For Coast Guard Rescue Swimmer, Finley Morris, life is good. She loves her job, is well respected by her peers, and has been given an opportunity to take her career to the next level. The only thing missing is the love of her life, who walked out, taking their daughter with her, seven years earlier. When Finley gets a call from her ex, saying their teenage daughter is coming to spend the summer with her, she's floored. While spending more time with her daughter, whom she doesn't get to see often, and learning to be a full-time parent, Finley quickly realizes she has not, and will never, let go of what is important.

Pursuit by Joan L. Anderson. Claire is a workaholic attorney who flies to Paris to lick her wounds after being dumped by her girlfriend of seventeen years. On the plane she chats with the young woman sitting next to her, and when they land the woman is inexplicably detained in Customs. Claire is surprised when she later runs into the woman in the city. They agree to meet for breakfast the next morning, but when the woman doesn't show up Claire goes to her hotel and makes a horrifying discovery. She soon finds herself ensnared in a web of intrigue and international terrorism, becoming the target of a high stakes game of cat and mouse through the streets of Paris.

Wrecked by Sydney Canyon. To most people, the *Duchess* is a myth formed by old pirates tales, but to Reid Cavanaugh, a Caribbean island bum and one of the best divers and treasure hunters in the world, it's a real, seventeenth century pirate ship—the holy grail of underwater treasure hunting. Reid uses the same cunning tactics she always has before setting out to find the lost ship. However, she is forced to bring her business partner's daughter along as collateral this time because he doesn't trust her. Neither woman is thrilled, but being cooped up on a small dive boat for days, forces them to get know each other quickly.

Arson by Austen Thorne. Madison Drake is a detective for the Stetson Beach Police Department. The last thing she wants to do is show a new detective the ropes, especially when a fire investigation becomes arson to cover up a murder. Madison butts heads with Tara, her trainee, deals with sarcasm from Nic, her ex-girlfriend who is a patrol officer, and finds calm in the chaos of police work with Jamie, her best friend who is the county medical examiner. Arson is the first of many in a series of novella episodes surrounding the fictional Stetson Beach Police Department and Detective Madison Drake.

Change of Heart by KA Moll. Courtney Holloman is a woman at the top of her game. She's successful, wealthy, and a highly sought after Washington lobbyist. She has money, her job, booze, and nothing else. In quiet moments, against her will, her mind drifts back to her days in high school and to all that she gave up. Jack Camdon is a complex woman, and yet not at all. She is also a woman who has never moved beyond the sudden and unexplained departure of her high school sweetheart, her lover, and her soul mate. When circumstances bring Courtney back to town two decades later, their paths will cross. Will it be too late?

***Mommies (Bridal Series book 3)* by Graysen Morgen.** Britton and her wife Daphne have been married for a year and a half and are happy with their life, until Britton's mother hounds her to find out why her sister Bridget hasn't decided to have children yet. This prompts Daphne to bring up the big subject of having kids of their own with Britton. Britton hadn't really thought much about having kids, but her love for Daphne makes her see life and their future together in a whole new way when they decide to become mommies.

Haunting Love by K.A. Moll. Anna Crestwood was raised in the strict beliefs of a religious sect nestled in the foothills of the Smoky Mountains. She's a lesbian with a ton of baggage—fearful, guilty, and alone. Very few things would compel her to leave the familiar. The job offer of a lifetime is one of them. Gabe Garst is a police officer. She's also a powerful medium. Her work with juvenile delinquents and ghosts is all that keeps her going. Inside she's dead, certain that her capacity to love is buried six feet under. Anna and Gabe's paths cross. Their attraction is immediate, but they hold back until all hope seems lost.

Rapture & Rogue by Sydney Canyon. Taren Rauley is happy and in a good relationship, until the one person she thought she'd never see again comes back into her life. She struggles to keep the past from colliding with the present as old feelings she thought were dead and gone, begin to haunt her. In college, Gianna Revisi was a mastermind, ring-leading, crime boss. Now, she has a great life and spends her time running Rapture and Rogue, the two establishments she built from the ground up. The last person she ever expects to see walk into one of them, is the girl who walked out on her, breaking her heart five years ago.

Second Chance by Sydney Canyon. After an attack on her convoy, Marine Corps Staff Sergeant, Darien Hollister, must learn to live without her sight. When an experimental procedure allows her to see again, Darien is torn, knowing someone had to die in order for this to happen.

She embarks on a journey to personally thank the donor's family, but is too stunned to tell them the truth. Mixed emotions stir inside of her as she slowly gets to the know the people that feel like so much more than strangers to her. When the truth finally comes out, Darien walks away, taking the second chance that she's been given to go back to the only life she's ever known, but she's not the only one with a second chance at life.

Meant to Be by Graysen Morgen. Brandt is about to walk down the aisle with her girlfriend, when an unexpected chain of events turns her world upside down, causing her to question the last three years of her life. A chance encounter sparks a mix of rage and excitement that she has never felt before. Summer is living life and following her dreams, all the while, harboring a huge secret that could ruin her career. She believes that some things are better kept in the dark, until she has her third run-in with a woman she had hoped to never see again, and gives into temptation. Brandt and Summer start believing everything happens for a reason as they learn the true meaning of meant to be.

Coming Home by Graysen Morgen. After tragedy derails TJ Abernathy's life, she packs up her three year old son and heads back to Pennsylvania to live with her grandmother on the family farm. TJ picks back up where she left off eight years earlier, tending to the fruit and nut tree orchard, while learning her grandmother's secret trade. Soon, TJ's high school sweetheart and the same girl who broke her heart, comes back into her life, threatening to steal it away once again. As the weeks turn into months and tragedy strikes again, TJ realizes coming home was the best thing she could've ever done.

Special Assignment by Austen Thorne. Secret Service Agent Parker Meeks has her hands full when she gets her new assignment, protecting a Congressman's teenage daughter, who has had threats made on her life and been whisked away to a Christian boarding school under an alias to finish out her senior year. Parker is fine with the assignment, until she finds out she has to go undercover as a Canon Priest. The last thing Parker expects to find is a beautiful, art history teacher, who is intrigued by her in more ways than one.

Miracle at Christmas by Sydney Canyon. A Modern Twist on the Classic Scrooge Story. Dylan is a power-hungry lawyer who pushed away everything good in her life to become the best defense attorney in the, often winning the worst cases and keeping anyone with enough money out of jail. She's visited on Christmas Eve by her deceased law partner, who threatens her with a life in hell like his own, if she doesn't change her path. During the course of the night, she is taken on a journey through her past, present, and future with three very different spirits.

Bella Vita by Sydney Canyon. Brady is the First Officer of the crew on the Bella Vita, a luxury charter yacht in the Caribbean. She enjoys the laidback island lifestyle, and is accustomed to high profile guests, but when a U.S. Senator charters the yacht as a gift to his beautiful twin daughters who have just graduated from college and a few of their friends, she literally has her hands full.

Brides (Bridal Series book 2) by Graysen Morgen. Britton Prescott is dating the love of her life, Daphne Attwood, after a few tumultuous events that happened to unravel at her sister's wedding reception, seven months earlier. She's happy with the way things are, but immense pressure from her family and friends to take the next step, nearly sends her back to the single life. The idea of a long engagement and simple wedding are thrown out the window, as both families take over, rushing Britton and Daphne to the altar in a matter of weeks.

Cypress Lake by Graysen Morgen. The small town of Cypress Lake is rocked when one murder after another happens. Dani Ricketts, the Chief Deputy for the Cypress Lake Sheriff's Office, realizes the murders are linked. She's surprised when the girl that broke her heart in high school has not only returned home, but she's also Dani's only suspect. Kristen Malone has come back to Cypress Lake to put the past behind her so that she can move on with her life. Seeing Dani Ricketts again throws her off-guard, nearly derailing her plans to finally rid herself and her family of Cypress Lake.

Crashing Waves by Graysen Morgen. After a tragic accident, Pro Surfer, Rory Eden, spends her days hiding in the surf and snowboard manufacturing company that she built from the ground up, while living her life as a shell of the person that she once was. Rory's world is turned upside down when a young surfer pursues her, asking for the one thing she can't do. Adler Troy and Dr. Cason Macauley from Graysen Morgen's bestselling novel: *Falling Snow*, make an appearance in this romantic adventure about life, love, and letting go.

Bridesmaid of Honor (Bridal Series book 1) by Graysen Morgen. Britton Prescott's best friend is getting married and she's the maid of honor. As if that isn't enough to deal with, Britton's sister announces she's getting married in the same month and her maid of honor is her best friend Daphne, the same woman who has tormented Britton for years. Britton has to suck it up and play nice, instead of scratching her eyes out, because she and Daphne are in both weddings. Everyone is counting on them to behave like adults.

Falling Snow by Graysen Morgen. Dr. Cason Macauley, a high-speed trauma surgeon from Denver meets Adler Troy, a professional snowboarder and sparks fly. The last thing Cason wants is a relationship and Adler doesn't realize what's right in front of her until it's gone, but will it be too late?

Fate vs. Destiny by Graysen Morgen. Logan Greer devotes her life to investigating plane crashes for the National Transportation Safety Board. Brooke McCabe is an investigator with the Federal Aviation Association who literally flies by the seat of her pants. When Logan gets tangled in head games with both women will she choose fate or destiny?

Just Me by Graysen Morgen. Wild child Ian Wiley has to grow up and take the reins of the hundred year old family business when tragedy strikes. Cassidy Harland is a little surprised that she came within an inch of picking up a gorgeous stranger in a bar and is shocked to find out that stranger is the new head of her company.

Love Loss Revenge by Graysen Morgen. Rian Casey is an FBI Agent working the biggest case of her career and madly in love with her girlfriend. Her world is turned upside when tragedy strikes. Heartbroken, she tries to rebuild her life. When she discovers the truth behind what really happened that awful night she decides justice isn't good enough, and vows revenge on everyone involved.

Natural Instinct by Graysen Morgen. Chandler Scott is a Marine Biologist who keeps her private life private. Corey Joslen is intrigued by Chandler from the moment she meets her. Chandler is forced to finally open her life up to Corey. It backfires in Corey's face and sends her running. Will either woman learn to trust her natural instinct?

Secluded Heart by Graysen Morgen. Chase Leery is an overworked cardiac surgeon with a group of best friends that have an opinion and a reason for everything. When she meets a new artist named Remy Sheridan at her best friend's art gallery she is captivated by the reclusive woman. When Chase finds out why Remy is so sheltered will she put her career on the line to help her or is it too difficult to love someone with a secluded heart?

In Love, at War by Graysen Morgen. Charley Hayes is in the Army Air Force and stationed at Ford Island in Pearl Harbor. She is the commanding officer of her own female-only service squadron and doing the one thing she loves most, repairing airplanes. Life is good for Charley, until the day she finds herself falling in love while fighting for her life as her country is thrown haphazardly into World War II. Can she survive being in love and at war?

Fast Pitch by Graysen Morgen. Graham Cahill is a senior in college and the catcher and captain of the softball team. Despite being an all-star pitcher, Bailey Michaels is young and arrogant. Graham and Bailey are forced to get to know each other off the field in order to learn to work together on the field. Will the extra time pay off or will it drive a nail through the team?

Submerged by Graysen Morgen. Assistant District Attorney Layne Carmichael had no idea that the sexy woman she took home from a local bar for a one night stand would turn out to be someone she would be prosecuting months later. Scooter is a Naval Officer on a submarine who changes women like she changes uniforms. When she is accused of a heinous crime she is shocked to see her latest conquest sitting across from her as the prosecuting attorney.

Vow of Solitude by Austen Thorne. Detective Jordan Denali is in a fight for her life against the ghosts from her past and a Serial Killer taunting her with his every move. She lives a life of solitude and plans to keep it that way. When Callie Marceau, a curious Medical Examiner, decides she wants in on the biggest case of her career, as well as, Jordan's life, Jordan is powerless to stop her.

Igniting Temptation by Sydney Canyon. Mackenzie Trotter is the Head of Pediatrics at the local hospital. Her life takes a rather unexpected turn when she meets a flirtatious, beautiful fire fighter. Both women soon discover it doesn't take much to ignite temptation.

One Night by Sydney Canyon. While on a business trip, Caylen Jarrett spends an amazing night with a beautiful stripper. Months later, she is shocked and confused when that same woman re-enters her life. The fact that this stranger could destroy her career doesn't bother her. C.J. is more terrified of the feelings this woman stirs in her. Could she have fallen in love in one night and not even known it?

Fine by Sydney Canyon. Collin Anderson hides behind a façade, pretending everything is fine. Her workaholic wife and best friend are both oblivious as she goes on an emotional journey, battling a potentially hereditary disease that her mother has been diagnosed with. The only person who knows what is really going on, is Collin's doctor. The same doctor, who is an acquaintance that she's always been attracted to, and who has a partner of her own.

Shadow's Eyes by Sydney Canyon. Tyler McCain is the owner of a large ranch that breeds and sells different types of horses. She isn't exactly thrilled when a Hollywood movie producer shows up wanting to film his latest movie on her property. Reegan Delsol is an up and coming actress who has everything going for her when she lands the lead role in a new film, but there one small problem that could blow the entire picture.

Light Reading: A Collection of Novellas by Sydney Canyon. Four of Sydney Canyon's novellas together in one book, including the bestsellers Shadow's Eyes and One Night.

Visit us at www.tri-pub.com

22499461R00238

Printed in Great Britain
by Amazon